Praise for Chey

"Anyone who enjoys Native American historical fiction should try Ms. Munn, who is second to none."
—*The Midwest Book Review*

"Vella Munn is a major talent in historical fiction. Her stories never fail to lift the spirit and warm the heart. The humanity of her characters simply shines. This author is destined to become a perennial favorite with readers."   —Susan Wiggs

"An exciting, action-packed, but deep look at the Cheyenne. Vella Munn paints an awesome landscape with strong portraits that show she is quite an artist when it comes to historical fiction."   —Harriet Klausner on Amazon, BN, paintedrock, and other websites, on *Cheyenne Summer*

"Effectively mixing western and romance, Munn tells a compelling and tragic tale."—*Booklist* on *Soul of the Sacred Earth*

"Vella Munn creates superior historical romances set among native Americans. *Blackfeet Season* is a story of political and spiritual intrigue."   —*Oregon Statesman Journal*

"This was a violent time in history and Ms. Munn records it well, without ever turning the reader off—and never shirking from her duty to portray everything both accurately and romantically."   —*Romantic Times* on *Wind Warrior*

"Vella Munn is one of today's best writers in providing her readers with an entertaining, fast-moving, and realistic novel. The protagonists are well drawn, empathetic characters, and the secondary cast provides a wealth of support to the story. The audience will appreciate *Daughter of the Forest* for the fascinating, well-researched, and exciting work of historical fiction that it is."   —*Affaire de Coeur*

By Vella Munn from Tom Doherty Associates

Daughter of the Forest
Daughter of the Mountain
The River's Daughter
Seminole Song
Spirit of the Eagle
Wind Warrior
Blackfeet Season
Soul of the Sacred Earth
Cheyenne Summer

CHEYENNE SUMMER

VELLA MUNN

A TOM DOHERTY ASSOCIATES BOOK
NEW YORK

This is a work of fiction. All the characters and events portrayed in this book are either products of the author's imagination or are used fictitiously.

CHEYENNE SUMMER

Copyright © 2001 by Vella Munn

A Forge Book
Published by Tom Doherty Associates, LLC
175 Fifth Avenue
New York, NY 10010

www.tor.com

Forge® is a registered trademark of Tom Doherty Associates, LLC.

ISBN: 0-812-57018-9
Library of Congress Catalog Card Number: 2001023202

First edition: July 2001
First mass market edition: July 2002

Printed in the United States of America

0 9 8 7 6 5 4 3 2 1

To my grandfather
Homer Eon Flindt.

If only you had been given more years.

PROLOGUE

One heartbeat there was nothing; the next, he'd walked from a place without form or smell and now stood, alone, on the plains. The grassland extended forever and was everything, had no beginning or—the seasons of his life had taught him—end. He was part of it and it owned him. Held him prisoner.

Heat and wind snarled, attacked. Growling back, he nevertheless turned his naked back on the torrent and bent his head to protect his eyes, nostrils, and mouth. He held two arrows in his strong right hand but had no bow. Even if he did, what use was a weapon against the wind?

The rest of his people were somewhere else, perhaps camped in a depression safe from the worst of summer, but he couldn't join them because—

Suddenly afraid, he fought to remember what had brought him here, but his mouth was parched, his head throbbed, and he could barely think. It wasn't until his belly cramped and he looked down at its sunken contours that he remembered.

He'd come to hunt buffalo because without meat, the Cheyenne would die. Why others weren't with him didn't matter, either that or the relentless flames of moving air had turned him into an animal concerned only with survival.

He sucked hot air deep into his lungs, felt himself drying out from the inside as well as the attack on his flesh. He wore a loincloth, but his feet were bare when he should have worn moccasins. His hair, held in two long braids, felt so heavy that if he'd had a knife, he'd cut them off.

A dream. Yes, this was *the* dream. Again. Inescapable.

Where was he? Fighting fear, he prayed to Heammawihio, the Wise One Above, because the sun represented the greatest spirit, not just to ask Heammawihio to cast a shadow over its flames but also because, overwhelmed, he couldn't concentrate on hunting.

The words were still forming inside him when a sound caught his attention. He turned, suffering a stab of fire-air across his face as he did. For a moment he thought he'd caught the distant thunder of buffalo hooves on packed earth. Trapped in silence, he didn't try to stop the tears that trickled down his cheeks, then evaporated.

He would return empty-handed. Old and young would stare at him with hungry, desperate eyes. There was no wisdom in his eyes; his hearing had failed him; he'd forgotten his bow. He had no horse to load meat on and his legs weren't powerful enough to—

"Heammawihio, where is your wisdom? I am Lone Hawk, a single warrior. If it was you who sent me out here, you are foolish."

Shocked by his sacrilege, he clamped his hand over his mouth. Palm and lips were so dry he couldn't tell where one left off and the other began. The wind instantly stole his tears. Eyes shut now, he lifted his head, opened his mouth, howled.

If the rains came, the buffalo would return and the land of the Cheyenne would again be rich, but what if this great drought never ended?

CHAPTER 1

Sweat ran down Lone Hawk's spine and temple, and his inner thighs stuck to his mare's back. Her deep, tired breathing had become part of him, but although heat stripped him of much of his strength, he had no wish to fall asleep.

Five other Cheyenne hunters, all members of the Bow String Society, rode nearby, not clinging to silence but not speaking either. Perhaps, like him, they'd been distracted by the hard, crackling lightning that occasionally sparked through the cloudless heavens. As long as it remained far away, there was nothing to fear, but if it came closer, touched the dry earth—

Each man wore his hair in long braids with at least one eagle feather woven into the dark strands. Their backs were straight, muscled legs part of their mounts, arms easy at their sides, fingers holding the leather reins with confidence. Except for their individually decorated loincloths, they were naked and nearly the same color as the sparse grassland.

The plains offered few hiding places, but from a distance, an enemy might mistake them for antelope. Even if they didn't, Lone Hawk and the others didn't fear attack, not just because Grey Bear, who'd scouted ahead yesterday, hadn't seen any sign of Pawnee, Ute, Crow, Omaha, Dakota, Shoshone, Arapaho, or Comanche. More important, Sweet Grass Eater, Grey Bear's priest grandfather, had prayed to and received a message from Maiyunahu'ta, Spirit Who Told Me in Sleep. No one had done anything to jeopardize the vital balance of the Sacred Arrows; this hunt was right. Necessary.

Lone Hawk, maybe because he'd been unable to shake the effects of his recurring nightmares, couldn't get his mind to settle and rest on Maiyunahu'ta's wisdom. Just the same, there was nothing he'd rather do than ride with his companions—unless it was to walk cradled in spring's gentle warmth. The land rolled in all directions, switch grass, bluestem, yellow prairie dock, crimson liatris, and buffalo grass fighting for space in the rich but ash-dry dirt.

Out of the corner of his eye, he spotted Grey Bear but made no effort to speak to the skilled horseman and fearless warrior. Grey Bear ran his left hand over his stallion's muscled neck. Whether he'd intended for Lone Hawk to note that Legs Like Lightning still moved with morning's energy, Lone Hawk didn't know. Still, it wouldn't surprise him, since Grey Bear's pride in his five-year old stallion was never-ending, as it should be.

The sound of approaching hoofbeats distracted him from his unwanted envy of Grey Bear's mount. Pulling on the rawhide around his mare's lower jaw, he waited for Porcupine to join him.

"The tracks are here," Porcupine said unnecessarily. The lean, short-legged warrior twisted his neck from side to side, working a kink out of it. "The buffalo wander toward the setting sun and then in the direction of summer and dryness, sometimes traveling over ground so packed their hooves leave no sign, but Sweet Grass Eater was right—Maiyunahu'ta blesses us. The droppings, although not morning fresh, have not lost all moisture."

Lone Hawk nodded agreement, but Grey Bear, who'd woven four white-tipped feathers into his thick hair, spoke before he could gather his thoughts. "You say this because your eyes have finally told you the truth?" Grey Bear asked Porcupine. "Did I not tell all of what I found? Perhaps you doubt the wisdom of my senses?"

"I would never question you." The slender warrior, who'd seen more than thirty winters and was married and the father of two children, didn't meet Grey Bear's sharp gaze. "All I said was that my eyes and nose have spoken to me."

Grey Bear looked as if he wanted to press the issue, not that that surprised Lone Hawk. Grey Bear had no need to discount his war and hunting skills and courage, and yet there was something about the solidly built warrior that reminded Lone Wolf of a searching child. He couldn't imagine Grey Bear ever doubting his prowess, and yet—

"I only wanted to settle in my mind how many buffalo we are following," Porcupine continued. "I thought I had brought enough arrows—" He indicated the quiver strapped to his naked back. "But I allowed myself to think we might be following a great herd. That was what I was looking for, understanding of how many lay ahead."

Lone Hawk stifled the urge to remind Porcupine that this time of year, with both water and grass in short supply, the buffalo had separated into small, far-ranging groups, but Porcupine, ten years his senior, knew that.

"Enough," Grey Bear said, his hand once again taking its measure of Legs Like Lightning's neck muscle. "There will be enough meat to feed everyone."

"I pray you are right." The words were out of Lone Hawk's mouth before he could judge their wisdom. As he expected, Grey Bear speared him with a probing glare. Then, perhaps because the hot wind had blunted even his keen awareness of his surroundings, Grey Bear turned his attention to ridding himself of several flies that had attached themselves to his chest, which he'd painted black. When he flicked them away, they headed for Lone Hawk. Lone Hawk waved them away, the effort increasing his awareness of how tight the dried red paint he'd put on his own chest made his flesh feel. The paint, which was the color of growth, protected him from wind and sunburn and signified his status as a warrior, but today it also added to his discomfort.

Grey Bear had dug his heels into Legs Like Lightning's sides and was quickly overtaking the peace chief Nightelk, who rode at the head of the small band. When he was out of earshot, Porcupine asked if Lone Hawk thought Grey Bear was displeased with him. Lone Hawk shrugged. "He is a man of much energy. Riding when he wants to hunt rests heavy on him."

Porcupine laughed. "That is not all that weighs on him."

"Not just him," Lone Hawk muttered under his breath, but although surely Porcupine remembered what it was like to be young and unmarried with need flowing through him, he didn't mention it. Porcupine's wife, Walking Rabbit, despite having given birth to two children and being a hard worker, hadn't grown fat and stooped, and Porcupine was envied by many.

"Grey Bear is not the only one who needs to exhaust himself in a hunt," Porcupine said. "Even I want that."

"You?"

"A warrior who sleeps with his wife before a hunt or battle risks weakening himself and getting killed."

"Walking Rabbit will welcome you when you return," Lone Hawk pointed out. "Those of us who are not married remain as children."

"True." Porcupine sighed. "I wish she had come with us, she and the other women."

"Summer has tired them. Until we have killed—"

A flicker of movement overhead caught his attention. Squinting, Lone Hawk made out a distant bird but couldn't tell if it was a hawk. If it was, he'd tell himself that the bird had been sent by Heammawikio, who was more powerful than the sun, as proof that he rode with his spirit's protection beside him.

Porcupine indicated the bird. "Perhaps it is a buzzard. We sweat so that our foulness has reached it."

"Perhaps." Lone Hawk started to lift his arm to smell himself there, then thought better of it. The sun was at the height of its journey, its heat relentless. The wind was gentle today, which made the sun even harder to bear. This morning he'd filled a buffalo bladder with water, but it would have to last both him and his horse until he returned home. "Does your head feel as if it would burst?" he asked.

Porcupine shrugged. "We endured the Sun Dance and carry its scars. Surely nothing can test us more."

He wanted to believe Porcupine, would have if it wasn't for his nightmares. He hadn't told anyone about them.

"I did not mean to complain," he told Porcupine. "I simply—sometimes summer makes thinking harder."

"True. So, when we reach the buffalo, will you go after a fat cow? Perhaps you dream of gorging on a great bull."

Bulls were avoided because their meat was tough and they were hard to kill. Lone Hawk's mouth watered at the thought of eating as much as his belly could hold, but the few buffalo he'd seen lately had lost their spring fat. A few days ago, he'd come across the carcass of a half-grown calf. The body had been torn apart and the bones picked clean so it was impossible to say what had killed it. Although wolves often took down newborns, they attacked larger animals only out of desperation, and that time hadn't come for them this season . . . yet. Perhaps the calf had injured itself and the wolves had taken advantage of its helplessness, but maybe it had died from lack of water and grass.

In that, the Cheyenne were like buffalo.

ALTHOUGH NIGHTELK KNEW who was approaching, the senior hunter didn't turn to acknowledge Grey Bear. When they'd started out, Grey Bear had led the way, pointing out the signs he'd found earlier, but then the younger, stronger warrior had given way to his elder. Alone with his thoughts, Nightelk had pondered not just whether this hunt would be successful but whether it was his last. Riding into his gray-haired years was a new journey; he hadn't thought he'd be taking it so soon—not with his back still straight and proud, his muscles firm, and his eyesight and hearing undimmed. If he could turn around and—

"I have been thinking," Grey Bear said as he drew alongside. "Perhaps I should ride on ahead again."

"Do what you want. I only caution you to conserve both yours and your horse's energy."

Grey Bear straightened, the gesture making his feathers dance. "My strength is as great now as it was when I first woke."

Perhaps. "And Legs Like Lightning?"

"I know what he is capable of, only I."

Already tired of the conversation, Nightelk closed his eyes. Just the same, he remained aware of his own horse's progress as well as the fact that his dog kept pace. Black Eyes meant as much to him as Legs Like Lightning possibly could to Grey Bear, and as long as Black Eyes gave no indication that game was nearby, he wouldn't push himself. Instead, he listened to his surroundings. Listened and tried to learn.

"I will not argue with you, Grey Bear," he said after a short silence. "I remember what it is to be a young warrior, full of oneself."

Grey Bear said nothing, prompting him to open his eyes. The handsome warrior who reminded him of a bull elk was staring at the horizon. In the distance, lightning, hot as death, flashed. Because there were no clouds, it gave no promise of rain.

"The time for action will soon be upon us," Nightelk continued, eager to think of anything except whether the lightning might catch the prairie grasses on fire. "And when it is, I may envy you, but that is not where my thoughts are now."

Grey Bear studied the horizon, but the lightning didn't repeat itself. His mouth pulled into a tight line, the young brave turned his attention to the wind-whipped tracks they'd been following. The so-called herd consisted of no more than five animals, two small enough that the others' hoof prints sometimes covered theirs. Grey Bear wouldn't be particularly boastful about finding so few animals, but with the band's meat supply nearly exhausted, even a single buffalo was important.

That's what he should be thinking about, the need to bring home everything they could. However, if he expended too much of himself in that, fear might take hold of him and result in his family's bellies going empty. When the time came to hunt, he'd become a predator. As for now—

"Perhaps not," Grey Bear said, his deep voice in rhythm with the sound of horse hooves.

"Perhaps not what?"

"It is not wise for me to leave the rest of you behind."

"Hm."

Apparently that satisfied Grey Bear because, after pressing the heel of his hand against his forehead, he held Legs Like Lightning back until Nightelk was once again in the lead. Alone, the forty-one-year-old warrior contemplated the many seasons that had taken him beyond where men like Grey Bear and Lone Hawk were in their lives.

To be a Cheyenne man meant facing danger and death; he'd known that from the time he'd left his mother's breast and joined the other boys. Their games had all been about fighting, hunting, attacking, and being attacked.

Not every warrior who rode out returned home alive. The uncle who'd afforded him his first hunting opportunity had died when a wounded buffalo trampled him and his horse. A brother had been buried following a Pawnee attack. There'd been others who would never see their twilight years, some of them riding with him in spirit today, others, he prayed, alongside his companions.

Breaking free of the thought, he jerked upright. His horse barely noticed but Black Eyes looked up at him. He returned the large, lanky animal's gaze.

"It is good to be a dog," he told Black Eyes. "Your thoughts go no further than this moment and what your eyes and ears and nose reveal to you."

That stopped him because as close as he and Black Eyes were, there were things he didn't know about him. On the other hand, there wasn't anything he wouldn't tell the animal.

"This may be my last hunt," he whispered. "I have stepped into another place in my life and must embrace the honor and responsibility." He swallowed to moisten his dry throat. "I who have always ridden with weapons must set them aside and sit with old men of the peace council."

Old men?

"I am the youngest," he said, reassuring not Black Eyes but himself. "Chosen because the one who was before me has died. Will you sit with me when the others and I talk of how to maintain peace within the band? Will you believe my wisdom? Think it was right for me to change from one thing to another?"

Black Eyes yawned, then lowered his nose until it nearly scraped along the ground.

Am I ready?

THE SUN WOULD soon leave the sky, and they still hadn't overtaken the buffalo. True, the droppings were fresh, but Lone Hawk had yet to hear the faint, telltale sound of chewing or spot the dust they constantly churned up. If they didn't come across the small herd before dark, the animals might escape.

Pondering that possibility, he looked around for Grey Bear, spotting him near Nightelk. Grey Bear and Nightelk didn't ride together often, but perhaps Nightelk was passing on wisdom. If that was the case, he should join them since Nightelk was both wise and courageous.

Heammawihio had breathed fresh life into the wind, and it rustled past the dead-appearing grasses. In an attempt to think of anything except how hungry and thirsty and hot he was, he cast around for someone to talk to, but the others looked half asleep. Even Black Eyes, whose greatest pleasure beyond guarding Nightelk was to track, seemed bored. Lightning occasionally danced above the plains.

At the moment, their journey was taking them toward the setting sun, making seeing difficult. As he'd done more times today than he wanted to think about, he surrendered to his dreams. When medicine men and priests dreamed, they knew what they meant, and their meaning, more often than not, touched the whole band.

Was he looking into his people's future? No! He was a warrior and a hunter, not a priest!

Still—

With a start, he realized his horse had nearly bumped into Porcupine, who was riding ahead of him.

"What is it?" he asked, embarrassed because Wolf Robe

and Woodenlegs as well as Porcupine had noticed his inattention.

Wolf Robe pointed at Grey Bear, who in turn was motioning for them to join him. Lone Hawk prodded his mare to get her to walk faster, aware that the others were having to do the same thing.

"I have decided," Grey Bear said when everyone had drawn close. "We must overtake the buffalo before dark."

"Why? How?" Porcupine glanced at Nightelk, but the senior warrior only studied Grey Bear. "If we ask our horses to run now," he continued, "they will be worthless during the killing. This heat—"

"Not all of them," Grey Bear interrupted, although to do so was rude. "Legs Like Lightning is still strong. Lone Hawk, you will ride one of the animals brought to carry the meat because they are fresher. You and I will ride ahead, see how much farther we have to go."

Lone Hawk wasn't surprised to have been chosen because, like his namesake, his sight was keen. Besides, despite his weariness, he wanted to be doing something—anything. "If it grows dark before we reach the buffalo, we will have to spend the night apart from the others," he pointed out.

"Yes."

Instead of acknowledging Grey Bear's curt response, Lone Hawk directed his next comment at Nightelk. "You have come to the same conclusion? This is what we should do?"

"Whether we sleep in one spot or two does not matter," Nightelk said. "Close to the buffalo, you will know where they bed down. If they start to leave in the morning, you can make them run back our way."

In his mind, he saw himself galloping beside a laboring buffalo, one with the creature, taking its spirit-strength. "That is good."

THE HORSE HE'D been riding since he and Grey Bear took off was somewhat fresher than his mare, but it didn't have the strength for a lengthy chase. Cantering had winded it;

even this trot couldn't last long. Horses were gifts from the creator Maheo, All Father, and although he often gave thanks to Maheo, he wasn't certain who he was praying too. As the God over all, Maheo was so great that he couldn't be fully described, and no one had ever seen him.

Mahoe and the Sacred Powers had given his people power for life and the wisdom to understand that that life is good. Everything that lived was related to everything else and had been created by Maheo, making everything part of a single living unity. Just thinking about Maheo's power and gifts humbled him. If Maheo was responsible for his dreams—

"This lightning," Grey Bear said unexpectedly. "I wish my grandfather had told me to expect it."

"No one controls what comes from the sky."

"You do not have to tell me that." Grey Bear glared at where the sky-fire had last shown itself. "If it frightens the buffalo . . ."

If it did, their effort might be for nothing.

"I want this hunt to be over." Grey Bear wiped sweat off the side of his neck.

"So you can fill your belly?"

"Not just that." He'd been riding a few paces ahead but now slowed Legs Like Lightning to the pace of Lone Hawk's mount. "I want to return to camp and see the girls looking at me. Wanting me to speak to them."

"Getting them to speak in return is not an easy thing."

"True." Grey Bear sighed. "I wish they would be digging turnip roots when we arrive."

There weren't any turnip roots left this time of the year, but that didn't stop Lone Hawk from imagining the fierce, mock attack the women would inflict on the men as part of a ceremony older than the oldest Cheyenne's memory.

The "attack" always began with the girls and women challenging the men to try to steal their just-dug roots, blankets, digging and pounding stones. The men responded by climbing onto scruffy old horses and taking up the challenge. For their pains, the men were pelted with sticks and dry buffalo dung. Only those who'd had a horse shot out from under them or been wounded in battle could dismount and snatch some roots—count coup.

"The last time I participated, I grabbed one of Seeks Fire's blankets," Grey Bear explained. "As I did, I lost my footing and dragged her down with me. Fortunately, her mother did not see. Otherwise, she may have stoned me."

What Grey Bear had done came close to being forbidden, not that he needed to tell him that. Neither did he point out that Grey Bear never lost his footing. "Did Seeks Fire say anything?"

"She warned me not to try to touch her again, but her body did not speak the same words."

Lone Hawk wasn't sure about that since the handsome Seeks Fire always conducted herself in the proper manner. Her mother daily tied her into her chastity belt, and not once had a single knot been disturbed.

"It is right that she and I be together," Grey Bear went on. "Our families are both wealthy and our children . . ."

Although his curiosity was enough that he wanted to prompt Grey Bear to continue, he waited.

"It is time for me to become a father. I watch my brothers and cousins with their children, see their pride and want that for myself."

"All warriors want children. When we are lazy, it is good to have someone to bring food to us."

"Not just that." Grey Bear touched his quiver. "Long life may not be the road I—or any warrior—walk. When I die, I want that not to be the end of me."

"No man or woman can say when their time on this land will end. It does no good to plan for what might or might not happen."

"I know. Still . . ." Grey Bear again fingered his weapons. "I fear nothing, have never run from a battle. Do not forget that."

"Have I said you did?"

Grey Bear shrugged. "We will find the buffalo, kill them, and return home. Before all the meat has been eaten, we will hunt again. Still . . ."

"Still what?"

Lightning spat, arched across the sky.

"Perhaps I want to stay with my wife," Grey Bear said. "Spill myself inside her and watch her belly swell with my seed."

"Your wife Seeks Fire?"

"Why not? She is everything I want, everything I deserve."

"And are you what she wants?"

His brow furrowed, Grey Bear stared first at Lone Hawk and then at their surroundings. Maybe it was a trick of the sun and the black paint he wore, but for a moment Lone Hawk saw Grey Bear not as a Cheyenne warrior but a shadow.

"No man knows what is inside a woman," Grey Bear said. "Perhaps you think you are different, that—do you love her yourself?"

"She barely looks my way."

"Hm. But you desire her, do you not? All men do because no other maiden's legs are longer. Her arms are both strong and slender. And her—her breasts are . . . only Touches the Wind can equal her in that."

If Seeks Fire didn't allow Grey Bear to court her, something Lone Hawk couldn't comprehend, would the warrior turn his attention to Touches the Wind? No, because Touches the Wind's family was poor, her mother crippled and her father cursed by a lifetime of bad luck. Despite her considerable domestic skills and the way Maheo had fashioned her, neither he or Grey Bear would seek her. Instead, she'd go to a lesser warrior or maybe an old man whose wife had died.

"We speak foolishness," Lone Hawk admonished. "If we return home empty-handed, what will we tell our people, that our minds were full of maidens and the buffalo wandered away?"

"No buffalo will escape my arrows."

Boasting was the way of a warrior and silenced fear, but Grey Bear never lost an opportunity to remind others that he was unequaled in fighting and hunting skills. Leaving him, Lone Hawk urged his horse to a faster pace. He'd gone only a few steps when he heard something that didn't belong to the wind. Behind him, Grey Bear hissed a warning. Stopping, they leaned forward, concentrating.

Human yells, distant and telling.

Buffalo dying.

CHAPTER 2

 Grey Bear reached for his weapons and fitted an arrow against his bowstring. At the same time, he dug his heels into Legs Like Lightning. The blood in his temples pulsed.

"Grey Bear, no!"

"Do not tell me no! This must not happen."

"Until we know how many there are of our enemy, we must be like antelope, silent and curious."

"I am a hunter, not an antelope!"

If Lone Hawk had said anything, Grey Bear would have thrown his words back at him. Silence, however, forced him to weigh what his companion had said. After releasing the tension on his bowstring, he urged Legs Like Lightning forward at a walk. Lone Hawk kept pace. Already he could smell buffalo excrement, blood, and fear. Their horses held their heads high, ears moving, always moving; their legs danced.

The swirl of dust that marked the killing ground took on form until, without having to say anything, the two men stopped. Lifting their hands to shield their eyes, they studied the scene ahead of and slightly below them.

The buffalo they'd been following had met up with more of their kind—and with death. Five buffalo had fallen, some unmoving, others stabbing and slashing their useless legs at the air. One bellowed, the sound thick as its lungs filled with blood. In the distance other buffalo milled as if unsure whether to flee or help their wounded or dead companions. The hunters paid them no mind.

"Pawnee," Lone Hawk whispered.

Grey Bear nodded agreement but didn't try to speak against the rage surging through him. There were eight of the enemy, two more than there were Cheyenne, not that that mattered because it was only he and Lone Hawk against those he ached to destroy. Those who'd laid claim to what his people needed for survival.

"They will remain here until they have skinned the carcasses," Lone Hawk said. "Through the night."

"And they will put down their weapons while they work. Be easier to kill." His throat tightened; he again reached for his bow and arrows.

"No."

"You would allow them to take what is ours?"

"That is not my thought. I—"

"You think too much! It is time to act.".

He started forward, but he'd gone only a few feet before Lone Hawk grabbed his rein and pulled Legs Like Lightning to a halt.

"Do not touch him!" he ordered. "You have—"

"What you are doing is foolish."

No one called him foolish! Not he who'd participated in his first battle when he was only thirteen. He'd ridden at the front of a line of warriors that distant day, been the first to bury an arrow into an Arapaho. No other Cheyenne brave had counted more coup in so few years, and the others eagerly followed him, agreed when he said it was time to go to war.

"You think you are so powerful you can kill eight of our enemy?" Lone Hawk asked, his tone calm and measured.

"You will not join me?"

"Today is not about avenging what the Pawnee have done. We are here to provide for our people, only that."

"The Pawnee killed—"

"I know." Lone Hawk divided his attention between Grey

Bear and the Pawnee who'd all dismounted and were intent on butchering. Already crows flew overhead, attracted by the smell. "Yes, they have taken what is ours, but I say we must use wisdom, not emotion."

On the verge of insisting Lone Hawk couldn't know what was going on inside him, Grey Bear thought better of it. He was a man of movement and action, doing and surviving because his priest grandfather Sweet Grass Eater showed him the way. Others might listen to the part of them that whispered of danger, fear, and the need for caution, but that had never been his way. Still, he had no wish to die today.

"This is not the end of it." Lone Hawk's tone became forceful. "Today is for the Cheyenne, not Pawnee."

BECAUSE THEY HADN'T gone that far ahead and the others were on the move, Grey Bear and Lone Hawk soon reunited with their companions. The explanation of what they'd found took only a few moments.

"Eight Pawnee?" Porcupine had rested his free hand on his shoulder and was massaging it. "And you say they killed only as many buffalo as they can carry away?"

Lone Hawk explained that perhaps half of the animals remained alive. As he did, the image of what he'd seen reformed in his mind, bringing with it not just sight but sound and smell as well.

Buffalo were gifts from Yellow Haired Woman who in turn had been gifted by Coyote Man who'd counseled her not to express pity for any suffering animal. Animals died to feed the Cheyenne, and the reality of their dying had always been part of Lone Hawk.

Beside him, Grey Bear waited. Grey Bear was like a wolf who conserves his energy until the instant of action. When he moved, it was with confidence and deadly purpose. Sometimes all instinct and little thought.

"Night stalks us," Lone Hawk said. "I sense its coming and ask myself whether it is our enemy or our friend."

"Explain yourself," Nightelk said, but before he could answer, Porcupine pointed out that if they hurried, they could attack before dark. If they were successful, they'd kill all of their enemy, but it was possible one or more would escape. If other Pawnee were nearby, they might attack in force.

"We must not risk looking for fleeing Pawnee in the dark," Porcupine finished. "If we do, we will be as vulnerable as our enemy now is."

"What are you saying?" Nightelk asked.

"They have taken what is ours and that should not be. I do not want to return home empty-handed. But . . ." Shrugging, Porcupine stared at Nightelk.

Nightelk held out his hands, palms up, his fingers curling inward as if cradling something. "We have several ways to walk," he said. "One." He lifted his right hand. "We attack now and trust that the gods and spirits will protect us through the night. Two." Up came the left. "We wait until morning."

"Morning!" Grey Bear shot back. "What if they have left?"

"Then we will overtake them. But there is another possibility." Nightelk clapped his hands together, staring at them as if they held wisdom. "There are more buffalo than we thought, enough for both Cheyenne and Pawnee."

"No!" Grey Bear glared at the senior warrior. "My grandfather's dream—"

"I know," Nightelk interrupted. "Sweet Grass Eater's message was that these are Cheyenne buffalo, but I say we should not risk Cheyenne lives if there is another way."

NIGHTELK HAD KNOWN only eight summers the last time the world had gone this long without tasting water. At first he'd given the drought little mind and had wished his parents would stop talking about dry water holes and air that leached the moisture from flesh and robbed creature after creature of life, but then his mother's breasts no longer held the gift of milk and his infant sister died. His parents' wailing and the desperate look in their eyes had taken him out of childhood and turned him into a warrior—a helpless warrior.

That year there'd been no rain until he'd begun waking to

chilled air and earth. His band, like the other Cheyenne bands, had been constantly on the move as warriors searched for the few buffalo that hadn't left or died of thirst, but finally .great black clouds filled the sky—first shaking the earth with thunderclaps like crashing boulders and great slashes of lightning ignited countless grass fires. The priests had prayed and sacrificed while the band gathered around them. Lightning and thunder had continued for days—it seemed like forever—and the wind growled in anger but finally, finally the heavens cried tears of life.

Shaking himself free of the memory, he focused on his surroundings. Lone Hawk and Grey Bear had stopped and were pointing. He joined them, his mouth watering at the sight of slabs of meat already on Pawnee packhorses; in his hand, he felt the weight of his cutting knife. Calf Woman had been his wife for so many years that their children—those who were still alive—were all grown, and he'd always been able to place food in their bellies. He didn't want to fail now, but neither did he want to leave Calf Woman a widow.

"Listen to me," he said. Around him the younger braves sucked in deep breaths, preparing themselves for battle. "Grey Bear has called this hunt, not me. I will not say that what he proposes is wrong, but I speak with the wisdom of my years."

No one interrupted, yet he sensed their impatience.

"As a young man my heart was filled with the need for hunting and war. I cared little for tomorrow, wanted only to be a Cheyenne man. But I would be dead if my heart had not learned how to beat another way. A cautious way."

"You do not wish to attack?" Grey Bear demanded. "To run like rabbits?"

"No, not like rabbits. Look." He pointed beyond the Pawnee to the small dust cloud that indicated where the surviving buffalo had gone. "Maiyunahu'ta spoke wisdom to Sweet Grass Eater. There is *our* food."

"No!" Grey Bear shook his head. "We are Cheyenne! We

do not go after what our enemy has no use for. We take what is ours! We take!"

"Do what you will," Nightelk said. "And call me an old man if that is what you wish, but I told my wife and others that I would bring back meat. That is what I do." He looked into each pair of youthful eyes in turn. "Decide. Follow me as hunters or Grey Bear as fighters."

With that, he pressed his heels against his mare's side and leaned forward. She sprang forward, alone. Behind him, the young men called out the names of their protector spirits; then the words changed and became a challenge.

As Nightelk galloped in a wide circle toward the living buffalo in the distance, Grey Bear again felt his body fill with hot and pulsing blood. The sensation took him out of himself, turned him into a grizzly, propelled him forward.

He howled and roared, and his head throbbed, and there was no taste of fear or even caution on his tongue. His body became wet with sweat; his lungs inhaled and expelled great drinks of air. The medicine bag his grandfather had tied around his neck bounced against his chest, and the bear symbols the old man had painted on his arms flexed and moved as if alive.

As GREY BEAR and the others galloped toward their enemy, the Pawnee abandoned their work and scrambled to retrieve their weapons. Their horses, still skittish from the killing, milled together. The Pawnee closest to Grey Bear appeared older than him, not as large or strong-muscled but with long arms and legs. The hair along his left temple was white as if coated in snow.

Grey Bear vowed the white would soon be covered with Pawnee blood, but before he could launch his first arrow, an enemy horse broke free of the herd and raced toward him. Anticipating a collision, Legs Like Lightning changed direction. If he and his horse weren't as one, he would have been unseated. As it was, he had to lean away from where Legs

Like Lightning now ran, making it impossible for him to keep his arrow aimed at Whitehair.

It didn't matter; he'd already found a new foe.

Another growl stretched his throat, and he bore down on the brave who was turning toward him, his stone knife his only weapon. His lips stretched over his teeth; he pulled his bow string as far as it would go, released. Saw it slice into the Pawnee's throat, watched dark flesh turn red.

He was Grey Bear! Hunter! Fighter!

A few feet away, Lone Hawk heard Grey Bear's triumphant cry but didn't try to see what had given it birth. He'd spotted another Pawnee who, instead of standing and fighting, ran toward the horses.

"See me!" Lone Hawk cried. "See your enemy!"

The Pawnee, naked except for a loincloth and without so much as a single line of paint, whirled around. He was short with legs better suited for a child, but his shoulders were broad and his neck thick. He gripped a bow and arrows in one hand; the other held his cutting knife. In his eyes, Lone Hawk saw something that briefly stopped his breath.

"I send you to the spirit world," he yelled at the Pawnee. With that, he released his arrow. It sped toward a naked belly and half hid itself in all-too-willing flesh. As he clawed at what was killing him, the wounded man's weapons clattered to the earth.

"You took Cheyenne buffalo!" Lone Hawk cried. "Took what Maiyunahu'ta sent us here to find."

The Pawnee stumbled forward, stopped, started to walk again, fell to his knees. He'd managed to pull the arrow out of him, but the hole streamed blood that ran down his groin and legs. Lone Hawk willed the man to end his dying and begin his journey to whatever spirit world waited for the Pawnee. While he did, he noted that the man's belly was sunken and his skin looked too big for his body.

THE SOUNDS OF battle raged behind Nightelk, but he forced himself to keep going. His mare had to be continually prod-

ded, and Black Eyes had already fallen behind; if he hadn't
filled himself with thoughts of those who depended on him
for food, he would have rejoined his companions. He wanted
to fight, wanted back the hot blood of his youth!

But he wasn't young.

Nostrils flared, he stretched out along his mare's back and
concentrated on what lay ahead of him. From what he could
tell, three were last year's calves; their meat would be tender.
He'd set a course toward the closest one when his attention
was drawn to a large cow. Under her belly he spotted smaller
legs, proof that she was trying to protect a calf. Thoughts of
the calf's meat started his mouth watering, but the cow represented more food.

"Maiyunahu'ta! Thank you!"

Perhaps the cow knew she was his target and that's why
she started to run. No matter, he needed this chase. Determination tightened his muscles as he set his horse after her.
She managed to keep her calf between herself and him, but
the youngster hampered her movements. Nightelk leaned to
the right, bow and arrow at the ready as he maneuvered so
the arrow would strike just behind the last rib between the
pelvis and spine where the liver lay. As soon as he hit her,
he'd turn his attention to the other buffalo because although
she might continue to run awhile after being wounded, she'd
soon die.

"Buffalo ! Hear me! This is your destiny! Your death for
my people's life!"

Close, so close now that he could smell her hot sweat. Not
enough air reached his lungs, and his horse wheezed. Still . . .

His prayer now silent, he released his arrow. He saw it
slice through the air, waited—

At the heartbeat before impact, the cow stumbled and lost
her footing. His arrow sailed over her back, struck—

Struck her calf!

The smaller creature squealed and pitched forward. The
moment its knees hit the ground, it righted itself, blood pour-
ing from the wound in its side. By then the cow had regained
her footing and wheeled as if to run down Nightelk's horse.

Wise to the ways of buffalo, he yanked his mount out of the way, then back around. Instead of continuing after him, the cow turned her attention to her youngster.

The calf stood with its legs trembling and its head down. Blood ran in a fine stream under its belly and onto the ground. Nightelk went back through the years of hunting, wisdom telling him that the young heart would soon cease beating.

Only then did he see what he'd hit.

What he'd done.

The calf was white.

Sacred!

Sick and terrified, Nightelk fled. Above, the heavens snapped and cracked, lightning threatening to set the sky on fire.

OUT OF THE corner of his eye, Grey Bear saw that Lone Hawk had drawn back from his dying foe and now stood motionless, but he had no time for the warrior whose sight was even keener than his own.

Nightelk had told them that their first concern must be for their families' needs. What the seasoned fighter had forgotten was that the Pawnee must be taught they'd been attacked by a superior force, pummel them as a mature bull elk beats a younger one.

"Grandfather, I ride for you! Fight because you have prepared me! And because a bear's courage flows through me!"

His words filled him, and the whisper of caution—not fear, of course—only caution, that he'd felt a moment ago vanished. Sitting tall on his stallion's back, he took in his surroundings. Although there were more Pawnee than Cheyenne, the element of surprise had tipped the balance. In addition to the two he and Lone Hawk had killed, another Pawnee lay as motionless as the buffalo. The ground seemed to be absorbing the dead, taking men and animals into itself, and yet cries and shouts and whinnies told him that the fighting continued.

What caught and held his attention was the sight of a Pawnee scrambling onto his horse's back, bending low over the animal's neck, whirling and racing away.

"Porcupine!" he bellowed because the older brave was closer to the fleeing Pawnee. He pointed and was relieved to see Porcupine charge. However, Porcupine's horse hadn't yet reached a gallop when he slid around to the animal's side, causing it to stumble.

"Do not—" Grey Bear started. His intention had been to order Porcupine not to let the Pawnee escape. The Pawnee had fired at Porcupine, but although the arrow hadn't been close enough to endanger him, Porcupine had nevertheless ducked. Now he stopped.

A quick glance told Grey Bear that not even Legs Like Lightning could overtake the rapidly disappearing foe.

"You did not think!" he yelled at Porcupine. "You let your body rule when your head should have!"

"I do not fight your battles, Grey Bear. Do not tell me how—"

The *twang* had barely registered as the sound of a just-released arrow when Porcupine jerked upright. One hand went to his side; the other gripped his mare's short mane. Porcupine's face registered surprise, the beginning of pain, and something else—horror and fear all mixed together in a great swirling. Walking Rabbit's husband looked down at what had been done to him, his gaze taking Grey Bear with him. Blood didn't flow but leaked, the deeply embedded shaft acting as a plug.

A moan, so low it might have come from the earth instead of Porcupine, pushed past his suddenly white lips. The wounded man continued to sit upright, allowing Grey Bear to take his eyes off him and search, quick and with desperate purpose, for the enemy.

Dying sunlight settled on black hair marred by a pale streak. Whitehair, angled so he was half hidden behind his horse, called. The words were taunt and challenge. Grey Bear didn't need to know any more.

Eyes locked on the rangy brave, Grey Bear sent a silent

message to Legs Like Lightning. His warhorse responded by tensing his muscles and lowering his head. Grey Bear reached behind him for another arrow.

"I—I die."

"No," he said over his shoulder at Porcupine. He continued to return Whitehair's gaze. They were two male bears, alike and yet not, fearless and knowing, all instinct and wisdom about the other.

"Tell—tell—Walking Rabbit . . ."

"No." *Go toward Whitehair*, his body told Legs Like Lightning. *Stalk him. Bring me closer so his flesh will eat what I have prepared for him*. The striped and sacred arrow his grandfather had blessed was now aimed at Whitehair's throat where the fragile breath of life waited.

"Grey Bear?"

"Soon," he told Porcupine. "I will come to you but first—" *First I kill*.

Whitehair's eyes narrowed, hiding and sheltering what he felt; his arrow gave out the same message Grey Bear's did. His body also said he also understood that the two of them were indeed bears.

A horse squealed; not far away, he heard Lone Hawk call out to the prophet Sweet Medicine. Porcupine again whispered his name, but those things barely existed for Grey Bear. This, the seasons and battles and wars had taught him, was why he'd been born and why he'd embraced the Sun Dance and become a man. Facing his enemy in honest battle filled him and made him whole. Tasted like spring and felt like rain.

"Face me," he told Whitehair. "Do not be a frightened bird. Look into my eyes and see the eyes of your death."

Whitehair again said something, but the words still meant nothing. Legs Like Lightning started toward the Pawnee. In contrast, the enemy's horse took one backward step and then another. His rider didn't try to stop him. Pawnee men became thickset soon after they reached adulthood, and yet this one reminded Grey Bear of a winter-barren tree, all dark and naked limbs.

"Perhaps we will die together," he told the Pawnee. "You and I, enemies, ending this life and beginning another today."

The corner of the Pawnee's mouth twitched; surely it wasn't the beginning of a smile. Grey Bear couldn't say why he'd put off this killing and didn't want to explain his actions to his companions. Out of the corner of his eyes, he saw movement; Porcupine was falling to the ground.

"You have killed him!" he bellowed. "Look into my eyes and know this—your life in payment for his."

After that, he had no need for speech. He concentrated on what his fingers were doing, the tension in his bow string, the bear-paw prints painted on his shoulders, the smell of blood.

He'd begun to release his arrow when Porcupine screamed. The sound cut into him, seared him and weakened his fingers.

Whitehair leaned to one side as Grey Bear's arrow flew past him. Lightning slashes fingered downward, the great energy filling the air.

CHAPTER 3

Stepping back from her family's tepee, Touches the Wind slapped the faded buffalo hide. The larger and newer tepees on either side provided her with a measure of shade, but she would gladly give that up in exchange for hides that hadn't been attacked by so many seasons that they'd become dry and brittle. On the brink of another slap, she thought better of it since she risked making the seam tear she was trying to repair worse.

Childish laughter distracted her. The tepee where Porcupine, his wife Walking Rabbit, and their two children lived was less than an arrow-flight away. Not only did its close proximity provide her younger sister Little Bird with constant playmates, but she loved watching the close-knit family.

"He has so much energy." Walking Rabbit chuckled as she pushed up the door flap to her tepee and stepped outside. "I should have let him go with his father, anything to keep him occupied."

Touches the Wind turned her attention to Knows No Fear who was chasing his younger sister Follower from one tepee to another. At eight, Knows No Fear was happiest playing with other boys and had little use for six-year-old Follower. Usually he wore a loincloth in imitation of the men, but on this hot day he was as naked as his sister, their sun-darkened bodies blending with their surroundings.

"I envy them," Touches the Wind admitted. "This heat—" She pulled up on her unadorned deerhide dress at the shoulders and shook it to allow air to circulate. "presses against me like a rock."

"I know what you mean." As her children raced past, Walking Rabbit reached out to stop them, but they easily evaded her.

Laughing, the tall, long-waisted woman joined Touches the Wind. Her dress, in contrast with Touches the Wind's, had been decorated with porcupine quills, horse hairs, and bluebird feathers. "You exhaust me with your energy." She indicated the tendon-thread Touches the Wind held. "I know I should be scraping hide, but it is so hot that all I want to do is sleep."

Torn between admitting she didn't dare put off her repair job and not wanting to talk about it at all, she gave Walking Rabbit a wry grin. "I could not sleep last night. Finally I brought my blanket outside where at least there is fresh air— some wind."

"And perhaps it was your father's snoring that kept you awake?"

Touches the Wind nodded and glanced at her family's tepee, but although the dark interior had felt suffocating to her, her parents remained inside—as they did most of the time.

She debated asking Walking Rabbit if she'd heard her father's snorts.

"Where is Little Bird?" Walking Rabbit asked. "I have not seen your sister today."

"I told her she could watch Rich in Hides paint a new design on Nightelk's tepee. I would love—"

"What would you love?"

She let a sigh escape. "For him to paint an eagle for me."

Walking Rabbit turned her attention to Touches the Wind's family's tepee, but her expression gave away nothing of her reaction to its dilapidated condition.

"I am glad Little Bird is not with your parents." Walking Rabbit shook her head. "I know they kept her with them yesterday, and I felt sorry for her."

"I told them a child cannot sit all day," Touches the Wind admitted. After stepping away from the hide shelter, she went on. "But our father wanted to talk about a long-ago hunting trip he had been on, and my sister needs to understand that there was a time when he was a part of hunting parties. It is not enough that she learns only from me."

"You teach her well. When you speak of Tomsivsi, Sweet Medicine, Thunder Spirit, and the Sacred Mountain, all children stop what they are doing to listen. That may be the only time Knows No Fear's arms and legs are at rest."

Touches the Wind laughed. "It pleases me to tell them about the beginning of the Cheyenne. When I do, I forget who I am, and in my mind I hear Great Spirit speaking. The priests gain power from passing on those things, but sometimes they drone on so. I try to make my telling different, alive."

Walking Rabbit reached out and squeezed her forearm. "It is not easy for you, is it, living with Long Chin and Kicked by Horse?"

This wasn't the first time they'd talked about that, but she'd always pulled back from complete honesty. She did the same today, distracting Walking Rabbit by pointing out that Knows No Fear and Follower were now hurrying toward Nightelk's tepee. That tepee was on the opposite side of the encampment that had been set up near a creek which kept the nearby grasses green and fed a few trees. The creek had become less and less as the long days passed. If it didn't rain, it would soon die and then—

"Come with me," Walking Rabbit encouraged. "Your work can wait while we look at what Rich in Hides is doing to my sister's home. This waiting for my husband is hard. I welcome any distraction."

It took only a few moments to walk from one end of the village to the other, but by the time Touches the Wind reached her destination, the sun had sapped her. Breathing deeply, she inhaled the smell of cooking fires, dirt, hides, and horses. A stiff wind would stir up debris, but she longed for the sense of energy that came with it—to touch it if only in her mind.

Rich in Hides, although too old to be included in hunting and fighting trips, remained a valuable member of the band because of his artistic talents. At the moment, he was applying his various colored dyes to the side of Nightelk's tepee that faced east. He'd already sketched the outline of a bull elk and was concentrating on antler details. A number of women, rendered lazy by the heat, watched and commented on the fine workmanship.

Touches the Wind didn't know how much Rich in Hides was being paid, but Nightelk was a wealthy man and could afford the best. Her parents complained, as they did about so many things, that some families had more horses, hides, weapons, and foodstuffs than they needed while others, particularly them, ate only because of the generosity of others, but she'd never begrudge Nightelk anything because he always saw that her family had a portion of whatever game he brought down. She thanked him in the only way she could, by telling everyone who'd listen that he'd make a wise peace chief.

As she studied the way Rich in Hides' life-gnarled fingers darted over his work, she contemplated what she could afford. If she wanted any kind of design on her tepee—her parents' tepee really although she'd long assumed responsibility for its upkeep—she'd have to ask Follower to do it.

"What do you think?" Rich in Hides asked Little Bird who was squatting nearby and working on her own crude design in the dust. "Have I made an elk? Perhaps you believe I am painting a lizard?"

Five-year-old Little Bird giggled. As recently as this spring, she'd hidden behind her big sister whenever an adult spoke to her, but she was losing her self-consciousness, much to Touches the Wind's delight. Because she too had grown up with Kicked by Horse for a mother, she knew how hard it was to walk with confidence.

Several young men, none wearing more than a loincloth, had gathered not far away, but she gave them little mind. Let them debate ways of assuring that their arrows would fly straight while they smoked their endless pipes; let them boast about whose body paint attracted the most attention.

Men teased women for gossiping, but women weren't the only ones who loved to talk about what others did or didn't do, the way people conducted themselves, how well they followed tradition, and who was the finest horseman—not that anyone doubted that that honor went to Grey Bear. Three peace chiefs were with the younger men and were probably imparting wisdom, but this wasn't a formal gathering; one wouldn't be held until those who'd gone in search of buffalo returned. When that happened, one subject would be on everyone's tongue—how much longer they'd remain here.

Her mind drifted to the effort of taking down tepees, gathering up belongings, and setting off across the plains, but not for long because just thinking about what she'd have to do gave her a headache. It was much easier to study her surroundings and imagine the twenty-two tepees, fire pits, hide-stretching looms, meat-drying racks, horse corrals, travois, dogs and children, parfleches, cradle boards, roots and other food stores, weapons and tools already set up at the band's new home—wherever that would be.

It was also easier to think about past rains than ask herself when the blessed sky-gift would come again.

"You do not need to put all your skill to what you are

doing," Calf Woman told Rich in Hides as she moved to the old man's side, nearly bumping him. "As soon as my husband has killed enough buffalo, I will begin work on a new home, and I will have you decorate it as befitting his place in the band."

Rich in Hides didn't look up from his task. In fact, he seemed oblivious to the women's presence, speaking only to the children.

"I told Nightelk," Calf Woman nevertheless announced to everyone within earshot, "that I do not want to have to drag this old thing with me."

Someone pointed out that even if the hunters managed to find more than the few buffalo Grey Bear was leading them to, there wouldn't be time to complete a new tepee before the band moved on. However, Calf Woman seemed not to have heard because she was now describing how the other women would help with stitching individual buffalo hides together—something no one objected to because it took many hands to complete such a large project and the other women's turn would come for needing help.

Although Touches the Wind wasn't wealthy like Calf Woman or the beautiful Seeks Fire whose brother Porcupine was married to Walking Rabbit, she'd be asked to join the others. Looking down at her hands, she took pride in their strength and skill.

Walking Rabbit nudged her. "That is all my sister talks about," she whispered. "Sometimes I think the only thing she cares about is having a large, well-made tepee and many belongings. It is a good thing her children are grown and no longer need her guidance."

Walking Rabbit had been born after her older sister had left childhood behind, the difference in their ages as much as there was between Touches the Wind and Little Bird. Touches the Wind felt more like a mother than a sister toward Little Bird, as did Calf Woman when it came to Walking Rabbit.

"Those who say the buffalo have all left are wrong," Calf Woman announced. "My husband will return with as much meat and hides as the horses can carry. Then I will have my new home and this one—" She gave it a disdainful look. "I will tear it down and leave it to the earth."

Touches the Wind forced herself not to stare at the structure, but that didn't stop her from imagining what it would be like to have something that large and well made for her and her family to live in. Calf Woman wasn't criticizing her present home; she simply had a deep need for secure surroundings. Just the same—

"Pay her no mind," Walking Rabbit whispered. "You know she will say the same thing over and over again until no one listens. Sometimes I feel sorry for Nightelk. My brother-in-law is rich in wisdom. He should be able to share that wisdom with his wife, not have to listen to her go on about things that do not matter."

"They seem happy enough."

"Yes, they do." Walking Rabbit shook her head. "Some things I may never understand."

Neither did she, Touches the Wind admitted. Nightelk's eyes were rich with knowledge, and although he was now a peace chief, his body was still that of a warrior while Calf Woman reminded her of a lumbering old buffalo.

"Have you noticed?" Walking Rabbit was still whispering. "Not once has my sister mentioned why the hunters must travel so far. Surely she feels the heat and wind, knows how long it has been since there has been rain, how little water remains in the creek. Is it possible that she lives in a world without drought?"

Touches the Wind couldn't answer that. What she knew was that the mention of summer brought reality rushing back to envelop her. In fall and spring, the boys played endless war and hunting games and the girls willingly helped the women. Even the band's oldest citizens seemed to have more energy, but these days their faces had a pinched look, and worry had settled deep in their eyes.

A thick layer of dust covered everything. As a result, all tepees were the same drab color, the distinctive decorations that said so much about each family nearly obliterated. Most women had given up trying to keep their deerskin dresses dust free, and although brushing one's hair was a daily ritual, no one's braids shined. The village's dogs frequently rolled in the dirt to rid themselves of flies and fleas, and if they fell asleep in the dry grass, they were hard to spot.

The band, which consisted of five kindreds of conjugal and composite families, numbered a little over a hundred men, women, and children. If a man married outside his band, he went to live with his wife's family, and nothing prevented people from moving to another village if they chose to, but for the most part, she'd known those here her entire life. All men of hunting and fighting age belonged to the ancient Bow String Society.

Today she took comfort from the familiar; even Calf Woman's unending chatter bothered her only a little. After all, Calf Woman had lost two children and still mourned them.

Lost in thought, she was slow to realize that someone had joined her and Walking Rabbit. Her first reaction upon seeing Seeks Fire was to walk away, but she reminded herself that as Porcupine's sister, Seeks Fire had probably come to see Walking Rabbit anyway.

Still, she couldn't stop comparing herself to the other maiden. In deference to the heat, Seeks Fire wore a dress that barely covered her knees, revealing her slender, strong legs. She'd fashioned thick fringe around the hem and the underside of her short, full sleeves and had incorporated trade beads and shells into the scooped neckline.

It wasn't that Touches the Wind wouldn't enjoy putting decorative touches on her clothing, but on top of everything else she had to do, there simply wasn't time. Besides, what was the point of sewing small bones, feathers, and other keepsakes into a dress that had belonged to her mother before she'd grown into it? No brave would look beyond her shabby clothing and see that her body and Seeks Fire's weren't that different—no longer those of children, not yet bowed by age, healthy.

"Does your sister wish to surprise Nightelk?" Seeks Fire

asked Walking Rabbit as she knelt nearby. As a maiden, she never crossed her legs, but if kneeling caused her discomfort, she gave no indication. "Is this her way of welcoming him back?"

"Perhaps." Walking Rabbit pressed her lips together. "But I do not think so. You know how she is when she wants something done."

Seeks Fire frowned, then nodded, the gesture drawing Touches the Wind's attention to the fact that her eyes were bright and her smooth-skinned face looked freshly cleaned. "There is no better painter than Rich in Hides," Seeks Fire said, "but she must have had to pay him a great deal to work today. I wonder if Nightelk knows?"

"My guess is he has more important things on his mind."

"Like preparing himself for a hunt," Seeks Fire finished for her sister-in-law. "I hope they took enough pack horses with them. If they come across more buffalo than they thought they would, it may take them days to prepare the meat for carrying." She sighed. "It will be good to have enough meat that everyone can again eat as much as they wish."

Touches the Wind sometimes wondered if Seeks Fire would turn out to be like Calf Woman, existing in the world inside her head. Perhaps not, because Seeks Fire was aware of the need for short rations, but instead of pointing out that the men might not come across any buffalo, she assumed the hunt would be successful. Sometimes Touches the Wind resented Seeks Fire for seeing spring in every day. Singing and laughing was easier for someone whose father was a respected and revered member of the council of forty-four, who had her pick of husbands instead of—

From where she crouched, Seeks Fire heard Touches the Wind breathing. Stifling the urge to study the other maiden, she concentrated on her surroundings. After a moment, she caught sight of her niece.

"Come here, little one," she called out. Giggling, Follower ran toward her and launched herself at her, nearly knocking her off balance.

"Oh, how strong you are!" she exclaimed. "Soon you will be stronger than your big brother."

Although Follower was already struggling to free herself, Seeks Fire held onto her a moment longer. Her niece was the delight of her life, and no matter what she was doing, the moment she saw the girl, everything else became unimportant.

"What do you think?" she asked Follower. "Perhaps you have grown so much that when your father comes home, he will not know who you are."

"No," Follower insisted. "Never."

"How right you are." She winked at Knows No Fear who stood behind his sister. "And what about you? How soon will it be before you hunt with your father?"

"I could now if I wanted."

"Oh, could you? You are ready to kill a buffalo?"

"Maybe not yet," the boy conceded. "But I could take care of his horse. And Grey Bear's stallion too."

Walking Rabbit and Touches the Wind laughed at that. "You can ask Grey Bear, my son," Walking Rabbit said. "But I do not think he wants a child to care for Legs Like Lightning."

"Your mother is right," Seeks Fire told Knows No Fear. "There are some things between a warrior and his war horse that are for them alone. When you have gone on your first hunt, you will understand."

Knows No Fear squared his shoulders. "I can ride Legs Like Lightning. I know I can."

"Can not," his sister taunted. "Can not, can not, can not."

With a growl, Knows No Fear rushed at Follower, but she evaded him by hiding behind Touches the Wind. As Seeks Fire watched, Touches the Wind pressed her hand against Knows No Fear's chest to keep him from getting at his sister. The struggle went on for several moments before Knows No Fear wiped sweat off his forehead, stuck his tongue out at Follower, and then wandered away, most likely in search of one of his playmates.

"He is a lizard-head," Follower announced. "A stupid lizard-head."

"Hush." Walking Rabbit attempted to cover her daughter's mouth. "Cannot you do something beside tease your brother?"

Follower rocked back on her heels and frowned. "Tell me about Sweet Medicine, please," she asked Touches the Wind. "And how—how the Sacred Arrows came to be and when Rustling Corn went to the Sacred Mountain."

"My daughter, Touches the Wind cannot spend all her time telling you about the beginning of us. If you ask and ask, she will grow weary and not want to do it any more."

"But I like—" Follower gave Touches the Wind a beseeching look. "No one tells the stories better than you. Please. Please."

Walking Rabbit sighed, then pointed out to Follower that her friend Little Bird was trying to get a butterfly to land on her finger. After Follower toddled off to join Little Bird, Walking Rabbit gave Touches the Wind and Seeks Fire a long-suffering look.

"When Porcupine returns, I will tell him he can watch our children while I hunt," she said. "Men think that hunting and fighting is work, but what they do is nothing compared to—I wish he was back."

Determined not to let the conversation settle on how long the men had been gone or whether they'd been successful, Seeks Fire cast about for something else to talk about, but the endless days and nights of no rain were on everyone's mind. Ever since the spring grasses that once fed great herds of buffalo had dried, the braves had ridden farther and farther in search of game, and priests and other old men had engaged in endless speculation about what should be done to insure that the sky would fill with rain-heavy clouds.

Staring at blue skies exhausted her. She wanted to play with her niece and nephew. More than that, she wished the men would return so she could flirt and pretend not to care that the unmarried ones tried to catch her alone so they could talk of inconsequential things that weren't inconsequential after all. So she could go back to enjoying being a maiden.

"It will not be much longer," she finally thought to tell her sister-in-law. "And when he does . . ." She'd nearly said that Walking Rabbit and Porcupine would wait for their children to fall asleep and then join their bodies, but modesty stopped her.

"Tell me," Walking Rabbit said. "Who do you want to see the most?"

After assuring herself that none of the older women could overhear, she leaned toward both her sister-in-law and Touches the Wind. "Grey Bear."

"Ha! Of course."

"Do not act as if I have told you a great secret," she admonished her sister-in-law.

"It pleases me to see your eyes dance when you speak his name."

With an effort, she kept from blinking. In her mind, she saw Grey Bear astride his powerful war stallion. Yes, he'd been hunting for days, riding hard with only limited food and water, but those things wouldn't bow his back. When he spotted her, he'd pretend to barely notice her. Still, if he managed to be at the creek when she went there alone for water or he handed her a piece of meat and their hands brushed—

Rich in Hides dropped unceremoniously to the ground, grunting as he did. "I am done," the old man announced. "Tomorrow I will do more but now I rest."

Without saying a word, Touches the Wind got to her feet and walked over to where Calf Woman had left a water bladder. She brought it to Rich in Hides and unfastened the rawhide thong around the opening so he could drink. As she did, Seeks Fire's gaze went to what she could see of the other maiden's legs. She was proud of her own limbs' ability to do what she demanded of them, sometimes drew comparisons between their slim length and the older women's fat-burdened calves, but Touches the Wind too could be proud of Maheo's gift.

Calf Woman had lumbered over to Rich in Hides and was

trying to get him to go back to work. Her concern, she insisted, was that the men might return tonight and Nightelk would be displeased because his spirit-animal was little more than an outline.

"Nightelk will not care about that," Walking Rabbit told her sister. "He has been without his wife for many nights and he will want—" She blushed.

"Look at her." Seeks Fire nudged Touches the Wind. "She believes such things are not our concern because we are unmarried, but what is more important than having the hunters back among us?"

Touches the Wind didn't respond, but then Seeks Fire didn't expect her to. They might be the same age, and they often hunted roots and other food together, but Touches the Wind went home to poor parents who kept to themselves while her tepee—her mother's tepee really—often held the Cheyenne nation's most respected men who came to council with her father. Touches the Wind spent her days tending to her parents' and little sister's needs while she helped her mother prepare enough food for respected peace chiefs— food they'd always had enough of.

Until this rainless summer.

Walking Rabbit had gotten to her feet and was looking around for her children. "Porcupine will want to see his son's new spear," she muttered. "I hope he has not broken it."

"And what does he want of his wife?" she couldn't help teasing.

Walking Rabbit blushed. "Thinking of that," she admitted, "allows me to forget my fear that he may return empty-handed."

Empty-handed. The word and reality behind it clamped down on Seeks Fire. Her mother had called her her laughing baby, and although she'd outgrown the nickname, she wanted to be that carefree infant again, would—

A moment ago the women and children had filled the air with their chatter, but they'd suddenly all fallen silent. Looking in the same direction they were, she spotted a mounted warrior. Shielding her eyes, she realized it was Lone Hawk, who had gone out with Grey Bear, Porcupine, and the others. Instead of acknowledging the villagers, he headed for the tepee where the band's most respected medicine man lived.

Walking Rabbit grabbed her hand and squeezed.

CHAPTER 4

People pressed around Nightelk, but his attention remained on Porcupine, who continued to breathe through tortured lungs. At the same time, he studied the way Porcupine and Walking Rabbit looked at each other.

"Have you nothing better to do than bother an injured man?" Calf Woman demanded of the women who'd crowded close. "Our hunters bring meat. You should be preparing it, not wasting time in things that do not concern you."

One woman grumbled that she didn't need Calf Woman telling her how to conduct herself, but Nightelk paid them little mind. He was vaguely aware of his wife staring at him, but he dismissed her as he did everything else—even Lone Hawk, who'd placed Porcupine on a hide blanket outside the wounded man's tepee and now cradled his head in his lap.

"Rest now," Nightelk told Porcupine, his words a repeat of what he'd already said many times during the ride home. "Turn yourself over to medicine and song."

"I—I try," Porcupine whispered. His eyes remained on Walking Rabbit.

"I know you do." Nightelk didn't know where the strength for his voice came from. "Think only that you are home, no longer forced to remain on horseback."

Porcupine said something, but Nightelk didn't attempt to hold onto the words. Instead, his mind replayed the nightmare of his arrow sinking into a white side, smelled fresh blood, felt his heart hammer and turn cold. Remembered the lightning.

No matter how many times he told himself he'd meant no harm, it didn't matter. He'd broken taboo. Porcupine's wound was proof of that—the consequences.

"Leave, leave," Calf Woman admonished when a trio of boys hurried up. "Learn from his injury and become wise and cautious but do not stand in the way of what must be done."

The boys grumbled, but when Lone Hawk repeated Calf Woman's order, they did as they were told.

"Where is my son?" Porcupine asked.

"I do not know," Walking Rabbit told him. "Perhaps he has taken our horses to feed and does not know you are back."

"I want—to see my children."

Instead of heeding her husband's plea, Walking Rabbit continued to kneel beside him and brush away flies. "Soon, soon," she told him. "But I want them to see a father blessed by the shaman, not—not the way you are now."

It was good to no longer have responsibility for Porcupine, Nightelk thought. Now that that had been turned over to others, he could . . . what? Something sharp bit into his knee and he shifted position, but he felt too old and weary to do more.

Because it had grown dark soon after he'd rejoined his companions two days ago, they'd remained where they were until morning. They'd prepared the meat for travel, and he'd lent a hand, his movements automatic. Most of his time, however, had been spent at Porcupine's side, and he'd led Porcupine's horse.

He'd said nothing about what had happened when he'd ridden off after buffalo instead of battling Pawnee—shame and shock silencing him—and Porcupine's wound had distracted everyone from asking about how he'd done. Porcupine's words, repeated over and over, had been about his wife and children, his fear that his wound was fatal. Nightelk had listened and nodded but hadn't been able to look into the injured warrior's eyes.

It was still like that.

"Go be with the men," his wife ordered him. "There is much boasting from the young, especially Grey Bear. You should add your wisdom and truth."

He lifted his heavy head and tried to focus. Calf Woman's mouth was firm, but her expression was one of concern.

"Soon," he said. "Porcupine, if you want something to eat—"

"Only water," Porcupine whispered. "My stomach . . ." When his voice fell away, Lone Hawk held a small bladder to his lips and helped him drink.

"Nightelk," Calf Woman insisted. "Think of yourself. You have not eaten, have you?"

He couldn't remember but didn't tell her that. He and Calf Woman had been together so long that it seemed she knew his every mood. He should walk away from her, let the camp absorb him and remind him of what it was to be a Cheyenne, but he didn't want to talk to anyone—especially his eldest son. The camp dogs, excited by the fresh meat, barked and snapped at each other. In the distance, wolves and coyotes, drawn by smells and sounds, howled. Squawking birds flew low overhead.

Somehow he found the strength to stand, but before he could decide what he should do, he caught sight of Knows No Fear and Follower hurrying toward their parents. He started to reach out to prevent them from getting too close, but no child could be protected from life.

"Father!" Follower wailed. "Oh, you—you . . ."

Dropping to her knees, she lay her head on her father's chest. Porcupine cried out, then pulled his daughter close. Knows No Fear remained standing, his fists clenched, feet digging into the earth.

"Come here," Porcupine said when he spotted his son. "I— it is so good to see—you."

Calf Woman clamped her hand over Nightelk's shoulder,

indicating she wanted him to go with her, but he shook her off.

"The painting I caused to have added to our tepee," she said into his ear. "I did it for you."

"Later."

Grumbling, she walked away, but he had no doubt she'd insist on an explanation for his behavior. The medicine man Easy Singer, who specialized in injuries caused by war, stepped out of his tepee where he'd been preparing himself and joined those grouped around Porcupine. Easy Singer carried a rawhide bag filled with Big Medicine, the dried and pulverized roots and leaves of a grasslike plant that grows near creeks. Before reaching into his pouch, however, the man, who'd painted himself white, checked the small fire burning near Porcupine.

"It is good," Easy Singer told the girl who'd been maintaining it. "The coals right."

As he threw a clump of sweetgrass onto the fire and began washing his hands in the smoke, Follower studied him with large, anxious eyes. Knows No Fear had settled himself near his father's feet, but although the boy struggled to remain motionless, his arms and legs twitched.

"Hear me, Wolf-Tooth," Easy Singer said, calling up the memory of his grandfather, who'd taught him his skills. "See this injured one and guide my hands in what I now do. The Big Medicine has been blessed and I believe in its power, but there is only a little of it left. I pray it is enough."

Under his guidance, the girl used the coals to heat a little water in a bladder-pot. Once the water was steaming, the medicine man dropped some of the Big Medicine in it and stirred it with a stick, creating a small amount of paste.

"We were born of the mud the Creator used when he fashioned the first man and woman," he intoned. "In that way, I use this medicine, but I do not say I create new life. My powers are limited; let no one doubt that."

Nightelk didn't want to hear that. Today of all days he needed to believe the medicine man could heal.

"This is medicine," the old man continued. "Powerful

medicine, and if Porcupine has walked the Cheyenne way and won the Creator's favor, he will live."

But what if the Creator was angry, not at Porcupine but at the man who'd killed one of his sacred animals? Nightelk felt hot. At the same time, he shivered.

"This is a holy place," Easy Singer said as he placed the paste over Porcupine's wound. "And Porcupine is surrounded by those who want only health for him. Who are ready to do battle against those responsible for his injury."

But it wasn't the Pawnees' doing this time! It was his!

Sick, Nightelk stifled a moan. Ignoring the medicine man's startled curse, he stumbled away. Only half aware of what he was doing, he headed toward where the meat had been piled in preparation for parceling out. Before he could put his mind to making sure everyone, rich and poor alike, got enough, however, Stands in Timber called to him.

"Have you forgotten where you walk now?" the senior peace chief asked. "You do not believe you have a responsibility to take a sweat with the rest of us?" Stands in Timber pointed at the sweat lodge built into the earth, which was used only during peace meetings. "Perhaps you want back what you were before."

"I accept my new position. Surely I already made that clear."

"You rode with the hunters."

"Yes." He had no wish to go into an explanation—about anything. "And now I have returned. But it was not wrong for me to see to Porcupine first."

Stands in Timber stared down his broad nose at him. Stands in Timber held an exalted position within the tribe, but that didn't mean he'd forgotten his days as provider and fighter.

"How is he?" Stands in Timber asked, indicating Porcupine.

"It is not for me to say."

"Hm. Do you think he will recover?"

"I do not know." The words made him sick.

"If he dies, our warriors will avenge his death."

Nightelk nodded.

"And no matter what happens to him, the Pawnee will avenge what was done to them." Stands in Timber sighed and suddenly looked ancient. "We must meet," he told Nightelk. "Decide how much longer we will remain here."

"Cheyenne are not afraid of Pawnee."

"I did not say we were. But there is one thing I fear, something you must too."

Did Stands in Timber know about the calf? Had the gods sent him the truth?

"Summer," the old man said softly. "Drought."

FROM WHERE SHE stood near her mother's tepee, Seeks Fire saw Nightelk and Stands in Timber talking to each other, but she had little interest in what the men might be saying. She wanted to ask Nightelk why he'd left her brother's side but lacked the courage—just as she'd been unable to stay with Porcupine herself.

"There is nothing you can do."

Startled, she whirled to find herself facing Touches the Wind. She opened her mouth to say she didn't know what the other maiden was talking about but couldn't. "He needs me," she whispered.

"He needs the medicine man and his family. You walk your way these days just as he walks his."

"We were so close as children," she admitted. At Touches the Wind's prompting, she started toward those who'd gathered around the meat; the other maiden kept pace.

"I know you were," Touches the Wind said. "I used to watch you and Porcupine and wonder if you would turn into a boy so you could hunt with him instead of taking on a woman's responsibilities."

"You did? Why did you not say—" She looked over her shoulder, but she couldn't tell what the medicine man was doing to her brother.

"I was afraid you would laugh at me or become angry."

"Maybe a little of both," she admitted. "Sometimes he

called me his puppy because I trailed after him like one. And then—and then we both grew up."

"He is grown," Touches the Wind said. "A husband and father. You and I are still . . ."

Still maidens, Seeks Fire finished silently, although today that didn't matter. "I do not want him to waste his strength thinking about me. He needs to speak to Walking Rabbit and their children."

"Can he?"

The question stopped her. Although she was aware that several young men were looking at her and Touches the Wind, she easily dismissed them. "I heard him say a little, not much. He called out when Knows No Fear came to him."

"Knows No Fear. A hard name for someone who has only seen eight summers to carry."

"My nephew thinks himself a grizzly, a bull elk."

"He is not the only one."

Wondering what Touches the Wind was talking about, Seeks Fire focused on her surroundings. As was the way of their people, the hunters had claimed prime pieces of meat for themselves and their families, but everything else had been placed in a pile and several peace chiefs were dividing it. Touches the Wind should be among the poor so she'd have a supply to take to her parents and little sister.

"He is watching you," Touches the Wind said.

"Grey Bear?" she asked without thinking.

"Of course. It is said that he alone caused the Pawnee to flee."

"Who said that? Him?" Despite herself, Seeks Fire strained to locate the young, powerfully built man. He wasn't in sight.

"Of course." Touches the Wind laughed. "Do you think he boasts too much?"

Porcupine, her brother, could tell her the truth about what had happened—or he would if he wasn't fighting to stay alive.

"You cannot help him," Touches the Wind said as if reading her mind. "All you can do is pray for him."

"I do not feel right being part of this celebration—" She indicated several boys who'd armed themselves with their small bows and arrows and were pretending to shoot each other while adults applauded their efforts. "Not while my brother lies bleeding."

"He would want you to walk your way."

Sometimes Touches the Wind's wisdom left her in awe. Not only could Touches the Wind faultlessly tell the tribe's history, but she seemed wise beyond her years in so many ways. Perhaps, she thought, she'd be the same if life had come harder for her.

"If the others see you laugh and smile, it will make it easier for them," Touches the Wind whispered as Calf Woman stepped away from the other women intent on cutting up meat and indicated she wanted them to join her.

"How is he?" Calf Woman asked once they'd come close. "Is the medicine working?"

Aware of how many were hanging onto her words, Seeks Fire explained that she hadn't wanted to distract Easy Singer from his work so hadn't stayed near her brother.

"Fine, fine." Calf Woman sounded distracted. "Watch that dog!" she ordered a girl. "Do not let him get close. Ha! Look at how close those birds come. Why should they fear dogs who think of nothing except their bellies?"

Seeks Fire started to look for the dogs; instead, she found herself gazing into Grey Bear's eyes. By tradition, she hadn't had a private conversation with him since her first bleeding and the four days she'd spent in the moon hut. What she knew of him came from her observations and gossip shared with the other maidens. Blushing, she tried but failed to lower her gaze.

Grey Bear had led this hunt. True, he'd done so at his grandfather's urging, but the other hunters had ridden with him because they trusted his courage and skill. She didn't know how many buffalo he'd killed but was certain it was more than anyone else. And the way he handled himself on horseback—

Needing air, she sucked in a lungful. The day was so hot!

Surely that was why she felt as if she might catch on fire.

Oblivious to what was going on, Calf Woman asked Seeks Fire if she wanted to select what belonged to Porcupine's family. "I know my husband will make sure they get their share," the older woman explained, "but I cannot help think that—that perhaps it will be a long time before Porcupine can hunt again."

Seeks Fire remained aware of Grey Bear's bold gaze, but she could no longer give it the attention she had a moment ago. How long would she feel like crying and laughing at the same time? Stumbling over the words, she asked Calf Woman to help her select the proper amount. As she did, she sensed Touches the Wind stiffen.

"What is it?" she asked under her breath so Calf Woman couldn't hear.

"Nothing. A thought I should not have."

Perhaps but an honest one nonetheless, one that comes naturally to a maiden who'd never been able to take food for granted.

"Not so much," Seeks Fire told Calf Woman when the older woman reached for a hindquarter. "My niece eats like a bird and Walking Rabbit—all she will care about is feeding her husband."

Calf Woman studied the remaining meat. The dogs, torn between hunger and fear of punishment, had slunk close, and noisy crows flew so low that Seeks Fire could make out their individual feathers. If it wasn't for the breeze, it would be insufferably hot. If only it would rain!

Instead, something that was both white and red zigzagged across the heavens. Lightning was part of summer. It also served as proof of the Creator's energy and power, the great bird Thunder who holds arrows in its talons and hurtles the arrows toward earth in the form of lightning capable of killing.

"NIGHTELK, BE STILL."

"I am."

"No, you are not. You cannot do his healing for him. Let him be."

Falling silent, Nightelk lay on his back and stared into the dark. Through the smoke hole at the top of their tepee he could see a small piece of the sky where a large number of stars rested. After his exertion of the last few days and the amount of food he'd eaten during the feast, he'd thought—hoped—he'd have no trouble falling asleep. He was wrong.

"Something is bothering you," Calf Woman said. "It has walked beside you since you got back."

And before that.

"What is it?"

This woman who was his wife and the other half of him didn't want to know the answer. "A man's thoughts," he told her. "What it is to become a peace chief."

She grunted. "You are still a hunter and a fighter, not old like some of them. You do not need me to tell you that."

The tepee smelled of buffalo hide, smoke, food, and other odors that added up to what he was. They should have comforted him.

"No one says you were wrong to go after buffalo instead of fighting Pawnee," she went on. "Each man makes his decision, and on that day *you* were a hunter, not a warrior."

They lay on a bed made of buffalo hide. In deference to the heat, many slept outside, but he wanted to be able to dismiss them. Maybe he wanted to dismiss Calf Woman as well.

"Do you believe you walked the wrong way?" she asked.

"What?"

"Do you no longer listen to me? I have become like the wind, a sound you ignore?"

"I do not ignore you."

Her harsh breath said she didn't believe him and that it didn't matter.

"Nightelk, you are not a man who holds your thoughts inside you. When our babies—when our babies died, we mourned together."

"Yes, we did."

"And when Two Coyotes was born, we held our healthy son and wept tears of joy. He still brings us joy."

"Yes, he does."

She'd lain as still as he, but now she turned onto her side. He imagined her heavy breasts falling forward and felt her belly brush against him. Like him, she was naked.

"Many call me foolish because I speak of things that do not matter," she said, "concern myself with painting designs on our tepee and how many eaglet feathers to sew into our grandchildren's cradles, but you never fault me for what I have become."

Why was it that she could say so many things when he couldn't?

"You know everything there is to know about me." She sighed. "Understand and accept me."

"You are a good woman."

"I am old and fat and tired, married to a man who walks as if he has not been touched by the same years. A man who believes the one wife he has is all he will ever need."

How had the conversation turned in this direction? Had his thoughts been trapped by the image of red blood on white hair?

"What is it?" She spread her hand over his belly; after a moment, her fingers trailed toward his limp penis. "What burden do you carry inside you?"

"Nothing."

"Nothing! A man's answer whenever he wishes to protect himself. Perhaps your fear for Porcupine is so great?"

Yes! "No. Not that."

"You have no fear for him?" Calf Woman cradled his penis in the palm of her hand.

"Yes, of course . . ."

"But that is not the only thing, is it, my husband?"

He didn't answer, but he didn't have to because his penis refused to respond to her practiced touch and in that she learned the truth.

CHAPTER 5

Conditioned by a lifetime of hardship and plenty, the Cheyenne ate as much as their bellies could hold. As a result, that night everyone fell asleep early. Now, although dawn had already given way to bright daylight, Lone Hawk sat alone outside his tepee. Except for a few dogs, the only other people outside were two pregnant women taking the early-morning walks that insured their babies would grow and be healthy.

Although he'd been raised in a Grey Hair band, he'd come to the Bow String Society with an uncle who'd wanted to learn at Sweet Grass Eater's side. His uncle had lost interest in determining the meanings of dreams and had returned home, but Lone Hawk had stayed and now lived with an elderly man and his two ancient wives.

In exchange for a place to sleep, he supplied them with meat and cared for their horses. Most of all, he listened when Sweet Grass Eater spoke and dreamed of one day being as wise and respected as Grey Bear's grandfather. Soon, he told himself, he'd walk over to Porcupine's tepee, but for now he wrapped the thought that Easy Singer's medicine had taken Porcupine onto the path to recovery around himself. The wind filled him with energy and he prayed Porcupine could feel it.

When he saw someone walking toward him, he gave brief thought to going back inside but couldn't stir himself to do so.

"It is quiet," Two Coyotes said as he joined him. "So quiet, one would think the Cheyenne care nothing about guarding against attack."

Lone Hawk waited until Nightelk's twenty-two-year-old

son had settled himself on the ground near him. "Guards were set," he said, although Two Coyotes knew that. "If the Pawnee come, they will find us ready for them."

Two Coyotes nodded, then glanced over his shoulder at his parents' tepee. "My father did not fight the Pawnee?" he asked. "Grey Bear said so, but I do not know more than that."

"Nightelk did not tell you of his decision to go after buffalo?"

Two Coyotes frowned, the gesture briefly disturbing his sober yet placid features. He scratched the side of his long neck, then ran his hand over his chest. "I have not spoken to my father since his return."

It was Lone Hawk's turn to frown. When he'd gotten married, Two Coyotes had moved into his wife's tepee, but last winter she'd piled his belongings outside, proof that she no longer wanted to be married to him. Her actions had come as a shock since Two Coyotes was a good provider and a hard worker; why would Leaf Fluttering leave him when there were more women than men?

At the time, she'd just given birth to their first child, but instead of joining the other young mothers in their daily activities, she'd spent much of her time washing and washing her infant girl. Some said childbirth had stolen her mind, and for a while Lone Hawk had accepted that explanation, but a few days after divorcing Two Coyotes, Leaf Fluttering had invited a Cheyenne from a band traveling through the area into her tepee. Now Leaf Fluttering and her daughter lived with her new husband and that husband's first wife some distance to the south. Two Coyotes had said little about how he felt about the divorce, just that it was right for his small daughter to be with her mother.

No one doubted that Two Coyotes would marry again, but in the meantime he'd moved back with his parents. However, like Lone Hawk, Two Coyotes spent little time inside.

To satisfy Two Coyotes' curiosity, Lone Hawk explained that Nightelk had said little upon his return to the hunting party.

"Nothing mattered except preparing the kill for travel and

getting Porcupine home," Lone Hawk said. "We did not want the Pawnee to return while we were still there so everyone worked. There was little talking."

"Hm."

"You think it should have been otherwise?"

"No, no. But last night there was much boasting and—"

"Boasting from Grey Bear."

"Yes," Two Coyotes said. "Perhaps my father is so worried about Porcupine and the Pawnee that he has not thought to talk to me and yet—it is his decision. I will wait until he is ready."

Lone Hawk, who hadn't seen his father since spring, wondered why Two Coyotes was concerned, but then Nightelk and Two Coyotes had always been close.

"He has much on his mind," he said. "We all do."

"Yes." Two Coyotes took a moment to study the cloudless sky. Then he wiped sweat off his temples and held up his hand so the wind could dry it. "My father carries new responsibilities. I do not want them to overburden him."

"He is ready to take his place as a peace chief. His wisdom and patience is like yours."

"I may be patient, but I am not yet wise."

Lone Hawk wasn't sure he agreed. True, Two Coyotes was only a few years older than he, but he absorbed a great deal from his surroundings and experiences. Other men became angry when their wives kicked them out, but Two Coyotes had only said he hoped she would find happiness. Even the unrelenting drought didn't seem to cause him to lose sleep.

"I wish I could accept what is the way you do," Lone Hawk admitted. "To never question what happens or want to change it—if I had made those things part of me, I would not be asking what more I could do to insure Porcupine's life."

"I want Porcupine to live." Two Coyotes turned his head one way and then the other, working a kink out of his neck. "And I want the Cheyenne to prosper. Do not think it is otherwise."

"You are not given to anger or the need for revenge. You

ask the men to decide whether their actions will cause harm to themselves or others before riding out on a war trail."

"Some say I am not aggressive enough."

"If we were all like Grey Bear, we would do nothing except fight."

"True," Two Coyotes said with a chuckle. "But we need men like Grey Bear, full of confidence and courage."

They could continue to discuss what each man brought to the tribe, but Lone Hawk's need to see Porcupine was becoming stronger with every breath.

"Your father will spend the day with the other peace chiefs, will he not?" he asked as he got to his feet. "Making the decision as to what we should do."

Two Coyotes nodded and also stood. "Perhaps that is what is on his mind, why he stares at me but does not speak. Why I did not hear him and my mother having sex last night. If he asked me, I would tell him we must move on now, but that must be his decision—his and the other elders." He brushed hair off his face. "The wind grows."

"If we wait a few days Porcupine may be stronger, more able to travel."

"True, but they must weigh Porcupine's health against the needs of many." Two Coyotes held out his hands, palms up.

TOUCHES THE WIND reached into a parfleche bag and pulled out a small amount of dried turnip. She placed it inside her bowl-shape grinding rock, then picked up another rock, which she used to pound the turnip slices.

"What are you doing?" her father grumbled, sitting up and rubbing his eyes.

"Preparing food."

Long Chin clamped his hands over his ears. "Why so early?"

"Because I promised Walking Rabbit I would do her chores so she can spend her time with her husband."

Touches the Wind's mother stirred on her separate bed.

"Walking Rabbit's relatives can do that for her," she muttered.

"It is something I want to do, a way of expressing my gratitude."

Kicked by Horse nodded but didn't say anything. Long Chin scratched himself under his loincloth. "Gratitude?"

"For everything the hunters do for us." She kept her attention on her work, grateful Little Bird had spent the night with a friend and was being spared this conversation.

"That they shared meat with us is only as it should be," Long Chin said. "I would have gone with them if they had asked but—"

"The hunt was for young men," Touches the Wind said, hoping to stop her father from whining that he hadn't been invited on a hunt for years, something she'd heard so many times she hardly listened anymore. "And a dangerous one."

"You believe me afraid to battle our enemies?"

She'd been a child the last time her father had gone to war, and she remembered little of what had happened. According to Long Chin, his horse had stepped into a prairie dog hole and had fallen on him, but she'd also heard that his horse had been running from a Crow and he'd fallen off and might have been killed if another Cheyenne hadn't speared his attacker.

"I did not say that," she told him. Satisfied that she'd ground the dried turnip into a powder, she poured it into the simmering buffalo broth. "I will place more rocks in the soup as soon as they are hot enough," she told her mother. "And I will put other rocks on the fire to heat, but you must keep the fire going."

Kicked by Horse sat up. "We have enough wood?"

"Yes," It was on the tip of her tongue to tell her mother that there'd be more wood if she hadn't had to collect it all by herself, but a glance at Kicked by Horse stopped her. Her mother had just married her father when she'd stepped behind a young stallion as Long Chin rode up on a mare in heat. The excited stallion had kicked out, striking Kicked by Horse on the head. Now blind in her right eye and unable to hear out of the ear on that side, she usually wore her hair pulled forward so it covered most of the indentation at her temple.

This morning, however, her hair matted away from her face, revealing discolored flesh and deformed bone. Kicked by Horse suffered from horrible headaches and sometimes became so dizzy she fell, but even when she felt well, she sat curled in around herself, waiting for pain.

Long Chin blamed himself for what had happened to his bride, the guilt adding to his burdens. He also resented Kicked by Horse because, according to him, she never opened her tepee to others for a feast. It was all Touches by Wind could do not to point out that her father didn't bring home enough meat to feed more than his family and usually not even that.

"You will do that?" she asked her mother. "Make sure the soup cooks and thickens."

Kicks by Horse nodded, then lay back down. Long Chin got to his feet and shuffled over so he could look into the cooking pot. "It is mostly water. It will have no flavor."

"Yes it will," she answered, although she knew better. When had anything she said changed his days from shadow to sunlight? "I have already put in some dried cactus fruit."

"How much?"

"Just a little," she admitted. "I want what we have to last as long as possible."

Long Chin frowned, then leaned forward to smell. "If—when—we move on, we will have to take wood and water with us—as much as possible."

"Yes, we will," she replied, not bothering to point out that the family's single horse would have all it could do just pulling the tepee. Their three dogs could each drag a travois filled with the rest of their belongings, but first she'd have to repair the travois. She'd ask her father to do that, but he'd only point out that that was women's work—work Kicked by Horse couldn't do because her vision was becoming more and more blurred.

"When will you be back?" her father asked when she started to lift the door flap.

"I am not sure. Maybe I will spend some time with Knows No Fear and Follower, let them do more than worry about their father. I will tell Little Bird what I am doing and ask if she wants to join me."

"You will be gone all day?"

"If necessary."

Long Chin glanced over at his wife, but if Kicked by Horse was aware, she gave no indication. Neither did she acknowledge her daughter.

"Good-bye, my mother," Touches the Wind said. "The hunters will surely continue talking about how they battled the Pawnee. Perhaps you would like to listen."

A grunt was Kicked by Horse's only response. As she stepped outside, Touches the Wind wondered, hardly for the first time, how much of her mother's behavior was caused by her injuries and how much came from within her heart and mind.

Some men might have divorced a deformed woman, but Long Chin had remained beside her. Some of it certainly was because he felt responsible, but he also believed he was cursed with bad luck, his belief so deeply ingrained that he no longer tried to step beyond it. Perhaps he believed no other woman would share his bed with him and by remaining married, he didn't have to risk rejection. Perhaps he was right.

Lifting her head, she looked around. A few people, mostly children, were beginning to move about, but even the dogs, their bellies swollen from gorging, were sluggish. The wind, however, was another matter. It felt angry, putting her in mind of a grizzly determined to destroy everything within its reach. She lifted her hand to shield her eyes from the dirt caught in the wind's grip but felt no desire to hide.

Wind was her spirit. It energized her and gave her strength when the burdens of her life threatened to overwhelm her. Perhaps it growled and snapped today so she could absorb its power and thus do what she needed to for Porcupine and Walking Rabbit.

"Thank you, Wind," she said. "I accept your gift and will use it for good."

If the wind heard, it gave no indication. It felt dry and hot against her and she imagined Wind spiraling down from the sky, carrying Sun's heat with it. So far she'd seen no sign of the lightning that had been around for several days.

As she stood outside Walking Rabbit and Porcupine's tepee, she heard female voices. After a moment, she recognized Walking Rabbit and Seeks Fire. From Seeks Fire's actions yesterday, she realized how much Seeks Fire hated seeing her brother injured, but the maiden had forced herself beyond that.

Although she never doubted she'd be welcome, she respectfully slapped the side of the tepee and waited for the door flap to open. The shadowy interior hid Walking Rabbit's expression, but the young mother held herself as if exhausted.

"Come in," Walking Rabbit said, and shuffled back.

As women always did when entering a tepee, she turned to the left. Then she spotted Porcupine lying near the middle, Seeks Fire kneeling beside him. The maiden stared up at her with none of the laughter that so often filled her eyes.

"I thought—" Touches the Wind started. "I came to offer to help care for him, but perhaps I am not needed for that."

"She has been here all night." Walking Rabbit indicated Seeks Fire. "We took turns bathing him with water; he is so hot."

Porcupine remained motionless, naked except for the covering the medicine man had put over his wound. "What does Easy Singer say?" she asked. "What more is he going to do?"

"He promised to return this morning." Walking Rabbit's voice sounded flat. "However, he told me that my husband's *tasoom* has left him and, if it does not return . . ."

No one could live without a *tasoom*, the body's spiritual essence. Sometimes a *tasoom* left an injured body, the shadow or shade traveling to a place of renewal. Many times it returned energized and able to keep life in the body, but sometimes . . .

"Do not talk of that." Seeks Fire started to stand, then settled back beside her brother. "My heart remains full of hope and good thoughts. It will not hear talk of . . ." She leaned forward and covered Porcupine's chest with her own. "I will protect him."

Touches the Wind wished she shared Seeks Fire's determination—or maybe the truth was, Seeks Fire knew what her brother should hear.

"You do not need me?" she asked Walking Rabbit. "Perhaps you and Seeks Fire would like to sleep."

Both women shook their heads. Feeling useless, Touches the Wind studied the dark interior. "Knows No Fear and Follower are not here?"

"I asked my son to see to our horses and told him to take his sister with him. They—I knew how they hate seeing their father like this."

Was Porcupine on a journey to a land beyond this one? Perhaps that's why he seemed oblivious to his surroundings.

"What about when the children return?" she asked. "What will they do then?"

Walking Rabbit gave her a blank look, glanced at her husband, seemed to draw into herself.

"I will go after them," Touches the Wind offered. "Tell Knows No Fear that it is right for him to spend the day with the other boys and then take Follower to see Little Bird."

"I—I do not want them to think they are not wanted here."

"They will not; I promise. And tonight they will be able to tell their parents what they did, share their adventures with you and Porcupine and maybe give you reason to laugh."

She thought Walking Rabbit might want her to tell her children something, but the young woman only looked at Seeks Fire, who stared back at her with eyes that spoke of the same fear and wild hope.

The wind again slammed into Touches the Wind when she stepped outside. Being near Porcupine had stripped much of the strength from her, making her wonder how long she could battle the unrelenting gusts. The tepees moaned and sagged under the blasts, and swirling dirt was rapidly turning everything gray/brown. She started trudging toward where the horses had been tethered during the night, only then realizing she hadn't tied on her chastity belt this morning. Most virgins' mothers did that religiously, but often Kicked by Horse was still in bed when she left to begin her outside duties, making it necessary for her to do the chore herself. No matter. As long as the wind was this angry, not many people would be about.

"How is he?"

Startled, she spun around. As she did, dust lodged in her eye; she worked at dislodging the irritation.

"I am sorry," Lone Hawk said. "I thought you saw me."

She shook her head, then struggled to see despite her tears. If someone had told her the young warrior would speak to her today, she would have done everything she could to avoid him, but he'd asked a question that demanded an answer—even if it meant two unmarried people spoke to each other.

"Easy Singer says his *tasoom* has left his body."

"No!"

Her voice unsteady, she told Lone Hawk that the medicine man had promised to come again this morning. Then she explained that although Porcupine appeared asleep, his sister and wife refused to leave his side.

"I think they do not want others there," she said, looking at the ground and not up at the handsome warrior. "Perhaps they believe his *tasoom* will find it easier to return that way."

"Perhaps. Nightelk has not come to see him?"

"I do not think so."

"He should. Just because he meets with the other peace chiefs does not mean he can forget he rode as a warrior on the hunt. Perhaps he—"

"Perhaps what?"

Lone Hawk said nothing, prompting her to glance at him. His jaw was clenched, and his eyes seemed darker. "It is not something that concerns a woman."

Then do not say anything to me.

"Where are you going?" he asked abruptly. "Walking Rabbit sent you for something?"

"No," she said, then told him about her plans for the children. It seemed strange but not wrong to be speaking to him, as if Porcupine's wound and their shared concern had changed something between them, at least briefly.

"That is good." Lone Hawk stopped staring at her and looked toward Porcupine's tepee. "Perhaps I will go with you and—"

"No!"

"No?"

"It—we should not be seen together."

After a moment he nodded. "I forgot. Or perhaps I would rather play with children than wait for my friend's *tasoom* to return."

If it is going to.

"The Pawnee," Lone Hawk said, freeing her from the unwanted thought. "They will regret what they did! I swear it!"

CHAPTER 6

 Legs Like Lightning snorted and threw his head. Grey Bear's fingers tightened on the rope around his stallion's lower jaw but didn't discipline his mount.

"He does not like the wind," Woodenlegs said unnecessarily. "He wants to stand with his back to it and sleep."

"He can sleep later," Grey Bear snapped. "Today I have need for him."

Woodenlegs grumbled something and Wolf Robe, who rode to Woodenlegs' right, laughed. With an effort, Grey Bear ignored both men. Legs Like Lightning was right; traveling with the wind blowing the way it was had become nearly impossible. Still, what choice did he have?

"My belly still aches," Wolf Robe said. He rubbed himself there. "And I could barely climb onto my horse this morning."

If Wolf Robe wanted sympathy, he'd have to look elsewhere. Last night as the members of the Bow String Society feasted together, Grey Bear had announced that the Cheyenne were foolish if they didn't at least determine where the Pawnee had gone. Wolf Robe and Woodenlegs had volunteered to go with him.

They should have left camp earlier in the day, but Wolf Robe wasn't the only one suffering the aftereffects of the huge meal. In addition, Grey Bear and his two companions had painted themselves so their enemies, if they came upon them, would know they were ready for battle, and that had taken awhile. As a consequence, the sun had begun its downward journey, its heat still powerful. Barely aware of what he was doing, Grey Bear reached behind him to touch the water bladder strapped to Legs Like Lightning's back.

"White Feather smiled at me," Woodenlegs said. "She was sitting with her sister pretending not to be listening to how we ran off the Pawnee, but I knew different."

"White Feather has yet to go to the menstruation lodge. She is a child."

Woodenlegs frowned at Wolf Robe. "Did any girl smile at you? Ha! They look at your untended hair and fat knees and run away."

"No maiden has ever run from me," Wolf Robe insisted. "I could be married many times over if I wanted, but I am in no hurry. When I touch a maiden's breasts, I want to know I have chosen well."

Although the thought of touching a woman's breasts quickened Grey Bear's breathing, he appeared to ignore his companions. Unlike the hilly area around their village, the land as far as they could see now was so open and flat that no enemy could hide from them, but they'd soon reach a series of valleys. In the meantime, he wanted to concentrate on what he should do if they came across some Pawnee. Porcupine's wounding must be avenged!

"Perhaps she does not know of your bravery," Woodenlegs was saying. "If not you will have to find a way of telling her."

Not sure whether Woodenlegs was talking to him, he waited.

"It is a shame it was her brother who was wounded," Wolf Robe pointed out. "Otherwise, she would care about more than that. If he dies . . ."

"If he dies what?" Grey Bear prompted.

"I was thinking of Walking Rabbit." Woodenlegs straightened, shielded his eyes, and stared around him. Apparently satisfied, he slumped again. "Of who will marry her and provide for her and her children."

"Perhaps you will marry her and then White Feather once she is old enough," Wolf Robe told Woodenlegs.

"Porcupine lives!" Something cold washed through Grey Bear. "Do not speak otherwise!"

Wolf Robe glared but didn't say anything. For a while the three men rode in silence as the wind made the dry prairie grasses moan.

"Seeks Fire spent the night in her brother's tepee," Woodenlegs said. "In the spring after the first great buffalo hunt when she worked with the other women, I remember"—he glanced at Grey Bear—"you watched her for so long that her father said something to you."

"Nothing of importance," Grey Bear retorted, hoping to satisfy Woodenlegs' curiosity. "He would not be displeased if I wanted to marry her."

"What father would? Choose some maiden, Grey Bear, so the rest of us will know which ones are left over."

Although he felt lethargic, Grey Bear threw out his chest. Seeks Fire might be distracted right now, but that wouldn't last long, especially if this journey resulted in revenge for what had been done to her brother.

* * *

AT LAST THE flat nothing took on definition as the three men entered the first valley. They stopped talking and spread out so they could more thoroughly access their surroundings. A lifetime spent in land like this had taught them that a quick glance was never enough; a seemingly small depression could turn out to be large enough to shelter buffalo or antelope—or those the Cheyenne were at war with.

Grey Bear indicated he intended to ride to the top of a roll of land. All around him, the grasses that fed the life-giving buffalo lay flat under the wind's weight. The sky to the north had taken on a slight haze, and someone not wise to the ways of nature might be fooled into believing the haze would become a cloud—and rain. But he didn't believe anything except what his eyes and ears told him. If it rained, he'd give thanks, but he knew better than to hope for what he hadn't seen for too long.

The village's old men and women—and sometimes Touches the Wind—told of when the Cheyenne lived in forests and lived off deer and elk, not buffalo. He tried to imagine what being surrounded by trees was like but couldn't. This open emptiness that wasn't was all he'd ever known. It suited him and yet—

Under him, Legs Like Lightning slowed, and his head came up. Taking his cue from his horse, he took careful note. Most of the prairie was a light golden-brown but some of the grass was darker, the why behind the deeper swaths unimportant. One did not question Maheo's magic. The creator, the One, was so great that not even the wisest man could fully describe Him so how could he think he understood why Maheo had painted some grasses darker than the rest. It was enough that—

Legs Like Lightning shook his head; his nostrils flared. "I thank Maheo for gifting you with a keen sense of smell," Grey Bear whispered. "What is it? Buffalo perhaps or—Pawnee?"

As alert as his horse now, he strained to see. He'd never tell Lone Hawk this, but he envied the other man's keen eyes. Perhaps should have asked him to come along.

Dismissing the thought, he pulled his surroundings into him and became one with the land and sky. At times like this, he thought of himself as an animal, all sensation and instinct. After riding a few more feet, he slid off Legs Like Lightning. With his bow and arrows strapped to his back and his knife secured at his waist, he crawled upward. When he reached the peak, he lifted his head and, like an antelope on the outlook for danger, took in his world.

There. Far enough away that even Legs Like Lightning would be winded by the time he'd run that distance was something.

"PAWNEE." GREY BEAR's voice was heavy with excitement. "As many as I have fingers on both hands. Painted and carrying many weapons."

"For war or because they hunt?" Nightelk asked.

"Hunt?" Grey Bear threw back. "There are no buffalo left there; even a foolish Pawnee knows that."

Several warriors nodded agreement. Nightelk studied those who'd gathered outside Grey Bear's tepee, most of them Grey Bear's age or slightly older. Only two other peace chiefs were in attendance, and so far they hadn't said anything. Lone Hawk and Two Coyotes sat next to each other, and Two Coyotes had just passed his everyday pipe to Lone Hawk.

"You are certain they did not see you?" Lone Hawk asked.

"Must I say it again?" Grey Bear shot back. "No, they did not."

Lone Hawk opened his mouth, but before he could speak, Two Coyotes touched his arm. "If Grey Bear says the Pawnee believe they are safe, I do not question his words." His voice, as always, was calm. Despite the heavy dread lodged inside Nightelk's belly, he didn't try to hide his pride in his son.

"Two Coyotes is right," he told the others, his attention directed at Lone Hawk. "No one should question Grey Bear in this."

"My words are guided by what happened the last time Cheyenne and Pawnee met," Lone Hawk said. If he felt chastised, he didn't show it. "Before, we attacked a few Pawnee and Porcupine was wounded. Now there are twice as many."

Grey Bear stared at Lone Hawk. "That matters to you? Perhaps you believe the Cheyenne incapable of winning a battle against so many?"

Lone Hawk's eyes narrowed, and the knuckles of the hand holding Two Coyotes' pipe turned white. "I am not afraid. But neither am I a puppy who believes he will not be hurt when he steals food from a much larger dog."

"You call me a puppy?" Grey Bear uncrossed his legs and made as if to stand. Nightelk held out his hand, stopping him.

After a moment, one of the other peace chiefs pointed out that Lone Hawk was wise to look at all aspects of what was being proposed. Revenge must be enacted; no one ever questioned that. However, was it wise to have many Cheyenne ride out after Pawnee now, when meetings to decide when or if the tribe should move on and where they would go were being held?

"Drinks Much Water is right." Nightelk indicated his fellow peace chief, a fat-bellied man who'd lost his front teeth. "Do we dare risk the lives of our bravest men? Revenge may have to wait until—"

"Wait!" If Grey Bear realized he'd interrupted his elder, he gave no indication. "Let Pawnee ride unchallenged?"

"We do not know what they are doing," Nightelk pointed out. "The meat we—you—provided will not last long. That is—"

"I *will* hunt again! Let no one doubt that." Grey Bear stared at each of the twenty-some men in turn as if challenging them to question his hunting prowess. When no one did, he focused his attention on Lone Hawk.

"I did not say this before because I wanted everyone, but mostly you, to hear this. To me, all Pawnee are the same, curs. But one stood out from the others—a warrior whose hair looks as if lightning has burned it white."

"Whitehair," Lone Hawk muttered. As he stared at Grey Bear, Two Coyotes drew his pipe out of his grip. "Whitehair," he repeated.

If a man wanted to hunt or go to war, he simply stated his intentions and others joined him if they were so inclined. The decision might be either applauded or questioned depending on the circumstances, but a young man didn't lay down his arms because his father or grandfather believed his actions rash or foolish. Without young men, the rest of the tribe would be unable to defend themselves, would starve. Thus, courage and daring were applauded.

Nightelk knew those things and remembered the days when his chest had swollen with pride as his own courage and daring was applauded, but he no longer walked in the past, and the horrible things he'd set in motion terrified him. Ruled by that fear and the reality that Black Eyes now avoided him, he argued that incurring even more of the Pawnees' wrath now was unwise. Neither Grey Bear or Lone Hawk, however, listened to him.

He understood why; Whitehair had wounded Porcupine.

"I WISH YOU were going with us," Lone Hawk told Porcupine as the injured warrior sat outside his tepee. "If Whitehair saw you, he would know the Cheyenne are mighty."

"I want him." Porcupine fisted his hand as if squeezing Whitehair's heart. "Want him to feel his blood flow from him as he made mine do."

"It will happen." Lone Hawk produced his pipe, filled the stone bowl with a mix of tobacco and kinnikinnick herbs, which he then lit. He handed his pipe to Porcupine, who took it gratefully. As Porcupine exhaled, Lone Hawk concentrated on the smoke, which was a breath of prayer and communication with the spirit world. The old men warned that too much smoking cut a warrior's wind, and with a hard ride ahead of him, he wouldn't take more than a few puffs, but it pleased him to see Porcupine sitting up and capable of smoking.

"Your side no longer bleeds?" he asked, indicating the wrapping over his friend's wound. "You will soon be able to join your wife in bed?"

Porcupine's smile was slow to come and didn't last long. "It is something we both want and for me to run with my son and hold my daughter, but it will not happen today."

Or tomorrow either, Lone Hawk admitted. Porcupine still looked pale and yet his checks held splotches of color. He'd already explained that Seeks Fire had insisted on the bandage because she wanted to make sure the medicine man's herbs remained in place. Seeks Fire had barely left her brother's side and was expected back from her visit to their parents before long.

"We will take you with us in spirit," he said unnecessarily. "Carry you in our thoughts and think of revenge."

"Revenge. It is always that, is it not."

Instead of responding to Porcupine's pensive tone, Lone Hawk explained that all except a few men would ride out in the morning. Several peace chiefs, Nightelk among them, had argued that hunting was more important.

"How can we go after food when we risk being attacked?"

"As we attacked the Pawnee." Porcupine chuckled, then coughed, the deep hacking bark leaving him gasping for breath. "I am getting old," he whispered when he could speak. "My body is taking so long to heal. Seeks Fire tells me I am ancient because she wants me to prove she is wrong, but her words are the truth."

"You are not old!" A moment ago Lone Hawk was looking forward to a glimpse of the maiden, but now he didn't want to see her. "Perhaps you would like to watch the men paint themselves for war?"

"No. No," Porcupine whispered. "Today they should be praying to their spirits and speaking of bravery, not having to look at me." Instead of taking another drag off the pipe, he returned it to Lone Hawk. "You should be with them."

Lone Hawk glanced over to where some ten men had gathered around Grey Bear's tepee. Not far away a group of boys, Knows No Fear among them, he hoped, watched the war preparations. "I will, soon. But I wanted you to know everything and to spend some time with you."

"I am grateful. I am surrounded by women these days, my wife and sister and Touches the Wind."

Lone Hawk frowned. "Touches the Wind?"

"She spends her time with Follower, taking care of her so my wife can be with me. Walking Rabbit says I am getting spoiled but—" He shifted position, and as he did, his features contorted and he placed his hand over his bandage. "But the women steal my energy. It is good to speak to a man."

The need to pray and boast felt strong in Lone Hawk. Grey Bear had already gone to his grandfather Sweet Grass Eater once and would undoubtedly seek spiritual guidance from him again. Lone Hawk wanted to learn from the old man's wisdom, yet doing so meant he'd have to be around Grey Bear. Whenever he saw him these days, the other man reminded him of lightning.

"I do not like the way the air feels," he admitted. "So dry, as if waiting for something."

"You feel it too?" Porcupine lifted his head and turned so he faced into the wind. "I thought perhaps it was my weakness that made me feel that way. My dreams are full of Maheo. That and nonsense."

"Maheo? He who created everything and is great beyond our understanding should fill your thoughts. That way His Sacred Powers will help you heal."

"I would like that, but I cannot tell Maheo what to do."

No one would even think to order the god over everything to do anything, and yet Lone Hawk couldn't help wishing he could speak to Maheo and learn from His wisdom. Ask whether Maheo and not Heammawihio the Wise One Above, had sent the nightmare of him desperately looking for food and water while the Cheyenne cried.

CHAPTER 7

When she'd seen Lone Hawk with Porcupine, Walking Rabbit had considered going back to her sister's tepee so the men could talk in private, but Calf Woman's chatter about how much work it was to take down a tepee and prepare it for travel had exhausted her.

It had been all she could do not to point out that all Calf Woman had to concern herself was her tepee while she had two children and an injured husband to think about in addition to moving, whenever that might happen. She hadn't because although Calf Woman's rapid-fire talk sometimes gave her a headache, she'd learned that her sister was concerned about her husband. Nightelk hadn't taken her as a man takes a woman since coming back from the hunt that had seen Porcupine wounded; that had never happened before.

Tears burned Walking Rabbit's eyes, but she brushed them away. How could she think of her own empty-armed nights and feel sorry for herself? Her husband's life was much more important. When he was healed, they'd make love and maybe another child would begin to grow inside her.

To her relief, Lone Hawk had left soon after her return. Porcupine had told her he wanted to go back inside, and although she hated the idea of being trapped inside the tepee, she helped him to his feet. This morning he'd been able to walk outside unaided, but now he leaned on her, shuffling and breathing heavily.

"What is it?" she asked once she had him settled on his bed and had given him a drink of water. "Do you want me to summon Easy Singer again?"

"No," he said after a too-long silence. "I—I feel hot, that is all. Perhaps a little more water."

She again held the bladder so he could drink, but he only took a single sip before stretching out and staring at the ceiling. "They fight for me." His voice sounded heavy. "Choose revenge against the Pawnee over hunting."

"That was their decision," she tried to tell him. "Do not carry the weight of it."

"I—I try not to but . . ."

"But what?"

"The Cheyenne call the Pawnee curs and cowards, but they are not. I fear—"

Her throat tightened. "What do you fear?"

For several moments he simply breathed, the labored sound tearing into her. She hated Lone Hawk for wearing him out.

"Too many things," he whispered. "I am so hot. So hot."

"Do you want to go back outside?"

He licked his lips, started to nod, then shook his head. He didn't look at her. "Perhaps later. Where are my children?"

Fear clenched her heart, held it. If only she'd stayed with her sister! If only Seeks Fire and Touches the Wind were here, but Touches the Wind had taken Follower with her to the creek and Seeks Fire—why had her husband's sister left?

"Knows No Fear is watching the men prepare for war," she told him. "Our daughter will be back soon."

"I hope so."

"You do not really want to be a man."

"I do too!" Follower insisted as she helped Touches the Wind lug a heavy water bladder to Porcupine and Walking Rabbit's tepee. "Men do not have to cook and sew and dig for roots and treat buffalo hides and look for firewood and stand over a hot fire. They—"

"Men hunt and fight."

"And laugh and boast and spend much of their time painting themselves and deciding what they should wear. What is there to boast about grinding turnips?"

Touches the Wind had no answer. Instead, she allowed herself to be distracted by the men gathered around Grey Bear's tepee. From here, she couldn't recognize everyone but spotted Lone Hawk who was walking, slowly it seemed, toward them. She'd just told the little girl that men hunted and fought and those things had sounded wonderful to Follower—as they surely did to the girl's brother—but Touches the Wind knew the truth behind those words. Porcupine's wound was proof of that; maybe Lone Hawk carried the weight of that truth on his shoulders today.

"I hope he is better," Follower said.

Knowing the girl was thinking of her father, Touches the Wind gave her a quick squeeze. "So do I. He will see how strong you are and that will make him happy."

Follower smiled, but the moment Touches the Wind saw Porcupine, she knew he was sicker than he'd been earlier in the day. Walking Rabbit locked frightened eyes on her but didn't say anything. Except for her father, Touches the Wind had never touched a grown man, not that she needed to because heat radiated from Porcupine, and he panted like a winded dog. Walking Rabbit asked if he wanted to go back outside where the wind waited.

"No," he muttered. "It is better that I remain in here where the men . . ." His eyes glazed and then focused. "Come here, my daughter." He started to hold out his arms to Follower, then let them drop. "You—you have been busy?"

Follower told her father about her morning, but Touches the Wind wasn't sure he was listening because his gaze kept flicking around the interior. Follower was still talking when Porcupine cleared his throat. "Touches the Wind, where is Little Bird? I—I think Follower should be with her."

Walking Rabbit gasped but didn't move from where she sat near her husband's side. Desperate to feel the wind on her flesh, Touches the Wind reached for Follower's hand. "Your father is right," she made herself say. "It is too fine a day to be inside."

"It is hot, not fine," Follower protested. "I want—"

"Do not argue." Walking Rabbit's tone was both sharp and tinged with tears. "You should—should . . ."

Silence hung in the air. After squeezing Walking Rabbit's hand and staring into Porcupine's unfocused eyes, Touches the Wind guided the girl outside. Although she sensed she was being watched, she didn't bother to look at the men. They were readying themselves for battle; that was all they should be thinking about.

Because Kicked by Horse had had some chores for Little Bird to do, she knew she'd find her younger sister near the family's tepee, so she led Follower in that direction. Follower's short, fat feet shuffled, and several times she glanced back over her shoulder but didn't say anything.

Once she'd found her sister, Touches the Wind told both girls that Easy Singer's puppies had just opened their eyes and they should be able to cuddle them. As was the way of children, Follower's mood turned to delight, and she and Little Bird ran off.

Instead of going inside to see what her mother wanted done, Touches the Wind turned toward Porcupine and Walking Rabbit's tepee. As she did, the wind slapped her cheek with a burning hand. She first recoiled and then pulled the air into her lungs.

"Are you going back to him?"

Startled, she faced Lone Hawk. Someone might think she'd allowed him to tug on her clothing if they saw them together. "H-him?" she stammered.

"Porcupine. How is he?"

"I—do not . . . He does not look well."

Lone Hawk's eyes darkened. "He seemed strong when I talked to him, and yet he did not want to smoke, and when I said I had to go, he did not ask me to stay."

"Perhaps talking to you exhausted him."

"Perhaps. I was hoping he would say something to us before we left."

Lone Hawk had painted his forehead red, and red and black stripes ran down the rest of his face, bold colors that said he was ready for battle. Only a loincloth covered him. Her father was a drab speck of a man who shuffled and whined and whose muscles had grown slack from inactivity. In contrast, Lone Hawk was all strength and energy. Fear touched her but was soon replaced by something she didn't understand.

"I do not know," she muttered. "He—you should ask him."

"Not if he is sleeping. Is he?"

"I do not think so. Please, I must go."

He blinked. "Of course. I am sorry." To her relief, he took a backward step. "I meant nothing improper by speaking to you again. I am worried about my friend but did not want to ask him how he felt." Something that might have been either a chuckle or a groan rolled out of him. "Some things one man does not tell another—admissions of weakness."

She'd never thought of that before, perhaps because it seemed as if there was nothing her father didn't complain about.

"You—the men will be leaving soon?" she stammered.

"As soon as Grey Bear says it is time. I wish—"

"What do you wish?" If someone saw them talking and told her father, Long Chin might force her to marry Lone Hawk. If that happened, he'd hate her. Still, she needed an answer.

"That Nightelk or another older man was going with us." His arms had been at his side, but now he folded them over his chest. "Someone wise and experienced who Grey Bear would listen to."

What men did when they rode out of the village was their concern. All she'd ever cared was that they returned alive.

"Grey Bear is unwise?" she asked.

Lone Hawk blinked, making her wonder if he'd spoken without first weighing the wisdom of his words. "Grey Bear is fearless and a proven fighter. You will tell Porcupine that my thoughts are of him?"

"Of course." After a moment of indecision, she backed

away from him, turned, and all but ran toward Porcupine's tepee. Surely she imagined he was still looking at her.

As MORNING MARCHED into the suffocating heat of afternoon, the warriors painted their horses and the decision to leave at dusk to take advantage of the cooler night was made. Inside his tepee, Porcupine alternately dozed and spoke to his wife and son. His words didn't always make sense, but Knows No Fear patiently answered his questions, even when they were repeated. Touches the Wind told them what Lone Hawk had said to her about Grey Bear, but neither Porcupine or Walking Rabbit asked why she and Lone Hawk had been talking. When, late in the day, Seeks Fire joined them, the conversation turned to what the peace chiefs must be talking about during the sweat.

Although Seeks Fire sat between Walking Rabbit and Touches the Wind, she kept glancing at her brother. Finally, bothered because he didn't seem to be listening anymore, she pressed the back of her hand to his forehead.

"He is on fire," she said.

Her lips moving soundlessly, Walking Rabbit did the same thing. Then she took hold of her husband's shoulders and shook them. He didn't respond.

"Summon Easy Singer," Seeks Fire ordered Knows No Fear. "Quickly."

As soon as the boy left, she removed the dressing. The torn flesh was no longer the same color as the rest of him but had turned black. It felt hot to the touch and was so swollen it looked as if he'd gained a great deal of weight there.

"My brother, please. Please." As Walking Rabbit had done, she shook his shoulders. He remained oblivious to his surroundings. "A fast," she managed. "He should have gone out by himself and fasted while praying for help from the spirits. I thought—I hoped Easy Singer's medicine would be enough but . . ." Shocked by her frightened tone, she fell silent.

"Do not blame yourself." Touches the Wind drew her away from Porcupine. "It was his decision to do what he did."

"He would have listened to me. If I had told him—he cannot die!"

"Hush, hush."

Touches the Wind wrapped her arms around her; she leaned into the other maiden's strength and, when she could, she looked at Walking Rabbit. The young mother had stretched out beside her husband and was slowly, lovingly running her hand over the barely moving chest.

"I love you," Walking Rabbit whispered. "I took your seed into me and you gifted me with two children. I want more, need all the years of my life with you. My husband, do not leave me. Please, do not . . ."

Porcupine died before his son could return with the medicine man. When Seeks Fire handed Walking Rabbit a knife, the new widow used it to hack off her long hair and slash her forehead in several places. Then Seeks Fire did the same thing herself. Holding onto each other, they stepped outside and walked to where Grey Bear and the other men were. No one spoke.

INSTEAD OF GOING off in search of the Pawnee that night, the men watched while Walking Rabbit and Seeks Fire dressed Porcupine's body in his finest clothing and wrapped him in several robes. Once that had been done, Porcupine and Seeks Fire's father and other male relatives placed him on a travois and carried him far from camp. Everyone took turns piling rocks on the corpse, and then a silent and grim-faced Nightelk slit the throat of Porcupine's favorite horse so the animal could carry his master during his spirit-journey. Porcupine's shield and war bonnet would go to Knows No Fear, but the rest of his weapons were left at the rock mound.

When Walking Rabbit started to slash her arms and legs because her husband had been killed by an enemy, Lone Hawk told her that wasn't necessary because the Cheyenne

men had already made the decision to seek revenge. That
seemed to satisfy her, either that or she didn't want her children to see her disfigure herself.

"It is done," Grey Bear said once everyone except Walking Rabbit and her children had returned to the village. "He
is at peace. Tomorrow—tomorrow we do what we must."

ALTHOUGH HE DIDN'T remember sleeping any during the
night, Lone Hawk was filled with too much energy for anything except getting on his horse and riding alongside Grey
Bear and Legs Like Lightning. Little wind had greeted the
morning, but that could change. None of the warriors had
said much and although the peace chiefs had had several
sweats and must have come to some decision about the
tribe's future, that would wait until the warriors' return.

Calmed by his horse's steady movement, Lone Hawk
found peace in knowing Porcupine's soul was on its way to
the Hanging Road where it would live forever with the Great
Wise One and the Cheyenne who'd gone before him. Porcupine hadn't committed suicide, which meant he'd be welcome in the afterlife. If he had, he wouldn't have been
allowed into Heaven but would have become nothing, a
thought that made Lone Hawk shudder.

"I wanted to comfort Seeks Fire," Grey Bear said. "If her
father hadn't been there, I would have."

"She has her family; Touches the Wind did not leave her
side."

"I know but—Knows No Fear should have come with us."

Although he'd been staring at the ground ahead of his
horse, Lone Hawk now glanced at the larger warrior. "The
boy has only been on one buffalo hunt and has yet to kill a
single calf. He is too young for war."

"For war, yes," Grey Bear agreed. "But he would have
brought his father's spirit with him."

That was true, not that he could imagine Walking Rabbit
agreeing to let her son come along. Now that they were no
longer in sight of the village, the warriors had spread out,

some traveling by themselves while others rode in small groups. Once they were closer to where Grey Bear had seen the Pawnee, they'd plan their attack, but for now, there was only greeting the morning and thinking about a man's death. Why he'd chosen to remain close to Grey Bear, Lone Hawk couldn't say. He should have sought out Two Coyotes.

"I saw you with Touches the Wind yesterday," Grey Bear said, breaking a silence of several minutes. "You spoke to her?"

"About Porcupine."

"Hm. She did not mind?"

He tried to remember what the maiden had said, but her words had faded. What he remembered was the way she'd kept her eyes on him instead of staring shyly at the ground. "Like me, her thoughts were of Porcupine."

"Hm. I do not understand the Pawnee."

Surprised by the sudden change in conversation, Lone Hawk took a moment to study the horizon and to go deep inside himself. Not sleeping meant he hadn't dreamed, and yet his hot and thirsty nightmare rode with him. He still hadn't told anyone about it, and if he decided to, it wouldn't be Grey Bear.

"Surely they know we would ride after them," Grey Bear went on. "Why would they come this close to a Cheyenne village?"

"The drought has touched them the same as it has us. Maybe they give little thought to where they go."

Grey Bear snorted. "If that is so, they are even more foolish than I thought. The buffalo have left this land; surely they know that."

"I cannot say what happens inside a Pawnee's mind; I do not want to know."

"If that does not matter to you, then *you* are foolish."

Fighting anger, Lone Hawk forced himself to study Legs Like Lightning. The stallion was restless and quick-footed today, probably because he'd thought he'd be traveling yesterday; that hadn't happened because Porcupine had died.

"Did you see Follower?" he asked. "As Porcupine was

being buried, she clung to her mother's legs, not crying but looking as if the earth had split open in front of her."

"Follower?" Grey Bear frowned. "No, I—wait, yes, she was there when I spoke to Walking Rabbit this morning. I did not know what to say to her so I left her to her thoughts."

"You and Walking Rabbit spoke?"

"Only for a moment. I wanted her to know I ride with her husband's memory beside me. Perhaps Follower heard and took comfort from that."

Grey Bear could be gentle; Lone Hawk had seen him around the tribe's boys and had been impressed by his patience and willingness to teach them certain skills. A girl was a different matter. Feeling overwhelmed by how one should comfort a child whose father has just died, Lone Hawk lost himself in his surroundings.

The Cheyenne traded with other Indians, even those they'd always been at war with. Some traders had come great distances and spoke of land covered by tall, fat trees fed by frequent rain. Although he'd been fascinated by the descriptions, Lone Hawk could never quite believe it was true. This land that sustained him and the rest of his people was all he'd ever known. Because he could see so far, his surroundings kept few secrets from him. Today it gloried in its hot, parched, waiting-for-winter patience.

Mutsoyef, Sweet Medicine, the ancient one who'd shown the Cheyenne many of the ways of remaining as one with their surroundings, had gifted them with Mahuts, the four powerful and mysterious Medicine Arrows. The arrows, kept wrapped in a fox-skin bundle, were guarded by priests and brought out only during the Arrow Renewal Ceremony held in early summer most years and attended by all Cheyenne. He'd listened carefully as the priests spoke of the wisdom Sweet Medicine had gained from the spirit Maiyun, heard again how two of the arrows had power over buffalo and two ruled human beings.

It wasn't the Cheyenne way to question anything a priest said or did. Still, he couldn't help wondering if perhaps the ceremony hadn't been conducted correctly this year, and that's why the buffalo had left. Maybe Maiyun and the other spirits had been angered by something the Cheyenne had done and were withholding what little rain they supplied. Maybe the spirits themselves were trying to warn him through his nightmare?

Certain the answer didn't lie within him, he stared at the sky. Porcupine was up there somewhere, traveling to the land of ancestors. A person who has died may feel sorrow at leaving those he loved but surely the journey brings him comfort, turned him from one thing into another. The journey—

The air felt suddenly alive, waiting. It might be warning of coming lightning, the energy of that great power filling him. Barely aware of what he was doing, he glanced at Grey Bear, who was studying his surroundings in his grizzly way.

"Do you feel it?" Grey Bear asked. "Something . . ."

"Perhaps the Pawnee are nearby."

"No. We will not reach where I saw them until tomorrow. This—this . . . The world waits for rain, an end to heat. The wind . . ."

As if in response to hearing its name spoken, a fire-burst of unseen air slammed into both men, rendering them and their horses breathless. Even as he fought, Lone Hawk imagined the same blast striking the Pawnee.

"Our enemies have come close because they are desperate," he said when he could speak. "We took the meat they needed and now they hunt—for anything."

"They will find only my arrows. Their bellies will fill, not with food, but with their own blood."

Grey Bear spoke as a Cheyenne warrior should, as all warriors were taught. Just the same, Lone Hawk thought not of killing those who'd killed Porcupine, but what would happen to empty-bellied Pawnee children if their fathers and uncles didn't return.

CHAPTER 8

The Cheyenne spent the night on a rock-carpeted rise with their horses tethered nearby. Two pack-horses carried water-swollen bladders while another's burden consisted of food. They'd stopped before dark so the horses could feed. By rationing the water, they could remain on the prairie for as many as five days, but as each man gave himself up to sleep, the common prayer was that that wouldn't be necessary.

Grey Bear had selected a relatively flat spot just large enough to accommodate his body. As a consequence, no one was so close that he felt their presence. Alone with his thoughts, he alternated between the anticipation of battle and asking himself whether Porcupine had completed his death journey.

Shortly before leaving the village, he'd sought out his grandfather and had lost himself in Sweet Grass Eater's stories of how, as a young man, he'd counted coup against the hated Crow three times—twice when he'd ridden into a Crow camp as part of a horse raiding band. Although Sweet Grass Eater had been wounded during a battle with the Kiowa, he'd remained untouched by the Crow, proof of his bravery and his spirit's power.

"You are of my blood," Sweet Grass Eater had told him. "More than your father is although he twice had a horse shot out from under him. In your eyes I see the fire that once burned in mine. It is good to know that fire has not died, that it will not die."

Wrapped in his grandfather's words, Grey Bear relived his own exploits. Although it would have brought him much glory to have the horse he was riding killed by the enemy, he was content to have counted coup several times, locating a small band of Crow hunters last spring, carrying a wounded companion out of another battle, and—once—charging two Pawnee while other Cheyenne warriors watched. His belly had tightened and his bowels loosened as Legs Like Lightning galloped toward the Pawnee, but he'd kept that emotion to himself, buried it under the act of reaching out and slapping first one and then the other Pawnee.

Tomorrow he'd do more than touch his enemy; tomorrow he'd kill—do to a Pawnee what had been done to Porcupine.

When the sun rose, Grey Bear sat up and stretched, acknowledged the wind. His back felt stiff and there was a rubbed spot on his right heel, but once he'd emptied his bladder and prayed, he felt ready to address the others.

"If this was another time," he began, "our people would have sent us off with songs of Wolf because Wolf guides the Cheyenne into war. Porcupine's death changed the usual order."

His companions nodded.

"It was time to mourn Porcupine, but now we must think only of why we are here. Fill your hearts with courage. Wolf rides with us."

"You prayed to Wolf?" someone asked.

"Before any other, as my grandfather said I should. I am your leader and I prepared for today, for all of us, by asking for help, courage, and wisdom."

After a quick breakfast, they broke camp and set off with Grey Bear still leading the way. Clutching his pipe in his left hand, he divided his attention between what he'd done to assure himself of success and what to expect when they came across the Pawnee. The tracks he'd made the other day had been blown away, and there was no sign of the Pawnee, but the enemy had been traveling slowly, hunting as they went, and he didn't expect that to have changed. Seeing their pitiful supply of dead rabbits and a single antelope carcass had made him laugh. The Pawnee were old women, not hunters like the Cheyenne.

Except that the Cheyenne had brought home buffalo meat just once since summer began and that had come about because the Pawnee had found the buffalo.

No! He wouldn't think about that! Today was for Porcupine, for being a Cheyenne warrior, for courage and success!

By the time the sun was high overhead, they'd passed the spot where he'd seen the Pawnee and were following their horses' tracks. Even a boy Knows No Fear's age could have no trouble determining which way to travel, but he continued to lead the way, the others riding single file behind him.

He stopped, sweat trickling down the back of his neck. "Listen," he started to say, but it wasn't necessary.

"Horses," Lone Hawk mouthed.

He nodded. Despite the heat, he felt alive. "Today Pawnee blood will flow."

PROTECTED BY THE undulating earth, the Cheyenne rode within sight of the Pawnee without being seen. It might have been because Grey Bear's prayers to Wolf had been answered, but when Lone Hawk saw that two of the Pawnee horses were lame and the others plodded with their muzzles almost dragging on the ground, the wind whipping their manes and tails the only sign of life, he knew that concern for their animals had kept the enemy from being as vigilant as they should have been.

There were nine Pawnee, their body paint nearly buried under layers of dust. Several horses carried small bags, which he assumed contained whatever they'd killed. The Pawnee themselves looked almost as spent as their horses; no one attempted to prod his animal into a faster pace, probably because the water bladders were nearly empty.

"These are Pawnee?" Two Coyotes whispered as he pulled alongside. "Surely they are not the same men you saw earlier, the ones who killed Porcupine."

Lone Hawk started to shrug but stopped when the sun

glinted off a swath of white hair on the Pawnee riding in front.

"They look half dead," Two Coyotes continued.

"They must be trying to get back to their people, but it may be too late—" He stopped speaking because Grey Bear was indicating he wanted them to gather around him.

"The spirits ride with us," Grey Bear announced. "And they have abandoned the Pawnee. These few are like buffalo standing at the edge of a cliff waiting to be stampeded over it."

"This is not war." Lone Hawk couldn't remain silent. "It will be a slaughter."

"Then we will slaughter our enemy! Be Cheyenne!"

Several of the younger braves echoed Grey Bear's words. Lone Hawk and Two Coyotes exchanged a look but said nothing. With an effort, Lone Hawk shook off the image of the trudging, desperate Pawnee and remembered Walking Rabbit's wails. He cast off the question of why there weren't as many as Grey Bear had told them about. Just the same, he was slow to understand that Grey Bear wanted them to surround the Pawnee and kill their horses.

Kill horses that were already dying? Cripple the Pawnee instead of facing them warrior to warrior?

His thoughts in turmoil, he nevertheless rode in the direction Grey Bear had indicated. The echo of Walking Rabbit's sobs faded; he could no longer hear little Follower crying over her father's body. Instead, his eyes locked on the two Pawnee horses barely able to keep up with their companions' slow pace. The Pawnee should have left the cripples behind, but they hadn't because horses sometimes meant the difference between life and death.

Whitehair's mount stumbled and pitched forward. Whitehair managed to jump off and then waited as the pitiful animal got its feet under it. Instead of mounting, Whitehair started leading the dust-colored creature. He seemed to be speaking to it.

Enemy, yes. Human, yes.

Grey Bear would wait until the Pawnee were in the valley

ahead of them before ordering his companions to ride down
on their enemy. As a child, Lone Hawk had been satisfied
to sit outside a prairie-dog hole until the curious creature
poked its head out and then shoot it, but he was no longer
a boy. He wanted the Pawnee to pay for killing Porcupine;
that would never change. But revenge should be a battle, not
slaughter!

He ground his heels into his mount's side. The horse, already alert, sprang forward. Lone Hawk's cry filled the air,
half howl, half warning. Instead of going after Whitehair, he
headed toward another man who dropped the rope he was
using to lead a pack animal and spun around to face him.
Although he was too far away for Lone Hawk to see into
the man's eyes, he read both fear and anger in the way the
Pawnee reached for his arrows.

Lone Hawk didn't give the Pawnee time to aim. Instead,
he yanked his own mount hard to the right and raced after
the now-loose pack animal.

Behind him, he heard other Cheyenne urge their horses
into a run. He'd been the closest to the Pawnee when he
revealed his position. As a result, by the time his companions
were near enough to attempt a coup or engage in battle, the
Pawnee had recovered from their surprise.

As if they'd already discussed what they should do if they
were attacked, the Pawnee charged. Startled, several Cheyenne horses tried to dodge out of the way. Although no
Cheyenne were unseated, controlling their mounts distracted
them.

"Do not let them escape!" Grey Bear bellowed. He thrust
his lance into the air. "They *must* not escape!"

"The horses!" This from Woodenlegs. "Do not—"

The rest was lost to Lone Hawk. He'd overtaken the pack
horse and managed to snag the rope before the animal could
step on it and hurt itself. Then, not thinking what he was
doing, or perhaps thinking too much, he began galloping
back toward the Cheyenne. Woodenlegs was now to his
right, Grey Bear, yelling, ahead of him. At the last instant,
he released the Pawnee horse so it continued to run at Grey

Bear. Legs Like Lightning planted his legs, and in his attempt to remain seated, Grey Bear took his eyes off the Pawnee he'd been about to attack.

"What are you doing?" Grey Bear demanded.

"The animal—" he began, then stopped; he wouldn't lie to Grey Bear. By way of answer, he turned and pointed toward the Pawnee. Although Wolf Robe, Two Coyotes, and several others charged after them, the Pawnee had recovered from their shock and lashed their horses in a desperate attempt to outrun the enemy.

"We are Cheyenne!" he told Grey Bear. "Warriors! We do not slaughter a helpless enemy."

A cry distracted him from Grey Bear's reply. Whitehair had managed to reach the top of the hill but instead of continuing to run, he sat tall and straight on his trembling mount's back. Whether the Pawnee had jumped onto his own horse or had grabbed another didn't matter. What did was the way Whitehair lifted his clenched fist over his head.

"YOU. YOU DID this!"

Lone Hawk didn't drop his eyes from Grey Bear's fierce glare. "I have said why." Although his insides felt as if they'd been caught in a whirlwind, he managed to keep his voice steady. "Those were not Pawnee warriors but wounded creatures run to the ground."

"They killed Porcupine!"

Wolf Robe hadn't returned yet, but Two Coyotes had given up chasing after the fleeing Pawnee and had joined the Cheyenne now grouped around Grey Bear and Lone Hawk. In his mind, Lone Hawk still saw Whitehair thrusting his arm skyward in defiance, but that wasn't all. He also remembered the spent horses, the Pawnee men's shoulders slumped in weariness.

"What we saw the day we took buffalo from them is not what the Pawnee are today," he said into the wind.

"They are the same!" Grey Bear jumped off Legs Like Lightning and stalked over to Lone Hawk. "They carry the same weapons! Porcupine must be avenged! He must!"

Lone Hawk dismounted. The two now stood close enough that they could have grabbed each other, but Lone Hawk had no wish to touch the man he'd considered his friend. His emotions tumbled inside him; he had no words for what he felt.

"You are not Cheyenne!" Grey Bear insisted. Heat lightning accentuated his words. "I see before me a snake, a small mouse fleeing an eagle."

"Grey Bear, no!"

Lone Hawk barely acknowledged Two Coyotes who'd angled himself so he could keep an eye on both men.

"I will *not* be silent! I cannot!" Grey Bear continued. He glanced at the others, then concentrated his attention on Lone Hawk. "We would have crushed them." He fisted his hand, the knuckles growing white. "Ended them. From this day forth, all would speak of Cheyenne courage."

"Cheyenne or you?" Lone Hawk demanded. "Attacking unprepared and defenseless Pawnee was what *you* wanted to do."

"That is wrong?" Before Lone Hawk could answer, Grey Bear forced his uplifted fist down by his side. He had to fight for each breath and his temples pounded. One unguarded word, another heartbeat and he'd strike Lone Hawk. Still, he couldn't stop himself. "We are Tsistsistas, The People. My chest"—he slapped himself there—"carries the scars of the Sun Dance."

"All of us do," Two Coyotes pointed out, his voice a soft owl call.

"Does he?" Grey Bear stared into Lone Hawk's eyes, seeing not the man who often sat at his grandfather's side but a creature he longed to crush. "I say he is a coward."

"Grey Bear, no."

His anger swung from Lone Hawk to Two Coyotes, but Two Coyotes hadn't warned the Pawnee. "My silence will not change the truth. This I say—say for all to hear." His nails bit into the palms of his hands, but he couldn't force his fists to relax. Lone Hawk's blood should flow into the ground. Needed to flow—at his hands.

"He—" He spat at Lone Hawk. "This one is *not* Cheyenne!"

Before he could collect the moisture he needed to spit again, Two Coyotes clamped his hand over his mouth. Grey Bear started to slap it away, then realized what he'd nearly done. If he'd struck Two Coyotes—

"Do not touch me," he mumbled. "I will—I must . . ."

Something that was a mix of summer heat and winter cold collided inside him, making him both sick and afraid—maybe of himself. Barely able to control his movements, he stalked away. His long and powerful legs carried him onto the plains but not fast enough that he couldn't hear what Two Coyotes was saying.

"This is not the Cheyenne way. There must be no fighting between us, ever."

The sun blasted down on him, and he tried not to feed off it, but it was so hard to let go of his anger's fire—so hard to remember that harmony within the tribe came before anything else.

SEEKS FIRE KNELT near the rocks marking her brother's grave. Her eyes glazed, but because she didn't care whether she saw anything, she didn't try to bring them back into focus. The relentless heat made her long for any shade, even the scant amount provided by her family's tepee, but she needed this time alone with Porcupine even more. Last night she and Touches the Wind had tried to distract Follower from her mother's grief by telling her to look for the silly man's face in the moon, but then Knows No Fear had come looking for his sister and talk had turned to why Porcupine had left his children.

"I had no answer for them," she told her brother's memory. "Your son looked at me with eyes so sad that I felt my heart break. You took such pride in his growing up but now he must do it without you and . . ."

Sensing energy, she readied herself for a repeat of the dry lightning that had been searing the sky since morning. She felt but didn't see it, then pulled back inside herself.

"What do you wish for them?" she asked. "Walking Rabbit tries not to cry when she is around her children, but even when her tears are not flowing, there is such sadness inside her that I fear she will die from it."

Maybe the dead didn't want to be reminded of the grief they'd left behind. Wondering how much Porcupine knew these days, she told him that a number of men, led by Grey Bear, had gone off after the Pawnee.

"They knew no fear, at least Grey Bear did not." Speaking his name aloud caused her cheeks to flame. "He is so brave, not a grub-eating black bear but a grizzly. When I look into his eyes I see—"

Another sound, this one nothing like the snap and snarl of lightning, silenced what would have been foolish words, and she quickly looked around. Calf Woman was lumbering her way, her breathing loud and quick.

"I look for my sister," Calf Woman said. "I thought she might have come here again."

"She did this morning, but when they kept after her, she went with the other women to dig roots," Seeks Fire explained. "It is something for her to do,"

"You did not go with them?"

"No, not this time."

"Perhaps it is well." Calf Woman stood looking down at the grave for several seconds and then cleared her throat. "I worry about my sister."

"So do I," Seeks Fire admitted as she got to her feet.

"I thought"—Calf Woman indicated the rocks—"your thoughts would be of your brother, not the woman he was married to."

"Walking Rabbit became a sister to me." Her throat caught and she had to struggle for the strength to continue. "Porcupine's death does not change that, and the children—"

"Knows No Fear is no longer a child."

"Eight is not a man."

Calf Woman appeared to consider that. "No, it is not. But my thoughts are with Follower. Knows No Fear plays with the other boys and looks after his father's horses and has more to do than just grieve, but his little sister—and her mother . . ."

Because Calf Woman's children were grown, and she spent most of her time with other women her age, Seeks Fire didn't often have reason to talk to her, but they'd been united by Porcupine's death; that bond was erasing the years between them. She wondered how Calf Woman felt about that, then decided it didn't matter. "I have seen your sister's tears," she admitted. "I do not know what to do to dry them."

"That is not for you to do." Calf Woman shifted from one leg to the other and rubbed her right knee. "Come with me, please. It is easier for me to walk than stand."

The two women traveled in silence for a while and then, as they neared the village, Calf Woman touched her arm. "Walking Rabbit will always love your brother."

"I know."

"But she must not spend her life clinging to that one love."

"I know."

NIGHTELK HAD SEEN his wife and Seeks Fire together and had no doubt that they'd been talking about Porcupine. He'd always been perplexed by women's conversations since they were so different from men's concern with providing food and engaging in battle, with boasting. Instead of announcing their accomplishments, women filled their days with gossip. Today, however, like too many other times, he couldn't free his thoughts from the image of the bleeding white calf. It wasn't until Calf Woman left Seeks Fire and came toward him that the image faded a little.

"I thought you were still at the sweat," his wife said. Her gaze remained on him.

"No." He didn't bother explaining that it had been so hot that once their business had been conducted, no one had wanted to linger around the heated rocks.

"Hm. Is it such a secret that you will not tell me what they spoke about?"

"What? No, there is no secret. We—"

"Never mind. I know what you are going to say, but that is not what we need to talk about today."

Something in her tone caught his attention. She knew something was bothering him; he had no doubt of that. But there was no way she could have found out—

"A thing that will change us," she said softly. "But must be."

WALKING RABBIT HAD indeed gone root digging, but by the time Nightelk found his wife's younger sister, she'd returned and was using twig brooms to remove the spines from several prickly pear cactus fruits. The sight of her meager supply sent dread through him, but he shook off the temporarily unimportant thought. Because Walking Rabbit was his sister-in-law, their relationship had been easygoing and light-hearted, but today he stood several feet away until she looked up.

"It is good to see you working," he said. "This is the first time since Porcupine's death, is it not?"

A shadow stole across her face and settled deep in her eyes. "I did not want to move, but the other women . . ."

"They were wise. You cannot spend your life lost in grief."

"Some widows do. When Last Runner died, his wife walked onto the prairie and did not return until spring came again."

"Night Woman cared for nothing except that her husband was a senior peace chief. When he died, there was nothing for her—except her grief."

Walking Rabbit nodded, and a faint smile touched her lips. "Last Runner's brothers made sure she always had something to eat and her family stayed nearby until they'd persuaded her to return to life. She would never say so, but she loved the attention."

"Your grief is real," he told her. "You do not shed tears so others will see them."

Her smile was gone, replaced by the glimmer of tears. "I do not know how to walk any more, how to be a mother, a sister-in-law."

He sat cross-legged opposite her, seeing in her high cheekbones and strong jaw a little of his wife, but where Calf Woman's bones were all but buried under fat, Walking Rabbit retained a young woman's angles. There'd been times when he'd envied Porcupine's right to sleep with her, and now . . .

"You will reclaim those things," he told her. "Grief is a season, a march of time that takes you on a painful journey, but at the end—"

Reaching out, she clasped his hand. "All these years and you still mourn your dead children."

Rendered briefly silent by the old pain, he nodded. After swallowing, he continued. "I will not try to tell you how long your journey will take, but listen to laughter. Take your children's laughter inside you and make it sing in your heart. The day will come when joy bubbles up from you and you will feel alive."

Still grasping his hand, she let her head drop. "You promise?"

How could he, who held himself responsible for Porcupine's death, promise her anything? And yet he had no choice. "Walk one moment, one day at a time," he said. "Ask no more or less of yourself."

"I—I do not know if I have the strength."

Walking Rabbit hadn't washed her recently cut hair since Porcupine's death. It lay limp and short and neglected, and Nightelk longed to ask her to tend to her personal needs.

"You may not have the strength for yourself"—The words came from somewhere deep and private inside him—"but for your children you must. That is what kept me alive when my babies died—knowing my arms needed to envelop a living child. When Two Coyotes was born—Walking Rabbit, you have a son and a daughter. They carry Porcupine's blood—and yours. Do not ever forget that."

"I—I know."

Difficult as what he'd been telling her had been, the next, he knew, would be even harder. Yet it had to be done.

"I am here—you must guess—today your sister came to me and—"

Walking Rabbit had let go of his fingers, but he still remembered how they'd felt cradled by her warmth. "When a woman's husband dies, she should not remain alone. Someone must provide her with what she cannot—some man must hunt for her. Care for her and sleep—"

Feeling foolish, he glanced at her, but she continued to stare at the ground.

"It is right that a man marries his widowed sister-in-law. Calf Woman wants that for you, and I—I wish to—to do what Porcupine no longer can."

Her head came up, but he couldn't read the message in her eyes.

"Knows No Fear and Follower need a father. I can be that man."

She blinked.

"I am not so old that I can no longer hunt. I want to do that for you and your children." He took what he prayed would be a calming breath. "And you should have more babies. I can—my seed—"

"No!"

Her cry caused his heart to lurch. "You do not wish—"

"Nightelk, if I cannot sleep with Porcupine, I will sleep alone."

CHAPTER 9

"Taxtavo is a gift from the spirit beings. It is part of *heammabestonev*, everything that is above the earth's surface. The Cheyenne breathe *taxtavo* and it makes all life possible. Tonight I will not speak of *aktunov*, which lies beneath the earth, because now only *taxtavo* matters. Open your mouth and nostrils and pull the sweet air deep into your lungs."

Grey Bear did as his naked, red-painted grandfather ordered, but although he welcomed reminders of Cheyenne beliefs, he continued to fight the need to confront Lone Hawk.

Since the warriors' return, he'd said little to those in the village, but others had spread the news of the abortive attack on the Pawnee and the near fight between him and Lone Hawk. He'd been aware of the way the maidens, particularly Seeks Fire, studied him, but although he'd longed to tell her about Lone Hawk's deception, he didn't trust himself to speak to her.

Only Sweet Grass Eater had demanded the truth. "There must be no disharmony," the old man had said. "Through peace within our people, the Cheyenne remain strong. Otherwise, we are open and vulnerable to our enemies."

"I know," he'd replied. "And I pray for peace within my heart."

"But has it come?"

When Grey Bear had been unable to give him the answer his grandfather needed, Sweet Grass Eater had gathered the men around him. Now Grey Bear sat to his grandfather's right listening to words that had been part of his entire existence. He felt comforted by the presence of so many others, but that didn't bury his sense of failure; the Pawnee had escaped. He avoided looking at Lone Hawk.

"My grandson is blessed by Heammawihio, the all-knowing High God," Sweet Grass Eater said in his familiar, singsong tone. "Heammawihio placed strength in his muscles and fed him with courage. We will not speak of what happened with the Pawnee; that time is behind us and we will move forward."

A sigh of relief rippled through the assembled men.

"I am also a peace chief," Sweet Grass Eater continued. "We have come together many times in the past few days because the decision before us is not easily made. I say this now; if anyone believes we have not chosen the right path, say so."

Several peace chiefs shifted position but no one spoke.

"This is good, how it should be." Sweet Grass Eater looked at each of the senior men in turn before pushing himself to his feet and placing his hand on Grey Bear's head. "This creek has been our home for many moons, but no longer."

Because he'd expected to hear that, Grey Bear remained silent.

"Buffalo are holy. They were born in the great underground cave and came to our ancestors so they would not starve."

"Yes, yes."

"But it is not the way of the buffalo to spend their lives in one place, just as it is the way of the Cheyenne to travel."

"Yes, yes."

"There is nothing here for us." Sweet Grass Eater sounded melancholy. "The graves of those who have died, yes, but not the food and water we need for life."

As if reinforcing what he'd just said, a lightning shaft spit across the sky.

"No rain," Sweet Grass Eater whispered. "And without rain what is left of the creek will dry; we will die."

The old man continued to talk. Although Grey Bear couldn't hold onto his every word, the essence of his words seeped into him. The journey had to be a wise one; otherwise, everyone's life was at risk. No one knew how long the tribe would have to travel before they found a new home. What was vital was making sure they had enough food and water.

"Because too many of our enemies lie behind us, we must go toward the setting sun, into land new to us, dangerous. We will take as much water as our horses and dogs can carry." Sweet Grass Eater waited for the other chiefs to nod agreement. "But there is not enough meat for a long journey."

Although his grandfather hadn't directed his comment at him, Grey Bear knew with proud certainty what was coming next.

"Because my grandson was gone doing what a warrior does, I went to the spirits for him."

In the silence that followed the latest, Grey Bear rose to his feet and stood before his grandfather. The past few days had tired him, but now he felt strong. "You did right," he said.

"I did what a man who has confidence in his grandson's abilities would do. I was ready to fast and pray for a vision if necessary but it was not. Instead, a dream came to me."

From the way the peace chiefs stared at Sweet Grass Eater, Grey Bear was certain this was the first anyone had heard of this particular dream. From what his parents had told him, Sweet Grass Eater had been the first man to hold him after his birth. The bond between them was powerful.

"What dream?" he asked, as was his right and responsibility.

"Your soul," Sweet Grass Eater mouthed.

"My soul?"

"Your *tasoom* came to me. My eyes saw the shadow, the shade of it, and I knew it had left your body. I was afraid for you."

Of course he was; if a *tasoom* left the body for too long, a person would die.

"My fear was short. Your *tasoom* came to me and told me

it had been to Heammawihio by way of *ekutsihimmiyo*, the Hanging Road where it spent time with the spirits of those who have died. Those spirits handed their strength to your *tasoom*."

Lightning again slashed at the sky. Grey Bear felt himself drifting upward and being strengthened by lightning's power.

"I bring to all of you the message that was given to me in my dream," Sweet Grass Eater said. "Grey Bear is mighty among men. He has the sight of the spirits; that sight will lead him to buffalo—buffalo enough for all of us. I cannot say how long the journey will take, but that unseen buffalo-place will become our new home. Grey Bear will find it, return to us, and guide all of us there."

Lone Hawk closed his eyes.

THERE WASN'T ENOUGH food in the village for a great feast, but everyone contributed what they could. Nightelk was pleased to see Walking Rabbit and her children among those who'd gathered outside Sweet Grass Eater's tepee that night, but much as he wanted to talk to the young widow again, other things were more important.

Once the majority of villagers had eaten and left, he presented himself to Sweet Grass Eater and Grey Bear. It didn't matter to him how many men remained in attendance.

"Your words have filled my heart," he told Sweet Grass Eater. "I have never questioned the power of your dreams, and my eyes have seen your grandson's great courage."

Nearby, Lone Hawk grunted but didn't say anything. Grey Bear shot a glance at Lone Hawk, then placed his hand on his grandfather's shoulder. "If I have courage," he said, "it is because my grandfather has long guided my steps."

Everyone looked at him, but although he'd often spoken before a large group, Nightelk had to struggle for each word. He loved being Cheyenne. Nothing gave him greater pride than to think of his place within the village and to know he contributed to its success. With a single act, however, none of that mattered; the only thing left to him was to ask forgiveness, somehow.

"Sweet Grass Eater," he began, "your words were that you prayed for keen vision for Grey Bear so he can find buffalo."

"Yes, yes."

"I do not doubt that your prayers were answered, and yet—" His heart thudded and he looked around for something, anything to calm himself. Beyond the circle of men stood his wife and Walking Rabbit—the sister-in-law who couldn't bring herself to marry him. There was no sign of Black Eyes.

"It is not the way of the Cheyenne to ask a single man to feed a village," he said.

Sweet Grass Eater frowned, the gesture highlighting uncounted wrinkles. "My grandson will do what he must, what the spirits have set before him."

"I know he will." If he'd been Grey Bear's father, would his chest swell at the thought of the younger man's reckless courage, or would his father-heart quake? Perhaps it was better to have a son like Two Coyotes, quiet and unboastful. "But did the spirits say he should ride alone?"

Sweet Grass Eater ran a hand across his leathery chest with its ancient Sun Dance scars. "That is for him to decide."

For him to decide. "Grey Bear." Nightelk turned his attention to the younger man. "This is what I must say to you. Your shoulders are broad, but they should not carry the weight of an entire band."

"They will carry what they must," Grey Bear said. "I do not shrink from the task."

No, you would not. "Neither do I." Nightelk's voice carried more conviction than he felt.

"What are you saying?" Sweet Grass Eater asked.

"That one man, even a man blessed by the spirits, is not enough. Summer bites with deadly teeth. If the Cheyenne are to survive, another must ride alongside Grey Bear. Me."

* * *

EXHAUSTION HAD CRAWLED under Lone Hawk's skin, but he fought to remain awake. When Sweet Grass Eater started to talk, and even when Nightelk proclaimed his desire to hunt with Grey Bear, he'd tried to distance himself from the conversation, from Grey Bear.

However, the other peace chiefs' refusal of Nightelk's offer meant he no longer could. Not looking at Grey Bear, he acknowledged every one of the peace chiefs in turn, saving his final look for Sweet Grass Eater.

"Grandfather," he began, calling the old man by the name often used for all elders. "I have listened to you since I first came here and am proud you consider me your grandson's equal." Sweet Grass Eater hadn't used those exact words, but the meaning had been clear. "I see myself as a humble man, an adequate hunter but not blessed in the way Grey Bear is. I have questions I wish to ask of you before I speak what is in my mind."

Sweet Grass Eater nodded. Clearly he enjoyed being placed in the position of making an important decision.

"You truly believe Grey Bear will accomplish more with another beside him than he could alone?"

"I have already spoken on this." Sweet Grass Eater sounded impatient. "My grandson is unequaled in courage and determination, but even I will not say that his senses are keener than any other. Your ears often hear what no other man can; no one's eyesight is better."

"I thank you for saying that. But there is another matter, one that both Grey Bear and I may wish to forget."

Grey Bear grunted but didn't speak.

"There has been disharmony between us. We do not walk as brothers."

"I know."

But did the old man, or anyone, fully understand how much distance existed between him and Grey Bear?

"If I do this thing—" Lone Hawk spoke only to Nightelk. "I do not want you to believe I question your prowess."

"I know," Nightelk said. "I only—the chiefs have spoken. They do not want me to hunt."

But you do. Why? Instead of pressing the question that he suspected Nightelk wouldn't answer, he walked over to Grey Bear and extended his hand.

"Our chiefs have spoken," he said. "Nightelk is now a peace chief, no longer a warrior. Still, they do not wish you to ride alone. I will not turn from their words. Will you?"

Grey Bear stared at him for so long that Lone Hawk felt the beat of unease from the assembled men. Finally, though, the other warrior rose and clasped his arm. "My grandfather has spoken. I take his wisdom into me, make it mine. Together—" He started to draw back and then, perhaps aware of the many eyes on them, continued to hold on. "If the spirits ride with us, we will succeed."

WORD THAT GREY Bear and Lone Hawk were preparing to travel as far as necessary in search of buffalo and thus a new home for the Cheyenne spread quickly. Touches the Wind's first thought was that her family's meager food supply couldn't possibly last until the two men found the buffalo of Sweet Grass Eater's dream, but the thought was a selfish one; she didn't like herself for it.

"I feel sorry for those who have much in the way of possessions," she told her mother. "It will take them much longer to get ready to travel."

"Travel?" Kicks by Horse looked around her, shuddering. "When?"

"I do not know. The chiefs have not said."

"It is too hot. How can we possibly carry enough water?"

Touches the Wind had convinced her mother to come outside this morning, but now she was sorry she had since the rising sun highlighted the contrast between her own dark skin and her mother's too-pale face. She wanted to tell herself that the old injury was responsible and that beneath the unhealthy-looking flesh, her mother's heart continued to beat as strongly as it ever had, but she couldn't.

"Mother," she said. "I will make sure you have what you need; I promise."

They'd been walking back from the too-little creek where they'd gone to wash, and although Touches the Wind had no trouble keeping her footing on the well-worn trail, her mother, walking slowly, held onto her arm.

"I am afraid," Kicked by Horse whispered.

"Of what?"

"I do not know." She laughed, but the sound was dry and joyless. "Perhaps it is only an old woman's fear."

"You are not old."

"Yes, I am. My eyes have seen countless homes from the time I was a small child, and I thought I would never mind that, but I want to stay here."

"Here where there is little water and no buffalo?"

"It may be a foolish woman's thoughts, but I do not know if I have the strength to—this is not what I want for you."

Puzzled, Touches the Wind waited for an explanation. The wind felt angry this morning and reminded her of a grizzly robbed of his kill. The sky too must be angry because lightning hissed and hissed again, but although its energy made her nervous, she also felt more alive than she had for days.

"You should be married," Kicked by Horse said.

"I will be when the time comes."

"The time is here." Kicked by Horse indicated her daughter's full breasts. "Your body is ready to carry a child, and you have the skills needed to care for your own tepee."

"Skills you taught me," Touches the Wind said, her mind only partly on what her mother was saying. If only she could jump onto a horse and ride into the wind!

"No. Those skills came from within you. I—I have not been the mother I should have been."

Kicked by Horse so seldom spoke about her feelings that the unexpected revelation took Touches the Wind by surprise and silenced her fantasy of galloping across the plains.

"I love you" was all she could say.

"And I love you, more than you can possibly know. Without you I—" The older woman pressed her hand against her cheek as if trying to cover the disfigurement. "I do not take a single breath without thinking about what happened to me and what I look like."

"The pain—"

"Pain has been part of me for so long that I should have placed it behind me."

"Do not ask the impossible of yourself. I know about your sleepless nights. In your eyes I see what you live with."

Kicked by Horse sighed and rubbed the scars with gentle, practiced fingers. "If I had known my life would have been like this, I would not have begged the medicine man to save me."

Touches the Wind started to speak, but her mother stopped her. "We must speak of this now because the time will come when I no longer speak of anything. No, do not tell me not to have these thoughts. I know what exists inside me, how much harder each day becomes."

Speechless, Touches the Wind drew her mother to her. The older woman's bones felt so fragile that they put her in mind of a small bird's. If only she'd been able to provide her mother with more meat, maybe . . .

"The spirits gave me a husband who did not divorce me when I became ugly, but it was not a good thing for you to see. I fear you believe only a poor, old, or lazy man will want you for his wife. I watch you when the young men are around, study the way you keep your eyes on the ground instead of smiling at them."

"I do not want to appear too bold."

"That is not it! Not all of it anyway. We are poor, yes, but a good man, a man worthy of you should not think only of that."

Touches the Wind didn't want to talk about her marriage prospects today, not with energy pushing and pulling at her and her mind on what it would be like to be either Grey Bear or Lone Hawk. They'd been chosen to seek buffalo because they were strong and courageous, Cheyenne men! How she envied them!

"Before I die," Kicked by Horse whispered. "I want to see you standing beside your husband."

"You—you will."

"But not just any man, lazy like your father."

"Mother!"

"I speak the truth."

"He is gentle" was the only thing she could think to say.

"Gentle! Long Chin is an old dog sleeping in the sun." Kicked by Horse had drawn back, but now she took her daughter's face in her hands. "Listen to me. Listen and take my words to heart. You deserve a husband with fire in his eyes."

NIGHTELK SAT BY himself beyond the village, his body if not his mind at rest. Because of the way the wind was blowing, he caught snatches of conversation and understood that nearly everyone was watching Grey Bear and Lone Hawk get ready to leave. The two young men had hurried through the process of checking weapons, gathering provisions, and preparing themselves spiritually because Sweet Grass Eater had been adamant that they leave as soon as possible. He supposed he should be grateful that his offer to accompany Grey Bear had been turned down; in truth, the prospect of such a lengthy and risky journey filled him with dread. But he'd brought the risk of starvation upon his people. He was responsible for the continued drought.

Childish laughter caught his attention, but instead of smiling, he felt old. So much needed to be done before they left. Some of the women were already gathering their seldom-used belongings together and tying them onto travois. Others had decided to spend the day looking for any roots their digging sticks might have missed. Although the adults felt more dread than excitement at the prospect of stepping into the unknown, it was different for the children—at least for most of them.

Sighing, Nightelk got to his feet and forced himself to turn in the direction of Walking Rabbit's tepee. Porcupine had had five horses, and although Knows No Fear had assumed care for them, the boy shouldn't have to do it all by himself.

He'd barely worked the stiffness out of his legs when he spotted Knows No Fear with several boys. One had painted his face to duplicate the decoration Lone Hawk had chosen while another had patterned himself after Grey Bear. Knows No Fear's unadorned features tore at Nightelk's heart.

"Have you used up all your paints?" he asked the boy with studied casualness. "Surely you can borrow a little."

Another child started to hand his paint to Knows No Fear but the half orphan shook him off. Even surrounded by his excited companions, Knows No Fear seemed quiet and subdued, prompting Nightelk to place his arm around his shoulder. The boy felt small to him, more child than man.

"Come," he said. "Walk with me."

Knows No Fear slanted him a startled glance. "I—you do not have—"

"I want to."

At first, Nightelk deliberately kept the conversation casual. By asking Knows No Fear where he thought Grey Bear and Lone Hawk would find buffalo, he learned that the boy had given the question considerable thought. Buffalo, he was told, were creatures of habit. In spring they gathered on the plains in great herds, but when the new grass turned dry and without nourishment, they sought higher elevations.

"Perhaps they can fly," Knows No Fear ventured. "How else can they darken the prairie with their presence one day and be gone the next?"

"Perhaps."

"My father—my father said that is not possible, but just because he never saw a buffalo fly, does not mean . . ."

"What is it?"

"Nothing."

He wondered if Knows No Fear had noticed that they'd been walking toward his father's grave. From what he'd heard, Knows No Fear hadn't gone back there since the burying ceremony.

"Listen to me," Nightelk said. The question of whether he had the right to tell this child anything momentarily stopped his words, but he surged on. "Everyone mourns in their own way. I cannot say what is right for you, but it must be done."

Knows No Fear walked slowly and studied the ground. The wind lifted his long, dry hair and made it stand on end, but Nightelk didn't feel like laughing. "I pray you will never have to walk in grief as many times as I have," he continued. "But I learned lessons I wish to pass onto you."

The boy remained silent.

"Saying good-bye is hard, but it must be done. When we leave, you, your mother, and sister will be leaving more than a place where you have lived for several moons."

"I know."

"Only you know the words you must say at your father's grave. Do not put it off too long."

His body suddenly stiff, Knows No Fear stared at what he could see of his father's grave. "Will he hear?" he whispered. "Maybe his soul has already left."

"A man will always hear his child's words. Your father wants only one thing from you, for you to walk into manhood."

Knows No Fear's breathing became ragged, and if he could have taken the child's tears and grief from him, he would have, but all he could do was hold him.

"I—I want—" Knows No Fear took a shuddering breath. "I am afraid to . . ." He aimed a trembling finger at the mound of rocks.

"Your heart needs to remember him alive."

A barely perceptible nod was the only response.

"If that is what your heart needs, then it is right. Tell him that."

THE CONVERSATION BETWEEN man and boy went on a while longer, with Nightelk searching through Knows No Fear's layers to the truth of him. The boy's greatest fear was that once they'd left the gravesite, his father could no longer see him. How lonely Porcupine would be then! Nightelk answered in the only way he could. A spirit was free to go

where and when it wanted. If Knows No Fear believed his
father was beside him, then he was.

"My father's heart has never forgotten my children who
died," he finished. "Sometimes there is much sadness when
I think of them, but at least I have the memories. As long as
I live, I will have that; so will you."

That must have been what Knows No Fear needed to hear
because when they went to Porcupine's grave, the boy didn't
cry. Instead, his voice proud, he told his father that he was
in charge of the family's horses now.

"If they are going to be strong for the journey," Nightelk
told Knows No Fear, "their bellies must be full."

"I have been taking them out to eat."

"Yes, you have. But you take them to places they have
already been, and little grass remains. A boy ready to assume
a man's responsibilities must not be afraid to lead a great
distance."

Although what he'd just suggested meant Knows No Fear
would have to spend the night away from the village, it was
something all Cheyenne boys did from time to time.

With the day marching on, Knows No Fear mounted his
own pony and started gathering the family horses around
him. Nightelk watched as any man would watch his son, and
when he smiled, it was a father's smile.

"Put the horses' needs before your own," he reminded
Knows No Fear.

The now-raging wind threatened to steal his words, and
when lightning scarred the sky, he remembered that the same
thing had happened the day he'd wounded the white calf.

"Be careful," he whispered.

CHAPTER 10

Touches the Wind gripped the small leather bag containing the turnip slices she'd dried last spring. Usually she added the turnips to soups to thicken broth, not to eat alone, but they were all she had. Grey Bear and Lone Hawk would soon leave. If she didn't approach them now, she'd miss her opportunity. Still, it was all she could do to force her legs to move. Her mother had watched her gather the small food supply but hadn't questioned what she was doing.

Was what she planned to do foolishness?

Hoping no one took note of her, she made her way past the randomly spaced tepees until she stood a few feet from where Grey Bear lived, but although she could hear him talking, she didn't approach. In her mind, Grey Bear was all dark energy, quick courage that frightened her as much as it fascinated. Lone Hawk, on the other hand, reminded her of his namesake; she had little to fear from a hawk.

Nothing except that a hawk's keen eyesight told it a great deal.

Her mouth dry, she changed direction, going now not to Lone Hawk's tepee but to where he kept his horses. Several boys had gathered around the two men holding the horses, but she forced herself to dismiss everyone except Lone Hawk, who was painting a lightning bolt on his mare's flank. From what she could tell, the symbol was nearly complete. The other man, Woodenlegs, gave her a curious glance.

"I—I do not wish to disturb you." She addressed Lone Hawk. "You have much to concern yourself with, preparations to make that—" Realizing she was babbling, she forced herself to start over.

"What you are doing is a great and brave thing. I know you have been told that by the men and perhaps that is all you care to hear, but—"

Lone Hawk handed his feather brush to Woodenlegs. "I do what is required of me."

"No. It is more than that—at least it is to me." Her burden had become so heavy she could hardly hold it, but she wasn't ready to call attention to it. Every word she spoke put her reputation at risk, but she couldn't bear the idea of his leaving without saying anything. "I am not like some, with a father who provides well. If not for the generosity and courage of men like you—Lone Hawk, if I could give you my eyes to aid your search, I would do so, but I cannot, so I—I hope you will accept this humble gift."

He stared at what she extended toward him. Fearful he might make fun of her pitiful offering, she lowered her gaze.

"For me?" he asked.

"If you have use—no one can say how long you and Grey Bear will be gone or how far you will have to travel. I—I wanted to do what I could to insure you will have enough to eat."

His bare feet whispered against the packed earth, signaling that he was coming closer. She fought to control her trembling. In a vague and unimportant way, she realized Woodenlegs and the boys had drawn away. To be alone with Lone Hawk—

"Thank you." He took her bundle and held it in his strong hand. "But will you and your family have enough?"

She didn't care what she put in her own belly and was weary of concerning herself with her parents' needs; only Little Bird mattered.

"Touches the Wind." His voice speaking her name sounded both soft and warm. "This is not an easy thing for you to do, perhaps not a wise thing. Your parents will disapprove of our speaking like this. If they learn it is not the first time . . ."

"My parents care about little except their own thoughts and concerns." Shaken by her admission, she lifted her head.

The wind that nourished and nurtured her was trying to steal his hair, and he'd spread his legs against the powerful gusts. His hawk-keen eyes were still on her.

"I did not wish to take your time," she told him. "I simply wanted to acknowledge what is ahead of you, say I realize it is not a journey easily taken."

"No, it is not."

"You—you have doubts?"

"Not that I can travel as long and far as I must, or that Sweet Grass Eater's vision was true but—" Lone Hawk glanced at Woodenlegs' retreating back. "What I do question is whether it is right for Grey Bear and me to be together."

"What? Why?"

"Our hearts do not beat the same."

"I—I heard that."

"Grey Bear is a warrior, only a warrior. It is not the same for me."

"Not—why are you telling me this?"

Why? Maybe it was no more complicated than she was a maiden and as such didn't concern herself with men's pursuits, but perhaps it went beyond that.

"I want to ask you something," he said, indicating his slight burden. "If Grey Bear and I do not succeed, if we do not return, what will happen to the Cheyenne?"

"We may starve."

"Yes." He took her words deep inside him. "Yes, that may happen."

"And you and Grey Bear will be dead."

"Death is no stranger to the Cheyenne, but to be responsible for so much—" He breathed in hot, electrified air. "You give me food your family cannot spare, but I will take it to remind myself of how much is at stake."

"For all of us." She started to extend her hand, then drew back. "Perhaps it is better to be a child. My sister cares only about play and being with her friends. I wish—sometimes I want to be like that again."

"So do I." He ran his hand over his Sun Dance–scarred chest. "But I carry proof of what it is to be a man."

She stared at his naked chest, seemingly unmindful of how the wind alternately lifted her skirt or flattened it against her body. "So do I," she said. "Not with scars but with what I have given you."

A nearby horse whinnied. Turning, he spotted Legs Like Lightning, ridden by Grey Bear, coming their way.

"It is time for me to leave," he told Touches the Wind. "But I will carry this moment with me."

"So will I." She met his gaze. "Lone Hawk?"

"What?"

"Be careful."

NIGHTELK STOOD TO one side of those watching Grey Bear and Lone Hawk leave. As the two men's horses carried them into the hot, dry prairie, the too-blue sky seemed to absorb them, and he tried to tell himself that today was no different from countless others when warriors—himself included—had gone off to hunt. Despite its vast clarity, the sky felt angry to him, thunder and lightning waiting.

A few minutes ago, he'd tried to get Black Eyes to walk alongside him so he could turn his dog over to Grey Bear and Lone Hawk, but for the first time in its life, the animal had growled at him.

"This is good," Sweet Grass Eater announced at last. "As it should be."

"I pray you are right," Nightelk said before he could judge the wisdom of his words.

"You doubt the power of my dreams?"

"Not that, but they are young and untested in many things."

Sweet Grass Eater shrugged, the gesture sending waves of movement through his loose, old skin. "They are part of *hestenov*, the universe."

"Yes, they are." Nightelk started toward his tepee.

"Nightelk," Sweet Grass Eater called out. "There are things we must speak of."

"What things?" he asked as first one and then more of the

other peace chiefs gathered around him and Sweet Grass Eater.

"Soon, perhaps by tomorrow if the women say they are ready to leave, we will turn our backs on this place and start after Grey Bear and Lone Hawk," Sweet Grass Eater said. "The journey will not be an easy one."

"No, it will not."

Although Nightelk had thought there couldn't be anything left for the peace chiefs to discuss, he soon learned he'd been wrong. There was the matter of the four Sacred Arrows, gifts from the prophet Sweet Medicine.

"BEFORE SWEET MEDICINE'S coming, the people were bad," Sweet Grass Eater told the assembled peace chiefs as they sat smoking outside his tepee. Everyone knew the story as well as Sweet Grass Eater did, but it was his right and responsibility to repeat it now.

"There was no law and much killing. Then a maiden who had not known a man gave birth and that child grew up to perform two miracles. As a young hunter, Sweet Medicine did not stay with the rest of a hunting party but went off by himself and killed a yellow calf."

Nightelk shuddered.

"Instead of sharing the hide with an old man the way he should have, Sweet Medicine hit the man. When others tried to punish him, he ran away and was gone from his people for a long time. When he returned, he told everyone of where he had been and what he had seen—the power that called him to the Black Hills. In the Sacred Mountain Noahvose, he found people who were not people; he also saw what has become our Four Sacred Arrows."

The elderly men nodded. Needing to feel part of the Chiefs' Medicine, Nightelk took his turn smoking the kin-nikinnick–tobacco– and sweet-grass–filled pipe.

"From the old ones who called him Grandson, Sweet Medicine learned the many things he took back to his people. First among those lessons was the truth of the Arrows, which are the Cheyenne's greatest power. Two are for hunting and two for war. All of our ceremonies are connected with them, and they symbolize our laws."

"Yes, yes."

Sweet Grass Eater spoke about the arrow renewal ceremony, which must take place if one Cheyenne ever kills another, but because this wasn't what today was about, Nightelk's thoughts slid to what Grey Bear and Lone Hawk were doing, the great sky all around them, their seemingly endless journey. If either of them questioned what they were doing or had doubts, they'd kept that to themselves—just as he now kept his own turmoil within him.

"Because of Sweet Medicine, the Cheyenne have rules to live by and ceremonies to renew us," Sweet Grass Eater continued. "Without the Four Sacred Arrows we would not be Cheyenne but small bird feathers tossed about by the wind. If we are to walk, alive, through this drought, the Arrows must be safeguarded."

"Yes, yes."

"By one who has just come to be a peace chief but still has the strength and memory of a warrior."

"No!" Nightelk blurted. "That responsibility—someone long schooled in Sweet Medicine's wisdom should carry them, not me. I—I am a child in this journey."

"You are a bridge," Rich in Hides said, "between the young men who provide our food and protect us from our enemies and the old. When I painted your tepee, I felt honored. You are strong, your eyes and ears keen. The Arrows will be safe with you."

No! You are wrong!

"YOU SPOKE TO him?" Seeks Fire asked Touches the Wind. The two women were standing in front of Walking Rabbit's tepee waiting to help her dismantle it. "Little Bird said she saw you and Lone Hawk together, but surely that must be a child's foolish talk."

Touches the Wind started to look around for her sister,

then remembered that Little Bird and Follower had gone after
Knows No Fear and the horses he'd taken in search of grass.
She should have told them that Knows No Fear had better
things to do than keep an eye on them, but they'd been restless and underfoot, driving her to distraction. Knowing them,
they'd grow weary and return before they'd gone very far,
but at least they were out of her hair for a short while. When
she'd mentioned this to Seeks Fire, the other maiden had
agreed.

"I spoke to him but briefly," she admitted, "when I brought
him a little food."

"I wish I had done the same with Grey Bear, but if I had—"
Seeks Fire fingered her chastity belt. "My mother would insist I marry him." She giggled. "Of course, that might not
be a bad thing. What did the two of you talk about?"

"Not much." She was hard pressed to remember the words
that had passed between her and Lone Hawk. What remained
clear was the way his eyes looked close up, his deep voice
and strong, broad chest. "Only a few things."

"He did not say anything he should not have? Perhaps he
believes he now has a right to touch your breast."

"No! I—I am sure he does not consider me his. I wanted
him to know he is doing a courageous thing and that I admire
him for that, nothing else."

Seeks Fire looked skeptical, but before she could say anything, Walking Rabbit stepped outside. She carried Porcupine's bow and arrows.

"I should have already given these to my son," she whispered. "If I had, he would know that in my heart he has
taken on his father's responsibilities."

"You can tell him that when he returns," Touches the
Wind reassured her friend. "He will not be gone so long,
maybe only until nightfall."

"He will if his sister and yours catch up to him," Seeks
Fire pointed out with a chuckle. "He will tell the horses to
eat fast so he can put responsibility for two silly girls behind
him."

Touches the Wind laughed and then turned her attention

to pulling the covering off the twelve poles that supported Walking Rabbit's tepee. The covering, which consisted of eighteen sewn-together buffalo hides, was so heavy that it would have to be strapped to a large travois and pulled by a strong horse. She wished she could say something light-hearted but feared nothing would distract Walking Rabbit from what she was doing—leaving the ground where she and Porcupine had last lain as husband and wife.

In silence, the three women pushed over the poles and wrestled the hides onto the ground before rolling them up. By then they were all sweating.

"You have done enough," Walking Rabbit said. "I can do the rest myself. Please, tend to your own tasks."

Instead of heeding her friend's suggestion, Touches the Wind found herself walking in the direction Lone Hawk had gone. She tried to imagine how far he'd gone, what he was thinking about now, whether he and Grey Bear would travel far into the night so they could take advantage of the cool-ness, but the wind was calling to her.

Leaving this place didn't bother her since to be Cheyenne meant calling no place home. Besides, no matter where her people went, the wind would travel with them, touch her and center her. The earlier blue-blue sky had taken on a hazy hue as if great amounts of dust had been sucked upward. That could be, she thought as her restless legs took her beyond noise and activity. If she went home, she'd have to listen to her parents; if she walked where the wind pushed her, she might become a child again in her mind, free like Little Bird.

Thoughts of what her sister, Follower, and Knows No Fear were doing sent her in a southerly direction but only for a little while because she didn't want the children—especially Porcupine's son—to think she didn't trust them. Instead, she heeded her namesake's whispers, walking rapidly as if her legs could take her as far as her eyes could see.

High above, a hawk rode on the swift, angry air currents, its eyes trained on the lone woman.

*　　*　　*

SEEKS FIRE FLEXED her fingers and rolled her shoulders in an attempt to release the tension in them. Dismantling Walking Rabbit's tepee had earned her a knot at the base of her neck. Her mother would want help taking down their own home, but surely that could wait until the worst of the day's heat had been spent.

Suddenly and irrationally angry at summer, she turned this way and that as if trying to escape herself, but wherever she looked, she saw activities that spelled the end to living in this place. She couldn't take her brother with her; his bones would be left behind. In her heart of hearts she accepted that, and yet walking away from him would be so hard.

So hard!

Was that why Grey Bear had been quick to embrace his grandfather's insistence that only he could find buffalo, not because he believed himself all-seeing but because he couldn't bear to look at Porcupine's grave?

Her head pounded, and she pressed her hands to her temple, but although she felt a little better, thoughts continued to stalk her. She felt like a young horse fighting its hobbles, like an eagle with a crippled wing.

No, not an eagle. A hawk.

As the creature circled high above, she laughed because the hawk was fighting the wind. A few breaths later, lightning seared the graying sky and perhaps frightened the hawk because it suddenly flew away. She was asking herself if there was a message in the hawk's behavior when it reappeared, a little closer to the earth now.

"What do you want?" she asked, glad she was by herself. "Hawk, what are you looking for?"

WIND CURRENTS RULED the predator, but a lifetime spent within what the Cheyenne called *taxtavo* had taught it how to live by those rules. When the wind was a sleeping child, the hawk took control by moving to its own whims and needs, but it knew in the instinctive way of birds that the child could awake at any moment and become a monster.

Today the hawk rode on a monster's back. Bowed before its master. Heard rolling, growling thunder, accepted the heat and snarling danger of lightning. It noted that the two women who'd separated themselves from their people were trying to make sense of what had happened to the day, but their concerns weren't its.

Neither did the hawk care what happened to the two silent warriors, the boy with the horses, or the two small girls who no longer hurried to catch up to Knows No Fear but stared upward, arm in arm and trembling.

CHAPTER 11

No spirit was greater than Heammawihio, the Wise One Above. It was he, embodying the power of Wihio, the spider who spins webs and walks on nothing, who carried the greatest intelligence. Heammawihio knew more about how to do things than all other creatures. Long, long ago, he'd left the earth and made his home in the sky, and the Sun came from him. He is more than the sky, more than words can express. The first pipe offering is always made to him.

Beneath the earth in the place called the Deep Earth, or *aktino*, is Akuniwihio, who is female, but as lightning and thunder continued their assault, Touches the Wind's mind lost hold of what had always given her a sense of peace.

"Akuniwihio must be very angry."

Suppressing a shudder, she acknowledged Seeks Fire, who'd joined her on a rise overlooking the village. "Maybe Akuniwihio commands Thunder to bring rain."

"I wish I could believe that," Seeks Fire said. "I want to."

So did she, but although the sky had darkened, there was no hint of moisture in the air, no rain-bearing clouds, no whiff of the wonderful smell foreshadowing a downpour. Instead, the dry thunder that followed on the breath of each light shaft seemed to mock them. The hard laughter made her glad for company.

"I keep thinking about Grey Bear," Seeks Fire said. "Legs Like Lightning does what his master commands him to, but horses can be foolish creatures, quick to panic. If the stallion started to fight him, would Grey Bear win?"

Touches the Wind couldn't concentrate on Grey Bear; instead, her thoughts were full of Lone Hawk, who was on the same journey and might have seen the same hawk she had a little while ago—the hawk that perhaps had come to warn of Thunder's fury.

"The last time the sky screamed like this," she admitted, "Little Bird hid behind me and covered her ears. She cried and begged me to make it go away, but of course I could not. I told her that once I had felt as she now did, and that the seasons had taken me past fear, but perhaps she heard something in my voice that spoke of the child still within me."

Seeks Fire nodded. "I was with my brother and his family. Follower begged Porcupine to shoot arrows at the lightning. Knows No Fear laughed at his little sister, but I told him her fear was real, nothing to make fun of."

The sky looked heavy; perhaps it had grown weary of bearing Thunder's weight. "I do not like this," Touches the Wind admitted. "I wish we were holding the Sun Dance now, finding harmony again. There is no—I reach out with my heart for harmony with the earth and sky, but although I pray for acceptance, I cannot find peace."

"Perhaps that is why the buffalo left." Like her, Seeks Fire's attention was on the horizon to the north where blackness grew. "Because there is too much anger here."

As if in response, a great rumbling roll exploded around them. Touches the Wind hunched forward, an animal fearing attack.

"Go away!" Seeks Fire cried. Then she clamped her hands

over her mouth. "I did not mean that," she muttered. "I would never think to command Thunder."

Thunder was a giant bird that carried arrows in its talons and sometimes hurtled those arrows—lightning—at the earth. Occasionally the arrows killed. Thunderbird, who was the leader of the sky creatures, fought Minio, the water monster living in lakes and streams. If Thunderbird could crush Minio, how could a maiden hope to stand before it? Surely Thunder knew Seeks Fire's unease had caused her outburst. Surely.

"I wish—" Touches the Wind said when only Thunder's echo remained to tease and taunt. "I wish I had not listened so closely to the old men's stories as a child."

"But you did. That is why you now tell the same stories to today's children."

"It is something I have always wanted to do because it brings me pleasure, but now—" Power was building again, the unseeable force seeming to suck strength from the earth itself. "I wish Little Bird was with me and I was holding her."

"Your sister and my niece will be back soon," Seeks Fire whispered. "Even now they must be running as fast as their legs can carry them, trying not to cry, no longer caring what Knows No Fear is doing."

Touches the Wind grabbed her friend's arm. "What if Porcupine's horses stampede? Knows No Fear does not have enough experience—"

"Thunderbird!" Seeks Fire cried out. "Be silent! Please, be silent!"

LONE HAWK'S HORSE trembled under him. To his left, Grey Bear fought to control Legs Like Lightning. The larger warrior seemed both part of his stallion and yet separate. Grey Bear looked, Lone Hawk thought with what little of his mind wasn't engaged in assessing his world, not quite human this afternoon.

"Thunderbird is awake," Grey Bear said. "His strength grows and grows. Maybe he will attack."

As a child Lone Hawk had believed heart and soul in what the storytellers said about the giant bird that carried lightning arrows in its talons. He still believed in lightning's power but now that belief was tempered with experience. "The chance that Thunderbird will hurtle his anger upon us is slight," he pointed out.

"Perhaps. Easy, easy!" Grey Bear ordered his stallion. "Feel me and take my courage into you!"

As Grey Bear continued talking to Legs Like Lightning, Lone Hawk guided his mare over the rocky earth. The sky was becoming like night, purple and black, not cloud-color but something perhaps of Thunderbird's creation. At the same time, the sun fought to cut through the heavy curtain, causing a glare.

"Maybe this is a sign," he made himself say. "If there is wisdom in the heavens, we should heed it."

"What sign? I see dry lightning and hear empty thunder. Heammawihio is at play, nothing more."

Grey Bear was probably right; yet that didn't silence Lone Hawk's doubts. He'd never question Sweet Grass Eater's wisdom, but perhaps the old priest had been wrong to order them to take off this morning. If Heammawihio meant for them to travel another day—

There, barely visible against the dark background, floated a hawk. Although perhaps he should point the bird out to Grey Bear, Lone Hawk kept its reality to himself. Hawks were solitary creatures, fearless hunters and killers of small animals, and he'd been named for the powerful, keen-eyed creature. Hawk didn't fear Thunderbird—

A great, multifingered spear of light sliced into the blue-black sky. Its white beauty went on and on, pulsing and fading a little, then seemingly feeding off itself and growing huge again. Lone Hawk smelled heat and power; his nerve endings pulled strength into him and for a moment he became more than he'd ever been.

Then thunder shook the world and he smelled something else.

Smoke.

"STOP IT! OH, please, stop!"

Before Knows No Fear could look around to see if anyone could hear, his father's horses screamed, their separate fears melting into a single sound. The flea-bitten old mare the others had been following reared on her stubby legs and pawed the air. Afraid she might bolt, the boy knew he should jump onto her back so he could better control her, but she danced just out of reach.

A moment ago he'd been torn between keeping the herd out here as Nightelk had advised and leading them back to camp since they were too nervous to feed anyway. Now he feared it was too late.

Thunder rolled on and on. Lightning came and went, came and went. There was no rain-smell.

Fighting his own terror, Knows No Fear looked around for the three-year-old mare his father had given him. He spotted her in the middle of the herd, her rein dragging on the ground between her prancing legs. He couldn't remember when or how or why he'd let go of her; the only thing that mattered was getting close enough to grab the rope.

"Do not run." He struggled to keep his voice a singsong. "There is nothing to fear, only sound and—"

Not just sound. Something red danced in the distance, embracing the earth and yet separate from it. His eight-year-old mind raced through memories and all too soon came up with the one thing he didn't want.

"Do not run." His words were part order, part plea. "Please, you must not run!"

His father's wisdom deserted him, replaced by hot emotion that snaked through him and tried to suck him into it. The lightning that had been building all afternoon hadn't been content to remain in the sky after all. It had stabbed the earth, more than stabbed.

Fire!

Once again the horses whistled their collective fear. He wanted to ask why they were so afraid because for this moment, this heartbeat, peace had returned to the sky, but the horses must not have cared because, like fawns fleeing wolves, they bolted. Instinct told him to grab his mare's rein, but how could he when the same fear that had invaded the horses attacked him? This land that was him, that had nurtured and nourished him had changed.

He hated the change, the smoke and flames.

Most of all he hated the wind!

"Help. Help—" The soft, distant whisper-plea drifted over him. He stopped, spun around, strained to locate the source.

"Oh, please, help." The second cry, if it existed, was no stronger than the first.

"Follower!" he screamed, confused. He tried to pull the sound into him, to clean the smoky air. "Where—"

"He-lp."

Taken out of himself, Knows No Fear ran a few feet in the direction he thought the whisper had come from. Then he stopped, started again, landed on a sharp rock. Breathing fast and deep against the pain coursing through him, he struggled to make sense of what was happening. Out of his reach now and rapidly becoming smaller and smaller raced the horses. On foot he had no chance of overtaking them, and their fear, he knew, might be enough to take them to their deaths.

Smoke grew and grew, became a great cloud that threatened to envelop him. The snapping, snarling flames fed off the wind and blossomed with the smoke. His mind told him these things even as he prayed for the strength to go on. He felt so small, an infant left alone to cry itself out, and yet he wasn't the youngest Cheyenne out here.

His sister—

Her friend—

"Follower!" he bellowed. "Is it you?"

"Please . . ."

"Mommy."

The little-girl voices came, he thought, from the middle of the smoke and flames. He stalked closer, his legs jerking, but even as he ordered himself to do what a man would, if he got any closer to the rapidly expanding heat-monster, it would consume him.

"Run!" he ordered the unseen and perhaps imaginary girls. "Run!"

NIGHTELK STOOD WHERE his legs had taken him and stared in the direction Grey Bear and Lone Hawk had gone. Today Heammawihio, the Wise One Above, had become powerful beyond his belief, but what held his attention wasn't the unrelenting lightning and accompanying thunder or even the spectacular colors painting the sky, but the wind borne smoke that billowed and whirled like an animal evading capture.

Lightning had set the prairie grasses on fire. At the moment, the flames were far enough away that the village wasn't in danger and small enough that he could see all of it, but if the wind continued to flex its great muscles . . .

"Aktuniwihio has unleashed his giant bird." Calf Woman slipped to his side and wrapped her arm around his waist. "Thunder commands the summer rains, but where is the rain?"

Nightelk inhaled deeply, then looked down at his wife. "I do not smell it," he said.

"Atch! Lightning but no rain." She squeezed him, hung on. "I am glad you did not go with Grey Bear and Lone Hawk. I need you beside me. This—this must be a sign, but of what?"

Of the gods' anger and hatred. On the verge of telling his wife about the white calf, he allowed himself to be distracted by someone running toward the corraled horses. He couldn't be certain but thought the runner was a woman. Another runner soon joined the first, both of them now trying to throw ropes over a couple of the animals.

A lifetime of responsibility kicked in, and Nightelk sprinted toward the frantic women.

"What is it?" he demanded once he was close enough to make himself heard. "Be careful! You will be hurt!"

Touches the Wind, her eyes wild with fear, whirled on him. "Little Bird!" she gasped.

Before he could speak, two horses reared. The other woman, Seeks Fire, jumped back. "Little Bird and Follower!" she cried. "We *have* to find them!"

"Find? What do you mean?"

Speaking rapidly and at the same time, the young women explained that the girls had gone looking for Knows No Fear. They should be back by now, distracted from their adventure by the angry, noisy sky, but they weren't.

Although they resisted, Nightelk took hold of the women's arms and guided them away from the horses. He heard his wife's heavy breathing behind him and was aware that Walking Rabbit had joined them, but he didn't have time to acknowledge either woman.

"The girls went after Knows No Fear?" he made himself ask. "You are certain?"

Looking miserable, Touches the Wind nodded. "They were underfoot. I had so much to do and I—I, Heammawihio, please, help them!"

"The fire grows."

Grey Bear shot Lone Hawk a look but didn't acknowledge what the other man had just said. From where they sat on their horses, they could see nearly to the village. Between the village and them flames fed. It had begun small, lightning's newborn. But the infant had dined well on wind and dry grass and had already become a laughing child. Soon it would turn into a man and then a monster.

"We must go back." Lone Hawk sounded weary.

"My grandfather—"

"Sweet Grass Eater's vision did not tell him of this," Lone Hawk interrupted. "The gods were silent on this."

If Lone Hawk said anything against his grandfather, Grey Bear wasn't sure he could keep from striking the other man. Gripping what self-control he had, he studied the flames as they reached upward and became smoke. He wasn't sure whether he smelled smoke or merely imagined it; it didn't matter.

"Sweet Grass Eater prayed to *maiyunahu'ta,* asking the guardian spirit to tell him what must be done so we would not starve. Perhaps, if he had asked if there was danger beyond that caused by the drought, *maiyunahu'ta* would have warned him, but he did not."

"You believe my grandfather should have asked to be shown everything?"

"I did not say that. But this"—Lone Hawk pointed at the fire—"comes before buffalo."

Grey Bear turned his attention back to the hungry flames. The wind pulled the smoke this way and that like a monster-child at play. It was impossible to say how long the game would continue or what might happen if it turned deadly. If the flames fed off themselves, they'd soon starve and die. "We will watch for a while," he said. "And if nothing happens, I will again follow my grandfather's words."

"No! Grey Bear, you know how quickly a fire travels. If it starts toward the village, they will need us."

"Our people need me to fill their bellies and show them the way to travel."

"If they are burned, it will not matter."

"My grandfather's spirit-dream buffalo will not wait for foolish men!" he insisted. To give weight to his words, he turned Legs Like Lightning from the fire.

He felt Lone Hawk's eyes bore into his back. "Go if you must," he said, "but Sweet Grass Eater is not the only one who has had a dream."

FEAR TIGHTENED WALKING Rabbit's throat. Time buckled and wove around her, making it impossible for her to say how long ago her brother-in-law had ridden off in search of

Little Bird and her children. She tried to tell herself that Nightelk had never failed in anything and wouldn't today, but these were her children, all she had left of Porcupine. Her life.

"Trust him."

"I—I want to." She glanced at her older sister, "but if the horses stampede, Knows No Fear may be hurt."

"No, it will not happen."

"How can you say that?"

Calf Woman opened her mouth and then closed it. For a moment they stared at each other. "I say what we both need to hear," Calf Woman whispered. "Do not fault me for that."

Walking Rabbit didn't but along with her memory of Nightelk's strong, straight back were others—Nightelk carrying her dying husband, Nightelk burying two of his own babies.

"I hate this—this standing here." More than that, she hated the terror bubbling in her throat.

Someone came up behind and gripped her shoulders so tight that she winced. She turned to see Touches the Wind.

"Please forgive me," Touches the Wind whispered. "I—if I had not told them they could go . . ."

Your fault. Your fault. Your fault. With an effort, Walking Rabbit buried the words deep inside her. "If the girls had come to me, I would have told them the same thing," she admitted. "They are old enough to go out on their own, have done so before. And Knows No Fear—" She had to swallow before she could go on. "He wants to be a man. Needs to walk in his father's footsteps."

Most villagers had hurried to a high point and were watching the not-distant-enough fire. On numb and trembling legs, Walking Rabbit joined them, flanked by her sister and Touches the Wind. Seeks Fire stood near Kicked by Horse who'd clasped her hands over her breast and was muttering "Little Bird" over and over again. Despite her own turmoil, Walking Rabbit wondered why Touches the Wind wasn't with her mother.

The smoke fascinated her. Because the wind was power-

ful, it held the smoke captive, played with it and threw it
about seemingly at whim. There was so much smoke, she
caught only glimpses of the feasting flames, but she could
hear their distant and yet distinct snapping.

"I remember," her sister was saying, "when some Sioux
set fire to the plains so they could chase buffalo over a cliff.
The wind shifted and the flames came back at the Sioux,
killing one man and several horses."

"That will *not* happen today!"

Silently echoing the words, Walking Rabbit looked around
until she locked eyes with Touches the Wind.

"Please," Touches The Wind went on, "do not speak of
death."

"I did not—have you heard the men?" Calf Woman demanded. "They speak of searching as my husband is doing,
but what if the fire comes our way? Who will help us move
our tepees to safety?"

"Your tepee!" Fear fed Walking Rabbit's outburst. "That
is all you ever think of! What do I care about hides and
poles? My children—"

"Walking Rabbit, please!" Seeks Fire interrupted. "Do not
be angry at your sister."

Holding back a sob, she reached for Calf Woman. They
clung together, staring out at the monster flames.

NIGHTELK HAD COVERED perhaps half the distance to the fire
before he realized that Black Eyes was running alongside.
The billowing smoke hid the village.

"Do you forgive me?" he asked the big dog. "Or perhaps
you are here because you want to see what else my sin has
led to?"

Black Eyes glanced up at him and then returned his attention to keeping pace with the excited mare.

"What does your nose tell you? Can you smell Porcupine's
horses? The children?"

Black Eyes whined. His tongue lolled out the side of his
mouth.

"Do not fail them. Please! If the gods seek vengeance, let it find me. Not the children. Please, not the children."

If Black Eyes heard the latest, he gave no sign. Instead of lifting his head so he could taste and test the air, he ran with his nose just off the ground. On the verge of telling Black Eyes how much he needed his keen senses, Nightelk remained silent. After a moment, he slowed his horse to a nervous walk. Black Eyes again whined.

"The flames make so much noise," he said by way of explanation, although he wasn't sure who he was talking to. "If I call out, will the children hear me? And if they do, will they know which way to come?"

His horse had begun to wheeze, and when Nightelk took a deep breath, he inhaled smoke. Only Black Eyes seemed unaffected. He struggled to remember more of what he and Knows No Fear had talked about, but he didn't think they'd decided on where the boy should take the horses. He'd deliberately left that decision up to Knows No Fear and now—

He'd been trying to make his way around one side of the fire, but the wind kept changing direction. He needed to get to higher land so he could better take in his surroundings, only he'd lost his bearings.

"Where am I?" he asked Black Eyes. He thought he'd put enough distance between himself and the worst of the smoke, but the wind suddenly threw a huge dark cloud in his direction. He tucked his chin against his chest, took a last, semiclean breath, and closed his eyes. His horse planted her feet and dropped her head as if taking from Black Eyes' wisdom. When he could no longer hold his breath, Nightelk let out the spent air and sucked in something that resulted in a spasm of coughing.

"Black Eyes," he called out. "Guide me. Help me find . . ."

Another coughing fit stopped him, but he hung on as he and his horse wheezed and fought for life-giving air. It came finally, but not until he felt exhausted. His eyes streamed tears.

The smoke was still there but less than it had been before. Although his vision was still blurry, he knew the wind now blew away from him. His horse continued to cough and seemed on the verge of collapse.

"Black Eyes?"

Hearing no answering whine, he looked around. The dog was gone.

CHAPTER 12

In Lone Hawk's dream, summer became Grizzly. When it had first invaded his nights, he'd fought the powerful creature, but after a while, he'd grown exhausted and learned to accept. There'd always been a measure of comfort in knowing the grizzly-dream never followed him into morning, but that had been yesterday.

When the fire began, he'd told himself it might be a little thing that couldn't find enough to feed off and thus would quickly starve to death. Now he knew how wrong he'd been.

"It is still not heading toward the village," Grey Bear pointed out. "I thank the gods for that."

When they'd begun to retrace their steps, Grey Bear had continued to question the wisdom of what they were doing, but he no longer did. Instead, the other man rode straight and tall, straining to see.

"It can turn at any moment," Lone Hawk pointed out unnecessarily. "Attack our people."

"Or us."

He grunted acknowledgment but didn't attempt to keep the conversation going. A couple of years ago, he, Grey Bear, and several other young and foolish men had cornered a sow with newborn cubs inside her winter cave. While the bear growled her warning, they'd challenged each other to be the first to send an arrow into the fierce heart. As it was, no one had fired because the sow had suddenly charged, scattering them and their horses. Lone Hawk couldn't remember whose horse had felt those powerful claws on its flank, just that no one had turned around to face their foe.

Today he and Grey Bear remained far enough away from the fire that if it charged, they should be able to outrace it, but the wind continued to grow in strength, perhaps feeding off the flames and reminding him too much of the great, deadly, twisting tornados that sometimes tore across the land.

Suddenly something felt different. After pulling his horse to a stop, he stood on the animal's back and took in his surroundings. Smoke filled much of the landscape, blanketing but not hiding the deadly flames beneath it.

"What is it?" Grey Bear positioned Legs Like Lightning so Lone Hawk's horse couldn't move forward.

"I am not—wait."

"What?"

"A wolf? No. Black Eyes."

Still not quite believing what he'd seen, Lone Hawk called out. The dog, who'd been trotting seemingly without direction, lifted its head and let out something that was half bark and half growl. By the time the animal reached them, Lone Hawk had dismounted. When he knelt, Black Eyes buried its muzzle in his chest.

"What are you doing here?" he muttered.

Black Eyes rumbled low in his throat.

"Where is Nightelk? Why are you not with him?"

Another rumble.

"I do not like this," Grey Bear grumbled. "Nightelk and Black Eyes are always together. Is it possible Nightelk declared to hunt with us after all and something happened to him?"

The seasoned warrior didn't do foolish things. Besides, Sweet Grass Eater and the other peace chiefs had decided he was needed at the village. "Nightelk must be nearby," he said, "but for reasons unclear to us."

Grey Bear frowned. "Perhaps he was sent to bring us back to the village."

The thought gave Lone Hawk pause. "Black Eyes." Still

crouching, he held the dog's head so they were looking at each other. "Where is your master? Take us to him."

STUMBLING A BIT, Kicked by Horse hurried back to the family's tepee with Touches the Wind. Instead of joining the men watching the fire's progress, Long Chin remained sitting outside his home. As soon as he spotted his wife and oldest daughter, he started to berate Touches the Wind for helping Walking Rabbit dismantle her tepee instead of taking down her own. Because of that, theirs would burn if the fire swept over the village. Although she usually deferred to her father, she held up her hand, stopping him.

"Little Bird is missing."

Before Long Chin could demand an explanation, she told him everything. "It is my doing," she admitted. Tears welled in her eyes. "Nightelk—Nightelk promised he would find her and Follower and bring Knows No Fear back as well."

"Nightelk should not look by himself! They"—Long Chin jabbed his finger at a knot of men—"they should have gone with him." He glanced over his shoulder at the small, sad tepee. "It is hardly worth taking down," he muttered. "But if you hurry, it will not take long."

A scream bubbled up inside Touches the Wind. She fought it but didn't completely succeed. "Little Bird is your daughter," she said through clenched teeth. "You will stay here, not look for her?"

"On foot? Or perhaps you believe our one old horse can carry me until daylight is gone? If she is worn out, how will she pull our possessions?"

This was all wrong! Nothing should matter except Little Bird's safety! Not trusting herself to say more, she slipped inside and began unfastening the ties that secured the hides to the lodge poles. She hadn't finished half the task before the small, dark interior closed in around her, and she rushed back outside.

Her father was nowhere in sight. Her mother stood a few

feet away, tears running down her cheeks, her hands pressed against her bony chest.

"What is it?" Touches the Wind asked.

Kicked by Horse held up her right hand, turned it this way and that as if seeing the thick knuckles and ragged nails for the first time. "My arms need to be around my baby."

The claustrophobia that had forced her to flee the tepee again clawed at Touches the Wind. "It *will* happen." Clutching her mother to her, she struggled for words. "I promise. Before the sun sets on this day, you will have her back."

How she hoped to accomplish that she couldn't say. What she knew was she couldn't remain in camp, doing nothing. Men might be the hunters and fighters, and she respected Nightelk, but this was her sister! With the vague thought that she'd cover more country on horseback than she possibly could on foot, she ran toward the corral. She prayed she'd be able to single their horse out from the others and if she killed the animal today, so be it.

"Touches the Wind, wait!"

Recognizing Seeks Fire's voice, she turned in that direction. Seeks Fire, Walking Rabbit, and Calf Woman hurried toward the horse corral. Although out of breath, Calf Woman explained that she wanted the younger women to take what of her husband's horses they needed.

"He was wrong," Calf Woman went on. "One man cannot find three children before the flames do. And if we waited for them"—she jerked her head at the men who seemed mesmerized by the distant fire—"it will be too late."

Men, if necessary, could move as quickly as any woman, but it was their way to discuss plans with one another, assessing and reassessing the proper course of action and putting great effort and ceremony into the act. Calf Woman was right. Little Bird, Follower, and Knows No Fear didn't have that kind of time.

When they saw what the four women were doing, a number of men, Sweet Grass Eater among them, gathered around.

"This is unwise, foolish. Your husband does what he believes is right." Sweet Grass Eater directed his criticism at

Calf Woman. "He has not yet agreed to take responsibility
for the Sacred Arrows because he does not know in his heart
whether he is worthy of the honor. By bringing the children
home, he will have given himself the answer."

"I do not care!" Calf Woman snapped. "Men! All you
think about is honor, proving yourselves!"

Sweet Grass Eater glowered at her. "You believe that is
wrong?"

"Today it does not matter! Do you not understand, it does
not matter! There." She pointed at a long-legged black mare.
"That one is big chested and can travel a long way. And that
one." She jabbed her finger at a compact pinto. "He too has
stamina." She glanced at Touches the Wind. "You wish to
go with my sister and Seeks Fire?"

"I must."

"So be it."

Before Touches the Wind fully comprehended what had
happened, she was on horseback flanked by Walking Rabbit
and Seeks Fire, and her mother had handed her a small
amount of water.

"My heart goes with you," Calf Woman said. She ignored
the men. "I know what it is to lose children. I pray that will
not happen here today."

Someone let down the corral's rope gate, and the three
women urged their horses forward. As Walking Rabbit rode
past Calf Woman, the sisters briefly clasped hands. Sweet
Grass Eater continued to grumble that Nightelk had insisted
on going out alone and his wishes must be followed. Although the men were obviously swayed by the priest,
Touches the Wind only wanted to be where she couldn't hear
him any more.

Walking Rabbit, who'd ridden Nightelk's horses in the
past, led the way, and she held to an easy canter until they'd
put the village behind them. By then Touches the Wind had
become accustomed to her mare's jerky gait and was able to
concentrate on her surroundings. The clan's tepees had been
placed on a relatively high, flat area within easy walk of the
creek with the result that she'd been able to look down on

the fire. Walking Rabbit had thought her son would have taken the horses east because the grass there hadn't been as heavily grazed as other areas, and that's where Nightelk had gone. Unfortunately, at the moment the smoke was blowing that way and reducing the visibility.

"The girls were on foot," Seeks Fire said. "I keep thinking their short legs would soon tire. They may not have traveled very far when the fire started."

Then why hadn't they come back? The possible answer— that Little Bird and Follower had lost their bearings because of the smoke—made Touches the Wind's heart beat so fast she wondered if it might break free of her chest. She remembered the way her mother had pressed her hands over her chest.

"I do not want them afraid!" she blurted. "This day—when this day began, they were excited about traveling, giggling and running about."

"The time will come when excitement again rules them," Seeks Fire said. "That is what we must think about, taking the children into tomorrow."

For the first time, she asked herself why Seeks Fire was with them. True, Follower and Knows No Fear were her niece and nephew, but Seeks Fire had always walked a woman's way; she'd never wanted to take on a man's tasks. All of them had defied Sweet Grass Eater because love and fear ruled them.

"Little Bird is in such a hurry to become a woman," Touches the Wind said. "She follows me everywhere, asking when she can prepare meals by herself, how many more winters she must live before she can help butcher."

The thought of never seeing her younger sister made her ill. In an effort to keep the fear under control, she continued talking. "I try to tell her it is not a wonderful thing to work from sunup until dark over great, smelly carcasses, but she does not hear my words. Little Bird!" she called into the wind. "Hear me! Hear and answer!"

One heartbeat and then ten passed.

"Follower!" Walking Rabbit's voice cracked. "Knows No Fear! Do not leave me, please! Do not die!"

SWEET GRASS EATER studied the departing women until he could no longer see them. Then, unmindful of the men, women, and children who'd gathered around him, he closed his eyes and prayed. With sixty-one winters behind him, only three other Cheyenne were older, and the others' minds were no longer sharp and clear.

It was different for him, he believed, because he'd spent his entire life in harmony with *hestenov*, the Universe. He also credited the fact that he'd never been badly injured and had always known good health, but his real strength came from the path he walked.

As day after dry day passed, his fear that it would never again rain had grown. Buffalo, in the instinctive way of beasts, had taken note of the drought long before humans had. Buffalo were travelers. As a consequence, the Cheyenne and other plains tribes followed them. It would happen again this summer; this he believed.

He, because of who he was, was expected to know where the game had gone. Prayers and dreams had shown him that the answer lay in his grandson's fierce courage. To keep peace, he'd agreed to let Lone Hawk accompany him, but the tribe's survival lay in Grey Bear's hands.

Had lain in Grey Bear's hands.

Perhaps buffalo-thoughts had blinded him to Thunderbird's presence. If he'd been more aware of his surroundings, would he have foreseen this fire? More than just the fire, should he have foreseen this danger to three children?

Heammawihio, guide my decision! Maiyunahu'ta, come to me not in sleep but now! These young lives should not, must not end today! Nightelk and the women search for them, but is that enough?

If anyone spoke, Sweet Grass Eater was unaware of it. Deep inside himself now, he pulled wisdom and experience around him and cast off his earlier words. He was body, heart, and soul Cheyenne! If his life had to end in order for a single child to live, he'd willingly plunge the knife into his own heart.

Heammawihio, what must be done?

Thunder had been quiet since the grasses caught fire, but it now exploded, the sound shaking the earth. Although his eyes remained shut, Sweet Grass Eater "saw" lightning scar the sky. A baby cried. Dogs howled.

"Go after them!" he ordered the men. "Ride with fear and courage beside you!"

"A DOG DOES not understand what you say to it!" Grey Bear insisted when Lone Hawk remained crouched beside Black Eyes. "This is only a foolish animal who has run away from his master."

Lone Hawk ignored Grey Bear, but the other man was right. They were wasting time here when they should be looking after the village's welfare. Still—"Where is he?" he once again asked Black Eyes. "You should be with Nightelk, not running from a fire."

The dog continued his singsong growl. At the same time, he lifted his large head and turned it in all directions. Finally he seemed to find what he had been looking for and trotted a few feet away. He stopped and looked back at Lone Hawk.

"He wants us to follow him," Lone Hawk announced. Without waiting to see what Grey Bear was going to do, he mounted and urged his horse after the dog. Grey Bear grumbled but caught up.

"This is foolish," Grey Bear said when they'd been traveling a few minutes. "Black Eyes has no wisdom. He follows rabbit scent."

"Smoke has buried any rabbit scent," Lone Hawk pointed out. "Do what you wish. Black Eyes and Nightelk are as one; that I cannot forget."

"Pray you are right, because if you are not, I will tell everyone you are one dog following another."

"You would say that? You hate me that much?"

"Hate? You are a coward. Afraid of the Pawnee. Hating a coward is not the way a warrior walks."

Lone Hawk started to pull on the reins so he could confront Grey Bear, but just then thunder killed the wind-sound.

"What is it?" Grey Bear taunted. "You shrink before Thunderbird's arrows?"

NIGHTELK'S MARE FLUNG her head as if trying to bite the sky. Already warned, he pressed his legs tight around her belly and pulled on the rein so she was forced to arch her neck.

"Do not be foolish," he admonished. "It is only thunder."

As if determined to make a lie of his words, the thunderclap was repeated. If anything, the sound was sharper this time. His mare trembled and pranced, and he prayed the children weren't as frightened.

At the moment the fire seemed to be standing in place, but as soon as the wind shifted, it would feed in that direction. In his mind's eye, he imagined Knows No Fear sitting astride the calmest horse while the boy tried to lead the other animals back to the village. If Knows No Fear had been aptly named, his self-assurance would be transmitted to the horses, but a child can't be expected to control panicked animals.

"Let them go," he said. "If they live or die, that is their doing. Think only of yourself. Your father wants *you* to live; he would not care what—"

His mare squealed, planted her legs under her, exploded. Intent on keeping her under control, he barely noticed the wolf racing past. If there'd been time, he'd tell his horse there was nothing to fear from a fire-fleeing wolf, but he was still forming the words when the mare suddenly plunged forward. Instinct catapulted him off her and onto safety, the crack of splintering bone barely registering. Once his feet were under him, he faced the now-thrashing animal. Her right forefoot flopped.

"No!" Despite the risk, he hurried to her side and straddled her neck, holding her against the ground. "Do not try to stand," he warned. "Lie still. Still."

Sweat streamed off the stricken animal, and her breath came in tortured hisses. Nightelk cupped a hand over the eye closest to him and brought his mouth near a laid-back ear.

"Do not be afraid," he crooned. "Calm yourself, calm. Think of when you were a foal, when your legs were strong and young and you could run all day. Think of your mother's milk and how it felt sliding down your throat and into your belly. There. There. Hear my voice, only my voice. It is all right."

Bit by bit the horse stopped struggling, but Nightelk continued talking to her, and as he did, he stared at her ruined leg. Above him the wind shifted direction. He smelled hot smoke.

CHAPTER 13

Black Eyes ran low and swift like a wolf. Twice rabbits fleeing the fire sprinted past him, but he gave them no mind. Hard behind him, Lone Hawk divided his attention between making sure he didn't lose sight of the dog and his surroundings.

Touches the Wind had been so named because as a small child she often danced to a breeze's tune. Instead of turning her back on winter storms when they threw snow at her, the girl had lifted her head and opened her mouth to capture as many flakes as she could. Lone Hawk wondered if Touches the Wind loved her namesake today.

"The dog has lost his senses," Grey Bear grumbled as he kept pace. "To run into smoke and risk being caught by flames—this is wrong! We should not be doing this!"

"Do what you wish." Lone Hawk didn't bother looking over at the other man.

"As soon as I have shown your actions to be foolish, I will head for the village."

Today shouldn't be about one man holding another up to ridicule! In yet another effort to dismiss Grey Bear from his mind, Lone Hawk again glanced upward. The smoky air contained the ashes that were all that remained of the summer dry grass. He felt soot on his face and in his hair and prayed the all too near flames wouldn't turn into a fire-river.

Black Eyes was getting farther and farther ahead of them; he'd urge his horse to a faster pace if he wasn't afraid the animal would step into a prairie-dog hole. Grey Bear must have the same thoughts; otherwise he would have urged Legs Like Lightning into a hard gallop.

Didn't Black Eyes understand the danger the fire presented? Was Grey Bear right: The dog had taken leave of its senses and was running to its death, taking him with it? If a *mistai* or ghost was nearby—

Movement overhead killed the thought. For a heartbeat, Lone Hawk believed he'd spotted a *mistai*, but his eyes soon brought him the truth. A hawk rode the smoke's edge, its small, sharp talons seemingly clinging to the blacked air. He nearly pointed the hawk out to Grey Bear, then decided to keep the sight to himself. He'd been named for the keen-eyed killing creature; this hawk was his!

Black Eyes had fallen silent once the men started following him. Now, however, he began to growl again, the rumbling sound nearly lost beneath the too-close flames' deadly snap and snarl.

"Foolishness," Grey Bear muttered. "Proven hunters being led by a flea-infested dog? Look out for a *minio*!"

Minio, horned hairy Water Spirits, were known to seize people in rivers and lakes. Parents sometimes frightened misbehaving children with tales of the frightening creatures. "Leave!" Lone Hawk snapped. "Ride your own way!"

Grey Bear snorted, then suddenly pulled Legs Like Lightning to a stop. "Look." He pointed.

Lone Hawk rubbed soot out of his eyes and focused. A horse lay motionless on a nearby rise; a man knelt beside the animal. Black Eyes stood at the man's elbow.

"Nightelk?"

The man's attention had been on Black Eyes but now he looked up. "I thought I heard hoofbeats," Nightelk said as they drew close. "But I could not be certain."

The fire was far enough away that Lone Hawk felt safe. Still, it remained an undeniable force, a prowling beast that might charge at any moment. Nightelk didn't have to utter a word; his eyes said it all. If the beast attacked, a man on foot didn't stand a chance.

"She is dead?" Grey Bear indicated Nightelk's horse.

"No. Her leg is broken."

She'd probably stepped into one of the prairie-dog holes littering the ground. "Come with us," Lone Hawk said. "We will take you to the village."

"No." Looking old and tired, Nightelk stood. When he did, the stricken mare lifted her head and stared at him.

"My prayer has been answered," Nightelk said. "You came."

"Black Eyes guided us."

Nightelk stretched out his hand, but his dog backed away. "I thank him for that." Sighing, he let his hand drop. "The ways of Heammawihio—listen to me!"

Sounding as exhausted as he looked, Nightelk spoke, and with each word, Lone Hawk's sense of dread increased. Little Bird, Follower, and Knows No Fear weren't in the village but somewhere on the plains.

"It was my duty to find them," Nightelk finished. He sounded as tired as he looked. "The only way I could think to atone for what I have done, but Heammawihio is not content simply to destroy *me*. The High God—no! I cannot accept that! The children must not die!"

SEEKS FIRE'S EYES burned. Her head ached. With every breath, smoke settled in her lungs and she fought not to cough. Had it only been a few days ago that her thoughts had gone no further than how she could get Grey Bear to smile at her? That maiden, that selfish child no longer existed.

They cannot die! They cannot die! pounded through her. Although she longed to give the words freedom, to cast them out of her, she didn't because to do so meant sealing them inside the hearts of the two women who rode and listened and stared and prayed with her.

She'd been given the wrong name! Her father had thought it funny that his barely walking daughter had been drawn to his wife's cooking fires, but that child belonged to yesterday, and the woman she'd become hated what relentlessly destroyed the prairie grasses. Still, if she could have appeased the fire god by throwing herself at it, she would have done so. Anything was preferable to the wall and weight of fear.

She'd never gotten close enough to a living antelope to touch it, but now two bounded by so close that they nearly ran into her horse. She barely glanced at them, cared only that the lean, swift animals were going in the opposite direction from the way they were traveling. If antelope feared being overtaken by flames, how could two small girls on foot hope to outrun the same monster?

Walking Rabbit started coughing. The spasm went on and on, forcing the young mother to grip her mount's mane to keep from falling off. Seeks Fire guided her own horse closer.

"Are you all right?" she asked when Walking Rabbit finally straightened.

Walking Rabbit looked at her but didn't speak. If she could have taken back the words, she would have. How could Porcupine's widow, the mother of two missing children, ever be all right?

Touches the Wind had taken the lead, and Seeks Fire followed her friend without question. Maybe Touches the Wind knew what was in her little sister's mind and heart and could thus determine where the girl would travel. As for Follower—Follower had been rightly named because usually the six-year-old tailed after her brother. But she was also a small leaf tossed about by errant breezes.

In Seeks Fire's mind, Touches the Wind became a tracking dog, more like a cougar on the scent or an eagle studying distant movements than a woman. She seemed to be taking in her world through her skin, assessing it, absorbing what she needed and discarding the unimportant. Seeks Fire gave Touches the Wind what she could of her thoughts and determination and prayed it would help. Prayed it would be enough.

Occasionally one or the other of them would call out, but mostly they listened, looked. Her horse wanted to return to the safety of the village or what the mare perceived to be safety. She needed to tell the awkwardly dancing creature that panic might kill it, and yet the taste of her own near panic kept her silent.

Fear was hot and bitter and yet cold. It nipped and bit, took chunks out of her heart and left hollow, bleeding wounds.

Follower was all legs and arms, wide, trusting eyes, and a high, sweet voice. This fire, this *mistai* couldn't destroy that sweetness! It couldn't!

"What—" Touches the Wind started to say. Her word fell away and somewhere in the middle of wind and flames, Seeks Fire heard something else.

"A horse," she said.

"In pain."

Unable to look Walking Rabbit in the eye, Seeks Fire strained to determine where the scream came from, but the wind bucked and whirled so that she couldn't be sure. When Touches the Wind urged her horse straight ahead, she didn't argue but, still trusting the other woman's instincts, followed.

Lead us to Knows No Fear, she prayed. *Make this animal his.*

But it wasn't. Instead, the sounds took them to Nightelk.

He must have heard them coming because he was looking in their direction, his arms folded over his naked, soot-caked chest. At the sight of the seasoned warrior standing near his

fallen horse, Seeks Fire nearly cried out. This man, this respected and trusted man, had vowed to find the children.
Instead—

"Where are they?" Walking Rabbit demanded before
Nightelk could speak.

"I do not know." His haunted eyes met hers.

Walking Rabbit slid off her horse and stumbled toward
Nightelk. "No," she whispered. "That cannot be."

But it could. His words, slow and deep, attached themselves to Seeks Fire's heart and left her both cold and filled
with a wild, perhaps irrational hope. After spotting the fire,
Grey Bear and Lone Hawk had turned back from looking for
buffalo. On their way to the village, they'd come across him.
If he'd insisted, they might have taken him to the village,
but after learning that three children were in danger and
heeding his plea to put their safety before anything else, the
two young men had ridden off in search of them. The last
Nightelk had seen, Lone Hawk and Grey Bear had been following Black Eyes.

"I am sorry." Once again Nightelk locked eyes with Walking Rabbit. Her strained features tore at him, reminding him
of how his wife had looked as first one and then another
infant had grown stiff in her arms. "I should have—"

His mare began thrashing again. Before he could grab her
head, she somehow got to her feet. The effort showed in her
huge, white-filled eyes and flared nostrils. Her shattered leg
had begun to swell. She bit at it, whimpered.

In the distance, wind and flames made noisy love, but
Nightelk paid no attention to the sound. Without looking at
the three women, he drew out his knife and approached the
mare. She tried to back away, nearly fell.

"It is all right," he lied. "Do not be afraid of me. I will
not hurt—listen to me. Listen and make my voice the last
sound you hear."

Begging forgiveness, he plunged the knife into the mare's
throat. Blood flowed from her. He heard Walking Rabbit's
heavy breathing and Seeks Fire's soft cry. Touches the Wind
was silent.

A moment later the mare's legs collapsed. She fell in a bunched heap and her head sagged forward.

Dropping to his knees beside her, he stroked her hot forehead. "It is over," he whispered. "The pain done."

He waited until she stopped breathing before pushing himself to his feet. Walking over to Porcupine's widow was perhaps the hardest thing he had ever done, but he had no choice. "I am sorry," he said.

"Sorry? You did what you must." She indicated the horse.

"No." He fought to raise his voice above a whisper. "Not that. The children . . ." He glanced at Touches the Wind. "I should have saved—I wanted—it was my duty. My atonement."

"Nightelk?" Walking Rabbit insisted. "What are you talking about?"

He couldn't answer.

"WHERE IS HE? I can no longer see—"

Not bothering to finish, Lone Hawk strained for a glimpse of Black Eyes before glancing at Grey Bear. If anyone had asked how long ago they'd left Nightelk, he wouldn't be able to say. Fighting to keep up with the dog and trying to see despite the smoke, but most of all worrying about the children, left no room for any other thoughts. Now, somehow, he'd lost sight of Black Eyes.

"He has run off." Grey Bear pointed to where a barely visible half-grown black bear stood on its hind legs staring at the fire. "Nightelk's dog saw or smelled that and fled."

Black Eyes couldn't abandon the children's scent! He couldn't! "Wait," Lone Hawk ordered when Grey Bear started off in another direction. "We cannot leave them!"

"I will never do that! But we saw nothing while we were following Black Eyes. We must try—try another way."

Grey Bear's hesitation distracted him from their desperate hunt. "That?" Lone Hawk indicated the direction Grey Bear had been going. "You think they may be there?"

The other man's silence lasted too long. Then: "I pray they

are. My thoughts—my thoughts are that Knows No Fear would have taken the horses some distance so others will think him resourceful. Nightelk thought he might have traveled east, but that is where the fire . . ."

Lone Hawk wanted to slap at the silence. Instead he forced himself to ask "What about the girls? Maybe Black Eyes has gone after them."

"If he knows where they are, why did he not wait for us?"

Like too much today, he didn't have an answer. Grey Bear continued to study both him and their surroundings, making him wonder if the larger man felt as helpless as he did. If it didn't take too much energy, he would have cursed Nightelk's dog and the bear that may have frightened him.

"Separate," Lone Hawk said. "We will cover more land than together."

"I know." Instead of riding away, Grey Bear turned Legs Like Lightning around and came so close that the two horses' noses nearly touched. "Your eyes are keener than mine," he said.

This morning Grey Bear had been full of youth and confidence. Now, however, his eyes mirrored the age and barely contained fear that had dominated Nightelk's. "I pray they will become hawklike," he said.

"And I pray your courage will flow to the children and keep them safe until you find them."

Grey Bear nodded but didn't say anything. For a moment, Lone Hawk thought the other man might reach out to clasp hands. Instead, Grey Bear made a fist, which he flattened against his chest. Soot continued to drift over and onto them. The prairie burned and screamed. With his mouth a harsh line, Grey Bear started backing Legs Like Lightning.

Instead of waiting to see where he intended to go, Lone Hawk looked around, hoping to get his bearings. Black Eyes had been trotting toward the valley called Low Green Rocks. Wrapping himself in everything it was to be Cheyenne, he started that way.

Since leaving Nightelk, they'd managed to stay a constant distance from the fire, but that no longer mattered. Although he had to fight his mare, who wanted nothing to do with this, he kept his mind free so he could open it to a child's thoughts. Knows No Fear had no equal when it came to the fighting games he and the other boys delighted in. He might be uneasy today, might have already lost his horses, but he wouldn't panic because his father had taught him well.

As for Little Bird and Follower—

"Send me your thoughts. Throw them into the air so the wind can carry them to me, so I will know what you are doing."

Nothing came to him, forcing him to admit he knew little about what went on inside girls' minds.

He called out several times, rode, called out again. The fire was to his left, closer than it had been earlier. If he continued on this path. . . .

"Are you here? Can you feel me, know I am looking for you? Stay far from the fire. Understand that it cannot be trusted, might attack."

The wind caught his words and swallowed them. He was still trying to sort through his mind for what he should say next when a ripple of something alive whispered over him. Thinking it might be a warning of danger, he again scanned his world. It wasn't until he looked up that he understood—or thought he did.

A hawk, perhaps the one he'd seen earlier, oblivious to the smoke that was the same color the thunder-heavy sky had been, floated ahead of him.

Not fully believing, he stared at the bird while his horse hissed in alarm. Whenever Massaum ceremonies were held to insure well-being, he took the role of Hawk and joined the other men imitating animals running from "hunting" members of the Bow String Society. Although Massaum was a time of fun and jokes, the meaning behind the ceremony remained serious. Other men might pretend to be shot, but he'd never allowed any Bow String Society warriors to think hawks easily fell to earth. This hawk, who might or might not be real, had come to him, him.

"Why are you here?" he demanded. "Is it because you

know my name or—please, I am only a man and do not understand messages from Heammawihio."

The hawk glided closer, so close now that Lone Hawk could look into its bright, black eyes. The flames were reflected in them.

"I fear—no, fear must *not* ride with me today! Only the children—is that why you are here? Because you know—because you have seen . . ."

Even a bird of prey needed to move its wings, but this creature had become more than its world. His heart thudded, and he couldn't give enough thought to pulling air into his lungs. The bird hung suspended, its wings cupping the air, its gaze still fixed. Its beak was slightly open, and Lone Hawk almost believed he felt its breath against his cheek.

"What do you want of me?" His horse had stopped moving, but he didn't care. "You are not of this world. I know—that I am certain of."

A breathy cry rolled out of the small throat. Lone Hawk opened his mouth to give thanks for what must be a gift from Heammawihio but nothing came out. Slowly, so slowly that it was beautiful to watch, the hawk turned. No bird could float like that and yet, and yet—

Lone Hawk touched his heels to his horse's sides. The animal shuddered and took a single step that was followed by another and then another. It occurred to him that horses and hawks might be able to speak to each other in ways that defied men's knowledge. When today was over, he'd tell Sweet Grass Eater what had happened and maybe the old priest would guide him to understanding.

Smoke became an even thicker blanket. Chased by the wind it was part of, it threatened to blind both him and his horse, and yet he gave no thought to running away; neither did the now strangely calm horse. He couldn't say whether he was traveling along flat land or traversing a rock-strewn gully. There was no world beyond the hawk and where it was guiding him.

His heart continued to try to break free of his chest, and his lungs hated the taste of what they were forced to accept.

His eyes burned, and his ears filled with snapping, snarling sounds. His mind—that uncontrollable force—held sweet images of a boy walking into manhood and two small, trusting girls.

A few days ago Little Bird had shyly asked if he'd help her move a boulder. He'd started to ask why she hadn't gone to her father, but then she'd slipped her soft hand into his and he'd spent much of the afternoon arranging rocks in a circle so she and her friends could do whatever it was little girls did inside rock circles.

Are you here! Little Bird, are you—

Lost in thought, he was slow to understand why his horse had suddenly stopped. On the verge of urging the animal on, he focused on the hawk. Its wings were still outstretched; it must have found a wind current to rest its nearly weightless body on. Cradled by what was beyond Lone Hawk's comprehension, it waited for him.

A moment ago his senses hadn't belonged to him, but now they came back, ears and eyes telling him what he needed to know. There, flat against the earth and curled into a small ball that reminded him of a sleeping newborn, lay someone. If he hadn't heard the barely whispered cry, he'd have believed the child dead. Relief briefly stripped all strength from him; a sob clogged his throat.

Forcing strength into himself, he jumped off his horse, but although his legs screamed at him to run, he'd spent a lifetime being cautious, and the lesson still ruled. Flames had licked their way across the land and were now so close that he recoiled from the heat.

Most summer days he didn't bother with moccasins, but he'd worn them today. Just the same, he felt the hard earth and dry, vulnerable grass the fire might soon consume. His horse must have freed itself from the hawk-spell because it again began whistling in alarm.

"It is me, Lone Hawk," he said to the child. He was now close enough that he could make out the line of the child's backbone beneath her faded dress. "I have come—" His voice caught. "Have come to take you home."

The girl didn't move.

"Do not be afraid. The fire cannot—are you hurt?"

Earlier the hawk's cry had captured him body and soul. Now the girl's whimper did the same. Unmindful of the wind-thrown sparks falling around him, he dropped to his knees and pressed his hand over the bony spine.

"Follower?" he whispered.

"No."

"Little Bird."

"Yes."

He'd yet to lay with a woman, but, thoughts of holding his own infant in his arms sometimes filled his mind. Children were the future of the Cheyenne and every life was precious. Feeling overwhelmed, he drew the small body to him. Little Bird responded by pressing her sweet mouth against him. Sobs shook her, and he wondered how long she'd held her tears inside her.

"It is all right," he crooned. "Easy, easy, you are safe." He resolutely kept his gaze on her and not their surroundings. "I will not let anything happen to you. I promise."

"I want—" She swallowed and started again. "I want Touches the Wind."

Not her mother but her older sister. "We will find her then," he promised with all his heart. "You—you are all right?"

He thought she was going to speak. Instead, her sobs, which had subsided a little, exploded again. He gave her his strength by holding onto her as he'd never held another human being. Ash had coated her hair and her arms and legs were gritty with it, but he heard her heart beating and nothing else mattered. Perhaps he called her by name; perhaps he did no more than repeat over and over again that she was going to be all right, that he wouldn't let anything happen to her.

Finally her emotional storm ended. Lying spent in his arms, she looked up at him. "I lost Follower," she whispered. A shudder coursed through her. "I lost her."

"Tell me about it," he said, careful to keep his voice calm. She did in the way of small children, jumbling the words and impressions in a way that confused him. Although he tried to get her to describe what the land looked like when she and Follower became separated, Little Bird couldn't remember. What she did remember was being terrified by lightning and thunder.

"I—I—Touches The Wind told me about *ekutsihimmiyo* where the souls of the dead travel to the afterlife. I thought, are souls ever angry? If Porcupine was angry because he is dead, maybe he commanded thunder and lightning to—"

"Little Bird, *Ekutsihimmiyo* is the Milky Way, the Hanging Road suspended between the Blue Sky Space and Earth. Together, the spirits of everyone who has ever died becomes Heammawihio, the Wise One Above. Heammawihio holds the Cheyenne in his hands and is goodness."

Little Bird gave him a confused look. "I could not remember all of my sister's stories."

Because the fear of being lost and alone had claimed her. "I understand," he said with his lips on her forehead. "Little Bird, Porcupine loved his children. He would never want harm to come to them, never . . ."

Looking up, Lone Hawk scanned the sky for signs of the hawk that had led him to the girl. Smoke painted the heavens and blocked out the sun. He'd managed to ignore the fire while calming Little Bird but couldn't any longer.

"Hawk," he called. "Hawk! Do you hear me?"

No matter how intently he stared, the smoke-coated sky kept its secrets.

"Without your guidance, I would have not found this child, but our task is not over. There are two more—please, show yourself. Take me to Knows No Fear and Follower."

The wind sucked in a breath and expelled it in a harsh and hot explosion.

"Hawk!" Still holding Little Bird in his arms, Lone Hawk scrambled to his feet. His horse snorted and backed away. "No," he commanded. "No, do not leave us!"

Whether the mare understood or couldn't decide between flight and staying with her master didn't matter. All he cared about was placing Little Bird on the mare's back and springing on himself.

"Hawk! Come to me, please! I need—*they* need you."

His eyes burned. The wind and flame sounds assaulted his ears and the great, black cloud enveloped him.

The hawk didn't return.

CHAPTER 14

Grizzlies were fearless. The great beasts ran from nothing. With claw, teeth, and muscle, they faced all danger. A hunger-driven wolf pack might attack a weak or injured grizzly, but although wolves were masters of attack and retreat, such attacks often proved fatal to one or more of the wolves.

Grey Bear thought of that as the hot, powerful wind pushed him and Legs Like Lightning. He was glad the heavens had grown silent, but the lack of thunder and lightning failed to calm his nerves. Slowing his breathing took effort, and he had no control over his rapid heartbeat.

There is nothing—nothing you can do. The danger too great. The fire may turn on you. If it does, not even Legs Like Lightning can outrun—

He shook off his unease, but it clawed at him again, and the battle weakened him. Legs Like Lightning snorted and pranced. If his stallion wanted nothing to do with this search and trotted with panic lapping at him, he should heed the animal's warning.

But what if he returned home empty-handed?

The thought of how his people would look at him if they believed him a coward kept him moving and searching, and when Legs Like Lightning tried to turn his back on the smoke, he ground his heels into the horse's sweaty belly.

His throat throbbed. He tried to moisten it, but he felt as parched as the air. The flames, visible beneath the swirling blackness, growled and challenged. Again and again, a fire-finger would race with incredible and random speed, consuming everything within its reach. Then that finger would either play itself out or grow disinterested in destruction, but as soon as it quit, another took its place, tasting, destroying. He told himself that as long as he remained alert, the killing fingers wouldn't reach him, but sometimes their speed exceeded what an antelope was capable of.

The children were dead. They had to be! It wasn't possible for three innocent and untested youngsters to outthink this monster!

As the image of charred flesh rose, clawed its way into his mind, he groaned, the sound somewhere between curse and prayer. He was powerful! No man equaled him in strength or daring! And yet this blaze laughed at him, turned him into a helpless newborn.

"Run!" he bellowed at the unseen children. "Run! Do not—do not let yourself be eaten!"

Surely Legs Like Lightning understood because the stallion lifted his head as high as he could. The sound he made was that of one stallion challenging another and yet different.

"I must speak of such things," he told him. "If I do not . . ."

Barely aware of what he was doing, he clenched his fists until the muscles in his arms and shoulders became like stone. Still, he felt helpless.

"It *must* not be like this! I am Grey Bear! Grandson of the priest Sweet Grass Eater. My heart has never known fear. I hunt and fight!"

What will you fight today?

Alarm slammed into him. If he dared take his eyes off the fire, he'd have looked around to see who had spoken. Then alarm faded a little and he knew the truth; he had asked himself the question.

Grandfather, when I became a man during the Sun Dance, I forced skewers through my own breasts. I, no one else,

*placed rawhide ropes through the holes I had made and tied
the ropes to the ceremonial pole. I danced and danced and
danced until the skin gave way and I was free. I did not
scream. Neither did I pass out or ask for water. If I can do
this, surely I can save three small children—or one.*

Legs Like Lightning pawed the earth and tossed his head,
but Grey Bear ignored him. He repeated his prayer, offered
it up proudly. But for too long, the only sound came from
the relentlessly feeding firestorm.

And then—

"What is it? A wolf?"

No one answered. He repeatedly blinked his smoke-
inflamed eyes and struggled to focus. And as the creature
he'd spotted continued to regard him from perhaps a hundred
feet away, he realized Black Eyes had returned.

IF ANYONE EVER asked why he'd followed Nightelk's dog
after ridiculing Lone Hawk for doing the same thing, Grey
Bear wouldn't have been able to say. In truth, he wasn't sure
he'd had any choice in the decision. Not only that, his stallion had ceased to be ruled by nerves and calmly trotted after
the rangy dog. In a dull way, Grey Bear was relieved they
weren't getting closer to the flames, but if Black Eyes had
chosen that direction, perhaps nothing would have changed.
Urgency continued to claw at his nerve endings, but he was
now doing something and told himself that was enough.

Legs Like Lightning had been traveling since morning and
now transmitted his weariness in the heavy way he lifted his
legs. Horses were life to the Cheyenne—yet he couldn't
bring himself to let the stallion rest.

Grey Bear couldn't say how long they'd been trailing after
the dog when Black Eyes stopped and howled. The throaty
sound hung in the air for only a moment before the noisy
fire swallowed it. Still, he continued to feel the howl deep
within him.

Black Eyes lowered his head and stared into the whispering, snaking smoke that perhaps served as warning of where the fire would head next.

"What do you want?" he asked. "My heart says you are guiding me, but I do not understand—"

A fire-charged blast of air stuck him in the back of the head. He swiveled and glared. He was Grey Bear, Cheyenne warrior! How dare the wind—

The second blow was even more powerful than the first, and this time it didn't die but continued to pound his flesh. Although he hated giving way before something he couldn't see and thus confront, he had no choice. Legs Like Lightning turned his rump to the wind and lowered his head at the same time; the stallion continued to stare at Black Eyes.

The wind flattened the dog's short hair against his lean body, but he seemed oblivious to it. He howled again, and as the sound echoed away, Grey Bear thought he heard something he hadn't before.

Wild, irrational hope heated him.

"Who is it?" he demanded. "Who . . ." Belatedly he realized that as long as he was speaking, he couldn't hear.

Spirit beings made up the world. Some, like Yellow-Haired Woman who gave the gift of buffalo, were always kind, but there were also great water serpents and the *mistai*, or ghosts. If a ghost had taken command of Black Eyes—

Fisting his hand, he slammed it as hard as he could against his chest. His Sun Dance scars were healed, but perhaps he'd struck himself with too much force because his heart first raced and then seemed to stop.

"Mistai?" he asked. "A fire-ghost born of flames and smoke? I do not fear you! I, Grey Bear, fear no one. Nothing!" He sucked in a deep, painful breath.

Something, part whisper and part beyond comprehension, floated through the air and all too quickly disappeared. Still, he understood—either that or his need to hope and believe made the whisper live.

"Knows No Fear?"

*   *   *

GREY BEAR FOUND the boy crumpled behind a boulder. Knows No Fear was so soot-covered that he barely resembled Porcupine's son, and at first Grey Bear had been afraid to dismount and approach the small, unmoving mass, but he walked one slow step at a time and dropped to the parched earth. When, finally, he touched the dirty shoulder, he was rewarded with a small squeak.

"Father?"

"No." *Your father is dead. Do you not remember?* "It is me, Grey Bear."

Knows No Fear seemed to shudder and draw into himself, but before Grey Bear could be sure, the boy lifted his head. His eyes were enormous and old, his right shoulder pockmarked with fresh burns.

"The horses," he whispered. "I lost—my father . . ." He started to reach for Grey Bear, then pulled back. "My father is dead."

The boy was eight, no longer a child. Last summer his mother had stopped holding him against her because Sweet Grass Eater and Porcupine had warned her that a boy can't become a man as long as he rests his head on his mother's breasts.

"What about the horses?" he asked.

"They—they are gone." Knows No Fear rubbed his hands over his eyes. The effort left dusty streaks. His lower lip trembled, and he clamped his teeth around it. "I—I could not hold onto them."

"The fire caused them to run?"

Knows No Fear nodded. "I heard one scream and scream—and then it stopped. I think—I think the fire caught it. When the herd started to run, I jumped on my horse, but it bucked and I could not—I fell off." He lowered his gaze. "The last I saw, it was running toward the fire. Horses— horses become crazy when they are frightened."

Grey Bear stifled the need to look at Legs Like Lightning to assure himself that his stallion had remained nearby and was safe.

"Fire is a wild animal," he told Knows No Fear. "It cannot be controlled."

"Like—" Knows No Fear sneezed. Black mucus shot out of his nostrils and barely missed Grey Bear. The boy wiped away what clung to his upper lip. "Fire is a grizzly," he said.

"Sometimes. Where is your sister?"

"My—my sister?"

"She and Little Bird came looking for you."

Knows No Fear's eyes became even larger and so dark Grey Bear could no longer see beneath the surface. Keeping the explanation as brief as possible, he told him that he and Lone Hawk had come across Nightelk, who'd been searching for all three children. When he explained that he and Lone Hawk had split up so they could cover more land, Knows No Fear struggled to his feet and looked around.

"I heard them. I think," he whispered. "But I saw nothing. I told—I told myself that their voices existed only in my mind."

"They were—are—real."

"I cannot see." His voice was barely audible. "Smoke covers everything. How can I ever find them?"

"You cannot." He had to force the next words. "We cannot."

"You think—" Knows No Fear clamped his hand over his mouth. Just the same, he knew the boy had been about to ask whether his sister and Little Bird were still alive.

"We must leave now." Grey Bear pointed toward the advancing fire. "Return to the village." To give weight to the words he hated saying, he placed his hand on Knows No Fear's shoulder and started to turn him toward Legs Like Lightning.

"No!" Knows No Fear jerked free, then looked around, confused. "My sister—she *must* not be out here!"

"Perhaps they have returned home."

Knows No Fear gaped at him. A tear puddled in his right eye and ran down his dirty cheek. "You think—you believe that?"

No.

"They are little girls, little more than babies," he said. "When the flames came, they would want to be with their mothers."

The boy nodded, but when he swiped at another tear, Grey Bear knew he hadn't convinced him any more than he had himself.

"Listen to me," he said as firmly as possible. "Follower and Little Bird are in the hands of the spirits. I thank those same spirits that I found you."

The boy remained out of reach, and Grey Bear was put in mind of horses and antelope, even buffalo. Fire terrified them; the same emotion had taken hold of Knows No Fear.

"Your father named you"—he held to the same firm tone he'd just used—"because he saw courage in your eyes and in the way you walk. Do not let that change now. Legs Like Lightning will take us home."

"But if my sister is not there?"

Then we will all mourn her. "Smell the smoke. Feel the heat. We must leave now!"

Like a trapped animal, Knows No Fear spun in one direction and then another. When his knees started to buckle, Grey Bear grabbed him and held on. "We must go now!" he repeated.

"But my sister? If the fire reaches her and Little Bird—" A sob shook him.

Fighting the impact that the sob had on his heart, Grey Hawk lifted Knows No Fear into his arms and strode toward Legs Like Lightning.

"You are a man," he said. He had to force the words past the sudden wound in him. "A warrior. Men do not cry."

ALTHOUGH THE VILLAGE'S women and children's too-loud voices were sharp with concern, Kicked by Horse paid them no mind. She'd barely moved since her daughter, Walking Rabbit, and Seeks Fire had ridden off. The day with its sounds and smells and awful heat felt unreal. Bands like tight rope circled her chest, and she had to fight to breathe, but she was only vaguely aware of her effort. Likewise, she'd paid little attention to what her husband had been saying and was glad when he left.

Someone cried out, shaking her out of herself. Her legs had turned into boulders; still, she forced herself to hobble in the direction of the new sound. At first, she couldn't make sense of what people were saying; then her vision cleared.

The black and red raging monster that was the fire no longer fed at a distance. A Maiyun wind had charged onto the prairie and taken control.

"It comes!" a woman exclaimed.

Several elderly men and boys raced for the horses. Long Chin suddenly appeared at Kicked by Horse's side. "What are they doing?" he asked.

Not bothering to explain the obvious, she stared at her husband. His face was red and sweat-stained, but beneath those things, he reminded her of a discarded hide long attacked by the sun. This man was the only one she had ever slept with, and yet he knew so little about her.

"We cannot stay here!"

Distracted by the unexpected voice, Kicks by Horse tried to concentrate on two women standing a few feet away. One was Calf Woman, but although she'd known the other her entire life, she couldn't call forth her name. She wanted to tell Long Chin that her mind felt like morning mist, but if she did, that might frighten her even more than she already was.

"Cannot stay?" Calf Woman questioned her companion. "If we flee, we will have to abandon our homes. And my husband—how will he find me?"

For two, maybe three heartbeats, Kicked by Horse had forgotten that her youngest child was missing. Reality slammed into her and stole her breath.

"Leave?" she managed. "Now?"

"We must," the original speaker said. As she did, her name, Willow Bark, came to Kicked by Horse. "If we do not, the flames will reach us."

"Flames?"

"The fire." Calf Woman pointed toward the smoke-monster. "Kicked by Horse, are you all right?"

"All right?"

A moment later she felt Calf Woman's arms around her but couldn't think how to lift her own arms to return the embrace. She felt so heavy and the weight in her heart . . .

"You are afraid," Calf Woman told her. "It is a mother's fear for her child."

"Yes."

"I am sorry. So sorry," Calf Woman continued. "The thought that you might never hold Little Bird again—"

"We *have* to leave!" Willow Bark insisted. "The wind—"

The village instantly became a disturbed anthill of activity as women raced about gathering up their children and what belongings they could carry. Some had already roped their horses and were either placing their children on them or hurriedly filling travois with clothing, food, and cooking utensils.

Girls shrieked, the able-bodied men who'd remained in camp cursed, a few women cried, two infants wailed. But Kicked by Horse was barely aware of those things. Even as Calf Woman dragged her with her toward the corral, she struggled to remember how to make her legs work.

"What are you doing?" Long Chin demanded as he plodded alongside. "How can you abandon our tepee? What about my pipe, my weapons?"

Conditioned by years of pacifying her husband, Kicked by Horse turned around. Long Chin glared at her, but he'd become a stranger.

"Your pipe!" she shot back. "Our daughter may be dead and you think of a pipe?"

"I *must* have it! A man cannot—"

Had the horse who'd ruined her face returned from the dead to kick her in the chest? Puzzled, she shook her head, but pain blurred her world. She couldn't get enough air into her lungs. Was the smoke thick enough to be responsible?

"What is it? What is wrong?"

"What—"

"Grab her!"

Voices buzzed around her, but Kicked by Horse couldn't make sense of them. A boulder dropped onto her chest and then another. She gasped, lacked the strength to push out the air she'd just inhaled.

When her legs went out from under her, someone lowered her to the ground. Although she couldn't be sure and it didn't matter, it seemed that the entire village had crowded around her. One face that might have been her husband's swam into view, then faded. It didn't matter. Nothing did except for the crushing pain and her terribly, horribly empty arms.

Little Bird!

WHEN CALF WOMAN ordered them to, two boys lifted Kicked by Horse's limp body onto a travois. One mounted the horse pulling the travois and joined the villagers fleeing the charging fire. Several households had already dismantled their tepees in preparation for travel so managed to haul their homes with them, but most were forced to run with little more than what they could carry.

Even with fear driving the horses, no one escaped the smoke's assault. Like an advanced warning, it rolled over the straggling, desperate group. The two infants who'd started crying when the alarm was given continued to scream. One first-time mother, her nerves raw, pinched her baby's nostrils until the lack of oxygen forced it to be silent. The other, distracted by the demands of her older children, ignored the wailing bundle in its cradle board.

A number of dogs ran off, but no one went after them. All boys old enough to be given responsibility for a horse were pressed into service. Women turned to the peace chiefs for direction. What they heard was short, urgent. "Flee!"

Elsewhere on the plains, the men who'd gone looking for the missing children took note of the fire's new direction. After praying for forgiveness, they abandoned their search and raced back toward camp. However, because the women and children had gone in the opposite direction, their paths didn't cross.

Their eyes streaming tears from the unrelenting smoke, Touches the Wind, Walking Rabbit, and Seeks Fire continued to plod on. As they did, fear and despair rode with them.

CHAPTER 15

"I am afraid."

"So am I," Touches the Wind admitted to Walking Rabbit. Although her mare staggered with weariness, she desperately wanted to turn the animal back toward the plains. However, they'd spent the terrifying, too-long day searching while trying to second-guess the fire's direction, and with night falling, they had no choice but to return to the village—if there still was one.

"Surely others have been looking for the children, Seeks Fire said. If they found them, they will be waiting for us."

In a dim way, Touches the Wind realized that Seeks Fire had been the voice of calm and reason when she and Walking Rabbit might have been overcome by terror. She gave her friend a grateful look.

"I wish Hawk had come to me again," she admitted. Every word had to be pushed past the too-familiar terror clogging her throat. "If he had, I could take comfort from the sign."

"Perhaps he tests your belief. It is the spirits' way to do that. Come, please. We should not be out after dark."

Touches the Wind had watched a lifetime of sunsets, but this one was nothing like the ones she both loved and took for granted. Because smoke coated the sky, today's sun looked weak. Barely able to show itself through the dense haze, its leaving was a whispering thing, a weary newborn falling asleep.

She started to explain how that made her feel but couldn't
hold her thoughts together enough to finish. Besides, Walking Rabbit probably wasn't listening and Seeks Fire wouldn't
care. When Nightelk ordered them to continue searching and
leave him to make his way on foot, Walking Rabbit hadn't
objected because nothing mattered to her except becoming a
mother again. That hadn't changed.

"If they are not there . . ." Why was she doing this? Giving
voice to her fear only made it harder to bear. She should be
like Walking Rabbit, silent.

They'd noted the wind shift in the afternoon and had expressed concern that the fire might be heading toward the
village, but from where they were, they couldn't be sure.
Besides, with the children missing, what did anything else
matter?

Night lapped at her. From childhood, she'd embraced
darkness and the opportunity to leave work and lose herself
in her people's legends, but today she hated it. If her mare
hadn't known the way home, they might become lost.

"Do you want me to go first?" Seeks Fire asked when only
a single gentle hill separated them from the village. "I will
learn the truth and bring it back so you do not have to
face . . ."

Much of the land around them had been scorched, forcing
them to take a circuitous route. Everything smelled of smoke,
and Touches the Wind's flesh felt caked with it. Chased by
the wind, the flames were now some distance to the south,
but the devastation—

"No," Walking Rabbit managed. "I cannot stand doing
nothing, knowing nothing. If my children . . . my arms *have*
to again hold my children. They have to!"

Although there'd been times during the day when Touches
the Wind needed to hear Walking Rabbit's voice, now she
hated it. Hated the truth of their shared emotions.

With hard night settling around them, the three women
returned to their people. Even before they reached them, they
caught the too-familiar stench of burned hide and recoiled

from the faint image of nothing where Sweet Grass Eater's tepee had been.

Struggling to breathe, Touches the Wind fought the swiftly approaching darkness. From what she could tell, the fire's path had taken it along one side of the village, wiping out everything in its way, but other homes had been left untouched, as had the horse corral. Her head aching from the effort of trying to see, she breathed through her mouth in an only partially successful attempt to keep the smell from overwhelming her.

"What have we done?" Seeks Fire whispered. "Is this the work of *mistai*? We have done something to anger the ghosts?"

"Do not say that!" Touches the Wind instantly wanted to beg forgiveness for her outburst but dread held her in its grip. She heard Walking Rabbit suck in one noisy breath after another.

"I did not mean—" Seeks Fire started. "Where are they?"

The answer came a few minutes later when what at first appeared to be burning embers a distance from the village turned out to be a campfire. Although usually each family maintained their own cooking fires, tonight only one burned, and a large number of people were around it.

"They see us," Touches the Wind said when Walking Rabbit stopped her horse.

"I know."

"They wait for us."

"I—I do not know if I can do this."

I do not know either. But before Touches the Wind could force herself to speak, she heard a child cry out.

"Little Bird!" she screamed.

Jumping off her horse, she ran on legs that had forgotten how weary they were. Reaching for the small blur, she clasped her sister to her breast. She couldn't breathe, couldn't speak. Her sister felt like the fragile-boned bird she'd been named for and smelled of sweat and smoke, but those things didn't matter. She was alive.

"Where were you?" Little Bird asked between sobs. "You were gone so long."

"I was looking for you. How—how did you get back?"

Still crying, Little Bird explained that she'd gotten separated from Follower but Lone Hawk had found her and brought her home. Although she couldn't bring herself to let go of the sweet child, Touches the Wind was aware that Walking Rabbit had her arms around Knows No Fear and they were surrounded by other villagers. She needed to cry in relief and thankfulness but first—

"Lone Hawk? He found you? But he and Grey Bear left to look for buffalo."

"He came back. Sister, I—"

Walking Rabbit's anguished scream cut through whatever Little Bird was going to say. With her legs threatening to collapse, Touches the Wind stumbled toward the young mother. Firelight bathed stricken features in red and deep orange.

"Follower!" Walking Rabbit wailed. "My baby—no! My baby cannot be dead!"

SHELTERED BY THE night, Lone Hawk watched as Touches the Wind released her sister to grab Walking Rabbit, who appeared to have passed out except for her pitiful sobs. Sensing Grey Bear's presence, he glanced at the shadow of the other warrior but didn't say anything. Coming from different directions, they'd reached the village within minutes of each other. By then most of the men, concerned about their families' welfare, had returned. No one had seen Nightelk, but Lone Hawk trusted that the experienced tracker and hunter would find his way home—if the fire hadn't overtaken him. The three women had returned and were now learning that their lives had changed.

"I tried," Grey Bear told him. "I looked for Wanderer. No one can doubt that."

"No one does."

"It is not my fault that the girls became lost and separated.

They should have stayed with their mothers. If they had—"

Their mothers? "We must face what happened, not try to turn it in another direction!"

"Do not tell me what to do! Mistakes were made today, mistakes that must not be repeated."

Unable to put up with Grey Bear's opinions, Lone Hawk let the night swallow him. Walking Rabbit was calling her daughter's name over and over again, the sound carving fresh wounds inside him, but at least she was surrounded by her family and friends and had her son to hold. He couldn't keep his eyes off Touches the Wind, who seemed to know that Walking Rabbit needed Little Bird nearby and was pushing other people away so Calf Woman could reach her sister.

Forcing himself out of the prison of his thoughts, he walked toward Touches the Wind. He told himself he wasn't the one to tell her what had happened in her absence, but before he could decide whether that was true, she acknowledged him.

"I—I do not know what to say." Her voice quavered. She drew Little Bird in front of her. "My sister would not be alive if not for you."

"It was not me who found her."

"What? But she said—"

"Hawk guided me to Little Bird."

There wasn't enough firelight for him to see her expression, but her quickly indrawn breath told him a great deal. "You saw a hawk today?" she asked.

"Not an ordinary hawk. I am certain of that."

"A—a spirit creature then?"

"Yes."

"Lone Hawk?" She swayed slightly, then steadied herself. Her hold on Little Bird didn't lessen, but she seemed to have forgotten where she was. When he stepped away from the knot of people around Walking Rabbit, she and the girl came with him.

"I saw him too," she whispered.

You are certain? he nearly asked, but it wasn't necessary.

"I am glad," he said instead. "I think—you and I must give thanks to Hawk."

"Yes. Hawk kept death from visiting—" She glanced in Walking Rabbit's direction. "I cannot say that, can I? If Follower—at least my sister is alive. For that I am thankful, so thankful." She bent down to kiss the top of Little Bird's head. "To have death's shadow cover me—I do not know how I could have borne it."

Closing his eyes, Lone Hawk searched deep inside him for what had to be said. He tried to tell himself that what she needed to know could come from someone else's lips, but he was a man, not a coward.

"Touches the Wind, your mother is dead."

For a long time, she stared up at him. Shock and disbelief, more illusion than reality in the firelight, faded to be replaced by acceptance and a terrible pain. She dropped to her knees in front of her sister. "You knew?" she asked Little Bird.

The girl nodded and buried her head in her sister's breasts. Touches the Wind held and rocked her now-sobbing little sister. Lone Hawk wasn't sure whether Touches the Wind was crying, but he didn't think so. Still, he'd seen how loving she'd been around her deformed mother.

"I am sorry," he said as he knelt with them. He patted Little Bird's heaving back and then, taking the risk, gently massaged Touches the Wind's shoulder. "One heartbeat she was standing and talking. The next she had fallen and no longer breathed."

"She—the fire did not claim her?"

"No. Everyone said the end came quickly—before she knew her daughters were safe."

Touches the Wind nodded, then her attention returned to the still-crying child.

"I thank Heammawihio and Hawk for looking after me," she whispered. "For keeping me alive so she will not be alone."

"You too have lost your mother."

"But I am a woman, not a child."

"That does not take away your grief."

"No." She studied his eyes for a long time, and he prayed she'd find some of the courage she was going to need in them. "It does not. I—" She shifted but didn't try to free herself from his touch. "Lone Hawk . . ."

"What?"

"I—" She again brushed her lips over the top of her sister's head. "Because of you and Hawk, I still have her."

NIGHTELK DIDN'T REACH camp until dawn. Half sick with weariness, he felt little when he saw that six tepees had been destroyed. He tried to tell himself the spirits hadn't completely abandoned his people as evidenced by how many homes, his included, remained intact and how few horses had been lost, but what did that matter if the children hadn't survived?

Most of the villagers were sleeping, and the few who were up paid him little mind as he plodded toward where his family's remaining belongings had been heaped. He'd thought he'd find Calf Woman there, but although she'd spread out his sleeping blanket, there was no sign of her.

He was still trying to decide where to look and whether he had the courage to ask certain questions when he spotted his son striding toward him. Even in his befuddled state, he felt a surge of pride in Two Coyotes' strength and health.

"I wish I had known where you were," Two Coyotes said as they clasped hands. "Grey Bear and Lone Hawk tried to explain where they had come across you, but by then it was night and my mother needed help . . . You are all right?"

I may never be all right. "My feet hurt, and I am hungry, but it is good—Grey Bear and Lone Hawk returned then?"

In a tone devoid of emotion, Two Coyotes told him what had happened. Everyone had fled the charging fire, certain the village lay in its path, but although the flames had tasted, it hadn't devoured. Once it had continued on its deadly way, they'd snuck back and were picking through belongings for what could be salvaged when Lone Hawk, Grey Bear, the children, and finally the women, returned. Despite his sparse words, Two Coyotes' eyes gave away his shock and pain.

"What about Walking Rabbit?" Nightelk asked when his son told him Follower was still missing. "She—how is she?"

"She is with my mother. They hold onto each other, crying but saying little."

Deeply grateful that at least Walking Rabbit had her older sister, his wife, to turn to, Nightelk was slow to realize that his son was still talking.

"Hungry?" he said in response to Two Coyotes' question. "I do not know."

"Is it that or you fear there is not enough food?"

Although the truth was he couldn't concentrate on his body's needs in the wake of what must have happened to Follower and Walking Rabbit's anguish, he forced himself to listen as Two Coyotes detailed the fire's damage. Some families had been able to save their entire food supply while others, having to choose between that and other possessions, had left a great deal behind when they fled the fire.

"The creek is filled with ash but it continues to flow a little; I thank Heammawihio for that," Two Coyotes said as several peace chiefs, led by Sweet Grass Eater, trudged toward them.

"It is good to see you," Sweet Grass Eater said. He rubbed his eyes with an age-spotted hand. "I spent the night in prayer hoping for answers and direction, but they did not come. This—such a thing has never happened to us before. My tepee . . ."

"My son told me." Despite the weight of responsibility that threatened to crush him, Nightelk's heart went out to the old man. "Do not think you must carry the burden for all Cheyenne."

"They turn to me for answers, but I do not have them today, do not know . . ." The priest stared around him, then blinked as if realizing how much he'd revealed. "The great Sweet Medicine learned many things when he was at Sacred Mountain, but the gods who passed on their wisdom did not tell him who commands fire or how to control lightning. If I knew that thing, if that wisdom had been passed onto the

Cheyenne, perhaps I—no, not perhaps! If I knew that thing, I could have prevented this." He stared at the ground; his hands trembled.

"You are only a man, a priest and dream-teller, yes, but still a man. If Sweet Medicine could not learn all things, do not tell yourself it should be different for you. Do not weigh yourself down this way."

Sweet Grass Eater lifted his heavy head and stared at him for a long time before nodding. His eyes were red from smoke and tears. "I want to hold your wisdom to my heart. I need to."

Wisdom? All he had was a crushing sense of guilt! "What will we do now?" he asked. "Has that been decided?"

It hadn't because the peace chiefs first needed to meet. In the meantime, the hard task of determining what remained of their possessions had to be done.

"You will meet with us?" Sweet Grass Eater asked. He sounded ancient and his voice was barely audible. "I know you are weary, but . . ."

"I will be there."

BECAUSE WHAT THE peace chiefs had to decide concerned everyone, the meeting was held in public. Although he'd eventually have to speak to Walking Rabbit, Nightelk remained with his son until Sweet Grass Eater called everyone together. The old man had managed to save his pipe and began by filling it with kinnikinnick and tobacco. His fingers shook as he lit it.

"My thoughts are of the first chiefs' meeting when Sweet Medicine called together the four who would sit with him. At that meeting, the Keeper of the Medicine was chosen and Sweet Medicine declared that any Cheyenne who attacks another will be considered an enemy and cast out. Because of Sweet Medicine's wisdom, there is harmony among the Cheyenne."

Nightelk joined in the grunts of agreement, but even when

it was his turn to smoke and meditate, he continued to look for Walking Rabbit and his wife.

"What happened during that first meeting became the path for all Cheyenne," Sweet Grass Eater continued. "Today is different because we are the Bow String Society, not the whole Cheyenne nation, but what we say and decide today will determine our path forever. We stand at the edge of a cliff with nothing behind us and a great hole ahead and yet we cannot remain where we are."

Uncharacteristically Sweet Grass Eater had little to say after that. Instead, he turned to the man to his left. Twelve peace chiefs made up the circle with the rest of the tribe standing around them, even the infants silent. The air, calmer than it had been yesterday, was still heavy with the stench of things burned, and no one, not even the young men who took such pride in their appearance, had changed from what they'd worn yesterday. The clan looked, Nightelk thought, like wounded deer surrounded by a wolf pack.

Shaking himself free of the image, he concentrated. Although each peace chief said it in his own way, their words were the same. There could be no staying here while hunters looked for whatever game remained. Today would be spent gathering belongings but tomorrow, after the water bladders had been filled, the entire clan would strike out. As for the direction they'd take—only the way leading to the setting sun, land unknown to them, held a chance of taking them into the future. Their enemies lay elsewhere, that and fire-ravished earth.

"My fathers, I must speak."

Surprised, Nightelk watched as Lone Hawk stepped forward. "I did not wish to do this," the young man said once he had everyone's attention. "I am a warrior, not a peace chief or even one born to this band, and should remain silent, but I cannot."

"Yesterday you saved a life," Sweet Grass Eater said. "Speak."

Instead of showing pride, Lone Hawk remained somber. "No one knows of my dreams. I did not tell you about them"—he indicated the priest—"because I believed they were nothing compared to your night-wisdom. No, that is not it! They frightened me and I did not want to know—I prayed they were meaningless, told myself that, but I no longer can."

"What came to you in your sleep?"

With his eyes downcast, Lone Hawk spoke of seeing himself searching endlessly for buffalo while his people hid from summer's heat and wind and his belly cramped from hunger.

"In my dream, we were in a new place. No buffalo trails were on the plains and my mouth was dry. If I look into our future . . ."

"What would you have us do?" Nightelk asked when it became obvious Lone Hawk had said all he could.

"I do not know. I have prayed and prayed for the answer, but it has not come. I only—perhaps I should have said nothing."

Nightelk waited for Sweet Grass Eater to speak, but the old man seemed fascinated by his hands. Their flesh reminded him of a dry and cracked creek bed.

"You did what you had to, spoke with a man's voice," he told Lone Hawk. "Yes, perhaps you have been seeing our future, but there is nothing else for us. We must leave this ruined place."

"No!"

Nightelk turned. Walking Rabbit stepped away from a knot of women, slipped toward the peace chiefs, and then stopped, alone.

"My daughter is here. I cannot abandon her!"

In the past he'd joked and teased with this woman. Once he'd taken her backrest and replaced it with a pile of cactus leaves, but she'd guessed who was responsible. Instead of saying anything, she'd slipped into his tepee—probably with Calf Woman's encouragement—and left dried buffalo dung in exchange for his shield. Looking at her hollow eyes and tear-stained cheeks, he wondered if she'd ever laugh again.

"The Cheyenne are one," he told her gently. "Today our hands and hearts are linked as they have never been."

"No, no."

"Do you think I wish to speak these words? My arms"—he held them toward her—"ache with the need to hold your daughter who was like my own."

A sob rolled out of her.

"Because she is not with us, my heart is empty and my fear"—he pressed his palms against his belly—"sickens me."

This time Walking Rabbit's sob was that of a wounded animal.

"But, please do not hate me for the words I must speak, she is only one child."

"She is my heart, my life!"

He nearly told her he understood, but although he'd buried his own babies, he hadn't carried them inside him—and both times he'd had a body to bury.

"Yes, she is." He stood and strode over to her. He thought she might bolt, but she only stared at him. "I have walked my own grief-paths, but yours is deeper; I cannot tell you where it will lead. What I must ask is for you to remember that you are Cheyenne. If you stay here, you will die."

"I do not care."

"I do not believe that." Dismissing their audience, he enveloped her. She felt so small, as if first Porcupine and then Follower's loss had sucked something from her. "You still have a son who needs his mother. You are young and should have more babies."

"No."

"Walking Rabbit, sometimes the truth is a nightmare, but we cannot hide from it. Lone Hawk placed his before us because he knew it had to be. Now I do the same."

"No."

She knows what I am going to say. "Follower belongs to the spirits. Perhaps they will find a way to return her to us."

Walking Rabbit sagged against him, and he understood her soul-deep need to believe him.

"If that happens, we will rejoice. But if she remains apart from us, if she has gone to be with her father, we must accept that."

"I want my baby."

She'd whispered the words, making him wonder if she'd intended them for only him. Afraid she'd collapse, he continued to hold her, but now he spoke to the entire tribe, spoke with his muscles and back still strong and his soul crying out for forgiveness.

"We are Cheyenne. We will walk into tomorrow."

Please.

CHAPTER 16

Seeks Fire settled herself on her mare and forced herself to take in her surroundings. Even when winter storms threaten to collapse the tepees, she'd always sensed their collective strength, but today, with Sweet Grass Eater's home reduced to nothing, she couldn't remember what that felt like.

Although everyone intended to follow the same trail, the individual families would set their own pace. Because the fire hadn't touched her parents' shelter, all their packhorses carried belongings, and her father, a man of action and planning, had been hurrying her and her mother ever since they got up with the result that they were among the first to strike out.

Strike out?

Nothing remained of the fire's heat so there was no need to ride around the burned land. There was also less danger of a horse stepping into a prairie-dog hole with no grass obscuring the opening, but she hated the idea of having to look at black, naked earth.

When she caught sight of a trio of boys, she guided her horse over to them, then realized they were watching Grey Bear, who was straightening an arrow shaft by forcing the heated stick through a bone with a hole in it. She wondered why he'd take time to do that now until she heard him address Knows No Fear.

"I watched your father work with his weapons because I wanted mine to fly as straight as his did," Grey Bear told the boy. "Some heat their shafts too quickly and the wood becomes brittle, but Porcupine understood the need for patience, and I learned from him."

Grey Bear could never be called patient. Just the same, she felt no desire to point that out.

"It is not a shaft's length that is important," he went on, "but its strength. Even when I know an arrow will be used to bring down a rabbit, I fill my mind with thoughts of the Sacred Arrows." Ignoring her and the other boys, he leaned close to Knows No Fear.

"When your father was a youth, he would pretend he was a great chief charged with safekeeping the Sacred Arrows."

"He did?" Knows No Fear asked.

"Indeed." Grey Bear nodded and acknowledged her with a wink. "He would pretend that a Cheyenne had shed another Cheyenne's blood."

"Why?" Knows No Fear sounded dismayed. "Surely he did not want that to happen."

"No. But remember, it was a game to him, one in which he was responsible for the four-day ceremony to renew the defiled Sacred Arrows."

"Did he throw away his arrows as the peace chiefs would if there was murder within the tribe?"

"Yes, only I saw him sneak out and take them back. I was a boy then, about your age, and I grew bored watching Porcupine make new arrows he said were sacred. Once he drove a large stick into the ground and tied his new arrows to them, two points up to bring good health and two down so we would have much fruit and game. He let me and my friends see them but not the girls because—"

"Because only men should touch Sacred Arrows," Knows No Fear supplied.

Anther boy piped up to say he'd never trust his sister to

carry his arrows because she might trip and break them. That made the rest laugh, and in their laugher, Seeks Fire's tears dried and the weight of what today was about became less. She was trying to think of a way to thank Grey Bear for bringing a smile to her nephew's lips when he reminded the children that they had work to do.

"Stay near your mother," he told Knows No Fear as the others scattered. "It does not matter whether she says anything to you; she needs to see you."

"She thinks I am a baby." Looking ashamed of what he'd just said, Knows No Fear stared at the ground. "A few days ago she could put her arms around three people. Now there is only me." His head came up and he stared into the distance. "How frightened my sister must be."

It took all Seeks Fire's strength for her to keep from crying. Her head pounding, she slipped off her horse and ran her fingers through her nephew's hair. "Do not wander off," she admonished. "You are right. You have become your mother's baby now."

"No," Grey Bear broke in. "He is a little man, a near warrior, fearless."

The warm thoughts she'd had for Grey Bear vanished; she wanted to tell him he was wrong to place that burden on the boy's shoulders. Instead, she told Knows No Fear that Calf Woman undoubtedly could use his help. To her relief, Grey Bear backed up her suggestion. It wasn't until the boy was out of earshot that she realized that left her and Grey Bear alone.

"I thank you for reaching out to him," she said, feeling awkward. "He misses his father so."

"His uncle should keep him at his side."

"Nightelk has done that," she countered. "But he must be many things these days and he is still tired."

"Nightelk carries new burdens that he keeps to himself."

So she wasn't the only one who'd noticed that. "Nothing is the same anymore," she admitted. "Everything has changed."

"Yes, it has. Before this drought and the fire, you and I would not be speaking to each other."

Ever since her first bleeding after which her mother had tied her into her chastity belt, she'd been aware of Grey Bear. Even today, being this close to him heated her skin and her throat was dry. She still thought he was wrong to push Knows No Fear out of childhood, but she couldn't put together the words to tell him that.

"What is it?" he asked. "Now that we are alone, you will not speak to me?"

"No, no." How could she be so self-confident around her friends and tongue-tied around him? "I—there is much on my mind. Whether we will have enough food."

"We will."

"How can you—"

He leaned over and grabbed the arrow he'd been working on. "This will find its way into an animal's heart. I will bring it to you and you will eat until your belly is full."

"Me? What about your family?"

"This is only one arrow. With my others, I will feed them."

He gripped the weapon so tight that the muscles in his forearm pressed against the dark flesh. Seeing her brother's body had served as a cruel reminder of how quickly life could end, and she wasn't sure she'd ever get over the terror that had clawed at her while she, Walking Rabbit, and Touches the Wind looked for the children. Images of Follower's sweet, innocent smile and the horrible question of whether she was still alive stripped strength from her and made her want to scream, but Grey Bear had never failed their people. He was courageous, so brave that maybe, she hoped, some of his courage reached Follower—if the girl's heart still beat.

Feeling as if someone else had taken control of her, she touched his forearm with her fingertips. Something that felt like lightning shot through her; she struggled for composure.

"Do not fear me," Grey Bear whispered.

"I—I do not."

"You tremble."

"So much unknown lies ahead of us." Her hand dropped to her side, but that didn't kill the fire in it. "I—I touched you in gratitude." *And because I had to.* "If it had not been for you, Knows No Fear would be dead."

He rolled the arrow around in his fingers. "When I was looking for the children, I thought of how your heart would break if I returned without them; I would not stop until I had found them—him."

"You—you thought of me? Not the children or their mothers?"

Instead of answering, he pointed to where Long Chin and Kicked by Horse's tepee had stood. Long Chin was on horseback, but it wasn't his old nag. From here, she couldn't see his expression, but he didn't appear to be bowed down with grief.

"I will never be like him," Grey Bear said.

"Like him?"

"With a weak heart. Not believing in himself."

Not sure how or why the conversation had taken this turn, she struggled to remember what they'd been talking about, but the air had become heavy with the weight of a hundred unspoken fears. As one family after another struck out, they left so much behind—not the least of which was a small girl.

"I will speak to your father," Grey Bear said.

"What?"

"About us."

"Us?" Her head throbbed and she couldn't think.

"It is right that you become my wife."

Speechless, she struggled to return his gaze.

"This summer attacks with cruel teeth, and we, all of us, must be strong if we are to survive. You and I, together, are part of that strength."

He didn't sound boastful so much as confident, but he didn't really know her so how could he say that about her? She asked him that.

"Did you stay in the village during the fire?" he replied. "No. You rode out."

"The children—I did what I had to because of them."
"And because, like me, fear is not part of you."

GREY BEAR STUDIED Seeks Fire until she'd joined her parents. Then, his movements automatic, he placed his new arrow in his quiver and slung it onto his back. The peace chiefs had concerned themselves with one thing—leaving. True, Nightelk had told the young men it was their responsibility to feed the tribe as best they could, but that was all.

It was enough. He'd told both the boys and Seeks Fire that his arrows would find the hearts of animals; that was what he'd do today and tomorrow and the days after that, somehow.

No! He wouldn't question, he'd succeed! There was no other way!

Instead of joining the men he hunted with or seeking out his grandfather and asking for words of wisdom—something he wasn't sure Sweet Grass Eater was capable of today—he touched the spot on his arm where Seeks Fire had briefly laid her hand. Her soft, small, gentle hand.

THE OLD WAY was gone. Today, instead of riding together as they'd done since taking on the responsibilities of manhood, the tribe's hunters traveled alone because very little meat remained and the need to replenish the supply had become urgent. Otherwise, they'd start killing dogs and even horses to survive.

With much of the surrounding land burned, they'd have to go great distances to find animals that had escaped the fire. More ground could be covered if each hunter went his own way. Also, the chance of finding Follower—if she was still alive—increased.

After making sure the stallion he rode today had drunk his fill and that he carried enough water to sustain both himself and his horse for a day and a night, Lone Hawk rode out. During a hurried conversation at daylight, the hunters had decided who would go in what direction, and he'd chosen east, which was the beginning. He constantly scanned the ground for tracks, breathing through his mouth to lessen the burned smell; he also often glanced up at the sky.

Whenever he did, thoughts of Hawk filled him, and he turned himself over to the spirit-bird that had led him to Little Bird. He wanted to call out for Follower, but if he did, he might warn a rabbit, antelope, or deer of his presence.

"My heart goes with you," Touches the Wind had told him that morning. "I cannot say if you will find Follower and place her in her mother's arms, but we both saw Hawk, and if Hawk hears my heart beating alongside yours, perhaps He will guide you to her."

He wanted to believe her, needed to believe! What neither of them had mentioned was that Follower had had no water for three days now and her legs were too short to outrun the flames.

The sun hadn't yet reached its highest point when he spotted a small opening under a boulder. When he pushed the rock aside, he discovered that it had served as a home for a family of foxes. Of the five small, reddish animals, four were dead—probably victims of smoke and heat. When he picked it up, the living kit tried to bite him, and he quickly broke its neck. After that, he filled a pouch with the carcasses and tied it to his horse. Then he held up the tail he'd cut off one of the carcasses, offering it to the spirits. As he did, he caught sight of an eagle. His hand moved to his bow, then stopped.

"You knew the foxes were here," he told the eagle. "Perhaps you think I pulled them out so you could feed, but you are wrong. This—this pitiful lot—will feed my people."

The eagle screamed, dipped lower, then rose. If it tried to take the foxes from him, he might grab the bird and strangle it so he could have its feathers, but perhaps not because although eagle feathers were sacred and highly prized, today they were unimportant.

"Go. Find your own food," he admonished. "Be glad the Cheyenne do not eat eagles. Otherwise, your body would already be in my sack."

The eagle followed him for a while, perhaps because the fire hadn't spared enough of the bodies of the animals it had killed to feed this bird of prey. Finally, though, it heeded his advice and floated away. Once he could no longer see it, he felt lonely; at least the would-be thief had been a living presence.

Flames had blackened so much. At times nothing for as far as he could see had been left untouched. Then, unexpectedly, he'd come to an area that, like much of the village, had somehow survived destruction. The wind, which was the fire's master, had been responsible. Although Wind merely toyed with him today, he'd never think he could rule it.

Too many thoughts! Rambling thoughts that blurred his vision and deafened him to what his ears might hear!

Despite the warning, though, a small part of him left what he was doing and went elsewhere. No, not just elsewhere—to Touches the Wind. He had no explanation for why Hawk had come to both of them and no words for what he'd felt when she'd thanked him for her sister's life. He hoped his presence had helped when he'd told her her mother had died and prayed she'd reconciled herself to having to leave Kicked by Horse's body behind. And if she occasionally thought of him and the thought gave her comfort—

Foolish!

The day pounded on and on, heat sucking at him and making him wonder how much longer he'd have the strength to go on breathing. His horse had started the day full of energy but now seemed to be sleepwalking. Follower could have escaped the worst of the day's heat by taking refuge behind a rock or in a depression, but without water . . .

Find peace, little one. Do not be afraid of death. Your father waits for you. He will—he will welcome you and the two of you will laugh together.

Yes, Porcupine and Follower would be happy in each other's arms, but what about Walking Rabbit and Knows No Fear? And what about him if he came across the girl's body?

"Hawk! Please!"

But Hawk must not have heard him. Either that, or the

spirit-bird knew there was nothing it could do so it remained where such creatures lived.

He twice stopped to stretch his legs and drink, but although his horse tried to get to the water bladder, he wouldn't let him. "Tonight," he told the animal. "After you have grazed."

Guided by the years that had made him as one with the prairie, his sense of where he was in relation to the tribe never wavered. The fire continued to live and feed, but it was now so far away that the distant smoke didn't interest him. The wounds it had left behind, however, were great. A snowstorm blanketed everything but fire—fire was a mischievous and deadly child.

He was pondering how Thunderbird's child had become so powerful when the stench of burned flesh assaulted him. His horse set his legs, and he had to prod him to start walking again. A flat area was ahead and to his left; his nostrils told him that was where the smell was coming from. At first he thought the fire might have trapped a few buffalo, deer, or antelope, but when he realized what he'd found, he sat with his hands splayed over his thighs, his stallion's nervousness seeping into him.

Five horses lay dead, grouped so close together that he knew they'd foolishly sought comfort in each other instead of calling on their legs and speed. The sun had already started to claim them, taking them from what they'd once been and preparing them to become part of the earth.

Markings on the flanks of two identified them as belonging to the Pawnee. Uneasy because Pawnee had been within a day's ride of his village, he concentrated on his surroundings. He soon discovered that dead horses weren't the only things the Pawnee had left behind. They'd camped here for a while, as witnessed by the rock-lined fire circle and heap of burned material that had once been a wind shelter. There were even several arrowheads, proof that they hadn't had time to gather all of their belongings before fleeing.

How many Pawnee and where had they gone?

Checking the dead horses to see if enough remained of

their flesh to feed his people—there was—was the last thing he wanted to do, but meat didn't belong to one tribe or another; it simply filled empty bellies.

"Thunderbird," he said softly. "I thank you for this gift."

His prayer caused him to frown because if the Pawnee were as hungry as his people, they might return for the meat. However, if they knew the Cheyenne were on the move and thus vulnerable, they might be planning to attack.

After making sure he could guide his fellow hunters here, he turned his back on the death scene. As he did, the smell came with him, part of his world.

Not just his world but the Pawnees' as well.

The last time he'd looked into the eyes of a Pawnee, it had been Whitehair, Porcupine's killer. But Whitehair was more than a killer; he and his companions had also been hungry and desperate—their condition touching his heart and making it impossible for him to attack them.

Had they all escaped the fire? When the flames raged, had each man jumped on a horse and raced to safety, leaving behind only extra animals? Or if he looked around, would he find the stiff, black bodies of those whose lives he'd spared earlier?

Although he searched for hoofprints fleeing Pawnee horses might have left, the earth's fire-wounds made spotting them impossible. If he turned around now, he could catch up to his companions before dark so they could start toward the horse carcasses, but perhaps it was better to delay his return while he searched to make sure the area was safe. Only how, in all this great nothing, could he find a few Pawnee?

From what he could tell, the fire had been moving in a northeasterly direction when it passed through here, which meant the Pawnee wouldn't have gone that way. However, eliminating one thing didn't give him the answers he needed, and he was once again struck by how deceptive this land was. If he stood and looked around, the plains appeared like a lake's surface, but if he started walking, he soon became aware of the subtle differences that led up to a great whole.

He'd been traveling about the amount of time it took to

paint his face for hunting when he decided to give his horse something to drink. He was getting ready to mount again when movement caught his attention. For a moment he thought the eagle had returned, but this bird was smaller, gray, not white-headed.

"Hawk? Is it you?"

The bird hovered over him but so high he couldn't see the message that might be in its eyes.

"Hawk? You have come to me?"

The bird continued its patient, weightless study of him, and in the silence that followed his question, he learned patience of his own. Finally the bird must have absorbed what it needed to because it started flying away, not the swift and deadly flight that was its kind's way but slow and measured.

Perhaps his horse heard the unspoken message because before Lone Hawk could urge it to do so, the stallion picked up its pace. The sound of horse hooves on hard ground briefly lulled him; then, in the space of a heartbeat, he came awake.

"Where are we going? Follower? Do you take me to her?"

Barely able to contain himself, he nevertheless concentrated on keeping the stallion at a steady pace. At the same time, he strained to hear something, anything that would tell him a little girl was nearby. As he did, he sent a thought-message to Touches the Wind.

Hawk has returned to me. If you had a hand in this, if Hawk saw into your heart and knows your soul is one with the earth, be with me in your mind today. Help me—help me find Follower.

Instead, what Hawk led him to made his heart hammer. Nearly twenty Pawnee warriors were on the move. Whenever a horse tried to stop and eat, he was prodded back into movement. The men's faces were painted for battle.

CHAPTER 17

Riding the horse Nightelk had given him, Touches the Wind's father traveled with Sleepy Foot and Sleepy Foot's three sister-wives, leaving Touches the Wind to make sure their dogs dragged their belongings instead of challenging other dogs or each other to fights. She tried not to ask herself why her father suddenly considered Sleepy Foot his friend, but it was impossible not to. Her mother had confided to her that Long Chin lived with a disfigured wife because he was too lazy and disinclined to court another. However, now that Kicked by Horse was dead, Long Chin had been forced out of his lethargy. As for what would happen now that he was a single man . . .

"You should not have to do that by yourself," Seeks Fire said as she guided her horse alongside Touches the Wind's lead dog to keep him from wandering off. She indicated the spare horse she was leading. "I want you to listen to me, not say anything until I have finished."

Touches the Wind nodded but concentrated on where she was going. The ground was rock hard and her moccasins so worn, she had to guard against injuring her foot.

"Your father accepted a horse-gift from Nightelk," Seeks Fire said. "I want you to do the same. My father—I reminded him that your mother had just died and you were still weary from looking for the children. Before he could say anything, my mother apologized for not having thought of that herself and told my father I could choose any horse I wanted. Even with the two we lost to the fire, we still have enough."

"I cannot—" Touches the Wind started, then stopped. "Thank you."

Neither maiden spoke while she mounted. "I have been

thinking," Seeks Fire said, "about how much has changed."

"Today feels as if nothing is the same as it once was," she admitted. "My mother—my mother is dead, but that does not wound me as deeply as what happened to Follower."

"I know. Even my brother's death—it is the not knowing, thinking about what could have happened to her that—" Seeks Fire guided her horse alongside Touches the Wind's and reached out to grip her wrist. "Am I wrong for telling myself it does no good to think about my niece? I should be sending her all the strength in me, but . . ."

But Follower has been missing for too long. "I understand," she admitted as she laced her fingers through Seeks Fire's. "I cannot get enough of holding my sister. Although she slept with me last night, and I felt her every time one of us moved, nightmares stalked me. I wanted her to walk with me today, but if she did, she might forget what it is to be a child. That is why I told her she could travel with Laughing Frog's children."

They rode in silence for several minutes before Seeks Fire spoke. Whispering, she explained that Grey Bear had told her he wanted to marry her. She'd tried to make sense of how she felt, but too much had happened lately.

"I thought," she admitted, "that if he ever approached me that way I would be happy."

"You are not?"

"I do not know!"

The sounds of movement were all around, but Touches the Wind easily dismissed them. Likewise, the relentless sun and her dry lips became unimportant. "Why do you not?"

That, she soon surmised, was what Seeks Fire needed to be asked and perhaps explained why the other maiden had sought her out. Seeks Fire's feelings for Grey Bear hadn't changed. In truth, she was even more awed by his prowess, but her world had darkened. Contemplating what joining her body with his would be like no longer dominated her thoughts.

"When my bleeding began," she explained, "my mother said I had taken the first step toward becoming a woman.

The next would take place when a man made me his wife, but I can no longer remember what it was to be a child. I—is it wrong to want that back?"

"Fear has become a weight around my heart too," Touches the Wind admitted. "So many things no longer are as they always were. Perhaps that is why I am drawn to our legends. They speak of a time that is finished."

"Yes, they do." Seeks Fire chewed on her lower lip. "Have you seen Sweet Grass Eater today? He looks so old, tired."

"He is an old man."

"His face speaks of the many seasons he has seen, but his eyes are still keen and when he speaks, it is with great wisdom. But—his tepee burned. Perhaps, for him, that is as great a tragedy as what happened to Follower is to Walking Rabbit."

"Perhaps." The question of whether the sweet child would ever laugh again slammed into her. "I—I have not talked to Walking Rabbit today. How is she?"

"She does not speak. Her tears have dried."

"She is not crying? How can that be?"

"Perhaps what she feels goes beyond tears."

Although dirt kicked up by the travelers blurred her vision, Touches the Wind scanned what she could see of her surroundings. They were in an area that reminded her of an old horse's sagging back, the land in all directions higher than the depression they'd entered. As a result, she couldn't see as much of the horizon as she had earlier in the day. Was Follower nearby but hidden from view and unaware of her people's presence? The hunters had vowed to look for her, but they also had the burden of searching for game.

"I want to talk to my father," she said. "Tell him to take the dogs so I can look for Follower."

"If you do, I go with you."

"You do not have to—" Remembering she was riding a horse that belonged to Seeks Fire's family, she stopped.

"I feel as if I will break apart and fly off in all directions," Touches the Wind admitted, her voice shaky. "Doing nothing—this doing nothing is—"

Before she could finish, shouts and cries filled the air. Alarmed, she looked around until she'd located where the sounds were coming from. A few moments ago, the land to the north had been empty of living things. Now it swarmed with men and horses.

"Attack!" someone shouted.

"Pawnee!"

Seeks Fire screamed and dug her heels into her horse. As she galloped toward her family, Touches the Wind desperately looked around for Little Bird. She'd been behind her, riding with Laughing Frog's nine-year-old daughter, but as people ran this way and that, everything became confusion.

Mindless of the danger in calling attention to herself, she pulled her horse around and kicked it into a run. A moment later she passed her motionless father. Most of the men were reaching for their weapons or already presenting themselves for battle, but he stared at her as if he'd never seen her before and his hands were at his side.

"Little Bird!" she cried. "I must—" She didn't bother to finish.

Terror clawed at her, but she fought it with the same strength she'd used to sustain her throughout that horrible day on the plains. Her only weapon, a skinning knife, was packed into one of the bundles; how could she have known the Pawnee would attack?

Curses and cries of disbelief filled the air. She felt the way she had when she'd seen what the fire had done to the village—disbelieving and yet accepting at the same time. She and this horse were strangers to each other; there was little communication between them as she yanked it about every time she spotted something that might be her sister.

Out of the corner of her eye, she saw a gray-haired Cheyenne running toward a mounted Pawnee. She didn't think the Pawnee saw the old man and his lance, prayed the weapon would find a home.

"Little Bird! Little Bird!"

No answering small-girl voice reached her. She struggled

to locate Laughing Frog's family, but grit in her eyes made focusing difficult.

How many Pawnee were there? As they rode and attacked and stole, they seemed to fill the earth, but she didn't think that more than twenty had charged over the rise. Twenty Pawnee against nearly a hundred Cheyenne? But most of these Cheyenne were women, children, and old men because the hunters were gone.

AGITATED BY WHAT was happening, the dogs reacted either by snapping at the closest horses' legs or running in useless circles. Seeks Fire leaned down and tried to swat the dust-colored dog running between her horse's legs but couldn't reach it. If the cur got stepped on, so be it.

"Stop it!" She didn't know who she'd directed her order at. When Grey Bear and the other men had taken off this morning, her heart had swelled with pride and confidence, but now she'd give anything to have them back.

One woman had been walking alongside the horse that dragged the travois holding her tepee. Now the woman was trying to keep a Pawnee away by throwing rocks at him. As the Pawnee's hard laughter slammed into her, Seeks Fire realized he wasn't interested in the dismantled tepee but the water bladder on top of it.

"No!"

The Pawnee, naked except for a loincloth and a strip of leather knotted around his upper right arm, stared at her. She was vaguely aware that another Pawnee rode behind him but didn't dare take her eyes off the closest one.

"That is *our* water!" she insisted. "You cannot have it!"

He said something and kicked his horse into a walk. The woman threw another rock, which glanced off the horse's chest.

"Not our water! We must have it. We must!"

The Pawnee's next words were harsh and few, perhaps an order. It didn't matter; if there was going to be a tomorrow for her people, she *had* to protect the precious water. Her world became a dust storm of movement caused by men, women, children, horses, and dogs. Her would-be attacker continued to advance on her, and she struggled to concentrate on him but danger could come from elsewhere at any moment.

In a vague way, she realized that a second Pawnee was headed toward the water. The would-be thief's lips parted—surely not in a grin—and she saw he was missing at least one tooth. If she'd ever hated anyone in her life, she didn't remember, but she hated this man with a fierceness that cleansed fear from her.

"Save the water!" she told the woman whose name she should have known as well as her own but didn't. "We must—"

WIND RUSHED PAST Lone Hawk but did nothing to cool the sweat that caked him. He was surrounded by the other Cheyenne hunters who'd gone out this morning. Their collective presence comforted him—but not enough.

"Why?" Grey Bear demanded.

He didn't bother acknowledging Grey Bear but concentrated on keeping his horse at a controlled canter. Surely Grey Bear knew that avoiding a fall was more important than any question. At the same time, he wasn't surprised at Grey Bear's confusion since it equaled his.

"They must be crazy." Grey Bear shouted to be heard above the pounding hooves from fifteen horses. "The fire overtook them as it did us. They should be heading back to their village, not coming after us."

Locating the scattered Cheyenne hunters and telling them what he'd seen had taken a too-large chunk of the afternoon. Even now he questioned the wisdom of what he'd done. Maybe he should have raced ahead of the approaching Pawnee to warn the travelers, but even if the women, children, and old men had known, they couldn't outrun their enemy or face them in an equal fight. Cheyenne warriors would do that—if there was anything or anyone left to fight for.

"You did not see how heavily armed they are?" Grey Bear asked.

"I told you." He tried to keep his voice even. "I saw bows and arrows and their faces were painted. It was enough."

Grey Bear sucked in a deep breath and ran his fingers over the side of Legs Like Lightning's neck. "Pawnee blood will flood the ground before today's sun sleeps. I vow that!"

Ignoring the boast, Lone Hawk glanced over his shoulder. The others, their features uniformly grim, followed close behind. All the horses were breathing heavily. If one or more faltered before they reached the tribe . . .

"Whitehair?" Grey Bear asked. "Was he among them?"

"I do not know." His throat tightened at the thought of the Pawnee he held responsible for Porcupine's death. "If he is, he is mine."

"Yours? Whitehair belongs to me, me!" Grey Bear thumped his chest.

"We will see."

"Listen to me," Grey Bear insisted. He rode bent over Legs Like Lightning's powerful back, his gleaming flesh stretched over taut muscles. "No Cheyenne warrior is my equal. I demand Whitehair's heart. It is mine!"

First you must kill him, if he does not kill you. In his mind, Lone Hawk saw the Pawnee descend on unsuspecting Cheyenne. This morning Nightelk had been riding in the lead, and if—when—the Pawnee attacked, the seasoned warrior would know how to organize the men, but the Pawnee could swoop down anywhere along the straggling line. If they aimed their arrows at women and children . . .

"You were wrong!"

"Wrong?"

Both grateful to be pulled away from the unwanted image and dreading what was coming, Lone Hawk glanced at Grey Bear.

"You let the Pawnee live when vengeance should have been ours."

Not that, not now!

"If Cheyenne hearts stop because you allowed Pawnee hearts to continue, the burden is yours."

His features set, Lone Hawk lost himself in his horse's rhythm. Slowly, too slowly, the land glided past. His people were ahead, Walking Rabbit with her twin griefs and soul-tearing fear, Knows No Fear with his boy-size weapons, Little Bird and the girlish laughter that always made him smile, Touches the Wind—

"Whatever Cheyenne blood is shed today is on your hands."

"Silence!"

"You say that because you know I am right." Grey Bear repositioned the bow slung over his shoulder. "Today I fight and kill because that is who I am—and because you made it necessary."

Faster, faster, faster! Why couldn't the horses fly over the land and—

"Stop!"

Recognizing Two Coyotes' voice, he waited for Nightelk's son to draw alongside.

"We are almost there," Two Coyotes pointed out. "But we must be of one mind."

"There is no time for that!" Grey Bear insisted.

Two Coyotes angled toward Grey Bear. "A wise man does not rush into an unknown."

"Pawnee attack. That is all I need to know."

Lone Hawk ached to order Grey Bear to listen to Two Coyotes, but Grey Bear wouldn't listen. And, although he wouldn't tell anyone this today, he wasn't sure he carried any wisdom with him.

Two Coyotes was talking again, his voice calm. They'd been making enough noise that they might nearly be upon the enemy without knowing it. They had to slow and listen, not argue about who'd draw first blood. And if they managed to run off the Pawnee without anyone being killed, that might be best.

"How can you say that?" Grey Bear insisted. "Have you become like Lone Hawk, a coward?"

Two Coyotes' features remained impassive. "Until rain blesses us, staying alive is what matters—not more of this endless fighting."

"Today the Pawnee attack, not us."

Grey Bear was right, but before he could decide whether to tell the other warrior he agreed, Lone Hawk heard something that turned his blood to ice.

No one said a word. Instead, as if astride a single horse, the hunters shot forward.

Grey Bear found a certain peace in being surrounded by other men who knew and accepted that their lives might end today. Their stolid understanding enveloped him, and although earlier had been spent thinking about Seeks Fire and their life together, he now lived for this moment, this afternoon. Legs Like Lightning kept pace with the other animals during the swift and yet measured approach, but when they came in sight of the battle between Cheyenne and Pawnee, the stallion raced to the front.

"Die!" he bellowed. "For this, you die!"

A handful of Cheyenne children who'd gathered together in confusion were the first to see their brothers, uncles, fathers, and cousins. Speaking all at once, they tried to explain what was happening. He swept his gaze over them trying to locate Knows No Fear, then turned his attention to assessing danger and seeking out weaknesses.

Because Legs Like Lightning held to his unerring pace, they were soon close enough that one of his arrows might pass through whoever he aimed at. This first arrow, the first taking of Pawnee blood became sacred in his mind. His warrior-honed senses told him that there were nearly the same number of Cheyenne and Pawnee fighters, that the Pawnee had scattered along the line of plodding Cheyenne and were wresting water bladders out of the hands of screaming women and children. Several Pawnee had already heaved bladders onto their horses' backs, but instead of riding off, they turned their attention to stealing horses.

"Belly-dragging lizard! Son of a snake!"

The enemy held the captured water bladder against his

belly, a spear in his free hand. Grey Bear's mind clicked through his options. If he fired without taking aim, his arrow might pierce the bladder. He could send his weapon into the Pawnee horse's throat, but the animal wasn't his enemy and this arrow, his first, should taste Pawnee blood.

Under him, Legs Like Lightning slowed and held steady just out of the spear's reach. The Pawnee's eyes flashed with a mix of confusion and determination. "Water is life!" Grey Bear shouted. "You take ours? No! I take yours!"

He didn't know whether this was the arrow he'd straightened while Knows No Fear watched; what he did know was that he'd done his job well because the arrow sped true, both an extension of him and free.

As the arrow punctured the front of his right thigh and came out the back, nicking his horse as it did, the Pawnee screamed and clutched at it. The water bladder fell from his grasp and plopped to the ground. The horse's dancing legs missed it, and after burbling for a moment, it settled serenely.

Blood welled around the dark shaft. His spear forgotten, the Pawnee tried to wrench it free. A moment later, squalling like an infant, he jerked his hand away.

"Taste my weapon!" Grey Bear told him. "Take it to death with you."

Although he said nothing, the wounded Pawnee's eyes told Grey Bear what he needed to know. It was possible for a man to survive being shot like this, but only if that man's faith in his shaman was total and that shaman a master of his art. If those two things didn't exist—

A woman raced toward them, her skirt threatening to tangle her legs. As the Pawnee's horse danced away, Grey Bear turned his attention to the woman. When she reached the water bladder, she looked up at him.

"Thank you," Calf Woman said. "Thank you."

"This was yours?"

"No! My husband would not allow the Pawnee to steal from us!"

Aware that he'd insulted Nightelk's wife, he looked around for the senior warrior but couldn't spot him. Perhaps

he should have asked Calf Woman where he was, but battle
called to him. Leaving her to her task, he rode toward a
tangle of bodies. From what he could tell, three people were
wrestling with each other.

He nearly laughed when he realized that two Cheyenne
boys nearly old enough to go on their first hunt had dragged
a Pawnee off his horse. Either that or the Pawnee had dismounted on his own and foolishly gotten too close to the
boys, not that it mattered.

As he looked down at the trio, his mood changed to alarm;
the Pawnee gripped a knife. Instead of jumping off Legs Like
Lightning, he urged him forward. The stallion moved cautiously, but his presence accomplished what he knew it
would because as soon as they realized what was happening,
the combatants scrambled away from the sharp hooves.
Crouching, the Pawnee looked up at Grey Bear.

"You fight children?" Grey Bear challenged. "You do so
because you are afraid to face men?"

The Pawnee probably didn't know what he was saying,
but there could be no doubt of the meaning. Not giving his
enemy time to reply, he reached for another arrow. The act
of pulling the arrow out of his quiver, settling it in his bow,
pulling the string taut, and releasing was one. Only a small,
resigned gurgle escaped the Pawnee's throat; the arrow buried itself to the feathers just under his rib cage.

Dismissing the man who'd sank back on his heels and was
staring dully at what had been done to him, Grey Bear studied the boys. One was wiping blood off a long scratch on
his forearm.

"He cut you?" he asked.

The boy nodded.

"When this is over, I will take you to Easy Singer to be
healed. You did not hear the Pawnee coming?"

"No. They—suddenly they were here."

Because the Pawnee had prepared themselves spiritually
and their gods rode with them? But if that was true, would
he have been able to wound two of them?

"They want water and horses," he said. "Anything else?"

Torn between needing to assess his wound and being questioned by the tribe's bravest warrior, the boy stammered. "I— I do not think so. Grey Bear, Smokes at Dawn is dead."

Smokes at Dawn was one of the peace chiefs. "They killed him?" he asked.

"He—I saw him run toward a Pawnee. Then the Pawnee ran his spear through him and he fell."

NIGHTELK HAD BEEN riding alongside Sweet Grass Eater when the Pawnee attacked, saying little and accepting that his thoughts remained locked on the image of his burned tepee. The priest had seemed almost unconcerned when the Pawnee raced into view, and Nightelk, terrified for his people's safety, had left his side. Torn between checking on his wife or Walking Rabbit first, but hating the thought of having to look into Walking Rabbit's grief-darkened eyes, he'd raced to Calf Woman. She was all right, frightened and angry, clutching her belly as she insisted she'd never allow the Pawnee to take what was hers.

When word reached him that Smokes at Dawn had been killed, he'd raced off in that direction. Several other peace chiefs had gathered around the body, insisting the Pawnee had done a terrible thing but doing nothing to avenge his death. He'd seen them for what they were, old men.

He hadn't stayed there either but had hurried this way and that until he spotted one of the enemy trying to take the horses of Seeks Fire's father's. "No!" he bellowed, and charged.

Caught off guard, the Pawnee attempted to confront him while still holding onto the lead rope. When the startled horses tried to run, their sudden movement jerked him off his horse. He landed on his feet and, bellowing, challenged Nightelk to battle.

A life spent doing and anticipating that took over, and Nightelk dismounted. "These are Cheyenne horses!" he insisted. "You will *not* take them from us! You will *not*!"

Whether the sharp-nosed Pawnee with a lightning bolt

painted on his upper arm understood didn't matter. He needed to say the words.

Although the Pawnee carried a bow and arrows, the man drew out his knife. If Nightelk sprang forward and slapped the man, he could count coup, but the thought was only a fleeting one; in his enemy's eyes, he read raw determination. Counting coup wouldn't end that determination.

"You are willing to die for water?" Nightelk asked as he slowly advanced. "What happened to yours?"

The Pawnee's gaze never wavered.

"It does not matter." His attention fixed on the knife; his thoughts went no further than what it was capable of. "This water is ours! It will not become yours!"

The Pawnee blinked and sucked in a deep breath. When he exhaled, Nightelk felt heat. Neither man moved. Then, swift as an antelope, the man spun on his heels and sprinted away. Nightelk stared at where his enemy had stood.

"My husband!" Calf Woman cried out. "Do not—please do not leave me!"

How she'd managed to find him escaped his comprehension, and there was no time to ask. As she wrapped her heavy arms around his waist, he assessed his surroundings.

"I will not lose you." Her too-loud voice hurt his ears; her weight trapped him. "Without you—you are no longer a warrior. Why cannot you accept that?"

Instead of fumbling for an answer, he peered over her head. Even as he looked for a Pawnee to fight, he'd been aware that the hunters had returned. Although he spotted Lone Hawk and Woodenlegs, he didn't see Two Coyotes.

"Come with me," Calf Woman insisted. "Please."

Do nothing while Two Coyotes' risked his life? Never! Wrenching free, he jerked a finger toward their belongings. "You left our tepee?" he challenged. "Does it no longer mean anything to you?"

"You mean more."

Speechless, he again indicated where he wanted her to go. At the same time, he took note of a flurry of activity a short distance away. Calf Woman shook her head and reached for him, but he stepped back.

"Do not do this!" Her eyes glittered with anger and pain.

"I am a man. I do what a man must."

"A foolish man! Crazy."

He didn't wait for what else she might say but hurried toward the activity. Because the Cheyenne had stretched out along the path, it was impossible to see whether Pawnee were attacking those ahead or behind his family. What hastened his steps was remembering that Calf Woman had convinced Walking Rabbit to travel with them; he hadn't seen the young widow since the Pawnee had ridden down on them.

FOR NOW AT least, her family's horses were safe. Seeks Fire sent a silent prayer of thankfulness to Nightelk, and then, although her mother ordered her to remain nearby, she went in search of her sister-in-law. She thought Knows No Fear was among the boys trying to control the dogs and comforted herself with the thought that the Pawnee wouldn't concern themselves with yapping curs. However, Walking Rabbit, wrapped in grief and fear, might be at risk, and even if she wasn't, Seeks Fire feared the attack would plunge her into a nightmare from which she couldn't escape.

Intent on the twin tasks of searching and making sure the Pawnee didn't notice her, she paid little attention to the ground. When her mare suddenly stopped, she had to grab the mane to keep from falling off. The animal pawed the earth and snorted nervously.

"What is it?" she began but there was no need to continue.

A Cheyenne lay unmoving, facedown with blood flowing from some unseen place to redden the earth. Although Pawnee sometimes scalped their vanquished foe so they could posses their enemy's soul, whoever had killed this old man had left him with his gray hair untouched. She thanked the spirits for that and then dragged her gaze off the figure. If more Cheyenne had been killed—

A woman screamed. Fighting panic, she stared in that direction. Three people were gathered around a horse hitched to a travois. One had hold of the rope around the horse's neck while the other two fought over whatever was on the travois. A second scream followed on the tail of the first, more desperate this time. Because the screamer could be Walking Rabbit, Seeks Fire fought the instinct and training that ordered her to flee. At her approach, one of the strugglers glanced her direction. The Pawnee—she had no doubt of that—grimaced and turned his attention back to whoever he was fighting with.

Now that she was closer, she saw that Four Toes and Stands in Water, Howler's two wives, were trying to prevent the Pawnee from taking a bladder strapped to the travois. Four Toes had hold of the horse while Stands in Water, who was pregnant, tried to push the Pawnee away.

"No!" Not questioning what she was doing, Seeks Fire clamped her knees against her mare's belly. The obedient animal trotted forward.

Growling something she didn't understand, the Pawnee shoved Stands in Water aside. A moment later he doubled up his fist and slammed it against her mare's nose. Squealing, the mare reared. Caught off balance, she reached for the mane but before she could right herself, the mare landed, hard.

Seeks Fire fell with her weight on her left knee, crying out as a rock ground into it. Despite the pain, she struggled to her feet. Standing on her good leg, she found herself face to face with the Pawnee. Someone had scratched him under his eye and blood trickled from the cut. He held a stone-headed club and was so close that his smell filled her nostrils.

"Die!" he said in Cheyenne. "Today you die!"

She tried to take a backward step, but her knee refused to obey. In a dim and unimportant way she wondered why he wanted to kill her. Four Toes still held the horse's head and seemed not to know what was going on. In contrast, Stands in Water had reached down over her belly to pick up a rock and was staring at the back of their enemy's head.

Desperate to keep the Pawnee from taking his anger out

on Stands in Water, Seeks Fire folded her arms across her breasts. She had to swallow before she could speak.

"Do not call yourself a man," she challenged. "If you do, it is a lie."

"I am a man!"

How he'd learned to speak Cheyenne wasn't important. Keeping him distracted was. "How can that be?" She tried to put a little weight on her left leg but was rewarded with shooting pain. "Only a dog attacks women."

The Pawnee's eyes hardened. He stepped closer, the club now aimed at her throat.

"Run," he taunted. "Run!"

She couldn't.

CHAPTER 18

Yellow Haired Woman, who gave the Cheyenne the gift of buffalo, was the daughter of the old man who dove into a stream and killed the great water serpent who'd grabbed one of the two young men sent to find food for their people. When one of the men agreed to marry Yellow Haired Woman, her father, Coyote Man, taught him how to plant corn and use buffalo for food. Although Yellow Haired Woman broke taboo by expressing sympathy for a calf who'd had dust thrown in its eyes after her father warned her not to feel pity for suffering animals, she was eventually forgiven.

Grey Bear's thoughts touched on Yellow Haired Woman and what she'd done for the Cheyenne before turning to another woman—a maiden really. Why his mind held onto Seeks Fire when he needed to concentrate on the Pawnee he couldn't say. He could only pray there was a reason—one that would soon reveal itself to him.

Legs Like Lightning was power under him, and he'd already seen Lone Hawk shoot one of the enemy, but the still-stealing Pawnee evaded him. Surely his warrior-honed senses weren't failing him!

Shaking off the question, he renewed his search. He spotted Nightelk and his wife together, then noted how quickly Nightelk hurried away from her. Instead of joining the seasoned warrior, he again gave Legs Like Lightning his head. At the same time, he strained to locate another of the enemy.

He'd started to tighten his grip on the rein when Legs Like Lightning suddenly snorted. Looking in the some direction as the stallion, he spotted several people near a water-pulling horse. The bladder had slipped to one side of the travois, but that wasn't what held his attention. He recognized Stands in Water because of the size of her belly, and yet that was only a small part of a larger whole. Although the Pawnee had come to steal water, he'd turned his back on what was within easy reach and focused his attention on another woman who, balancing her weight on one leg, refused to back down.

Seeks Fire.

Alarmed, he urged Legs Like Lightning closer. When the Pawnee spun toward him, Grey Bear smiled.

"You die," he said, his voice calm.

Seeks Fire reached out as if to take the club out of the Pawnee's hand but collapsed and fell. The Pawnee swiped at but missed her head.

"No!" Grey Bear yelled. "You will *not* count coup on her!"

He was off Legs Like Lightning and facing the Pawnee before his mind fully recorded what he'd done.

"Grey Bear!"

He glanced down at Seeks Fire, seeing pain in her eyes along with something else he chose to believe was relief, pleasure, and pride.

The Pawnee's fingers moved almost imperceptively as he increased his grip on his club, but Grey Bear had lived to adulthood because he let nothing escape his notice. Instinct for survival took over, and he dismissed Seeks Fire.

His enemy was far enough away that a single leap wouldn't bring them together. One or both of them could have drawn bow and arrow and fired but only if the other didn't charge. For a moment Grey Bear contemplated doing that, but this man, this dung-eating man had hurt Seeks Fire and tried to count coup on her.

"I am Grey Bear!" he announced. Calm and yet with every ounce of him focused on his would-be killer, he pointed his knife at him. "No Cheyenne has faced more of the enemy. No other Cheyenne's heart beats as fearlessly. What about you, dung-eater? Has your puny weapon ever tasted blood?"

The Pawnee might not understand the words, but he obviously knew he was being insulted. His features had a pinched quality and his eyes were sunken in their sockets as if moisture had drained out of him. His lips were cracked, and there were healing burns on his forearms.

Grey Bear indicated the burns. "Did you do battle with the fire? Were you that foolish?"

"What are you talking about?"

Not looking at Seeks Fire, he told her to study the Pawnee's arms.

"I—did not notice," she said softly, almost sadly. He waited for her to continue, but she didn't because—he told himself—she knew what he had to do.

"You are a snake," he told the Pawnee. "A buzzard who steals what is dead and rotting. But you made a mistake today that will kill you."

Grey Bear's moccasins slid easily over rocks and dirt. He stopped just out of the club's reach. The Pawnee said something he didn't understand, something that didn't matter. The man licked his lips, and one of the cracks seeped blood.

"This"—Grey Bear indicated the precariously placed water—"is not something the Cheyenne have discarded so buzzards can feed. It is precious to us, life."

Again the Pawnee's tongue flicked over his lips, and this time he winced. He lowered his club a little so it was now aimed at Grey Bear's face.

"You thought our hunters would not know what you were

doing," Grey Bear went on. Never before had he taken so much time talking to someone he intended to kill; the maiden was the difference. "But Hawk warned Lone Hawk—us. You will not touch what belongs to the Cheyenne, you will not!"

In a dim way he realized others were headed his way, but if he allowed himself to look at them, his enemy might attack. He ordered his senses to tell him whether the newcomers represented friend or enemy, but they remained silent, useless.

"No coup will be counted today," he told the Pawnee. "Instead, I kill you."

Perhaps something in his body language transmitted itself to his foe because the other warrior leapt at the same time he did. Grey Bear's knife slid under the Pawnee's skin at his side, nicking a rib but going no deeper; Grey Bear dodged in time to prevent the club from crashing into his face. Just the same, it hit him a glancing blow on the shoulder, numbing his arm. He felt his knife start to slide out of his grasp, gripped it.

A woman screamed. He didn't think it was Seeks Fire. The Pawnee stumbled back, but although he briefly pressed his free hand over his wound, he didn't look at it. Instead, he kept his gaze locked on Grey Bear. One of the newcomers spoke—in Pawnee.

Fortified by the growl rolling up from deep inside him, Grey Bear lowered his head and slammed it into his enemy's belly. As they fell, he sought a new home for his knife, but his tingling fingers were too slow to heed his command. Dropping the useless weapon, he wrapped both hands around the Pawnee's throat as blows from the man's club slammed once, twice, three times onto his back.

Pain sent strength to his fingers, and he pressed so hard he wondered if he might tear off the man's head. Fighting was done with bows and arrows, counting coup and escaping, not in hand-to-hand combat. Yet because as a child he'd often wrestled with the other boys, he knew how to use weight and leverage.

The Pawnee tried to take a breath, but Grey Bear held it

trapped inside the vulnerable throat, pressed his body along the other's length, his legs straggling the naked ones as they began a wild spasm. Hard fingers gripped and tore at his arms and shoulders and tried to reach his neck, but when he dug his thumbs into the Pawnee's windpipe, the man's strength ebbed. The Pawnee's body bucked and jerked, fought to dislodge him. Through blurred vision, Grey Bear tried to focus on his enemy's features. He saw a desperately opened mouth, nostrils spread wide, eyes that looked deep inside to where his world was turning black.

The spasms became a shudder that grew weaker and weaker.

Strength held Grey Bear in its grip, and he reveled in it, let that strength plant his feet under him, stand, and assess his surroundings. Three Pawnee stood not far from where Seeks Fire sat. One looked at her, but the others kept their eyes on him.

"See what I have done!" He pointed at the motionless Pawnee. "With my hands I stripped life from him. Come, so I can do the same to you."

None gave any indication they understood, prompting him to reach down and grab his knife. Blood had made it slick.

Stands in Water hadn't moved during his attack on the Pawnee. Now, however, she clamped her hands under her belly and moaned. He accepted the sound for what it was, unimportant, but all three of the Pawnee glanced at her, and he took advantage of their momentary distraction by kicking the discarded club toward Seeks Fire. He didn't wait to see what she would do with it.

The dominant male wolf asserts his authority by challenging anyone who questions his superiority. Where a wolf uses teeth and fierce snarls, Grey Bear threw out his chest and spread his legs. The enemy was armed, but he pretended not to care. He held up his free hand and slowly closed his fingers as if encircling another throat.

"Come! Fight! Let me kill again!"

*   *   *

LONE HAWK WAS hard-pressed to make sense of everything. Impressions came at him as if from a nightmare: A Pawnee, intent on ripping a food-laden parfleche off a girl's back, knocked her to the ground, and his horse's front hoof struck the girl's ankle, causing her to cry out; an elderly woman determined to keep her burden-dog with her was being dragged about by the excited animal; four boys, armed with their child-size bows and arrows, ran about trying to get close to the enemy; Long Chin stood motionless and confused in the middle of his small heap of belongings. No one was interested in Long Chin's possessions, but he didn't understand that, a thought that saddened Lone Hawk and made him wonder, briefly, what having Long Chin for a father was like for Touches the Wind.

Touches the Wind! He prayed she was all right, hadn't sacrificed herself to protect her little sister.

"They leave!" someone shouted. "Stop them!"

Alerted, he took note of three fleeing Pawnee. Because his mare had started to limp as they reached the would-be thieves, he'd exchanged her for a fresh mount. Now he sent the tall black mare after the men who were making off with a string of horses. Two Coyotes also galloped toward the thieves, but he was far enough away that they didn't try to speak.

The Pawnee kicked their mounts, but the weary animals barely cantered. As a result, Lone Hawk and Two Coyotes quickly overtook them.

Two Coyotes' features gave away nothing of his thoughts, but Lone Hawk read his mood in the straight, hard line of his naked back. Horses were life; without them the Cheyenne would die.

"The rope." He pointed at the cord holding the horses. Two Coyotes nodded, but instead of trying to grab the rawhide, he raced ahead before wheeling around to confront the enemy. The horse handler reined in, slowing the string. At the same time, the two other Pawnee flanked him and aimed their arrows at Two Coyotes.

His attention divided between Two Coyotes and the enemy, Lone Hawk absorbed and assessed. Two Coyotes, looking no more concerned than if he'd come across some prairie dogs, studied the Pawnee. He held his bow and arrow ready. Although the horse handler was distracted by the need to maintain control of the six mares and two foals, the other two men were trying to keep Two Coyotes and Lone Hawk within sight, no easy task since Lone Hawk had now positioned himself behind them.

"It is too hot a day for fighting," Two Coyotes said, his tone indicating nothing more important than deciding whether he should take a nap or go for a stroll was at stake. "These horses do not want to run. I say we sit down and talk."

Whether the Pawnee understood didn't matter; what did was that Two Coyotes' words seemed to be having a hypnotic effect on them. One man separated himself from his companions and came a little closer to Two Coyotes, but then he stopped and looked around.

A mare whinnied; her foal, who'd wandered away, scampered back to her side. Another mare stomped the ground while a third lowered her head and tried to feed. Something about the horse handler nagged at Lone Hawk.

"The fire," Two Coyotes went on in his singsong tone, "is behind this. I understand that. My friend understands that. If you had come to us wanting to trade, we would do so, but you are thieves."

The man closest to Two Coyotes muttered something over his shoulder that Lone Hawk thought might be a translation.

"Does the word 'thief' anger you?" Two Coyotes asked. "What else would you call yourselves then?"

As the foal who'd rejoined his mother jumped away, the horse handler glanced at the skittish creature; the relentless sun highlighted his features. Lone Hawk took note of strong bones and a large nose beneath ebony eyes, but he dismissed them; only one thing mattered.

Whitehair.

Two Coyotes continued, now talking about how Lone Hawk had come across the burned-out Pawnee camp and dead horses, but he paid no attention. In his mind, he replayed the day he'd first seen Whitehair, the day Porcupine had started to die. Perhaps Whitehair too remembered because the Pawnee stared at him with raw wariness and determination.

"I believe you understand my words," Two Coyotes said. "My words are for one thing—to let you know this drought has touched Cheyenne and Pawnee alike."

The thick-kneed Pawnee who'd remained near Whitehair said something to him. Whitehair nodded.

"When there is no water and the grass has died," Two Coyotes continued, "the buffalo leave because otherwise they will die. It is the same for us, the same and yet different."

Two Coyotes' words buzzed and hummed. Now Lone Hawk held onto them, pulled them into him, followed them.

"If buffalo do not have enough food and water, they die. I cannot say whether they know what is happening to them, but people do. You come for horses and water because you want your people to live, but if we allowed that to happen, our bones will soon be bleached by the sun."

Thick Knee prodded his horse forward until he'd joined the Pawnee closest to Two Coyotes. Lone Hawk and Whitehair stared at each other.

"Cheyenne men are fighters. It is their responsibility to risk their lives for their people. Sometimes they die. It is the same for the Pawnee."

The translator said something to Thick Knees.

"But I do not want today to be about death." Two Coyotes sounded sad, and yet his arrow remained aimed at the translator. "Pawnee loss will not become Cheyenne loss. This I say: Today Cheyenne horses will *not* replace dead Pawnee horses."

"We take!"

"No, you do not."

The translator stared at Whitehair, who increased his grip on the rope but said nothing.

"These are my final words." Two Coyotes turned his horse

so the animal served as a partial shield. "Leave. Now. Empty-handed."

Although he continued to hold his bow and arrow ready, Lone Hawk assessed how long it would take to drop them and pull out his knife. He still wasn't sure what Two Coyotes hoped to accomplish, but obviously he'd confused the Pawnee.

Time beat at him, urging him to do something, anything, but when he looked into Two Coyotes' eyes and saw the patience in them, he accepted that wisdom. In contrast, Thick Knees and Translator's horses moved nervously, obviously absorbing their masters' moods. Whitehair seemed to have better control over his emotions, perhaps because he risked losing six mares and two foals.

Lone Hawk didn't hate Whitehair. At first the realization confused him and he tried to cast it away, but Whitehair was who and what he was, a warrior from another tribe, nothing else. He'd wounded Porcupine because Cheyenne and Pawnee had always been at war. He'd attacked defenseless Cheyenne because they had something his people needed.

"Aee!"

Thick Knees' horse squealed and gathered herself to rear, but Thick Knees released his arrow before the mare's feet left the ground. The arrow flew straight for several feet, but as it neared the neck of Two Coyotes' horse, it angled to the right and lost speed. Just the same, it found a precarious home in the pinto's chest. The pinto jumped, and when she landed, the arrow was knocked loose.

Two Coyotes' own arrow shot forward and buried itself in Thick Knees' side. Two Coyotes reached for another arrow. By then Thick Knees had dropped his bow and grabbed the arrow protruding from him. Instead of trying to pull it free, he cradled it; his mouth hung open, yet nothing came out.

Translator dragged his disbelieving gaze off his companion. His own bow and arrow quivered. He started to speak, but the words died as his horse lowered its head, exposing him to Two Coyotes' weapon.

Lone Hawk took advantage of the distraction by charging not Whitehair but the horses. At the same time, he grabbed his knife. He heard the discarded weapons hit the ground and then forced his attention, his entire being, on what he had to do.

Whitehair waited for him, thrusting his spear as Lone Hawk reached out to slice through the horse-rope. He feared the spear would strike his mare, but it missed. Had Whitehair deliberately avoided—

Up and down. Resistance and then nothing! He struggled to focus on what had just happened, but his mare had gone from standing to a hard run, and he was hard-pressed to remain on her. His knife had connected with the rope, but whether it had severed it or simply slid off it, he didn't know. Earlier he'd laid the rein over his mare's neck, but it slipped off. Just the same, he managed to slow and turn her with the pressure in his knees.

The foal that had been reprimanded for getting too far from its mother now pranced in a small, mindless circle. As other horses tried to avoid the unruly youngster, they became tangled in the rope holding them together. Whitehair tried to bring order to chaos by yanking on the lead, but when he did, the rope snapped.

Suddenly free, the horses looked about in confusion. The lead mare tried to back away, but she remained lashed to the others. Whitehair threw the useless rawhide at Lone Hawk.

"Go!" Lone Hawk ordered. "Leave!"

Twang!

Alarmed, Lone Hawk shot a look in Two Coyotes' direction; he'd released his second arrow. Like the first, this one found Pawnee flesh to feed on. Blood stained the pinto's chest.

"I did what I must!" Two Coyotes declared.

"Do you see?" he asked Whitehair. "Your companions are wounded. Do you want the same for yourself?"

Whether Whitehair understood didn't matter because the truth lay in what the other Pawnee were doing. Translator had been shot in the upper right arm, and it hung at his side, dark blood running along the embedded shaft. Thick Knees had managed to pull the arrow out of his side, but he'd slumped forward and looked in danger of falling.

"I do not want to kill you," Two Coyotes said. "Not today."

Whitehair's horse had a scar on his left shoulder, and the hairless strip stood out in contrast to the rest of the sweat-soaked hide. If Whitehair was afraid or felt sorrow because his companions had been wounded, his expression gave no hint. Looking calm and resigned, he returned Lone Hawk's gaze.

"This is all that remains of the horses you took." Lone Hawk indicated the useless rope. "Today they are not yours. I give you your life because . . ."

He was still searching for an explanation when Translator took hold of Thick Knee's horse and began leading it away. Whitehair watched the departing men for a few moments, then lowered his spear and started after them. When he looked back at Lone Hawk, Lone Hawk couldn't see his eyes, but the Pawnee's back remained straight.

WHEN NIGHTELK HELD out his arms, Sweet Grass Eater placed the bundle containing the four Sacred Arrows in them.

"I thank the spirits for this moment," Sweet Grass Eater said. His eyes were red-rimmed, his voice strong. "It is not for me to look inside your heart and know what has changed, but it is right that today these become yours to safeguard."

Although a few minutes ago he'd been so tired he hadn't been sure his legs would hold him, Nightelk felt stronger and more alert than since shooting the white calf.

"I do what I must." Slowly, undeniably, the arrows were becoming warmer. Still, he cradled them as a father cradles a newborn. "What is right for the Cheyenne."

Night had begun stalking over the land, but although he looked forward to the accompanying coolness, a great deal needed to be done before then. Just the same, he knew not to hurry this moment.

"I should have known the Pawnee would attack," Sweet Grass Eater continued. "I did not open myself to the truth in time because my heart was heavy. The seasons of my life are upon me these days, and I fear . . . I hate the dying of innocent children."

He looked around at the handful of old men grouped around them. "I never thought the weight of those seasons would change me, but if I do not face that truth, the Cheyenne will suffer—suffer more than they already have."

Today had been heat and pain, death and loss. But those things weren't Sweet Grass Eater's fault. Perhaps, Nightelk told himself, they weren't his either. Perhaps.

"The Pawnee did not take the arrows from us," he told the somber peace chiefs. "Yes, grief is all around us, and we mourn the end to a life just begun, but in that one thing we can be happy."

Sweet Grass Eater continued to express concern that his mental state had prevented him from knowing the Pawnee were going to attack, but as the other men reassured him that no one could see everything, Nightelk concentrated on the slight weight in his arms.

Not even the oldest Cheyenne had been born when Maiyun gave the four arrows to Sweet Medicine, so no one had seen them being made. Over the years they'd become fragile and whatever moisture might have once lived in the wood had been sucked out. Like bird bones, they needed to be protected and sheltered.

By him?

Usually the peace chiefs would talk until they fell asleep, but tonight other things came first. Cradling the blanket-wrapped arrows as if they were thin sheets of ice or a sleeping child, Nightelk made his way through the ragged camp to where his wife had placed their belongings. She said nothing as he laid the arrows alongside his weapons, but when, numb, he turned to leave, she blocked his way.

"How many?" she asked.

He sucked air deep but not deep enough into him. "Three."

"Three dead." She started to lift her head, then stared at the ground. "Who?"

Looking at and yet not seeing her dry, gray hair, he began. Smokes at Dawn had probably been the first casualty, followed by Red Water, whose body had been pierced by no fewer than five arrows. His brother Black Hairy Dog had been wounded at the same time and might not survive.

"And . . ." Exhaustion surged through him, wounding and aging. "Jumps Like Ants."

"No! That cannot be!"

"Her father—her father said she was near the horses when a Pawnee came for them. The Pawnee did not see her." He blinked. "Either that or the enemy did not care that a little girl stood in his way."

"She was only three!" Calf Woman clamped her hand over her mouth. "I do not want my sister to know this. If she hears that a child has died—"

"You cannot keep the truth from her. Where is she?"

Calf Woman pointed vaguely. "Afterward, when everything became quiet, she came to me, holding onto Knows No Fear so tight it must have hurt him. Then she walked away."

"She left Knows No Fear with you?"

Calf Woman nodded. "Perhaps she has gone looking for Follower."

"If she does, we may never see her again."

Her, Follower, and Jumps Like Ants.

CHAPTER 19

 Grey Bear stalked from one end of the camp to the other on legs that existed beyond his control. He couldn't control the way his heart hammered—or the hatred raging through him.

The sun had gone to its resting place, and the faint light that remained would soon disappear, but he still saw the fear, disbelief, and grief in his people's eyes. Jumps Like Ants' parents sat across from each other with their tiny daughter's body laid out between them. He stopped his pacing long enough to stare down at the inert blanket-draped mound, then stalked off again.

The land had shrunk! Either that or he'd grown larger than the largest buffalo. If he knew how to make it happen, he'd turn himself into Thunderbird so he could fly over the Pawnee and release lightning-arrows that would burn and burn until nothing except the stench of charred flesh remained.

"Grey Bear, wait!"

Barely able to contain himself, he waited for Two Coyotes to join him. "Where are you going?" Two Coyotes asked.

I do not know. "I heard"—with an effort, he kept his voice low—"about what Lone Hawk did not do."

"We have back our horses. He made that happen."

"Lone Hawk looked into a Pawnee's eyes, but did he kill him? No! Once again he let our enemy live."

"So did I." Two Coyotes kneaded his left thigh.

"Perhaps. And maybe they will die of their wounds."

"Maybe."

"Tell me, did Lone Hawk stand like a warrior or did he run?"

"Stop it."

"Stop? How can you say I have no right questioning what he did?"

Two Coyotes' sigh cut through the near night. "Today we turned from strength and became a people who may not live. What does the action of one man matter now?"

In a dim way Grey Bear knew Two Coyotes was right, but if he allowed his thoughts to settle over their future, he'd feel useless, frightened. It was easier to blame.

"If Lone Hawk had killed the Pawnee when we went after them before, if he had not warned them so they could escape, today would not have happened."

"It did. That is our truth."

Two Coyotes' words reminded him of drumbeats so he fought their impact in the only way he could, by whirling and striding away. Pulling air into his lungs hurt, and his head felt as if it had been trampled.

Several men had stationed themselves around the camp in case the Pawnee tried to return, and he'd be expected to join them. He wanted to be part of that armed force, to do something! But first he had to find a release for the energy that threatened to tear him apart.

With little thought to what he was doing, he made his way to where he'd last seen the Pawnee. From what he'd heard, the enemy had made off with three water bladders and at least four horses. Three water bladders weren't that many, he tried to tell himself. More than twice that many remained, and if the horses were given just enough to stay alive . . .

But eventually the water would be gone, and if he—*he*—hadn't found—

As the first star slipped into the sky, he dropped to his knees and buried his head in his hands. He was alone, safe from prying and knowing eyes. Trapped by something without words.

SEEKS FIRE ROLLED onto her back and stared upward. The night had felt endless, but finally, thankfully, it was over. Before much longer the sun would begin its cruel attack, but for these first few minutes she could pretend it was spring.

No, she couldn't, she admitted as she got to her feet. She wasn't sure whether Jumps Like Ants' parents had cried through the night; maybe she'd simply imagined she'd heard their sobs.

Someone had told her Lone Hawk and Two Coyotes had confronted the Pawnee who'd taken the horses responsible for the little girl's death. Although the Cheyenne men had gotten the horses back and wounded several thieves, they hadn't killed them.

Touches the Wind had insisted Lone Hawk and Two Coyotes couldn't have known what had happened to Jumps Like

Ants because they would have avenged her if they had, but she didn't care.

Although her stomach grumbled, she made no effort to find something to eat. What did her own needs matter in the face of the needs of children and pregnant women? Instead, she walked to the edge of the camp and looked out at the plains. She'd grown up accepting the endless sweeps of grass for what they were, her world, giver of what she and her people needed to survive, but this morning the vastness made her feel small and insignificant.

Her father and grandfather spoke of when the Cheyenne lived near mountains and great lakes where there were few buffalo but endless geese, ducks, fish, large deer, sheep, even handsome elk in addition to wild rice growing in the lakes. Winters there were harsh with much snow, but there'd never been a lack of water and families lived in houses made of elm and birch bark. If they hadn't been forced to leave by heavily armed Sioux, Assiniboin, and Cree, she'd have grown up surrounded by trees.

Unable to comprehend what that was like, she feared the endless nothing that trapped her as surely as trees and mountains could, prayed that Follower had somehow found shelter and sustenance in the nothing or was walking along *ekutsih-immiyo*, the road that leads the souls of the dead to the afterlife.

Sounds of activity alerted her to the fact that her people were getting up. Everyone would soon meet to decide what they needed to do—and take stock of what and who had been lost. Instead of joining them, she continued to stare at her surroundings. Walking Rabbit had wandered off yesterday, and from what she could tell, her sister-in-law was still gone. If this was any other time, Walking Rabbit would have never risked exposing herself to the Pawnee, but maybe she no longer cared what happened to her.

Maybe Follower had cried out to her in her mind and she'd had no choice but to search for that spirit-voice.

"I want to be with you," she whispered. "With you and your daughter, my niece. And yet . . ."

She stared down at her feet but couldn't think what she should tell them to do. The land was Mother; she'd grown up hearing and believing that. But this land, this cruel master, had taken Follower!

Not caring whether anyone saw, she crouched and slammed her fist against the ground. Pain shot through her arm; although she'd never thought she'd want to hurt Mother-Earth, she felt somewhat better.

By the time she joined the haggard Cheyenne gathering near where Sweet Grass Eater had spent the night, her hand had stopped stinging. With an effort, she tucked thoughts of Follower and Walking Rabbit against her breast and turned her attention to what was being said. Stands in Water had given birth, and mother and son were fine.

Sweet Grass Eater began by explaining that Nightelk had assumed responsibility for the Sacred Arrows.

"My heart is at peace because of what he has done," Sweet Grass Eater said. "But although I am ready for another, perhaps him, to speak with wisdom for all of us, that may not be possible. That is what this morning is about—to find the path we must walk."

Jumps Like Frogs' parents sat near Sweet Grass Eater. The little girl's mother had scratched her arms and legs because her daughter had been killed by the enemy while Calls Grouse expressed his grief by letting his hair flow instead of braiding it.

"I wish to say something," Calls Grouse said. "I am not the only one who has lost someone, but my grief will not let me think about them. I mourn because my daughter's life had just begun. I do not want to leave her here, alone. But I must."

Sensing movement, Seeks Fire reached out and drew Knows No Fear to her side. A few days ago, the boy wouldn't have wanted anyone to see the gesture, but so much had changed. If his mother didn't return—

"You are certain on this?" Nightelk asked Calls Grouse.

"My heart is so heavy I wonder if it may stop beating, but yes, we will do what we must."

"So be it." Nightelk glanced at Sweet Grass Eater, who nodded at him before stepping back so Nightelk now stood alone in the center.

"I am new to this path," he said. "Because I watched and learned from my elders, I know the wisdom of letting everyone speak their mind, but this is not a day for long debate; there is not enough water for that."

Knows No Fear straightened a little, but his still child-soft body remained pressed against Seeks Fire's.

"Today must be about finding water, nothing else."

What about Walking Rabbit? We can't—

"How?" someone asked, distracting Seeks Fire.

Nightelk's suggestion was simple. Men had to ride out, not just west in the direction Sweet Grass Eater believed the buffalo had gone, but everywhere except back toward the abandoned village. Because the Pawnee might still be around, no one should travel alone. At the same time, a number of warriors had to remain with the women and children to guard against attack.

Lone Hawk stepped forward. "The Pawnee are not our enemy today," he said when Nightelk acknowledged him. "After what happened yesterday, they will not return."

"What happened? What did you do to make the Pawnee fear us?"

Startled, it took Seeks Fire a moment to realize who'd spoken. Grey Bear, one side of his face painted black, stared at Lone Hawk. He'd armed himself with bow and arrows, a knife, even a spear.

"Do not listen to this man!" He jabbed a finger at Lone Hawk. "Two times now he has refused to shed Pawnee blood. Why? Why?"

"Grey Bear," Nightelk warned. "This is not the time for this."

"Yes, it is. It must be."

Although the peace chiefs muttered nervously and Nightelk positioned himself between Lone Hawk and Grey Bear, Grey Bear continued to glare at Lone Hawk.

"I *will* be listened to!" he insisted. "My ears will *not* accept what this one says and my heart is *not* fooled by his lies."

"Grey Bear, do not—" Nightelk started.

Before he could finish, Sweet Grass Eater grabbed Nightelk.

"This is my grandson," the old priest pointed out. "I say we will hear him."

Next to Seeks Fire, Knows No Fear stiffened. Warned by the boy's discomfort, she struggled to keep her own emotions under control.

"Sweet Grass Eater," Nightelk said. "I do not want to fault your words, but I fear that what your grandson says will tear the Cheyenne apart when we must walk as one."

Sweet Grass Eater started to nod. Then his gaze fixed on Grey Bear and he shrugged. "You speak with the wisdom of your years," he told Nightelk. "But my grandson is our future. He must be heard."

Was Grey Bear truly the future? This morning with death and loss all around her and fear in everyone's eyes, she didn't know. Nothing should matter except finding what they needed to survive, to guard against more Pawnee raids—and bury the dead and leave behind Follower, and Walking Rabbit if necessary.

"I look at Lone Hawk's heart," Grey Bear said, his somber tone tearing her free from questions of whether Walking Rabbit was still alive, "and I see a Pawnee heart."

Lone Hawk started toward Grey Bear, but Two Coyotes clamped his arm around his wrist.

"You stop him?" Grey Bear asked Two Coyotes. "Why?"

"I was there, remember," Two Coyotes pointed out. "I know what you are going to say, that because Lone Hawk did not cut the heart out of a Pawnee, he can no longer be called Cheyenne, but yesterday was not about revenge."

"Not revenge? How can—"

"It was about keeping our horses," Two Coyotes continued. "Which we did."

"Not all of them." Then, although everyone was looking at him, Grey Bear glanced her way. His features, half touched by sunlight, the rest hidden by the black paint, belonged to a stranger, and yet he'd told her he wanted to marry her.

"I do not say you and Lone Hawk should have recaptured all our horses," Grey Bear went on. "But this I believe: The Pawnee have no fear of us because he"—he again stabbed a finger at Lone Hawk—"because he has forgotten what it is to be a Cheyenne warrior."

Lone Hawk returned Grey Bear's stare. "I am Cheyenne," he said, his voice both calm and commanding. "I will never be anything else."

"Words do not change the truth," Grey Bear countered. "I look around me and see fear and desperation and grief on the faces of people who live in my heart. My heart bleeds because it did not have to be like this. We face death because *he* is a coward!"

Despite Seeks Fire's effort to keep what she was feeling from Knows No Fear, a spasm shook her. The boy squeezed her hand and got to his feet.

"I do not want to be here," he announced. "I want to lead my father's horses to food and water so his spirit will know I have not forgotten my responsibilities, but I cannot do that because there is no water."

Some of Grey Bear's anger seemed to slip out of him. "Your father will always be proud of you," he said.

"Will he if his horses die?"

A small sound like a sigh or maybe a strangled sob followed on the heels of Knows No Fear's words. It was followed by a low buzz of conversation.

"My son speaks with a man's wisdom," Walking Rabbit said. Looking haggard, she nevertheless held herself erect as she came to stand beside Knows No Fear. "My thoughts have become wild things, and I feel as if I will drown in them. Last night they would not let me sleep. My daughter . . ."

Tears filled her eyes and she looked about to collapse. Hurrying forward, Nightelk wrapped his arms around her. She didn't appear to notice but, after a moment, went on.

"I believed my daughter was calling me. It did not matter

if the Pawnee found me," Walking Rabbit went on. "But—but I was wrong."

"Do not do this to yourself," Nightelk cautioned.

"Do you think I want to say these words!" Eyes blazing through her tears, she pulled free and faced him as a mother deer faces a pack of wolves. "My heart—my heart bleeds! But although I do not know how this is possible, it continues to beat."

Nightelk started to reach for her again, then stopped.

"My daughter is not here," Walking Rabbit whispered. "There is no reason for me to stay. For any of us to."

Knows No Fear wrapped his arm around his mother, and they clung together, crying. Unable to remain a bystander, Seeks Fire got to her feet and stumbled toward them. Holding them as best she could, she stared up at Grey Bear.

"Please," she whispered. "Make her words your truth."

WHEN THE GATHERING broke up, Lone Hawk started after Walking Rabbit and Knows No Fear, but then Touches the Wind joined them, and he stopped. The other warriors were already gathering up their weapons or going after their horses. He was expected to join them, wanted to so no one would think he was hiding from Grey Bear's accusation. He'd only intended to tell Walking Rabbit not to lose hope—somehow.

No, tangled thoughts weren't what kept him where he was. If he approached her now, he'd have to acknowledge Touches the Wind as well, and she might see beyond his hollow words.

He was still staring at Touches the Wind when she slowed and turned toward him. He'd faced Grey Bear unflinchingly, but that had been a simple matter of believing he'd been right not to kill a Pawnee. Talking to her was different, harder in a way he barely understood.

Her eyes questioning, she joined him. "I thought you would be with the other men," she said softly.

"I will, soon."

"It is what you want?"

"It is what I must."

She nodded, then cocked her head and looked up at him. As a child, he'd sometimes wondered if there was anything his mother didn't know about him. Today, with Touches the Wind, it felt the same.

"You will ride alongside Grey Bear?" she asked. "Put your argument behind you and do what is expected?"

Because nothing, really, had changed, they'd continue to search for water where Sweet Grass Eater's dreams had told them to. He could, if riding alongside Grey Bear was impossible, join the men who chose to ride with the women and children, but that wasn't what he wanted to do.

"I will pray to Hawk," he told her. "Hawk guided me to the Pawnee; perhaps Hawk will also show me where to find water."

A gust of wind brought the smell of morning prairie to his nostrils. Touches the Wind must have smelled it too because her frown lessened.

"We should not be talking," she said. "My mother—" Catching herself, she rubbed her forehead. "My mother is dead. It is strange to no longer be a child but not yet a woman. I do not always know what I should say or do. One thing . . ." She turned her head so she looked into the wind and took a long, slow breath. "If I speak what is in my heart, you will not be angry?"

"What is in your heart?" he asked. He'd weathered Grey Bear's attack. Nothing she said could possibly cut that deep.

"I have been thinking about Hawk. When the wind calls as it does today, my thoughts ride on its currents. When that happens, I have little control over them but—"

"Touches the Wind, we do not know when we will be together again." *Maybe never.* "What is it?"

Her breasts rose and fell, rose and fell. "Hawk took you to the Pawnee, yes. But Hawk could not stop what happened yesterday."

For a brief, unguarded moment he thought he hated her, but how could he hate the truth? "No, He did not."

"Why? Have we angered the spirits? Walked a path we should not?"

"I do not know."

"I do not want children to die!" She reared back as if trying to escape her own words. "Children have always died, but it does not make the burying easier. If I could die in their place, I would."

In his mind he saw the way Walking Rabbit had looked when she'd returned from her search for her daughter. The image faded but was immediately replaced by one of Jumps Like Ants' too-small blanket wrapped body.

"Do you blame me for Jumps Like Ants' death?" he asked.

"Blame?"

"Maybe I should have avenged her. Shed Whitehair's blood."

"Whitehair?"

"A Pawnee." He couldn't bring himself to tell her that Whitehair was also responsible for Porcupine's death. "It does not matter to Grey Bear that I did not know about Jumps Like Ants when Whitehair and I faced each other. I begged Hawk to tell me whether I was wrong in what I did, but"—he shrugged—"he did not answer."

Her head still uplifted to catch the breeze, Touches the Wind pressed her fingertips to her temples and closed her eyes. "I am a woman. My body was made for creating life, not taking."

"Because of that, we walk paths that do not cross?"

"I do not know!" She increased the pressure on her temples.

"You do not wish me to ask that?"

For a moment she gave no indication she'd heard. Then she lowered her hands and fixed him with a level gaze. "I wish that when we talk to each other it is about other things, things of little consequence that make us laugh."

"And for there to have been no deaths?"

"And no deaths." She shook her head. "Do you still dream? Last night did you see men hunt for buffalo that are not there? Were their throats dry and their horses dying? And the wind—had the wind become everything?"

His first impulse was to tell her he'd been too exhausted for anything except sleep, but the lie wouldn't come. "It was different, yes. But no less unsettling."

"You tried to send it away?"

"Over and over again, but it refused to leave."

"Sometimes dreams are like that."

When she slid closer to him, everything except for her faded. In an unimportant way he realized that Seeks Fire had come into view.

"Grey Bear wants to marry her." Touches the Wind indicated Seeks Fire.

"Marry?"

"Not now, of course, but later after—after we have found a new place to live and our cooking pots are full."

"What—is it what she wants?"

She regarded him so intently that he was forced out of himself and his bombarding emotions. "You concern yourself with what a maiden wants?" she asked. "Perhaps you thought she would marry you."

Once, maybe, a lifetime ago. "No, no."

"Then what is it?"

"Grey Bear is . . ." He nearly called him a wild animal but stopped himself. "A warrior. Full of the need to fight, unafraid to kill."

"Yes, he is."

"Without gentleness in him."

She sighed, her breath a warm caress on his flesh. "Are you afraid for her?"

He'd never known a Cheyenne woman who was afraid of her husband. Although a man was expected to be fierce and brave, he left those things behind when the hunting and fighting was over. If a wife didn't like her husband's behavior, she placed his belongings outside her tepee and was done with him. But what if Seeks Fire married Grey Bear without knowing the full truth about him—because not even Grey Bear knew how much violence lived inside him?

"I—I am glad they will not marry for a long time." The

world and its weight pressed down around him; it was all he could do to brace himself against it.

"So am I."

"Why do you say that?"

"There is something in his eyes that . . ." Her words trailed off and she stiffened.

"What is it?"

"The men are ready to leave."

When he saw that they were mounted and either saying good-bye or already riding away, he couldn't believe he hadn't been aware of that before. Not sure what, if anything, he wanted to say to Touches the Wind, he started toward them.

"Wait!"

"What is it?" he asked without looking at her.

"Your dream. Tell me."

He did, his words without emotion. "Except for birds, the plains were empty. They were not hawks but buzzards, buzzards feeding on a single body. I do not know who that person was. Maybe me."

As THE MEN painted and otherwise prepared themselves, Nightelk had busied himself with securing the Sacred Arrows to his steadiest mare and watching his wife encourage Walking Rabbit to eat something. He'd told Walking Rabbit he wanted her to ride next to him, but although she agreed, not once did her eyes stop scanning her surroundings. He wondered how long she'd go on looking for her daughter and when she'd finally accept that Follower was dead.

Now Nightelk walked over to where Two Coyotes and Lone Hawk were talking to each other. Grey Bear stood nearby, surrounded by the youngest warriors, not looking at Lone Hawk or Two Coyotes.

"I wish I was going with you today," Nightelk said.

"I know you do." Two Coyotes inclined his head in Walking Rabbit's direction. "But she needs you. Everyone does."

If they knew what I did, they wouldn't. "What you are doing is more important."

Two Coyotes flashed him a smile that took him back to his son's childhood, or would have if Two Coyotes' eyes had carried his mouth's message.

"Do you believe in Sweet Grass Eater's wisdom?" Lone Hawk asked. "That we must still ride toward the setting sun?"

"I do not know." Nightelk struggled not to stare at Two Coyotes or ask himself if he'd ever see his son again. "I want to trust his dream; everyone does."

"Not all dreams speak the truth."

"No." He'd limited himself to a few sips of water so there'd be enough for the warriors and children, and his throat was dry. "They do not, but what else is there?"

"That is what Lone Hawk and I were talking about," Two Coyotes admitted. "To head anywhere else may be foolish, dangerous, and yet . . ."

Nightelk's thoughts fixed on the word "dangerous," and he checked to make sure the two men wore their medicine bundles. "Some believe the Pawnee are far away, that they will not again test our strength, but . . ."

"To believe that is foolish," Two Coyotes finished with another of his mouth-only smiles. "My father, I will be careful."

So long ago that the memory had dimmed, Nightelk had told his own father the same thing. At the time, he'd believed his father didn't trust him. Now he understood that love had been behind the words and hoped the time would come when Two Coyotes said the same to his own son.

"I know you will," he muttered.

Something brushed against his leg. Looking down, he saw Black Eyes. The dog hadn't come near him yesterday, and he didn't know where he'd been during the fight. He slowly extended his hand. Although Black Eyes didn't nuzzle his fingers, neither did he move away.

"Take him with you," he said. "Let his eyes become yours."

CHAPTER 20

After the great prophet Sweet Medicine died, a young man dreamed that he should organize the Cheyenne men in a way they'd never been before. He told his companions about the dream and chose four to go with him to the Sacred Arrows priest, but because the Arrows were the highest authority, nothing new could be done without permission of the man responsible for them. When the priest heard what the young man wanted to do, he refused to give his approval.

The next day at dawn, the priest noticed the young man standing at the top of a high hill, surrounded by every dog in camp. Realizing he'd been wrong, he gave approval for the new society. After four days of ceremony, costume making, and teaching, the fearless Dog Men came into being.

As Black Eyes trotted ahead of Lone Hawk and Two Coyotes, Lone Hawk contemplated the Dog Men, who were members of a band who lived many hard days' journey south of where he was today. As a boy, he'd dreamed of going to live with the Dog Men so everyone would think him among the bravest of the brave.

After yesterday's endless riding and searching, he had little interest in anything, in part because hunger and thirst gnawed at him. He'd taken those sharp teeth to bed with him last night as he and the others camped near a dry creek bed. He wasn't sure who'd spotted the creek, but although several said they hoped being near it would bring water-wisdom, it hadn't happened.

One long day behind them, but how many more? How many?

"Lone Hawk?"

With an effort, he shook himself free. Two Coyotes still had a mark on his cheek from where he'd slept using his hand to cradle his head and, like the others, hadn't bothered with fresh paint.

Two Coyotes glanced up at the newborn sun, acknowledging its power. If he feared that power, he didn't show it. "You called out during the night," he said.

"Did I?"

"You had a dream?"

As his companion had done, Lone Hawk turned his attention to the sun. A little night remained in the sky, but the sun would soon burn that away. Yesterday's hot wind had pushed past his flesh to heat his lungs. The breeze had died during the night, but he had little doubt it would soon be back. Although Two Coyotes had made the hard decision to withhold water from the horses, Lone Hawk suspected Grey Bear had given some to Legs Like Lightning because the stallion was the only horse not anxiously sniffing the air. Grey Bear's head moved constantly as he searched his surroundings, not that there was anything to see. Nothing except endless dead grass, ageless rocks, the vast horizon.

"Yes," Lone Hawk said. "A dream."

"The same as before or new?"

Lone Hawk sighed, then explained that last night's image had been a repeat of the one he'd had the night after the Pawnee attack. "I told myself it was nothing to try to make sense of. So much had happened that day; surely everyone saw dark, violent images."

"For it to visit you twice—you would be foolish to dismiss it."

"I do not." He closed his eyes, concentrating. "I do not know who the lone rider who came to me is; maybe me. When he first spots the buzzards, he wants to turn another way but something pulls him near them. When he can see into the buzzards' eyes, they hop away from what they have been feeding on and he sees—what remains of a Cheyenne warrior."

Two Coyotes was silent for a moment. Then: "Can the rider see the face of the dead man?"

"No."

"Lone Hawk?"

"What?"

"The next time, keep yourself in the dream. Look into those dead eyes so we will know who it is."

KNOWS NO FEAR had wanted to remain beside his mother, but once the band was under way, Walking Rabbit told him to spend the day with his friends. Once he was gone, instead of joining the other women, she gave her horse its head. At first it simply followed behind the rest of her family's horses, but after a while its nose led it over a rise and down a long, narrow depression. Her body moved in time with her mount's steady plodding. When she'd returned from her futile, nightlong search for her daughter, she'd told the tribe she accepted that Follower was in the hands of the gods. At that time, exhausted beyond grief, she'd believed her words, but her mother's heart continued to bleed and cry.

She couldn't remember when she'd become aware of Porcupine. Her girlfriends had gossiped endlessly about who'd catch the eye of the tall, handsome young man and had begged Seeks Fire to speak kindly of them to her brother. Although her parents would have been ashamed of her if she appeared too bold, she hadn't been able to stop thinking about him or trying to be where he was. After he'd announced his desire to marry her, he'd admitted he'd been aware of the attention the girls gave him but hadn't known what to do about it. He'd noticed her, not because of the care she'd given her appearance or because Seeks Fire had pointed her out to him but because he admired her ability to work from daylight to dark after a buffalo kill. She'd teased him that he only wanted a hard-working wife, but although that might have once been the case, they'd fallen in love.

Now Porcupine, who'd planted two seeds inside her and had carried her firewood and water for her while she was pregnant, was dead. She'd known that could happen and had kept a small part of her heart separate from him.

What she hadn't prepared herself for—what her mother's heart recoiled from—was why she was out here today.

Follower, you are my baby. You give warmth to my arms and a reason to laugh. I need you! Do you not understand, I need you!

The too-familiar sob clawed at her throat. Her head pounded, and her heart hurt. She wanted to hurtle a spear into her world and wound the cruel earth and air that had stolen her baby. And, in an insane way, she wished she'd never met Porcupine or slept with him or given birth to his children.

Realizing her horse had stopped walking and was trying to feed, she ground her heels into the mare's side. Before Porcupine's death, she'd had little use for this particular horse because, although the mare had seen five summers and had allowed stallions to mount her, she'd yet to become pregnant. If they needed to kill a horse for food, this one would be the first.

She wasn't sure why she'd chosen to ride her this morning—maybe because the mare had been closest. Now, for the first time, she became aware of the broad back and easy gait. Unlike many horses, this one's backbone wasn't so prominent that she felt compelled to wear a saddle. Also, unlike mares with foals, she hadn't grown scrawny since giving birth. Although she had a few scars and a small wound on her left flank, probably from being bitten by another horse, she was relatively free of fleas, and flies seldom clung to her belly.

Maybe, Walking Rabbit told Porcupine, *your son and I will not eat this one after all.*

Her son? What about her daughter?

In an effort to combat the hot wind, she continually blinked moisture into her eyes. Shielding them with a hand that shook, she probed her surroundings. Something had happened to her while she was assessing her mount's worth, either that or pain had so deeply wounded her that she'd separated herself from it to survive. Whatever the reason, she was both grateful and sad because she now felt nothing. The wind danced with the grasses, the rolling, waving movement beautiful. Often the horizon turned hazy as dust was thrown about, but her world looked clean and clear this morning, beautiful.

Although she couldn't see the tiny insects that lived near the earth, she heard their low, collective hum and recalled the booms and foot-stomping dances of male prairie chickens in spring. She caught a glimpse of movement on the ground to her left—a prairie dog or rabbit or mouse, proof that some creatures didn't care whether it ever rained again.

The two distant dots might be hawks or eagles. She had no doubt they were aware of her presence and felt comforted by the thought that their eyes shared the world with her. Then, as peace wove itself around her, something else invaded. Fighting to keep her mind in the nothing place it had gone to, she formed a mental image of a mosquito or bee. She'd been bitten or stung, that's all.

No, not all!

Nothingness had been warm, soft, slow. What now slapped and bit had sharp teeth. She flashed on an image of how her world had looked as smoke and flames consumed it, but that wasn't it. No fire? What then?

Stopping, her horse threw up her head. The solid body trembled, and she breathed in short, loud gasps.

"Easy, easy." Walking Rabbit tightened her grip on the rein and wrapped her fingers around the length of mane. Her leg muscles tensed.

Suddenly the mare screamed, high and harsh. At the same time, she flung her head as if trying to bite the sky, then, almost the same movement, she gathered herself and shot forward. Walking Rabbit leaned along the broad back and looked back as the panicked mare thundered across the plains.

Grizzly!

* * *

THIS MORNING NIGHTELK rode at the rear. When he'd gotten up, Calf Woman had asked if he intended to travel with Sweet Grass Eater, but he'd told her no. Sweet Grass Eater had the other peace chiefs to talk to, and he had no wish to hear endless opinions of what should be done to entice buffalo to show themselves.

"But where the buffalo are, so is water," Calf Woman had pointed out.

"I know," he'd snapped, then regretted his outburst; years of marriage had taught him that she knew how to examine his words for the truth about him. She'd given her opinion of Sweet Grass Eater's insistence that the young men continue to travel in the direction revealed by his dreams, and he'd wisely heard her out. When she started talking about Walking Rabbit, however, he'd found an excuse to leave.

The tall grass underfoot was alive with spiderwebs, but he missed the countless bobolinks and meadowlarks that once had filled the air with their song.

He hadn't seen Walking Rabbit today but that wasn't surprising. Knows No Fear, leading his mother's packhorses, had ridden with him for a while, but he hadn't been able to think of much to say, and before long the boy had left.

No one would question why he'd waited for everyone to pass before setting his own pace. Someone needed to remain at the rear to watch for the enemy, and who better than a seasoned warrior?

A warrior whose arrow had killed a white buffalo calf.

Should he go to Sweet Grass Eater and tell the priest what he'd done? Maybe the only way he'd find forgiveness was by riding off by himself, riding and riding and riding until his horse collapsed and they both died.

By his own reckoning, he was certain he'd asked himself that question more times than he had years of life, but that didn't mean he was any closer to an answer. When he looked for missing children or accepted responsibility for the Sacred Arrows, he almost forgot what rested on his shoulders, but the moments of forgetfulness didn't last long enough and when the truth returned . . .

Sighing, he tried to put his mind to how much longer the water might last. Everyone was rationing their supply, but even if certain horses and dogs went without any, it would all be gone in no more than three days. And then . . .

Dust kicked up by the hooves of the horses ahead of him coated his sweaty face, arms, and chest, adding to his discomfort. His horse complained with whistling breaths. He wanted to order her to be silent but knew it wouldn't do any good. Occasionally he studied those ahead of him, but they were far enough away that he couldn't identify them. Besides—

The sound of rapidly approaching hoofbeats sent a shock of alarm through him. Alert, he turned around, removed his bow from around his chest, and reached for an arrow. A rider came into view, the horse slowing as it approached.

"Walking Rabbit," he called out. "What is it? You—where have you been?"

She dismissed his question with an absent wave. Her eyes, which had been dim and dark lately, looked huge.

"A grizzly." She drew her sweating, gasping horse alongside his. "I saw a grizzly."

"Where?" he demanded. "Is it attacking?"

"No, no," she assured him. Then, her words rushing together, she told him she'd been out by herself when a bear had suddenly risen up from behind a rock. She hadn't waited to see if it intended to attack but had fled.

"I could not stop my horse," she admitted. She was still breathing rapidly but a little of the white had left her eyes. "I did not try." She chuckled briefly. "I—I do not know who was more afraid, my horse or me."

"Did the bear follow you?" Although her mare showed no inclination to do anything except stand on widespread legs with its head nearly on the ground, he took the rein.

"No. After I had gone a short distance, I looked behind me. I did not see anything. Maybe. Maybe—"

"Maybe what?"

Walking Rabbit straightened and sucked in a breath. When she looked at him, the full force of everything she'd been through lately slammed into him. "I was going to say that maybe I only imagined what I saw, but I did not." She patted the mare's neck. "She did too."

"It is over. You are all right."

"No," she whispered. "I am not."

He hadn't touched her since Porcupine had been wounded, but he couldn't stop himself now. Taking her hand, he placed her palm against his chest.

"I know," he said.

She blinked rapidly several times, but he saw no hint of tears and wondered if she had none left to shed.

"Nightelk? What if that grizzly found my daughter?"

Not giving himself time to think about what he was doing, he vaulted off his horse, reached up to place his hands around her waist, and drew her down to him. When he again looked into her eyes, he saw a small, hurt child.

"Listen to me. We are far from where we last saw Follower. She could not have walked all the way here."

"You—you do not know that."

"Yes, I do. When the life went out of my babies, I held them next to my heart and prayed that my strength would go into them. I was a warrior and knew that once life leaves a body, it does not return, but I was also a father."

She continued to stare up at him, but he couldn't tell whether she understood what he was saying. He wondered if she at least understood how terribly hard it was to speak.

"I did not know how I could go on living." His voice dropped to a whisper. "If I could have died so they would live, I would have ridden unarmed into a Pawnee camp or thrown myself in front of stampeding buffalo."

Even now, years after he'd buried his babies, the pain was as fresh and sharp as it had been then. Still, he believed she needed to hear this. And he needed her to know how terribly, terribly sorry he was.

"For a long time after, my children came to me in my dreams, sometimes even when I was awake and doing things they had been no part of. I heard their cries and laughter and felt the warmth of them. I prayed and prayed that they were safe, and although I knew they were happy living with their ancestors, I could not eat or sleep because I was fearful for them—wanted to protect them from Heammawihio."

"Heammawihio, High God? How can that be?"

"I was not myself," he said. "Grief had turned me into someone I did not know and could not control."

He thought she might not understand, but after a moment she nodded. "It is like that for me."

Pulling her against him, he offered his strength. "The grizzly you saw did not kill your daughter," he told her. "Whatever happened to her, it was not that."

"I—I know." Walking Rabbit shuddered, and he sensed her battle with tears. "I hurt." She moaned. "Hurt has become my world. I want it to stop!"

"It will, someday."

"You promise?"

"You want me to promise you spring and a return to what you once had, but I cannot do that. What I know, what I offer, is that the day will come when you can hold your pain in your hand and it no longer crushes you."

She didn't say anything, and Nightelk told himself she was taking his wisdom into her so it would become her strength. What he didn't say was that at least he'd had Calf Woman; she would have to bear her burden alone.

He wouldn't ask her to marry him again, not he whose sin was responsible for her grief, but she shouldn't be alone. She deserved a husband, a good and compassionate husband.

Like Two Coyotes? His son.

ALTHOUGH GREY BEAR'S determination hadn't once wavered throughout the long, blistering day, he'd sensed Legs Like Lightning's fatigue. He'd given his stallion water when there hadn't been enough, but Legs Like Lightning was part of him; how could he find buffalo without the stallion's strength?

That night he slept restlessly, and although he hated admitting it even to himself, fear lay beside him. He'd never been afraid of an enemy faced on a battlefield, but how does one attack nothing?

At dawn he walked away from the others and sat watching the world come to life. There was little tall grass or the fragile fringed orchid here. He missed the taller-than-he bluestem. His belly rumbled, but it was hardly the first time he'd been hungry, and he remained motionless; someone looking at him might think he'd fallen asleep, but he was thinking—going through his life to battles fought and won, successful hunting trips and some that hadn't been.

He'd told Seeks Fire he wanted to marry her because it was time for him to become a husband and father and she was the most beautiful maiden in the village. But that wouldn't happen until summer was over, until everyone's belly was full.

He stretched out his legs and stared at them, seeing dark flesh and hard muscles. His chest was scarred from the Sun Dance, and he had other scars but none on his legs. Slowly, almost hesitantly, he slid his hand under his right thigh and pushed upward. Many women and some of the old men were fat but only a little lay beneath his skin. With his free hand, he reached for the knife at his waist and placed the tip against the skin of his inner thigh.

"Erect Horns, hear me this morning!"

He closed his eyes to slits and went back in his mind to the time before his birth, when famine had come to the Cheyenne and the warrior Erect Horns had traveled to a sacred mountain near a great body of water to ask help of Maiyun and the Thunder Spirit. At Sacred Mountain, Erect Horns had been taught the Sun Dance and Maiyun had given him a sacred horned buffalo-skin hat.

As Erect Horns was leaving, Maiyun had said: *Follow my instructions accurately, and then, when you go forth from this mountain, the heavenly bodies will move. The roaring Thunder will awaken the sun, moon, and stars, and rain will bring forth fruits of all kinds, animals will come forth and follow you home. Take this horned cap to wear when you perform the ceremony, and you will control the buffalo and*

*all other animals. Put the cap on as you go from here and
the earth will bless you.*

There wasn't time for the ceremony, but the sacrifice necessary to gain favor of the great powers, yes!

Silent, Grey Bear shoved his knife into his thigh, not stopping until he'd skewered himself and driven the tip into the
ground.

"Maiyun! See what I have done! Touch my wet blood and
know my courage. Honor my sacrifice by giving my people
what they need to go on living."

ALTHOUGH GREY BEAR made no attempt to hide his wound,
no one mentioned it because a sacrifice, even one done to
benefit a great many people, was between a man and the
spirits. At first the puncture caused little discomfort, but as
the day wore on and Legs Like Lightning started to sweat,
sweat and horse hair resulted in so much pain that he fought
to keep it manageable. He did so by thinking of Seeks Fire
and the admiration he'd see in her eyes when she realized
what he'd done. When thoughts of her caused his penis to
pulse, he embraced his grandfather's wisdom.

By that evening there'd still been no sign of buffalo, but
the next morning Grey Bear again got up early and stood on
a boulder so Maiyun would have no trouble spotting him.
He started to touch his swollen and feverish leg, then thought
better of it.

"Are you not satisfied?" he asked. "I have not shed enough
blood? Do you need more proof of my bravery?"

As he waited, he spotted small dark spots hovering just
above the earth. Crows, maybe.

Crows traveled with the buffalo.

CHAPTER 21

Seeks Fire ignored the first growl. She paid no more attention to the answering yip and was only mildly surprised that the dogs had the energy. The lacing on her father's left moccasin had become loose, and she needed to thread new strips of leather through it, but the hours of walking had exhausted her. All she could think about was how glad she was that they'd stopped for the night. Although she'd recently had a sip, she couldn't get her mind off water. If only there was enough to wash up in!

An explosion of furious snarls brought her to her feet. Two dogs, both the color of dust, were fighting, neither slowed by the travois still strapped to them. She thought the dogs belonged to Long Chin, not that it mattered. Waving her father's moccasin over her head and yelling, she stomped toward them, but they ignored her. The smaller had clamped his teeth into the loose flesh under the other one's neck, but from what she could tell, he hadn't inflicted much damage. The larger dog jerked his head up and down in a futile attempt to break free. Each time he flung his head upward, the movement pulled the other off its feet.

"Stop it!" She struck the larger one's face with the moccasin. "Fighting will not put food in your bellies!"

Her logic made no impact. She might have left them to settle their argument themselves if she hadn't been worried they'd ruin the travois in the process. She considered Long Chin lazy, but she loved his daughter, and Touches the Wind had little enough in the way of possessions.

Afraid one of the dogs would grab her father's moccasin, she tossed it away and cast around for something else. At that moment, the travois strapped to the larger dog broke, scattering food preparation tools everywhere. Furious, she snatched one of the framing poles and wacked the dog in the side with it. Yipping, he tried to back away. The other dog, startled by the change in his enemy, let go of him and faced her.

"Do not threaten me!" she warned. "Show your teeth and I will pull out all your hair!"

Whether dogs understood what people said to them had always been a mystery to her. Perhaps these two were impressed by her tone—and maybe they'd simply forgotten what they'd been fighting about. Whatever it was, they both dropped to their bellies and stared up at her, panting.

"You are so foolish. Look what you have done." She indicated the carrying bags strewn about. "Do you know who will have to fix this? Not Long Chin. He will only complain. His daughter, the woman who feeds you, will say nothing against him, but she should."

The larger dog cocked his head as if considering that.

"All this work will fall on her shoulders," she continued. "On Touches the Wind whose mother has just died."

Dealing with the dogs had, for a few moments, taken her from what her life had become, but her words brought everything rushing back. Remnants of the long, unbearably hot day settled around her, and she dropped to her knees. Fortunately, she was out of the dogs' reach since both tried to lick her without getting to their feet.

"I am so tired," she whispered, taking comfort from the fact that the dogs would keep her secrets. "I miss my brother so, and whenever I think of Follower I—"

Her world blurred and with that, she lost touch with today and those that had come before it. If she put her mind to it, she could remember how long it had been since they'd gotten under way, but it didn't matter.

"I do not want to die, but if I must, I do not want it to take a long time," she admitted. "If that is a coward's way, so be it. What purpose would be served by slowly starving, by having nothing to drink? If that is our end, I want it to come now, not days and days—"

A current seemed to be rippling through the camp, but there'd been no lightning today so that wasn't it. Grateful for the distraction, she forced herself to stand. Her knees itched from being on the ground and she absently rubbed them.

Someone was coming.

THE HUNTERS HAD found three yearling buffalo around a small, muddy pool. Because the horses were too weary to follow it, one buffalo had escaped, but they'd killed the other two. By the time they'd prepared the carcasses for travel, the mud had settled, and they'd filled their bladders. Returning had taken an entire day.

"Maiyun revealed the buffalo to me," Grey Bear boasted once everyone had gathered around. Although his leg was stiff and sore, he took care not to let anyone know. He looked into one face after another and threw back his shoulders to emphasize his broad chest.

"It is not for me to know what is in Maiyun's heart, but when I cut the heart out of the buffalo I had killed, its warmth and strength went into me." He shot Lone Hawk a glare, daring him to mention that it had taken both their arrows to bring down the animal, but Lone Hawk only returned his stare.

"Grandfather, Maiyun sent your buffalo-dream to you."

Sweet Grass Eater, who no longer looked as bowed down as he had after his tepee burned, nodded. "Maiyun has blessed us. Our time of being tested is over."

As Lone Hawk continued to study him, Two Coyotes stepped forward. "Tonight is a time for celebration, yes," Nightelk's son said. "But we are wrong to think that two small buffalo and a little more water means summer is done with us."

"Maiyun walks beside me," Grey Bear said. "He will do so as long as he sees that I am fearless and a great hunter. I make this promise." He held up the pipe his grandfather had just handed him. "I will provide for my people. As long as life is in me, I will do that."

No one called him boastful, and surely that wasn't doubt he saw in his grandfather's eyes. After cutting the heart out of the buffalo, he'd smeared its blood over his legs. Much of it had flaked off, but he could still feel it. Believe in its strength.

"I am Grey Bear." He spotted Seeks Fire flanked by Touches the Wind and Walking Rabbit. "Warrior and fighter. Hunter. Tonight we eat and drink. Tomorrow—" He paused until he was sure he had everyone's attention. "Tomorrow the Pawnee will feel my strength."

"What do you mean?" Lone Hawk asked.

"Pawnee stole from us. Like coyotes and buzzards, they attacked when we were vulnerable. That cannot be! They must pay!"

"No!"

He scanned the crowd, certain someone would warn Lone Hawk not to bring disharmony to the tribe, but no one did. Although he'd been raised to never lift a weapon against another Cheyenne, he couldn't let Lone Hawk continue to defy him.

"What would you have happen?" he taunted. "For Pawnee to call Cheyenne belly-slinking dogs?"

"You and I have spoken about this," Lone Hawk returned in his maddingly calm tone. "I will say the same words I did before: Before anything else, we must have food and water, a place to live where our horses can find enough grass."

"A safe place? There can be none as long as the Pawnee see us as a wolf sees newborn fawns, vulnerable and helpless."

Lone Hawk closed his eyes and folded his arms over his chest. "The Pawnee who attacked were not wolves. Desperation made them do what they did."

"They killed a child. Stole our horses and water."

"My grandson is right," Sweet Grass Eater said. "If Pawnee believe there is no punishment, they will return."

One after another, the tribe's young men echoed Sweet

Grass Eater's sentiment. In contrast, the peace chiefs pointed out that punishment and revenge must wait until they'd found a new home, not that Grey Bear had expected it to be different. It had always been the way of old men to walk softly and think of caution, but they no longer risked their lives defending their people, and they should step aside and leave the decision of whether to fight to those who did.

"I have listened long enough," he said at last. "These are the years of my youth. I am strong today. Maiyun and Heammawihio ride with me and fill me with courage today. Was it only an accident that I found the buffalo? No! Has luck kept me alive? No! This has."

He clenched his fist and lifted his arm over his head. "Our enemies know and fear me and those who ride with me. The foolish Pawnee have forgotten their fear. That is why they attacked women and children, killed and destroyed and stole. I will punish them for that—alone if I must."

"When?" Lone Hawk asked. "Now?"

"Yes!"

"Even though there is not enough water and the meat will last only a short while?"

Fear lapped at Grey Bear, but he turned his back on it. "The Pawnee have our water. I will take it back."

"They did not take that much. It is gone now."

"Then they will pay for that! What about the horses they stole?" he challenged. "Do they mean nothing to you? You hand them over to our enemies without demanding anything in return?"

"Do not speak my words for me, Grey Bear. Or think you know what is in my heart."

A ripple of unease washed over the assembled Cheyenne, distracting Grey Bear. As far as he knew, Seeks Fire hadn't once taken her eyes off him. Surely she believed him the bravest of the brave.

"What lives inside you is not my concern," he said. "Tomorrow I will make my preparations to find and punish the Pawnee—to take back what belongs to us. Those who believe as I do can ride with me. The others"—he deliberately fixed his gaze on Lone Hawk—"can stay here and eat the meat I provided."

"LONE HAWK?"

Recognizing Touches the Wind's voice, Lone Hawk stood in the dark, waiting.

"I must talk to you."

She was like a small owl whose flight is silent until it wishes to make its presence known. A fire had been built so the women could roast some meat, but only a few coals remained to cast a quiet light over those closest to it. The rest of the camp was blanketed in black, as was she.

"You are all right?" he asked. "At peace with your mother's death?"

"At peace? Yes, I think I am. Life did not give her much laughter, and she was often in pain."

"What about Little Bird?"

"She mourns her mother, but from infancy she reached for me when she needed to be held, and having her around gives my days purpose."

"I am glad."

A sigh light as a feather floated over him. Although he couldn't see her, her presence was everywhere.

"I did not know I was going to tell you that," she admitted. "It is one thing for a woman to share what is inside her with another woman, but for me to say to you I could not love my sister more if she was my daughter—do you and Grey Bear hate each other?"

"Not hate." He spoke slowly as he waded through his emotions. "We are very different men. And those differences touch everyone."

"Yes, they do. Much of what Grey Bear says is wise. We will suffer if the Pawnee or others believe we have become frightened deer, but in some ways we are."

Instead of prompting her to explain, he waited.

"Deer who have nowhere to live and only a little to feed on. My sister's life means more to me than anything else. I want her to have water and food, a tepee to sleep in. All women feel that way."

When had he stopped thinking of her as a maiden? Maybe at the same time she had. "Grey Bear and many of those who ride with him believe I have become a woman because I say the time is not right for revenge," he told her.

She sighed. "I cannot say which way is right. Mine is a woman's heart. But you are a warrior. You fight and hunt. Only a man can do those things."

He'd never doubted his right to take his place with the tribe's men, but hearing her say that filled him with new resolve.

"It is a man's way to do what he wishes, either alone or with those who want to join him. Grey Bear will ride against the Pawnee, taking with him others who do not care what made the Pawnee act as they did, just that they must be punished. I have said everything I am going to say and will not try to stop them."

"Will you ride with them?"

"I do not know."

"No," she whispered. "I believe you do."

"You can see inside me?"

"You are a Cheyenne man. You cannot remain here while others risk their lives." She slid a little closer, her presence both a blanket and unseen lightning. "It is the same for me. Because I am a Cheyenne woman, I have become my sister's mother."

LULLED BY HER mother's droning voice, Seeks Fire was nearly asleep when she heard a horse approaching. Her belly ached from the amount she'd eaten, and although she'd hated the argument between Lone Hawk and Grey Bear, she'd contributed little as her parents later debated which man had spoken with the most wisdom. The moon had been slow to waken tonight, but it now revealed their visitor.

"Grey Bear," her father said as the warrior dismounted. "It is good to see you."

Because they slept in the open, her father couldn't formally invite their visitor to sit in the guest place. Just the same, he made a show of indicating the spot on his left that was the place of honor.

Grey Bear settled himself after ground-tying Legs Like Lightning a few feet away. Even in the dim light, Seeks Fire saw he'd painted sun symbols on both Legs Like Lightning and himself. In addition, eagle feathers had been woven into mane and tail. As always, the stallion held his head high and alert. Her heart skipped a beat.

"I have thought much on this," Grey Bear said after her father had lit his pipe and passed it to his guest. "I have long known I should take a wife, but I wanted the choice to be a wise one, one that will benefit the Cheyenne."

Seeks Fire swallowed and her hands began to shake.

"Your daughter's modesty is legendary. She has never done anything to bring shame to her parents, but that is not all."

Without looking at her mother, Seeks Fire knew she'd leaned forward and was concentrating on Grey Bear's every word.

"There is no maiden more beautiful. Gentle and accomplished in women's skills, she proved her bravery during the fire."

"She loves her niece and nephew," her father said. "I knew she would do everything she could to try to find them."

"She did. Many men would like to marry your daughter," Grey Bear continued. "But many are afraid to ask."

"I know." Her father chuckled. "Because I am rich."

Grey Bear inhaled deeply and then released the smoke in a long, thin stream. "So is my family. My wealth is beyond numbers of blankets and the size of my tepee. To the woman I make my wife, I offer courage and strength, success in hunting and fighting skill."

"I would never say different," her father admitted, "but a man who seeks a wife must pay for her. You want my daughter; what do you give for her?"

"A new saddle I will pay Rich in Hides to cover with bird

and animal designs, buffalo-bone dice my grandfather has blessed, a slate pipe with eagle heads carved into it and a soft fur bag to carry it in, seven horses."

"I have many horses."

"You do not have Legs Like Lightning."

"Your stallion is part of the bride price?"

Nodding, Grey Bear glanced at the dark animal. "He has already spilled his seed inside my family's mares and is proven. When Seeks Fire becomes my wife, he will mount yours."

Although discussions of a family's wealth or poverty had always been freely discussed, this conversation made Seeks Fire uncomfortable. It was almost as if the two men considered her one of her father's possessions.

Grey Bear's offer of Legs Like Lightning didn't mean he'd relinquish ownership of the magnificent stallion. Once Grey Bear became part of her family, everything her family possessed would be his as well.

She needed to see her mother's reaction but didn't want to call attention to herself. Besides, it was too dark to see anyone's expression. She thought Legs Like Lightning might grow bored, but the well-trained fighting horse remained where his master had left him. Would Grey Bear help her onto the stallion's back, let her experience his great speed?

Her father and Grey Bear were still talking. Maybe her father had brought up Grey Bear's bravery, because the younger man had positioned his arms as if preparing to release a tautly held arrow.

"Maiyun stood beside me and guided my weapon," he said. "Others fired upon the buffalo, but *my* arrow pierced its heart. It ran only a little distance before dying."

Her father nodded. "Because of you, tonight our bellies are full, and when you attack the Pawnee, they will shrink in fear."

A few minutes ago her father had admitted he had concerns about the timing for seeking revenge. Now, it seemed, he walked with Grey Bear. Seeks Fire wasn't sure how she felt about that.

"They will do more than run from me." Grey Bear threw back his shoulders and held his breath to expand his chest. "At my hands they will die."

"Good!"

Seeks Fire's mother started, but although she had an opinion about everything, for once she said nothing. Seeks Fire had no doubt that her mother wanted her to do the same.

Again she struggled to keep up with the conversation. "A man who kills a Cheyenne child cannot be allowed to live," Grey Bear insisted. "I, a Cheyenne warrior, vow before Heammawihio that Pawnee blood will flow so Jumps Like Ants can go to the afterlife knowing her death has been avenged."

"It was an accident," she offered. "The Pawnee did not see Jumps Like Ants, did not know the horses ran over her."

"Horses he stole! I spit on that man and everyone he has ever ridden with or calls him a relative."

"But to punish many for the act of a single man—"

"If I do not, more Cheyenne children will die."

Overwhelmed, Seeks Fire fell silent. The thought of mourning another child was almost more than she could bear, and yet some of the Pawnee Grey Bear wanted to kill had to be fathers. Their children would cry and grieve. And— and surely the Pawnee who'd survived Grey Bear's killing would vow revenge.

Maybe it would never end.

BY THE NEXT morning, word of Grey Bear's marriage proposal had spread throughout the camp. If Seeks Fire accepted the proposal, which everyone believed she would, the marriage would take place as soon as a new home had been found. In the meantime, the women debated what she'd wear when she mounted her handsomest horse and rode with her friends and family around her to where Grey Bear waited. The women, glad for the distraction, had already begun considering what gifts of dresses, shawls, rings, bracelets, leggings, and moccasins they'd present and who would braid her hair and paint red dots on her cheeks for her first night as a wife.

Nightelk listened with half an ear as Calf Woman and her friends debated how large a tepee the young couple would have and how soon they'd fill it with babies. He wished Grey Bear had waited to announce his intentions because his mind should be on how he intended to find the Pawnee and what he and his companions would do once they had, not baby-making.

Whether his son went with Grey Bear was Two Coyotes' decision. Just the same, when Nightelk saw Two Coyotes checking his horses' hooves and eyes, he couldn't remain silent.

"Has Grey Bear said how he hopes to find the Pawnee?" he asked.

"He plans to consult with Sweet Grass Eater; perhaps he has already done so since he says he wants to leave before nightfall."

"You heard Lone Hawk's caution. Surely you believe his words carry wisdom."

"I do. In fact—" Two Coyotes looked around, assuring himself that they were alone. "When the men met, I spoke of the need for all of us to travel together, the dwindling water, but Grey Bear and several others spoke of Jumps Like Ants, and Sweet Grass Eater said her soul can find no peace until she has been avenged."

"When Sweet Grass Eater looks at his grandson, he sees what he was as a young man. He wants to live that life again, through Grey Bear."

"What he was, or what he wishes he had been," Two Coyotes said.

After acknowledging his son's wisdom, Nightelk watched as Two Coyotes ran his fingers up and down a rangy mare's legs. He'd heard that Lone Hawk had offered to lend his keen eyes and sharp ears to the journey for reasons known only to that man and wondered if Two Coyotes would have to mediate between Lone Hawk and Grey Bear. He wanted to pass on the wisdom of his years so Two Coyotes would know what to say and do, but his son was no longer a child.

"Grey Bear may believe his grandfather can point him where he needs to go or that the spirits will guide his steps, but that may not be enough," he said.

"No, it may not. You will not go with us?"

Nightelk shook his head. "This is a journey for young men."

"Men who could use your wisdom."

Filled with love, Nightelk placed his hand on Two Coyotes' shoulder. Too late he asked himself whether his touch would bring bad luck to his son.

Only much later did he remember that he hadn't asked Two Coyotes whether he had any feelings for Walking Rabbit. Now he could only pray he'd return so he could.

CHAPTER 22

They found the Pawnee camped at the edge of a long, narrow gully covered with old deer and buffalo tracks. As was their custom, the Pawnee had positioned two men at each end of the camp to act as sentries, but on this moon-bathed night, the sentries looked half asleep, not surprising since they probably hadn't seen any living creatures larger than a rabbit for several days. Just the same, as he slowly skirted the enemy, Lone Hawk searched the ground for anything that might cause a noise and give away his presence.

Fully alert, he took note of the sleeping and nearly sleeping men. Scouting the area had taken longer than he'd hoped, but he now knew there were eleven Pawnee and an equal number of horses. They had few belongings beyond the weapons a hunting party needed. Each man slept on a hide bed, but in deference to the heat, they'd placed nothing on top of themselves. They kept their bows, arrow, and spears within reach.

Seven Cheyenne had accepted Grey Bear's challenge to find the Pawnee who'd attacked and stolen—and killed. Although Grey Bear had been disappointed in the limited amount of food they'd been able to take with them, it was probably more than the Pawnee had. In an unguarded moment, he pondered why Cheyenne or Pawnee would care what the other did during this summer of want, but then he thought of Jumps Like Ants and the violent end to her hopping, happy ways and how close people he loved had come to dying from thirst because of the Pawnee. Still . . .

An owl hooted, long, low, and mournful, only no night bird had made that sound. After a moment he answered with a single note of his own. One of the sentries lifted his head and looked around before slumping forward again.

When Grey Bear joined him, a silent shadow in a shadow world, Lone Hawk indicated the dozing Pawnee. Grey Bear nodded and then pointed to another sentry.

"I will take him," Grey Bear mouthed. "This one is yours." *Yours to kill.*

Grey Bear left before Lone Hawk's thoughts stopped echoing. Alone again, he cast around for a glimpse of the man he'd traveled for two days and nights to find. Whitehair had caused Jumps Like Ants' death, but all Pawnee were linked together in the same way he was linked to his people.

A Cheyenne child had died at Pawnee hands. He was a Cheyenne man, responsible for giving that child's soul peace and avenging her death.

But it was more than that, emotion woven so tightly into his relentless dreams that he wondered if he'd ever be free.

After shifting his grip on his knife, he inched, snakelike, toward the sentry. Although he couldn't see Grey Bear, he knew he was doing the same thing.

Jumps Like Ants would never become a woman, a mother! Whitehair, a Pawnee, had killed her!

Launching himself at the unsuspecting sentry, he drove his body into him. His forward movement smashed the Pawnee's face into the ground. Despite that, the man managed to turn his head. Ordering himself not to think, to be, Lone Hawk slid his knife under the vulnerable neck and upward until he met resistance. *Resistance. Life.*

Bellowing, the Pawnee wrenched himself onto his side and lashed out, his forearm and elbow catching Lone Hawk in the chest.

Grey Bear was still thirty feet from his Pawnee when the cry brought the man to his feet. With no more thought to hiding, Grey Bear stood and faced his foe; the sound that burst from his throat was more growl than shout. The Pawnee had been using his spear to lean against. Now it was aimed at Grey Bear's chest.

The Pawnee, straining to make sense of what was happening, looked off balance. He was shorter than Grey Bear, but his shoulders were broad and his legs thick. And there was that spear.

Knowing little except he wouldn't allow himself to die tonight, Grey Bear circled, keeping out of the spear's reach. He was still looking for an opening when the Pawnee yelled loud enough to summon the others.

Pushing off, Grey Bear exploded. Taken by surprise, the Pawnee barely had time to reaim his spear before Grey Bear's knife sliced into the underside of the hand holding it. The Pawnee cried out, stabbed. Ready for him, Grey Bear ducked out of the way. He sensed movement everywhere.

No longer an attacking dog, Grey Bear became a deer surrounded by wolves as three Pawnee rushed to help their fellow hunter. In the moonlight, he couldn't be sure whether they were armed.

Help! The cry pressed against his clenched teeth, but he wouldn't, couldn't let it escape. Praying the warriors who'd agree to let him and Lone Hawk slip into camp and disarm the guards understood they'd lost the element of surprise, he assessed his attackers. The newcomers were still pulling themselves out of sleep which meant the spear-man constituted the greatest danger.

"Have I wounded you?" Grey Bear taunted. Never still,

he studied the spear-man's movements and learned from them. "Hurt you and stripped strength from you?"

Blood oozed from the man's hand, but his grip didn't slacken. Even more telling, the other three Pawnee slowly, cautiously approached. One stood near the spear-man, but the others had spread out and now came at him from both sides. Grey Bear shifted his weight. As he did, the still-healing thigh wound protested, forcing him to stumble.

The man next to the spear-man sprang forward. Too late Grey Bear saw he held a club. Although he ducked, the club caught him on his left temple. His vision blurred, and he couldn't feel his legs. A moment later something slammed into him and knocked him to his knees. Bodies were everywhere. A hand tried to grab his knife-arm, but he yanked free and propelled himself at the new attacker. He thought his knife struck flesh, but even if he'd killed that man, there were still three others.

Wolves circled trapped deer, their teeth tearing into tendons, crippling the panicked animal.

"No!"

He was back on his feet without knowing how he'd accomplished that. His world was still consumed by Pawnee, but at least—

Night was for sneaking up on the enemy, but it had become *his* enemy. Fighting the shadows, Grey Bear struggled to learn everything he needed to stay alive. Because he'd twisted and turned avoiding the spear and club, he was no longer certain where he and Lone Hawk had left the others. The first shout had come from where he'd last seen Lone Hawk. If he was dead . . .

It didn't matter, not now!

A figure stepped toward him, feet dragging along the ground and hunched over as if trying to protect chest and belly. Thinking the others would take advantage of the distraction, Grey Bear was torn between the desire to stand and fight and the need, the primitive and unthinking need to run.

In the end, he stood where he was and watched the slowly approaching figure. Seeking to surround him, the man's companions spread out. And the other Pawnee—where were they?

Grandfather, if I die before you, so be it.

Movement to his left distracted him from what might be his death-prayer. Spinning in that direction, he sent strength into his arms and legs and fought dizziness. His vision was still clearing when he sensed another presence, this time on his right.

One of the men said something. If he'd been able to concentrate, he might have understood the words, but he felt fragmented. During a buffalo hunt, he concentrated on a single animal and made it his prey, but these men weren't stupid, frightened beasts.

"Grandfather, tell me—"

Something flew through the air at him. He ducked and it sailed past. He instantly righted himself, but as he did, a fresh stab of pain shot through his wounded thigh, forced him to stop.

They were all around now—one behind him, one in front, the others on either side. No matter which way he turned, he couldn't see all of them. They came closer in a strange, disjoined dance. He couldn't run.

Run?

Sudden fury replaced indecision. Snarling, he launched himself at the man ahead of him. They were too far apart, distance giving the Pawnee enough time to dodge. As Grey Bear pounded past, the man struck him on the side of the head—counted coup on him!

"No!"

Fighting his thigh, Grey Bear whirled and came at the man he hated as he'd never hated before. This time the enemy wasn't quick enough, and his knife found a home, buried itself in all-too-yielding flesh.

The Pawnee's squeal reminded him of a squalling bear cub. Blood pooled up around the knife wound as he continued to press down. He felt his enemy give way, struggle to keep his footing, lose the battle.

Slowly, almost gracefully, the Pawnee slid to the ground.

As he did, he reached for Grey Bear and his nails left thin lines of scratches. The smell of blood filled Grey Bear's nostrils; a moment later that scent was joined by the stench of half-digested food.

"You eat my knife, do you?" he taunted. "How can you say you have counted coup on me when I have killed you?"

Too late he remembered the other men. They came at him in a rush, but although they got in each other's way, they managed to drive him back down to the earth. His momentary triumph forgotten, Grey Bear slashed and slashed again until weight piled around and on him and he couldn't move.

"Help!"

Galvanized by the words he never believed he'd say, Grey Bear forced himself to wait until a face came close. Rearing up, he clamped his teeth around a long, sharp nose. Screaming, the Pawnee struggled to pull free, but he refused to let go. The others were still trying to overwhelm him, but the anguished howl distracted them; as it went on and on, they slipped back to watch.

Help! he cried again, silent this time because he could no longer speak. The Pawnee he was biting began pummeling him about the face. Several blows struck others who'd gotten too close, but maybe he couldn't make himself stop, couldn't think beyond this agony. The three who'd helped take Grey Bear to ground had finally made sense of what was happening. In the wordless way of those who'd spent their lives together, they now worked together to render their foe helpless. One grabbed his hair and forced his head back. Another wrapped his fingers around his throat and squeezed. Deprived of oxygen, Grey Bear's movements became disorganized. He let go of the man's nose.

The injured man staggered to his feet. Holding onto his bleeding, throbbing nose, he tried to kick his tormentor but struck the man trying to choke Grey Bear. The choker hollered a protest.

The world slid away, leaving Grey Bear alone in a pain-filled and formless place. Nothing mattered except getting air into his lungs—not the pounding in his head, not the powerful forces anchoring him to the ground, not even the flickering images of his grandfather. He was dying, dying slowly. He hated and feared the dying, wanted to cry and sob and cling to his mother's breast.

Most of all he needed to breathe.

ALTHOUGH HE MIGHT never fully comprehend how, Lone Hawk had managed to keep his hold on his knife. As a result, even with the pain in his chest, he'd slashed the Pawnee's throat. Surprised because his intention had been to simply disarm the sentry, he'd watched as the man tried to stem the flow of blood. At length, he had focused his attention on him. They were staring at each other when Lone Hawk realized their struggle hadn't been a silent one. The Pawnee were awake.

Fortunately, the waiting Cheyenne had sensed what was happening and had rushed forward to grab horses while the Pawnee were still confused. The man he'd wounded presented no immediate danger; besides, it wasn't Whitehair. Lone Hawk took in his surroundings. Sounds told him a struggle was taking place where the other sentry had been stationed.

If Grey Bear was in trouble . . .

Making his way in the dark took a long time. Finally, though, the stars revealed the truth.

Several Pawnee were running after the horses now back in Cheyenne hands. Lone Hawk comforted himself with that thought, then accepted that he couldn't call on his companions to help him rescue Grey Bear.

"Heammawihio, I kill to save a life!"

His bow twanged and his arrow flew. As it struck one of the Pawnee crouched over Grey Bear in the back, the man jerked and spun around. Surprised, the other Pawnee stared at their companion. Open-mouthed, the wounded man stared into the dark.

Again Lone Hawk withdrew an arrow. His second victim's cry was a twin of the first, but because the arrow struck the

Pawnee's breastbone, it didn't penetrate as far as the first had. Screaming, the Pawnee yanked it out and flung it from him. To Lone Hawk's surprise, he then cupped his hand over his nose.

"Grey Bear!"

Instead of rushing Lone Hawk, two Pawnee gathered around the one with an arrow in his back, their voices a torrent of sound. Horses snorted and stomped. Lone Hawk noted another figure nearby; this one twitched one way and then the other. The man moaned.

"Lone Hawk? Grey Bear? Where are you?" Two Coyotes called.

"Here." Unwilling to risk taking his eyes off the Pawnee, he answered without looking around for Two Coyotes. Grey Bear's attackers stared in the direction the voice had come from. At the same time, the hoof sounds became organized.

The Pawnee who was maybe dying continued his broken dance. Grey Bear sat up.

"What is it?" Lone Hawk demanded. "What have they done to you?"

Instead of answering, Grey Bear scooted around until he was on his hands and knees. Lone Hawk thought he'd get to his feet; instead, he remained like a dog, his head low and his breathing tortured.

A whisper of movement from the nearest Pawnee distracted Lone Hawk. The one with his arrow in his back staggered forward a few feet, then stopped. When he turned toward one of his companions, the other man clutched his arm. Someone shouted in Pawnee. Lone Hawk understood two words: "horses" and "Cheyenne."

"We take your horses!" His gaze never wavering from the three Pawnee, he repeated his taunt. Then he pointed at the now-motionless figure. "Take my words into you," Lone Hawk continued. Whether they understood didn't concern him; he needed to say this.

"Make my words part of you for as long as you live. One of you, a warrior whose hair has been touched with snow, killed a Cheyenne girl. Tonight is our revenge. A Pawnee life in exchange for hers. And horses to replace those Whitehair and others stole."

Grey Bear rocked back and pushed himself to his feet. The Pawnee stared at him, but before they could do more than that, whoever had warned that Cheyenne were taking horses shouted again. The one Lone Hawk had shot in the chest continued to cup his hand over his nose; the one with an arrow in him gave no indication he cared what was happening. The others, however, started running in the direction of the horses. Night swallowed them, and a moment later, Two Coyotes emerged from the shadows. He ignored the wounded Pawnee.

"We must leave, now! Grey Bear—"

"I—hear."

That small, strangled squeak couldn't belong to Grey Bear, could it? On the verge of again asking if he was all right, Lone Hawk turned his attention to what Two Coyotes was saying. Several Pawnee weren't in any condition to fight and one might be dead, but the rest were still dangerous.

"We *must* leave," Lone Hawk told Grey Bear.

"No." Grey Bear rubbed his throat and tried again. "Whitehair—"

"We have not seen him," Two Coyotes replied. "Besides, it is too dangerous."

Danger? Danger wasn't being able to breathe and his head threatening to explode and waiting for the Pawnee to kill him. Grey Bear's vision remained blurred, but his ears told him what he needed to know. If Whitehair was here tonight, he'd be with the horses.

Not caring what, if anything, Lone Hawk and Two Coyotes did, he ran in that direction. His wounded thigh cramped, sending shockwaves of pain into his groin; he stumbled.

Help me.

Heat flowed through him. Refusing to recoil, he gave himself up to the sensation, let it surround him, became that heat. He was a warrior! A fighter! He'd come here to avenge

Jumps Like Ants' murder, not have his own life ripped from him.

Not stand face to face with fear.

He no longer felt his thigh or the effort and courage it took to breathe. Drawn to the milling, shouting Pawnee like a wolf pulled to the smell of blood, he kept up the pace. His hands held no weapons, but he'd take what he needed from his enemy, use the man's knife to kill him.

Laughter bubbled up from his chest and exploded as something close to a cougar's cry. By now all Pawnee had armed themselves and were determined to keep control of the animals that made the difference between life and death on the plains. He could have waited until he was sure they wouldn't note his approach, but his fevered system wouldn't allow that.

On legs that knew nothing except fighting and killing, Grey Bear who'd had coup counted against him and had believed he was going to die, launched himself at the objects of his hatred. Behind him Lone Hawk watched, learned, feared.

CHAPTER 23

 Woodenlegs had suffered a dislocated shoulder while wrestling for control of a pregnant mare. Lone Hawk guessed five Pawnee had been killed, not that he could be certain since once the Cheyenne had grabbed the horses, they'd galloped away. Grey Bear had been the last to leave; he might still be there if Two Coyotes hadn't threatened to take Legs Like Lightning.

Lone Hawk doubted that Grey Bear noticed, but the others had left him alone with his thoughts as they put distance between themselves and their enemy. Because Woodenlegs hadn't been able to guide his horse, Lone Hawk had ridden beside the tight-lipped man. Although they'd talked of many things, neither mentioned Grey Bear.

Once it was light, they took turns sleeping. Because he'd been too keyed up to rest, Lone Hawk offered to stand the first watch. Grey Bear acted as the other sentry, but they didn't speak to each other. Just the same, he remained aware of Grey Bear's restlessness. Grey Bear had always boasted after a battle, but not this time. Instead, he acted more like a trapped cougar; Lone Hawk wanted nothing to do with a dangerous, sharp-clawed predator.

When Two Coyotes offered to take over, Lone Hawk stretched out near Woodenlegs, who was trying to rest while propped against a rock.

"Although I dread having to get back on a horse, all I can think about is getting back to our people," Woodenlegs admitted as the weight of sleeplessness settled over Lone Hawk. "I can hardly wait for Easy Singer to put my arm back in place—and for Seeks Fire to hear how I was injured."

Lone Hawk yawned. "Seeks Fire?"

"I know." Woodenlegs looked around, then whispered. "It is foolish for me to think of her, but I cannot help it."

"She and Grey Bear . . ." Another yawn stopped him.

"Grey Bear. I do not know him anymore. The way he acted—as if he would kill every Pawnee—is it possible that a *minio* has taken possession of him?"

Lone Hawk didn't know; neither did he want to think about the rage surrounding Grey Bear. For a few minutes he thought sleep might elude him, but he concentrated on the wind's deep whistling and made it his song, lost himself in melody. His last thought was of Touches the Wind; perhaps the wind sang to her today.

The dream came, bold and clear. In a dim way he realized it wasn't the one that had been part of him since the drought began, and at first he simply watched. He saw something floating above the earth, not a rainbow because it was all gray and yet similar in shape. Then the distant downward arch flattened and began to angle upward, losing itself in something that might be clouds. Someone—perhaps he—was walking along the mistlike path. The person's bare feet occasionally slipped through the mist, forcing the walker to struggle to stand. A sense of dread permeated the mist-world's dry heat, and the person kept looking behind him.

A voice, so low that it was more hum than words, was born from the mist. As for the speaker himself—the path-walker strained to see the newcomer, but that person or creature remained out of sight, either that or the speaker was without form.

This is ekutsihimmiyo. *Sacred.*

"How can that be?" the walker asked. "*Ekutsihimmiyo*, the Hanging Road, is only for the dead and I am alive."

Are you?

The walker swallowed. He tried to speak, but no words formed. His feet no longer sank into the mist but found firm earth—or was it earth?

"Where am I going?"

Ekutsihimmiyo *feels your footsteps. Follow it into the sky.*

"I do not want to die! I am not ready! I want—want to live!"

Ekutsihimmiyo, *pathway of all souls. Come into the afterlife.*

WHEN WORD OF the men's return reached camp, Seeks Fire's heart felt as if it might climb out of her throat. Like nearly everyone, she'd been traveling on foot today, and her feet hurt. Her long, heavy hair hung limp against her neck, and although the wind dried her sweat as soon as it formed, she felt sticky and dirty.

According to the boy who'd spotted the men, everyone who'd gone after the Pawnee and horses had returned, and no one appeared to have been badly wounded.

"We should have a feast," Calf Woman exclaimed. "It is not enough that they will sit and smoke while they tell us what happened; there should be food to celebrate."

Instead of joining in with those bemoaning the lack of food, Seeks Fire slipped away. She wouldn't risk running toward the men, thus giving people a reason to gossip about her, but she was too agitated for anything except being alone with her emotions.

Grey Bear wanted to marry her. He'd look for her, study her face for her reaction to seeing him. What she didn't understand was how she felt.

Still waiting for her heartbeat to return to normal, she studied the dust kicked up by the horses. Just looking at it made her mouth feel even drier. The horses! She'd think about them, not what had happened when Cheyenne and Pawnee came together.

Grey Bear, on Legs Like Lightning, was in the lead. It seemed that the others held back from him, but perhaps she only imagined it.

"Grandfather!" Grey Bear called out. "Your prayers and dreams have brought success to the Cheyenne! Never again will Pawnee take from us."

Several boys, Knows No Fear among them, hurried forward to take control of the horses. The men dismounted, and Lone Hawk and Two Coyotes helped Woodenlegs slide off his mount. Grey Bear didn't seem to notice but remained on Legs Like Lightning until his grandfather came to stand at the stallion's head.

Grey Bear smiled down at the old man, then looked around. When he spotted Nightelk, he acknowledged him with a nod. He continued to smile but when, finally, his eyes met Seeks Fire's, she saw that they were guarded.

"You attacked the Pawnee?" Sweet Grass Eater asked loud enough for everyone to hear. "Tell us, did they easily give up the horses?"

"No," Lone Hawk said when Grey Bear remained silent. "They did not. Pawnee died."

After that, the questions came one upon another until finally Sweet Grass Eater held up his hand.

"There will be no more traveling today," he announced.

"My grandson needs to rest. While he does, he will tell us everything."

The other men had as much right to tell their stories, Seeks Fire thought. She waited for Grey Bear to point that out, but he didn't. After acknowledging his grandfather, he slipped off Legs Like Lightning. From where she stood, she could no longer see him, and the murmur of voices buried anything he might be saying.

"It is all right. No one will say anything against you if you join them."

Wondering how Walking Rabbit had gotten so close without her knowing it, she gave her sister-in-law a brief smile. What she got in return was only a memory of Walking Rabbit's earlier broad grins.

"I know," she said. "It is just that . . ."

"Just what?"

"Sometimes when men come back from hunting or fighting, they look and act like strangers, as if they have seen things women will never understand."

"It was like that with Porcupine."

"I never—once he became a man, I no longer knew what was in my brother's heart. But you were his wife. Did he tell you of his thoughts?"

"A little. Perhaps as much as he understood." Walking Rabbit sighed. "I think it is harder for men to know what is in their hearts. Either that or they are taught not to listen to their hearts so nothing will stand between them and bravery. I see that happening with my son."

"Perhaps . . ." Seeks Fire stared at the ground for a moment. "I do not want to have to say this, but perhaps Knows No Fear does not know how to get past your sorrow, or how to deal with his own. He walks behind the men hoping to become brave that way."

Walking Rabbit pressed her hand over her eyes. "Maybe." When her hand dropped to her side, Seeks Fire saw that her eyes had filled with tears. "I—I do not want to think about that today because if I do—if you marry Grey Bear, he may tell you things no one else knows."

As a girl, Seeks Fire had given little thought to what men's lives were like, but that had changed this summer. "Becoming a woman is not so easy either," she said, trying for a light tone.

"No, but women do not face death the way men do. We die from sickness or injury or sometimes while giving birth, but we do not ride to war and we are not expected to kill animals that might kill us."

The conversation had become heavier than she'd wanted, but she couldn't end it yet. "Was Porcupine ever afraid?" Seeks Fire asked. "When plans were being made to attack, did he ever want to remain behind?"

Walking Rabbit shook her head. "He did what a man had to, but sometimes, in my arms, he became a little boy again."

"Did he?" Seeks Fire had never talked to Walking Rabbit about her and her brother's intimate relationship and wasn't sure how much she wanted to be told.

"I think all men are like that." Walking Rabbit went on. "In bed they can forget about wrapping courage around them. If you marry Grey Bear—I was going to say you will understand once you and Grey Bear sleep together, but perhaps he is different. Perhaps, like his namesake, he has never tasted fear."

IT WAS ALL Grey Bear could do to sit waiting for his turn to pull the pipe's sweet smoke into his lungs. When he finally inhaled, he felt tobacco and herbs spread throughout his system, but the expected relaxation didn't come. Instead, he continued to feel as if he might shatter. If he allowed his thoughts to return to those unreal moments of battle—and his helplessness . . .

At his grandfather's prompting, he and the other warriors detailed what had happened after they'd found the Pawnee. Sweet Grass Eater insisted on offering prayers because only Woodenlegs had sustained an injury, and a peace chief suggested that Pawnee had died because their gods had deserted them in the face of the more powerful Cheyenne gods.

Everyone except for Nightelk had laughed at that, and yet although he loved the sound of that laughter, Nightelk's somber features more closely matched his own emotions.

Occasionally a blast of hot air slammed into him; twice he felt lightning's energy, but if lightning was searing the sky, from where he sat surrounded by his people, he couldn't see it. Just the same, he wondered if it might be searching for him, wanting to feed off the strength of his emotions.

Finally, when he thought he couldn't stand it a heartbeat longer, Sweet Grass Eater announced that his grandson needed to sleep and should be left alone. Grey Bear knew his grandfather didn't understand his prolonged silences, but if he ever told him why, it wouldn't be today.

His legs had become numb while he was sitting, but although he had trouble standing, none of those he'd ridden with offered a supporting hand. Determined not to look at Lone Hawk, whom he both hated and feared today, he scanned his surroundings until he spotted Seeks Fire. She was sitting beside Walking Rabbit and staring up at him with probing eyes.

He'd nearly died. If it hadn't been for Lone Hawk, his blood would have stained the earth. A Pawnee, now dead, had counted coup on him. If Lone Hawk or Two Coyotes told anyone—

Bears were strength! A bear fought and killed, feared nothing. The beast ruled with claws and teeth, ripped and tore. When a grizzly walked about, all other animals cowered, and when a grizzly charged another creature, that creature knew it was doomed! Nothing, not even a pack of wolves, could bring down a young, healthy bear.

And he was one!

Looking around, he realized he'd stalked away from everyone, even Seeks Fire, and had come close to the horses. As he was trying to decide what to do, he sensed something behind him and whirled, ready to fight. Black Eyes stared at him in the dog's all-knowing way.

"Leave me," he ordered. "You do not understand! You cannot possibly understand."

Black Eyes' mouth opened and his tongue lolled out the side of his mouth. His gaze remained steady.

"I warn you! Do not look into me. Do not think you understand—"

Black Eyes growled and something in the sound took him back to the day when the dog had led him to Knows No Fear.

"I do not hate you," he said, his voice low and tightly under control. "I know what you did and thank you for that, but today—today I am different."

Different? How?

The dog couldn't possibly have asked the question; it must have been he—his lightning-burned thoughts.

"I am trapped within myself," he whispered. "I hate it here—must find my way—must be free."

INFLUENCED BY WHAT Walking Rabbit had said about a man's secret thoughts and what that man might share with the right woman, Seeks Fire took note of where Grey Bear had headed. Careful not to draw attention to herself, she waited until the others had either returned to their belongings or broken into small groups to talk. Then, no longer aware of her sore feet, she went after Grey Bear.

She spotted him not far from the horses, and it seemed that he was talking to Nightelk's dog, but then he spun away from Black Eyes. She couldn't possibly sense the impact his weight made on the earth, and yet she felt that weight and power—the press of emotions.

As she approached Black Eyes, the dog regarded her with a somber expression. Even as a puppy, Black Eyes hadn't exhibited the goofy, carefree behavior of most young dogs, and she'd sometimes wondered if he was saddened by what he saw.

When Black Eyes gave no indication he'd try to stop her from following Grey Bear, she continued on. However, although she told herself to pay the animal no more mind, she glanced back at him. He'd plopped onto the ground and rested his head on his front paws. The folds of skin above his eyes sagged.

Was he weary, or resigned?

Unable to shake off the question, she matched Grey Bear's pace. If someone asked why she was following him, she wasn't sure she could tell them—or herself. He looked as if he carried a great weight; she couldn't ease his burden the way Walking Rabbit had eased her husband's, but . . .

"Grey Bear?"

He whirled, crouching as if ready to attack. Above and beyond him, the sky was a clean and relentless blue, serving as sharp contrast to his dark features. Slowly, like an animal gaining understanding of its surroundings, he straightened.

"What are you doing here?"

"I—ah, I did not have a chance to add my voice to those who praised you."

"Praise me? What for?"

"For—for your courage."

His nostrils flared. His smile, if that's what it was, sent alarm through her. "You were not there so how can you know?" he asked.

"Grey Bear, what is it?"

Perhaps she'd said the right thing because his storm-features seemed to soften a little. "I did not mean—you have been all right? You are not too tired?" he asked.

Compared to what he'd been doing, her exertions were nothing, and she told him so, careful to keep her tone light. "I feel sorry for those who are with child. Their backs are tired and they must wonder whether they will put up their tepees again before giving birth."

"Hm."

"I know. Those are women's concerns, not men's."

"A birth blesses all of us." He looked around, perhaps realizing how far they were from the rest of the tribe. "I killed Pawnee. Not Whitehair because I could not find him."

"Whitehair?"

"It does not matter."

His hand settled over the knife at his waist. After a moment, he held it up. When he ran his fingers over the tip, she wondered if he might press down hard enough to injure himself.

"I am glad you are back," she said when the silence became too much for her. "I wondered where you were, what you were doing, whether you were safe."

"Why do you think I would not be?"

The thunderclouds had returned to create a storm in his deep-set eyes. "You are human."

"I am Grey Bear!"

"I know." She took a backward step, then had to struggle not to do it again. "Grey Bear, my whole life, I looked up to my brother. I believed he was stronger than the strongest buffalo, and his family would never know hunger, that only old age would take him from me, but I was wrong. The world is beyond our control—his death taught me that."

He'd continued fingering his knife while she was talking, but now he stopped. "Porcupine died because he did not prepare himself for battle the way he should have."

"Do not say that! It was—his death was an accident."

"An accident? The gods knew he was afraid. That weakened him and made him vulnerable to—"

"And you have never been vulnerable?" It was all she could do not to rake her nails over his cheeks. "You are so fearless, so powerful you do not know what it is to be human?"

"I am Grey Bear." He put his knife away and stepped toward her. "When I say it is time to fight our enemies, the men follow me. Our enemies tremble in fear of me. I have counted coup—yes, I am powerful! Fearless."

"You are human."

"I am a Cheyenne warrior."

"I know. I would never say otherwise, and yet—this summer is a monster. I ask myself if we will survive until it ends or if . . . If I sound as if I doubt who and what you are, it is because heat surrounds me."

Seeks Fire couldn't tell whether he understood what she'd

been trying to say, but his eyes seemed to have lost a little of their anger.

"Our world is," she continued. "It is useless to try to change it or to want to become anything except what we are. When I see my family and friends, I feel blessed. Children make us wealthy, and I can—" She'd been about to tell him she longed for the day when she held her own child, but he might think her too bold. "How can I be anything but afraid? How can anyone?"

"A warrior rides surrounded by courage."

"If fear can enter your grandfather—"

"You are wrong! After the fire, Sweet Grass Eater turned to prayer and opened himself to dreams that would tell him which way the Cheyenne should walk, that is all."

From infancy she'd walked with gentle steps. Defeated and confused, she indicated the direction he and the other men had come from.

"You were looking for Pawnee and horses," she said. "But did you see any sign that buffalo or other animals were nearby? Was that what the Pawnee were doing, hunting?"

"I do not care about the Pawnee. Whether they return to their people or die where we left them is not my concern."

Until now she hadn't considered how the Pawnee would fare without horses. She should have since that was why Grey Bear and the other men had gone after them instead of concentrating on providing the tribe with meat.

"Do not think about Pawnee," Grey Bear ordered. "They are less than us, insects and snakes." He ground his foot against the earth. "What matters is that I defeated them."

"You and the others."

"You sing their praises? Is that why you came here, to tell me I would not be alive if not for them?"

"No." Confused, she shook her head. "I would never say that."

He pulled in a long, deep breath, almost as if he were inhaling her words. Not saying anything, he closed the distance between them. Uneasy, she stepped back and looked around. They were alone, so far from the others that no one would hear even if she shouted.

His size intimidated her. When he'd left, he'd painted bear and arrow designs on his face and chest, but sweat had smeared the colors so they reminded her of mud.

"I hunt and fight," he said. "Attack and stand against attack, count coup and—that is my life, everything."

"Is that how it feels?"

"It is! Do not say otherwise!"

What had she done now to anger him? On the verge of asking, she instead hid behind silence.

"You cannot possibly understand. You, a maiden, will never walk in my footsteps."

"No."

"You are safe because each day I risk my life for you."

"I—I am grateful."

"Do you think I need a woman's praise? Ha! I am Grey Bear!"

She recoiled from the last, but before she could decide whether to run, he clamped his hand on her shoulder.

"Grey Bear. We are not married. We cannot—"

"I cannot sleep." His eyes glazed over. "My nights are full of fighting and more fighting."

"I did not know."

"I am not afraid! Never!" Under his grip, her shoulder started to go numb.

"No one said—"

"Last night when the dreams would not stop, I walked off by myself. Then I looked up at the stars and saw . . ."

"What?"

"You."

Leave. Just leave. "I—if that helped you through the night, I am glad," she managed.

"A man should not need a woman that way." His voice was so low she wondered if he was talking to himself. "I am a man, a man. That is enough."

Her throat muscles constricted and although she finally managed to swallow, her mind was too jumbled for words

to form. Maybe if she spoke in a mother's soothing tone—
but this was Grey Bear, fearless warrior.

"I did what I must—rode in search of Pawnee and brought
back the horses they stole from us." He shook his head; when
his eyes again locked on hers, she saw nothing of the man
she thought she knew in them. "My success—I deserve to
be praised for that."

"I did. I do."

"It is not enough."

"What do you want?"

Again that shaking of the head. This time when he was
done, he pressed his free hand against his forehead, leaving
a white mark.

"What do you want?" she repeated.

"To have no thoughts."

He turned her away from him and started fumbling with
the knot on her chastity belt. All instinct now, she struggled
to break free. A scream expanded inside her, but she couldn't
give it freedom. If someone heard . . .

Her mother's elaborate knots defied him. After jerking her
about in frustration, he wrapped an arm around her neck and
pulled her, off balance, against him. With the other hand, he
used his knife to slice through the long, thin strips of deerhide.

She couldn't breathe. In contrast, his breaths were quick
and noisy things that echoed and added to her terror.

"I want!" he hissed. "Need . . ."

"Grey Bear!' Her outburst sent pain shrieking along her
throat. Desperate to release the awful pressure on her throat,
she clamped her fingers over his forearm, but the lack of
oxygen stripped her of strength. She felt her legs give way,
realized he was holding her up—that the shredded chastity
belt lay at her feet and he'd worked his hand under her
dress's neckline. Fingers as rough and as dry as untanned
hide raked her breast.

No, no, no!

CHAPTER 24

Lone Hawk hadn't acknowledged her since his return, but that wasn't what sent Touches the Wind out on a solitary walk. Although a woman's need for a spirit-guide wasn't as strong as a man's, since her mother's death, she'd wanted to go on a fast and spirit-prayer. If things had been different, she'd be doing that now.

These days the wind rested. Although Wind simply was and it would never occur to her to hate it for what it had done, the gentle, sometimes almost imperceptible breezes made her as uneasy as its earlier rage had. Wind reminded her of dogs—sleeping most of the time but given to sudden bursts of energy and quick, loud, sometimes deadly fights.

Her habit of watching for a hawk was an unconscious one that left her mind free—too free. She wasn't the only one worried about the dwindling food and water supply. If she could say something to Lone Hawk—not beg him to make sure she had enough food, of course, but simply to ask what plans the men—

Puzzled, she stopped and tilted her head to one side, listening. The sound wasn't easily identifiable, which immediately put her on alert. She couldn't imagine the enemy stirring themselves for an attack on this hot afternoon, but that very thing had happened not that long ago and she knew better than to . . .

Was that a scream? No, not a scream; it was too muffled for that. Just the same, the fear that someone, or maybe an animal, was being attacked galvanized her. A glance over her shoulder reaffirmed what she already knew—the camp was too far away for anyone to hear her cry. Besides, if she yelled, the attacker might hear and come after her.

After picking up a large rock, she headed toward the disturbance. If she was a man, she'd know what she should do, but endless days of hunting for roots, prickly pear cactus fruit, milkweed buds, and chokecherries hadn't prepared her.

"Wind," she said under her breath. "Fill my eyes with your strength and make them keen. Teach me to listen so . . ." With a rueful shake of the head, she admitted that talking to her spirit only prevented her from listening.

The moccasins she'd debated wearing made no sound, but her ears roared, and she was afraid that whoever was out there could hear her breathing. She was foolish! She should run back to—

Follower?

An involuntary shiver shook her, but although she admonished herself that the child couldn't possibly be here, logic didn't completely still the wild prayer. If Follower had somehow survived . . .

Her emotions barely clamped into submission, Touches the Wind measured her forward progress one step at a time. She crouched and kept her head low, but before long her back started to ache and she risked standing a little straighter. It took several concentrated blinks before her vision sharpened and she was able to dismiss the heat waves.

There, movement.

Even more nervous than she'd been, she forced herself to come closer. To see. To understand.

Her eyes took in what was happening, but her mind was slow to accept the unacceptable. Although she'd been taught to guard her virginity, she knew what went on between a man and a woman; given the crowded living conditions, it couldn't be any other way.

But this wasn't the sex her parents had indulged in, albeit only infrequently in recent years. This—this grunting and struggling and a man's thrusting rear end and a half-naked woman under him shouldn't be!

Shocked and fascinated, she couldn't do anything except watch. The man's back was to her, what she could see of his legs young and strong. She accepted that he had his fingers around the woman's outstretched arms and was holding her down. Her legs were wide apart, bent at the knee, heels digging into the ground. The man grunted, grunted, gasped, gasped again.

The woman was crying.

Touches the Wind pressed her hand against her belly, but although the urge to flee became stronger and stronger, she didn't move. What these two people were doing was between them—or it would have been if she hadn't sensed the violence. Hadn't heard the woman's sobs.

Seeks Fire's sobs.

Only dimly aware of what she was doing, she lifted the rock over her head. For a moment she hung there, certain she couldn't possibly do what she was thinking of, calling herself crazy, and then—

The rock smacked the man between the shoulder blades. Bellowing, he sprang off Seeks Fire and whirled toward his attacker.

Grey Bear!

Touches the Wind opened her mouth but only a moan escaped. Grey Bear, shaking his head, crouched naked before her. Seeks Fire was barely visible behind him, and she'd stopped crying. Touches the Wind wondered if the three of them would remain like that forever, but she really didn't care because this couldn't be happening, and she must be dreaming, and before long she'd wake up and not remember—

Grey Bear pushed himself to his feet. His penis hung between his legs, and he made no attempt to cover himself. He continued to shake his head, and she saw slowly dawning realization in his eyes. He glanced down at the rock she'd thrown, then, graceful beyond belief, he broke into a run—not toward but away from her.

Seeks Fire had rolled over onto her side, but she didn't seem to be looking at anything. Her whimper sounded too much like Walking Rabbit crying for her husband and daughter.

"I am here," Touches the Wind said as she dropped to her knees and tried to put her arms around Seeks Fire.

Jerking free, Seeks Fire slammed her fist into Touches the Wind's shoulder.

"No, no," she soothed. "It is me, not him. You are all right, all right."

Seeks Fire sobbed, and yet her eyes remained dry. Although her fingers were still fisted, she no longer held them up defensively. When Touches the Wind tugged on the hem of her dress, Seeks Fire took notice but made no move to help cover herself. Her face looked blood-drained.

A million questions raced through her, but she couldn't form the words to ask them. She wasn't sure which of them was shaking more or whether it made any difference. Suddenly afraid Grey Bear might return, she stared where she'd last seen him.

"He is gone?" Seeks Fire asked.

"Yes." *Please.*

"He—he—you are alone?"

Grey Bear's discarded loincloth lay a few feet away, and she wondered if the lump under it was his knife. If he returned, did she have the courage to pick up the hated garment and grab the weapon?

"I am alone," she remembered to tell Seeks Fire.

"I did not—I did not want him to—"

"I know."

"You believe me?" She sounded like a frightened child. "You do not think I acted in an unchaste manner?"

"No, no. Never."

"He hurt—why did he hurt me?"

GREY BEAR RAN until his lungs felt as if they'd burst. He'd cut his right instep and had cramps in both calves, but as long as a shred of strength remained in him, he'd been unaware of those things. Now, however, he had no choice but to sink to his knees and reach behind him to massage his calves. He didn't know how long he'd been running or where

he was. His dry mouth cried out for moisture, but how could
he return to camp this way—naked?

Naked.

Sobbing, the warrior slumped forward until his forehead
slammed into the ground. He tried to command his arms to
push himself up, but for too long he couldn't remember how
to make his muscles work. The sun beat against his naked
back and rear end.

He'd removed his loincloth during his frenzied taking of
Seeks Fire. His knife must be with it; if he wanted it back,
he'd have to ask her—

Touches the Wind!

If she'd bruised him when she threw the rock at him, he
couldn't feel it now, not that such a small injury mattered.

His mind emptied out and became nothing. He straightened, then remained motionless as the sun and wind died his
sweat-slick body. Everything ached and the need for water
ate at him, but he remained in the lifeless cave of his mind
for as long as he could.

When a tiny spider started climbing up his leg, he watched
until it neared his penis before blowing the insect away. He
started to reach for his penis and then stopped, confused.
From the time he'd stopped thinking of himself as a boy, he'd
covered himself there.

Finally, although if he could have done anything else he
would have, he struggled to his feet and looked around.
The land looked as naked as he was, exposed and vulnerable. He wanted to tell himself that at least he was alive while
the land appeared dead, but with his mind shut down, he
couldn't.

LONE HAWK WAS watching the sun set when Touches the
Wind and Seeks Fire walked into camp. He thought they'd
join one of the groups of women or go to eat with either
Seeks Fire's parents or Little Bird and Long Chin's relatives,
but although Touches the Wind waved at her younger sister,
she and Seeks Fire remained apart from the others.

Touches the Wind glanced at him, but before he could
acknowledge the look, she'd returned her attention to Seeks
Fire. Seeks Fire looked as if she'd shrunken into herself in
much the same way Walking Rabbit had. Possibly they'd
gone looking for Follower and the unsuccessful search
weighed on Seeks Fire, but surely she already accepted the
little girl's death.

As the sky turned from blue to red and orange, he started
toward them. Somehow he'd find the words to tell Seeks Fire
that the man she intended to marry had sliced open a Pawnee's neck, cupped his hands over the fresh, hot blood, and
rubbed it over himself. The Pawnee might have still been
alive when Grey Bear started kicking him, but Lone Hawk
doubted he'd heard Grey Bear insist that no Pawnee would
ever touch him again. Lone Hawk and Two Coyotes had
finally pulled Grey Bear off the corpse and forced the frenzied warrior onto his horse.

All the way back, Grey Bear had stayed tight inside himself, and no one had attempted to break past the barrier of
his burning eyes. When the tribe's voices reached him, he'd
taken note of his surroundings, and by the time everyone
gathered around, Grey Bear's voice had been calm, boastful
as always. Just the same, Lone Hawk held onto the image
of blood coating a powerful chest and the thud, thud of feet
striking a helpless foe. Seeks Fire needed to know that.

Caught in that tangle, he'd nearly reached the two maidens
before he saw Touches the Wind's warning stare. *Go away*,
she mouthed. *Leave us.* He'd tried to look at Seeks Fire but
Touches the Wind positioned herself so that wasn't possible.

"I MUST TALK to him," Nightelk said. Before he could get
to his feet, Two Coyotes lifted a restraining hand.

"Not tonight," his son warned. "Grey Bear was like a man
in hibernation when we left the Pawnee. I believe he is returning to what he has always been, but the journey is not
yet complete. Until it is, he will not hear your words."

What Two Coyotes said made sense. Just the same, the

burden of what he had to do weighed on Nightelk. When Two Coyotes had indicated he wanted to talk to him in private, he'd thought the opportunity had come to ask what his son's feelings were for Walking Rabbit, but then Two Coyotes had described Grey Bear's behavior.

Father and son had expressed the same disbelief; no matter what one enemy does to another, some things are beyond revenge. A man might take a defeated enemy's hair because that's where the soul resides, or cut off a finger to prevent him from using a weapon in the afterlife, but a ghost or *mistai* must have taken possession of Grey Bear. Nothing else explained his behavior.

A *mistai* sent by the Sacred White Calf?

"Where is he?" Nightelk forced himself to ask. "I have not seen him since the gathering."

"I saw him walk away, in that direction." Two Coyotes pointed. "If this was anyone else, I would have gone to Sweet Grass Eater, but . . ."

"But what?"

"Is it possible—could Sweet Grass Eater have performed magic to turn his grandson into a monster-warrior?"

"No," Nightelk whispered. "That is not it."

"You know what it is?"

He couldn't answer.

GREY BEAR DIDN'T know or care how long it had been dark before he slipped back into camp. His mouth watered at the smell of food, but he didn't trust his belly to accept anything. If there'd been any other way, he wouldn't have returned to where he'd assaulted Seeks Fire, but he couldn't come home naked. He'd found the loincloth and knife where he'd left them.

Despite his prayer that he'd be left alone, his grandfather was waiting for him. He heard the old man's breathing but couldn't put his mind to the sound enough to determine Sweet Grass Eater's mood. The familiar scent of tobacco and herbs told him he was smoking.

"You return," Sweet Grass Eater said.

"Yes." His legs trembled, and he dropped to the ground across from the man who'd led him into adulthood. When Sweet Grass Eater handed him some water, he drank until his throat closed.

"Why did you not stay here? Everyone wanted to hear about what you did; when the other men started to speak, I told them the words had to come from you."

Did his grandfather suspect it hadn't been an ordinary raid, that something no one wanted to talk about what had taken place? Unable to put his mind to the question, Grey Hawk shrugged. Surely Seeks Fire had returned. Should he try to speak to her? But what words could possibly explain—

"The Pawnee are behind us," his grandfather said. "We must not waste energy thinking of them."

"I will not."

Sweet Grass Eater was silent for a long time, but he couldn't think of a way to break the silence.

"You are different." Sweet Grass Eater inhaled and passed the pipe to him. "You have always been a young grizzly, but today you are like one whose muscles and eyes have seen too many years."

"I am tired."

"Hm. Rest then but first—do you know how little water remains?"

Water? Hunting? "What do you want?"

Sweet Grass Eater's explanation, as did most of what he said these days, took a long time. Grey Bear remembered little of it, just that starvation once again stalked the tribe. Sweet Grass Eater would continue to pray for revealing dreams, but he and the other young men had to be his legs.

"I was only a small child when our people left the mountains," Sweet Grass Eater said in a melancholy tone. "But I remember that water was everywhere, water and trees to protect us from the sun. I wish—it is foolish to wish to return there." He sighed. "Still, it is easier to think about what is familiar than wonder what waits in land we have never seen."

Confidence had always radiated from Sweet Grass Eater;

this fearful tone disturbed Grey Bear. If he'd been able to pull himself out of the quicksand of his mind, he'd probe for the reason. Tonight, however, he couldn't think beyond how fiercely Seeks Fire had fought—and what he'd done to her.

His grandfather's voice droned on. Tomorrow he'd be expected to lead the men in a far-ranging hunt to the west, but his thoughts refused to go beyond rape.

Rape.

Sin.

Unforgivable.

Why then had he—

Something to do with the eyes of a man determined to kill him and feeling helpless and afraid and somehow surviving and needing, as he'd never needed anything in life, to be strong again.

ALTHOUGH SHE HADN'T asked her to, Touches the Wind remained beside Seeks Fire. When Little Bird joined them, Seeks Fire stirred herself enough to talk to the child and even hold her as Little Bird fell asleep. After kissing her, Seeks Fire settled Little Bird on a blanket and then sat with her hand on the small chest.

Seeks Fire's family had come by to ask where she intended to spend the night. When she hadn't answered, Touches the Wind said their daughter would be sleeping with her and Little Bird. That hadn't satisfied Seeks Fire's mother, who'd obviously sensed that something was wrong, but at least the older woman hadn't pressed for an explanation. Now, although a few people were still about, most had gone to bed.

"I cannot talk to her," Seeks Fire said, breaking a long silence. "If I look into my mother's eyes, she will know . . ."

"She knows you are burdened."

"But she does not . . . You—you will not tell her, will you?"

"No. I wish—I want to force Grey Bear to explain himself. I do not understand! I cannot."

Little Bird stirred, prompting Touches the Wind to lower her voice. "He was like a stallion who senses a mare is in heat. I have never—no Cheyenne man would do such a thing. Perhaps—" Hoping to gather her thoughts, she pulled in the cooling air. "He *is* Cheyenne, but what he did—it was as if he hated you."

"He—he wanted to marry me."

Seeks Fire sounded as if the life had been stripped from her. Touches the Wind wanted her to scream and yell, to pick up a knife and attack Grey Bear.

"You will not marry him now," she said. It wasn't a question.

"No! Never!" Seeks Fire sagged forward, the hand that had been rubbing Little Bird's back falling still. "I—I should not have gone after him. He must have thought—he must have thought me bold."

"You had not seen him for days and simply wanted to talk. He knew that."

"Did he?" She straightened. "What is inside him? Today I saw things I had not before; he was different, dark like a cave."

"What did you talk about?"

"I do not remember. Everything I said was wrong. Darkness continued to surround him, but it was more than that."

"In what way?"

Seeks Fire took a shuddering breath. "I do not know. Please, what did I do wrong?"

Suddenly angry at her friend, Touches the Wind grabbed Seeks Fire's wrist. "Listen so I do not have to say this again. You did *nothing* wrong. The sin is his."

Seeks Fire pulled free, but although her wrist must ache, she didn't rub it. "We cannot both remain here," she said. "What happened today is against everything Cheyenne, a sin in Heammawihio's eyes. If I kill myself, he can go on living."

"No! You cannot—" Little Bird squeaked and changed positions, distracting Touches the Wind.

"Our people need him." Seeks Fire's voice was thick with conviction. "I am only a hungry mouth."

Eventually Touches the Wind got her friend to promise to put distance between herself and the rape, but she herself felt little different from the way she had when she'd found Seeks Fire and Grey Bear.

At Touches the Wind's prompting, Seeks Fire stretched out beside Little Bird and fell asleep with her body wrapped around the smaller one. Touches the Wind prayed the maiden would find a small measure of peace in sleep, then, driven by the reality that Seeks Fire was no longer a maiden, no longer pure and chaste, she stood and started walking.

They hadn't talked about the possibility that Seeks Fire might be pregnant. Maybe Seeks Fire hadn't thought about that yet, but she would and when she did, Touches the Wind would tell her babies couldn't possibly be conceived in anything except a loving union, but was that true?

"Wind. Wind, talk to me tonight. Touch me not with restlessness as you so often do, but so I can be what my friend needs. So I can look at Grey Bear who puts food in my sister's mouth and not want to kill him."

The wind remained silent.

"IT HAS HAPPENED!" Sweet Grass Eater announced early the next morning. "Last night Grey Bear and I smoked together, and I prayed to Heammawihio and Aktinowihio. Then I pulled sleep around me and dreamed."

The gathered men, women, and children leaned forward almost as one, eager to hear what their priest had to say. Nightelk and several other peace chiefs sat nearby, but Sweet Grass Eater didn't need to ask wisdom of any of them. The nagging sense that something was wrong with his grandson continued to bother him, but his dream had been so powerful.

"Thunderbird came to me, not once, not twice, but three times."

Several women gasped. The peace chiefs, except for Nightelk whose eyes were nearly as dark as Grey Bear's, nodded expectantly.

"The stream that has long been part of my dreams promises cool sweetness."

He waited for someone to ask how that could be in the wake of unrelenting rainless days, but no one did.

"It still keeps its location secret, but I saw an eagle flying over it. When the men are close to it, Eagle will come to them just as a hawk came to Lone Hawk when he found Little Bird."

If he'd expected an enthusiastic response from Lone Hawk, he was wrong. When this meeting was over, he'd ask the warrior if he doubted his words—something the younger man never would.

"Eagle will look down upon my grandson and know him for the powerful warrior he is." Sweet Grass Eater thought he'd spotted Grey Bear as people were arriving, but why wasn't he sitting in front, as was his right and responsibility? "Which is good because the buffalo herd has grown."

He waited for his announcement to sink in, then continued. "This is what I saw, what waits for us. Where we are going, in the direction of the setting sun, the days are cooler and the land a little higher. The earth is not flat like here but has many hills covered with grass so tall it brushes the buffalos' bellies. My dreams show me that."

At that, many eyes widened. He wondered where Walking Rabbit was; surely she hadn't wandered off again. Did she and Jumps Like Ants' parents speak of their shared grief?

"There are as many buffalo around the stream as there are Cheyenne," he finished. "Waiting for us."

"How is this to be done?" a peace chief asked.

"Nothing has changed. We will continue to travel, walking slow so we will not tire. As for the hunters—"

No matter how he strained, he couldn't see his grandson. "Grey Bear will say when the men will leave, how fast they must ride, how many provisions they should take with them. That is his decision, his."

CHAPTER 25

Afternoon's heat had put an end to the day's travel, and most were either dozing or caring for their belongings. Whenever she thought of her dwindling food supply, none of it meat, panic lapped at Touches the Wind.

Although she was at a loss as to how she might help Seeks Fire, she'd invited her to walk with her and Little Bird. Neither woman had said much, and when they heard that the hunters would take off once the sun set, Seeks Fire admitted she was glad she wouldn't have to look at Grey Bear for several days.

Touches the Wind had felt the same way, and yet her relief was tempered by unexpected concern for Grey Bear. No matter how much she despised what he'd done, she couldn't forget that he'd stood by himself as his grandfather described his dream and that he looked exhausted.

He should! After what he'd done, he should hate himself! Maybe more than hate.

Seeking distraction from the heat and their uneasy parents, several children wandered over. In an attempt to accommodate them, Touches the Wind passed on something that had happened to her grandfather. While out hunting, he'd come across strangers building something they called a fort. One of the newcomers, Sieur de La Salle, had said he'd traveled from a distant place called France and wanted to trade his knives, axes, pots, and guns for furs.

When the children pressed for a description of the fort, she drew what she hoped was an accurate representation in the dirt before admitting her throat was too dry for any more storytelling. Little Bird left with Laughing Frog's daughters;

Seeks Fire's eyes drooped, but Touches the Wind knew she couldn't sleep.

Although the act of walking drained her of what little energy she had left, she found it easier to think while walking than while sitting and staring at nothing. The horses were grazing nearby, slowly spreading out as they searched for enough to fill their bellies. The wind came at her from behind, pushing her away from her people.

The land here was uneven enough that what from a distance appeared to be flat turned out to be an endless series of dips and rises. For a while her thoughts went no further than that, and she idly wondered if Heammawihio had had a hand in its design. If not him, then who?

The sun, hot and relentless, would soon kiss the horizon and then go to sleep. She pondered whether the wind would become stronger once the sun no longer sucked the life out of everything. That was another question, if Wind felt heat. Wind carried heat with it, yes, but as for whether it was strengthened or weakened by Sun . . .

She'd been concentrating on her footing but now something drew her attention upward. The small hawk hadn't been in the sky when she'd started on her walk; she was sure of that. But she'd learned not to be surprised by anything Hawk did.

For several moments it rested on unseen currents, and she envied its lack of concern about the world below it, but then it angled toward her.

Feeling more energized than she had all day, she clamored up a mound and scanned her surroundings. Behind her, the people she'd known her entire life sat or lay surrounded by their belongings. They looked small and brown, in part because their brightly painted tepees had been tied into compact bundles, perhaps in part because all except the smallest children understood how dire their straits were. She wanted both to hurry back to them to comfort and be comforted and to walk away from the responsibility and fear, perhaps forever.

What was she thinking? There was nowhere else for her to go.

Belatedly remembering that Hawk had brought her here, she scrutinized her surroundings. For too long, she saw nothing to hold her interest when she noted that someone else had left camp and was heading not toward her but a little to her left. Grey Bear.

Shocked, she dropped to a crouch, but even as she wondered whether he'd seen her, she realized he was taking no note of his surroundings. Instead, he walked with his head down like an old and tired man; his feet dragged and each step took great effort.

In her mind, she saw herself running up to him and striking him over and over while demanding to know how he could have turned his back on everything Cheyenne and become an animal. Once he lifted his head and she studied his features, no longer young and strong but reminding her too much of her mother's ruined face. Were those tears?

Alarmed, she concentrated. She still hadn't changed her opinion that he should bear the weight of responsibility for having raped the maiden he'd declared he wanted to marry, but she'd never heard of a Cheyenne man doing that horrible thing, couldn't understand it. Perhaps he'd decided to go on a spirit quest during which he'd seek guidance and forgiveness, although she didn't see how that was possible. If that was his intention, his quest would have to be a brief one since he was expected to lead the hunt this evening. If he had to ride out sleepless and distracted from the mission his grandfather had handed him, would he fail to see the dream-buffalo and water?

Fear had already knotted her stomach when she saw the knife.

"LONE HAWK? PLEASE, I need—I must speak to you!"

Lone Hawk looked up from the arrows he'd laid out around him to see Touches the Wind, her face sweat streaked and breathing heavily, hurrying toward him. Although several men were working nearby, she paid them no mind. When she fixed him with a dark, frightened stare, he got to his feet, and they walked out of earshot of the others.

"Grey Bear," she blurted before he could ask for an explanation, "is out there." She pointed.

He shrugged. "Perhaps he seeks guidance from his spirit."

"No, no! That is what I first thought but—" She swallowed and started to reach for him, then stopped.

"You followed him?" he prompted.

"No, no." She looked around and then up at the sky. "He—he has a knife."

"No man would be without one."

If Touches the Wind heard, she gave no indication. Instead, she clamped her hands over her elbows and squeezed. Then she rocked back and forth. "There is—I must tell you something."

"Must you?"

Acting as if she hadn't heard him, she again looked around. "A thing happened—I promised I would not say anything, but if I do not . . . Lone Hawk, I fear Grey Bear plans to take his life."

Something slammed into his chest. He fought it, concentrated. "Why?"

"Because of what he did. Seeks Fire, I am sorry. Please—" She lurched toward him, so close now that he felt her warm breath. "Please keep this within yourself. I beg you. Yesterday Grey Bear raped Seeks Fire."

Although his chest continued to throb, in a strange way he wasn't surprised. There were a hundred things he could say, questions to be asked. Instead, he waited. The telling came quickly, her words jumbled and incomplete.

"Please, go after him," she finished.

THE WIND LENT strength to his legs as Lone Hawk raced in the direction Touches the Wind had indicated. She'd said something about seeing a hawk and the bird alerting her to Grey Bear, but he had no time to think on that. His mind spun, making it nearly impossible for him to concentrate on

what he was doing, or why. It was easier to simply run, to
be, to note how little sound his feet made.

He found Grey Bear where Touches the Wind had seen
him. Perhaps the warrior hadn't had the strength to go any
farther. Grey Bear stood with his back to his people, but
whether that was because he couldn't bring himself to look
at them or because something else held his attention, he
couldn't say—didn't care.

The knife, if Grey Bear held it, was hidden by the broad
back. He'd hunched over and had spread his legs slightly.
Although he looked as powerful as he always had, bearlike,
there was something terribly, terribly lonely about him.

Lone Hawk opened his mouth to call out. Instead, he
slowed to an uneasy walk that brought him so close to the
other man that he couldn't understand why Grey Bear hadn't
heard him. Unseen insects droned in their endless way and
the grasses brushed against each other, creating a rustling
sound. He heard a bird trill, but except for those things, the
plains were silent. He couldn't hear his own breathing, or
Grey Bear's.

Then Grey Bear straightened, stretched out his arms like
a man accepting a gift. In his hands he clutched his knife—
pointed at his chest. His shoulder muscles tensed.

"Forgive me!" Grey Bear cried.

"No!" Lone Hawk sprang forward.

NIGHTELK RODE LEANING forward so he could see his
horse's hooves because Black Eyes ran just ahead of the
mare, sometimes so close he was afraid the dog would get
stepped on.

A few minutes ago he'd been sitting with his wife. Then,
as Calf Woman was saying perhaps the time had come for
her to talk to her sister about remarrying, Black Eyes had
trotted up. At first the dog had done nothing more than lift
and cock his head, listening in his intent way. Then, apparently satisfied that he'd made sense of whatever it was he'd
heard, he closed his mouth around Nightelk's wrist and

started pulling. When Nightelk got to his feet, the dog released him, only to propel him toward the horses by butting his nose into the back of his knees. The dog had growled and stared until Nightelk mounted.

Now he, who could think of little except a Sacred White Calf and his great sin, was following the dog that knew of that sin and hated him for it. He hadn't tried to explain himself to his wife, hadn't looked to see if anyone noticed what he was doing. Instead, he gave himself up to Black Eyes' wisdom. If Black Eyes was guiding him the same way the dog had guided Grey Bear to Knows No Fear . . .

"No!"

Jerking the mare to a stop, Nightelk strained to listen. The sound had come from a distance, but he thought the voice was Lone Hawk's. If the Pawnee—

Black Eyes whined.

"What is it?" he asked. By way of answer, Black Eyes trotted ahead, looked over his shoulder, growled.

His legs once again young, Nightelk dismounted and started running. Why he'd decided to go on foot, he couldn't say.

All too soon, he'd erased the distance between himself and what he'd been brought out here to find. Two men, Lone Hawk and Grey Bear, knelt in a strange embrace. Because their backs were to him, he couldn't see their expressions, not that he needed to. Lone Hawk bore Grey Bear's weight and had folded himself around the limp warrior much as a parent comforts a crying child.

"What is it?" he demanded.

For a long time Lone Hawk gave no indication he'd heard. Then, slowly and halting like an old, old man, he lay Grey Bear on the ground and looked up. Nightelk saw no hint of recognition in his eyes, didn't need to see the knife protruding from Grey Bear's chest for reality to sink in.

Lone Hawk shifted position, but instead of sliding away from Grey Bear, he took hold of the knife and pulled it out. Blood bubbled up from the wound and added to the red staining the broad, unmoving chest.

"Tell me," Nightelk said.

Tell me.

It all came back to Lone Hawk, his desperate attempt to reach Grey Bear, the warrior's powerful hands fisted around his knife, the point piercing and then plunging into the healthy young chest, a strangled cry followed by a look of acceptance and peace.

For a warrior to die in battle brought great honor to him and his family. Men who'd done something to bring shame to themselves sometimes chose war as a way of committing suicide, but what Grey Bear had just done went against everything Cheyenne.

As had the rape.

"Tell me." Nightelk repeated. He sounded almost gentle.

Grey Bear killed himself.

But if he said that, Nightelk would demand to know why, and Seeks Fire would no longer be seen as a maiden. Soiled, she'd spend the rest of her life bearing that shame. Maybe her parents would turn their backs on her, cast her from the band.

And Sweet Grass Eater would no longer be seen as priest and visionary. He'd become the grandfather of the man who'd raped a maiden and then killed himself.

"Lone Hawk?"

"I killed him."

NO MATTER WHERE he looked, Nightelk saw into a deep, dark cave. He'd felt hot for so long it seemed part of him, but he'd been shaking since finding Lone Hawk and Grey Bear. His heart hurt, and he tried not to think about how his own father had died with his features contorted in pain and his fingers clawing at his chest as if trying to get to the damaged organ that was killing him.

He'd taken the knife—Grey Bear's knife—from Lone Hawk and ordered the younger man to follow him back to camp. First Black Eyes and then the mare had trotted after them; several times Black Eyes had rubbed his head against Lone Hawk's side.

Others must have known that something terrible had happened because, silent and somber, the band members watched as he'd made his way to where Sweet Grass Eater dozed. Lone Hawk had stood beside him, bent and colorless.

"Your grandson is dead," Nightelk told Sweet Grass Eater. "At Lone Hawk's hands."

Sweet Grass Eater crumpled into himself, wounded in ways the loss of his tepee hadn't touched. When he held out a trembling hand for the blood-caked knife, Nightelk had no choice but to give it to him. The old man used the tip to slash his arms and legs, crying great wracking sobs as he did. Everyone, except for Nightelk and Lone Hawk, it seemed, was unable to control their grief.

Still crying, Sweet Grass Eater pushed himself to his feet and stumbled toward Lone Hawk. With palsied fingers, he pressed the knife against Lone Hawk's throat.

"End me if you must," Lone Hawk whispered. "If my death brings you peace, I will not try to stop you."

A shudder shook the old man; he dropped his head and began muttering. No one spoke during the prayer, and when it was over, Sweet Grass Eater handed the knife back to Nightelk.

"Cheyenne do not kill Cheyenne," Sweet Grass Eater said, the words so low they barely registered. "Such murder is against everything the gods taught us. My grandson's death will be the only one."

His speech seemed to exhaust him. When he sagged, several hands, Lone Hawk's among them, reached out to support him. Leaning against Two Coyotes, the priest asked for the Sacred Medicine Hat bundle. After blessing it, he unwrapped the buffalo-hide bag and pulled out the Hat. He then turned the Hat, made of buffalo fur from the top of a buffalo head with the horns attached, to one of the peace chiefs and held up the largest of the four ancient hollow bone pipes made from antelope shanks. Using a tobacco mixture someone else gave him, he filled the fragile pipe and lit it with a shaky hand.

"We are part of *hestenov*, the universe. We stand on *heammahestonev*, the surface, and never see *aktunov* which is below. We have been given *taxtavo* to breathe but as long as we live, we will never be in *setovo*, the Nearer Sky Space because that is the home of birds and why we hold them sacred. At night we see *aktovo*, Blue Sky Space where the sun, moon, and stars live. Those things are part of our harmony, as are our sacred ceremonies and the Sacred Arrows."

Nightelk looked around until he spotted Calf Woman. She nodded, letting him know he could easily get his hands on the Sacred Arrows.

"They have been defiled." Sweet Grass Eater's voice became stronger. His wounds no longer bled freely. "They must be purified."

An Arrow Renewal Ceremony took many days and involved every Cheyenne band. That great coming-together with hundreds of tepees facing east to greet the rising sun had to take place near water, where there was enough forage for the horses. This summer there was neither.

"I must pray and smoke on the purification," Sweet Grass Eater said. "If the Renewal cannot be done properly, it should not take place because the gods will be displeased. But"—he faced Lone Hawk—"there is something that *must* happen."

THAT *SOMETHING* MEANT Lone Hawk would be cast out from the tribe, Nightelk thought as energy and anxiety took him back to the killing site. Grey Bear's body was no longer there. His family had come for it and were preparing it for the kind of burial befitting him, but Nightelk didn't need physical proof of Grey Bear's death for the memories to flood back.

Despite himself, he built fragments of that image one upon another. When it had been happening, he'd been too disbelieving to focus on details, but time had, he prayed, taken him to understanding.

In this summer of drought, the band had lost its most accomplished hunter. That that loss had come at Lone Hawk's hands was still incomprehensible—or it would be if he hadn't killed the Sacred White Calf. Others might look at Lone Hawk and ask themselves how this young warrior could have killed a fellow warrior and hunter, but they didn't know what Nightelk did.

The ground had swallowed much of Grey Bear's blood but enough remained to stain the spot where he'd fallen. His relatives had left their footprints so it was impossible to determine which indentations had been made by the two men. Because Grey Bear had been carried off, there were no drag marks, no sign of struggle.

Grey Bear wouldn't impassively wait for Lone Hawk to kill him.

Puzzled, he went back to studying the ground, but before he could pull reality around him, he saw something shimmering on the horizon.

The distant spot was white.

"White Buffalo Calf." He swallowed and tried again. "Is it you?"

Only the wind responded. Unable to make sense of its message, he repeated his question. The shimmering white didn't move, was so far away he could have told himself he was mistaken.

Only he wasn't.

"Lone Hawk!" he cried. "This is not your sin; it is mine."

Something, a presence of some kind, shared this space with him. He needed to acknowledge it, but not until he'd finished his prayer.

"Heammawihio, take me! You are the Wise One Above and are more powerful than the sun. You are responsible for the Sacred White Calf coming to life; I beg forgiveness for killing your child."

Could Heammawihio sense the connection between them?

Surely the Wise One Above knew he'd held his own dead children. "Is it not enough?" he begged. "My infants' lives for the Calf's? Must your anger spread over Porcupine, Follower, Jumps Like Ants, and now Grey Bear? When will it be enough? When?"

When I am dead?

When the entire band is?

"I want to hand you my death." The thought of dying didn't bother him, never seeing or speaking to his family again did. "But if it comes at my own hands, it is a sin. I am now a peace chief, keeper of the Sacred Arrows. I no longer ride to war so how will my death come? How do I make my heart stop? Please, tell me! How do I make my life end?"

The strain of trying to focus on the distant white caused his eyes to blur. After rubbing them, he scanned the horizon for what had been so clear before, but he could no longer see it.

His legs felt like rocks, and yet he forced himself to turn back toward the camp. He was struck by how small and colorless his people and their possessions looked from this distance, now that the sky surrounded them.

Then he heard something.

Grass. It is only the grass moving under the wind's beat. Just the same, he lifted himself onto his toes and looked around. At first he saw nothing that hadn't been there before, but then his life-taught eyes found what was different about the grass to his left. Instead of waving gently like everything else, a large gold-brown circle remained motionless.

Grizzly.

The creature rose, the rich coat catching the last of the sun's rays. It lifted its massive head so it could test the air, not that it had anything to fear.

When it growled, the low rumble vibrated through him and stripped him of everything except the instinct for survival. Perhaps Heammawihio had sent the bear as death-giver; perhaps he should walk toward that death.

But Nightelk didn't.

Couldn't.

Instead, as the great creature rose onto its hind legs, he sent a prayer to his legs and ran.

CHAPTER 26

As the sun set, Grey Bear's father and uncle carried his body to the camp's eastmost spot and lay it on the ground. His mother, who'd collapsed when she heard of his death, trudged to the burial spot, surrounded by female relatives. When she looked down at the bundle that was her son, she moaned and sank to her knees.

Walking Rabbit hadn't joined the mourners but stood at a distance, her features an unreadable mask. Seeks Fire, drawing strength from the young widow, forcefully reminded herself of how little she'd lost in comparison. Still, she couldn't make herself participate in the burial and didn't care what the others thought of her behavior. She'd seen Grey Bear's body when it was carried into camp, but while the sight caused many to wail or immerse themselves in prayer, she'd felt as if she was staring at something that had never known life.

She shouldn't feel this way. The tribe had lost much more than a son; its finest hunter had died.

A hunter who'd defiled her.

Sensing Walking Rabbit's eyes on her, she returned her look but made no attempt to join her. The exhaustion that had been part of her since the rape had become almost familiar.

Shouldn't it be different now? She could pretend to be his grief-stricken intended, and the others—except for Touches the Wind—would accept any behavior, but first she'd have to feel something, anything.

Grey Bear, dead.

At Lone Hawk's hands.

"You are all right?" Touches the Wind asked softly.

"No." She couldn't think of anything else to say.

Touches the Wind's breathing was quick and labored. Someone spoke to Walking Rabbit and the young widow started toward the speaker. The fog began to lift, allowing her to think, forcing her to ask the question.

"Did you tell Lone Hawk? Is that why he killed Grey Bear?"

Touches the Wind dropped to a crouch, and after a moment, Seeks Fire joined her. All around them, the sounds of loss rose and fell, rose and fell.

"I told him, yes, but . . ."

"You said you would not."

"I had no choice."

"No choice?"

"Listen to me, please. You do not know what happened."

By the time Touches the Wind had finished, Seeks Fire felt no longer just empty but utterly drained and hollow. She hadn't wanted her mind to paint images to go with her friend's explanation but had no control over what formed inside her.

"The look on Grey Bear's face frightened me," Touches the Wind said. "He looked like a man who has stared into the eyes of his own death."

"He—he wanted to die?"

"I believe he did. When I saw what he was doing, I could not think, ran. I saw Lone Hawk, and the words tumbled out of me. Before I had finished, he started running toward Grey Bear."

Seeks Fire sucked in a deep breath and let it out. "Then Lone Hawk did not kill Grey Bear."

"I will never believe that."

Prompted by her aching knees, Seeks Fire got to her feet. She felt the heat of a hundred eyes on her. Only one pair mattered, but although she searched for him, she saw no sign of Lone Hawk.

"Where is he?" she asked. "Have you spoken to him since—"

"Afterward, I tried to talk to him, but he turned his back on me and would not speak. I am afraid—what if he follows Grey Bear's footsteps?"

Fear as powerful as what she'd felt when she realized Grey Bear intended to rape her nearly brought her to her knees. She felt night closing down around her, isolating her. What did starvation or no water matter in the face of this great storm of emotion? Seeking escape, she started walking, running almost, but before she'd gone more than a few feet, Touches the Wind grabbed her arm.

"What are you doing?" Touches the Wind demanded.

"Let me go!"

"No! Where are you going?"

"I do not know! I must—what have I done to deserve this?"

"You?" Touches the Wind's voice was laced with anger. "This is not about you."

Seeks Fire wanted to tear at her friend, not stopping until she'd shredded her flesh and silenced her. Then, as quickly as the rage had come, it vanished. Still shaken by the emotion, she flattened her hand over her throat.

"You are right," Seeks Fire whispered. "Lone Hawk tried to stop Grey Bear from killing himself, and now . . ."

"I know."

THEY FOUND LONE HAWK by himself so far from camp that it was almost as if he'd never been part of it. He barely acknowledged them but continued to stare at the ground.

"Why did you not say anything?" Seeks Fire asked.

When he remained silent, Touches the Wind told him that Seeks Fire knew the truth.

"I thank you for what you tried to do," Seeks Fire said. She nearly touched him but pulled back in time. "Because

of your silence, our people may never know what he did—
that for a few minutes he was not the warrior everyone
thought him. When—when Touches the Wind came to you,
you could have told her that this thing was between Grey
Bear and me, but you did not. You acted."

"He is still dead."

"You—you do not believe I did something to bring this
upon myself?"

"No. I know what he was like."

"Like?"

"Not the warrior everyone believed him to be. His body
and mind had filled with battle. He kept reliving what had
been done to him and what he had done to others. Hot blood
pounded through him, and he did not know what to do with
that."

The explanation sounded so simple, so easy for her to
accept.

"When the fire was out, after he had raped you, his guilt
overwhelmed him. He could not live with it."

Seeks Fire never thought she could feel sorry for Grey
Bear, but she now did. To be a warrior was sometimes a
horrible thing.

"Lone Hawk, you must tell them," she insisted. "Make
them understand Grey Bear was not himself and that he—
that he raped me and then hated himself for it."

"You want him to say those words?" Touches the Wind
asked as Lone Hawk stared at her.

Although it was nearly dark, Seeks Fire closed her eyes
and went deep inside herself. The thought of everyone knowing how she'd ceased to be a maiden made her shake, but
what if she remained silent?

"It can be no other way." She forced the words. "If people
understand I did nothing wrong, they will—they must—"

"No!"

Startled, she opened her eyes and struggled to read Lone
Hawk's emotion.

"I have thought about this and little else since Grey Bear's
death," he said. He sounded calm and resigned. "Death waits

for all of us if we do not soon find water and food. Perhaps we have only one hope—Sweet Grass Eater's dreams."

She nodded.

"What will happen to everyone's faith, to their hope, if they know that his grandson, the man he molded into a fearless warrior, committed an unforgivable sin?"

Seeks Fire's throat threatened to close down. "They—they will doubt our priest."

"Yes." Lone Hawk glanced at Touches the Wind, who stood a few feet away, her face uplifted as if she were opening herself to the evening breeze. "But not all," he continued. "Some will accept the truth, but others, those who have long turned to Sweet Grass Eater and Grey Bear and placed their trust in them, will continue to believe I killed him."

He held out both hands as if hefting weights. "Our people will be divided. Facing death and no longer as one."

LONE HAWK WOULD have given a great deal to speak to Touches the Wind in private, but she'd left when a somber Seeks Fire did. Because he'd already thought long and hard about what he had to do, he'd turned his back on the night-peaceful plains and returned to his people. Now, surrounded by those he'd long considered his clan, his family, he'd never felt more alone.

A couple of peace chiefs suggested he be tied up so he couldn't leave before the public meeting that would declare him an outcast, but Nightelk asked if he accepted his punishment, and Lone Hawk said yes. As he explained, he'd gone off by himself during Grey Bear's funeral out of respect for the dead man's family.

After that, no one looked at or spoke to him. In the dark, he couldn't tell where Touches the Wind had gone, had no way of looking into her for the truth of her emotions.

Unable simply to sit and wait, he gathered his belongings together. He was checking his mare's legs when he heard someone approach.

"The peace chiefs will speak to you at dawn," Nightelk

told him. "They agreed with me that your banishment will take place before everyone is up, in private."

"I see."

"Banishment for what you have done is for four years. You understand?"

Four years. "I do what I must."

Something that was a cross between a sigh and a groan rolled out of Nightelk. "My son told me what happened during the raid against the Pawnee. Grey Bear had coup counted against him and was nearly killed."

Lone Hawk nodded.

"It is my doing, my sin."

"Yours? You were not there."

"Not my flesh but—" Nightelk sighed. "I must tell you something. Beg your forgiveness."

At the older man's words, Lone Hawk's exhaustion faded into nothing. Stepping away from his horse, he indicated the ground, and after Nightelk sat down, he did the same. The stars and moon touched the older man with a pale, silver light.

"Everything that has happened to the Cheyenne beginning with Porcupine's death is because of me," Nightelk began.

"No! How can you say—"

"Listen. Listen and understand."

In detail, Nightelk described how he'd accidentally shot a Sacred White Calf and his desperate prayers for forgiveness. Deaths and the threat of starvation were proof that his effort at atonement hadn't satisfied the gods.

"I wanted to hand them my life in exchange for the Calf's, but although I prayed for guidance on how that should be done, those prayers too were not answered. At the same time, I told myself I was needed, that I had been made a peace chief and could not turn my back on those responsibilities. I was handed the Sacred Arrows, Sweet Grass Eater's tepee burned, and he lost faith in his power, I spoke for him . . ."

Nightelk crossed his legs and leaned forward. He looked old, smaller.

"For a man to die in battle brings glory to himself and his

family, but I could not walk that way because my worth is no longer as a warrior. I did not know how to bring about my death and—no! I lie."

Lone Hawk waited.

"I do not want to die. Calf Woman and I are like two halves of one thing. She has already lost enough; I do not want her to have to mourn me as well, to know what I did. When I look at Walking Rabbit, I see a woman alone because of me, a woman I should marry but who does not want any man. It—if I am no more, will the Cheyenne find peace? Would my death bring rain and cause the buffalo to return?"

"I do not know," Lone Hawk said. Then because tonight was about the truth, he told Nightelk how Grey Bear really had died.

"I cannot say why so much that is bad stalks us," Lone Hawk finished. "It is not for me, or you, to understand the ways of the spirits. What I do know is that I no longer have a home."

"LONE HAWK?"

His eyes opened and he started to sit up. Despite herself, Touches the Wind scooted away.

"What are you—" he began. "You should not be here."

"It is all right. No one will see us."

Despite her reassurance, he glanced around, but he'd placed his sleeping blanket near his horse which he'd tethered at a distance from the others. Grey Bear's family was still awake, but everyone else must have given into exhaustion, as evidenced by the many snores.

"You will leave in the morning?" she asked.

"Once the peace chiefs have said what they must."

"This is my fault." Tears welled up in her throat, but she fought them. "If I had not sent you after Grey Bear—"

"Stop! You did not rape Seeks Fire."

"No. I—will I ever see you again?"

"I do not know," he said, and it took every ounce of strength in her not to lean into him. From earliest childhood, she'd believed that fighting and hunting were the most courageous things a man could do, but now she knew it took greater courage to walk away from people who'd become part of him.

"I do not want you to be alone," she told him. "To be banished for something that was not your fault. I—I should go with you to keep you from being alone, but Little Bird . . ."

"This must not touch her. You and I have spoken on this before. I do what I must."

"I wish . . . so many things. For so much to be different."

"That cannot be."

"I know, but at least let me give you a story, something to hold with you so you will never forget what it is to be Cheyenne."

"I never will."

"I, ah—" Touches the Wind fought tears. "Where will you go?"

He shifted his weight so he now supported his upper body with his right arm and his legs were stretched out near hers. "Perhaps to the Great Lakes. I would like to see land our ancestors knew."

"The Sioux, Assiniboin, and Cree are there."

"Once, yes, but perhaps they have moved elsewhere."

"You do not know that. Lone Hawk, the Great Lakes are so far away. You will never make it."

He didn't agree or tell her she was wrong. Instead, he occupied himself by studying the stars. "I am ready for what I must do." His tone was soft, resigned. "The time will come, in four years, when I will be forgiven."

Do not say it! Do not— "If you are still alive. If any of us are."

Taking her hand, he held it against his warm chest. "Yes," he said. "If any of us are. I tried to sleep so perhaps a dream would visit, but I cannot quiet my thoughts enough for that. Maybe it is better not to know what waits for any of us."

"Perhaps."

He increased his hold on her hand. "Take care of yourself. Please, promise you will."

"I do not matter. You are the one in danger," Touches the Wind murmured.

"We all are."

NIGHTELK STUDIED LONE Hawk until he could no longer see the young man. He wondered if the pain he felt at this moment could be any greater if his own son had been cast from the tribe. Then, because the day's heat was going to be relentless, he turned to what he had to say.

Grey Bear, he reminded the gathered men unnecessarily, could no longer lead. The hunt required by Sweet Grass Eater's dream and by necessity was the most important ever undertaken.

"We must have a new leader," he said.

He waited for Sweet Grass Eater to agree with him, but the priest continued to stare fixedly at where his grandson's body lay.

"Someone who will not stop or turn away." Nightelk took a breath. "Someone who knows what is at stake."

The young men muttered among themselves, but although several shifted position and he thought they might get to their feet, none did.

"I understand what is in your hearts," he went on. "That no one can take Grey Bear's place, and without Lone Hawk, we have lost keen sight and hearing, but it is the Cheyenne way to follow a man who is not afraid. Or if he is, that man knows how to ride with fear."

"Father?"

The sound of his son's voice freed Nightelk from the remnants of his conversation with Lone Hawk. Two Coyotes stood near the back of the hunters, his gaze steady.

"I have given this a great deal of thought," Two Coyotes said. "Asked myself whether I am the one the others need or want. I have hunted since I was old enough to sit a horse, but I have always asked myself if there is a way other than war. That is why I questioned whether I should be leader."

"No, do not doubt," several men muttered.

Two Coyotes acknowledged them with a nod. "I have fought, and if I must, I will fight again. But if there is a choice between drawing weapons against our enemies and riding another direction, I will turn my horse. If there are those who cannot follow a man who believes that, speak now."

No one did, the silence filling Nightelk with both pride and dread.

Please, he prayed. *Do not let my sin touch my son.*

CHAPTER 27

Nightelk wasn't sure whether Walking Rabbit had paid any attention to the men's plans, but when he walked over to her and her son, she indicated she wanted him to sit on one of her blanket bundles. Knows No Fear, whose features displayed a maturity they hadn't had before, stopped what he was doing to watch.

"I heard," she said. "You and Sweet Grass Eater are going with the hunters."

He nodded. "Many asked him to lay aside his grief and use his dreams and prayers to protect them."

"I hope he can, but I do not understand why you are going."

He'd hoped to confine the conversation to questions about how she was doing and whether she needed any help. "My heart cannot do otherwise," he told her.

"Your heart?"

"I need to hear Sweet Grass Eater's words and know we are truly following his dreams. Danger may come if—*when* we reach the buffalo," he said with as much conviction as he could. "We must prevent the Pawnee from stealing from us."

Walking Rabbit studied him for a moment. "And perhaps it is easier for you to ride with the hunters than remain with the women and children—near me."

"I do not fear you."

"Not me but my grief. Mine and that of Jumps Like Ants' parents."

She no longer reminded him of a shadow figure, making him wonder if his prayers had been answered and that was why she was starting to become more than just a woman without a husband or daughter.

"Is that true?" she asked. "Looking at me is too hard?"

"I do not want this for you."

"I wish you success and for your arrows to pierce the hearts of many buffalo. I wish I could give you more than that."

"It is enough." He turned his attention to Knows No Fear. "Others will tell you to walk in your father's moccasins and look after your mother, but I do not. If this was another time, I would take you with me."

Walking Rabbit straightened protectively.

"But too much is at stake," Nightelk went on. "You must remain with those who follow. But before I go, I give you something so you know my heart walks with you."

Before either of them could ask what he was talking about, he reached into his quiver and drew out three arrows.

"These are not the Sacred Arrows, but arrows represent what I feel for you. I hope you will take them, feel their strength and protection."

After a moment, Walking Rabbit took them from him. She gave two to Knows No Fear. The third she held in both hands.

"Be careful," she said. "Ride with wisdom and a pure heart."

*   *   *

SEEKS FIRE HADN'T meant to see what took place between Nightelk and Walking Rabbit. She'd simply been on her way to her sister-in-law to ask if she needed help getting under way. However, watching the way Walking Rabbit and Nightelk stood with their heads close together sent a sharp bolt of pain through her.

That could have been her and Grey Bear! If he hadn't died, she'd be spending these minutes with him. Perhaps they'd speak of practical matters, but maybe they touch on what their lives would be like once they were married.

Grey Bear would never marry anyone. He was dead.

Not sure where she was going, she turned and headed onto the plains. She was careful not to let her feet take her near Grey Bear's grave, but that didn't stop her from asking herself whether she'd kneel before it and offer up a prayer before leaving.

What would she say to Grey Bear's spirit? That she forgave him? That she understood he hadn't been able to distance himself from the heat and horror of battle? Maybe, but she also needed to ask him if he'd thought, even for a heartbeat, of her.

If he hadn't killed himself, if instead he'd listened to Lone Hawk's warning, Grey Bear would be alive. Would he have taken his usual place of leadership, or would his memories have made that impossible?

Worn out from the endless questions and her equally endless turmoil, she tried to lose herself in her surroundings. A high haze was in evidence, and the sky had lost a little of its blue, but although she welcomed the change, the haze carried no rain in it. The wind bit with hot teeth, but she paid it little mind. This morning she'd stood passively as her mother tied her into her chastity belt, but if Grey Bear had planted his seed inside her . . .

Frantic, she spun away, but there was no escaping the question. A child born to a Cheyenne woman believed a virgin was almost beyond her comprehension. If she could hand the infant to Walking Rabbit to replace Follower, perhaps she'd be forgiven, but what if Walking Rabbit didn't want a child born from sin?

"Do not let it be! Grandmother Earth, you are both supernatural and living and care for everything living. Please, do not let this be."

Sick, she ground her fists into her stomach.

From nearly a quarter of a mile away, a Pawnee watched. When the wind sent his hair into wild tangles, he smoothed it down, his fingers lingering over a large white patch at his temple.

IF HE'D WANTED to, Lone Hawk could have stayed near camp until the men left, and as long as he remained hidden, he could have followed them to see if Sweet Grass Eater's telling-dream spoke the truth.

Instead, he headed in a northeasterly direction. At first his mare had resisted because she wasn't going with the other horses, but he'd convinced her to walk where he wanted her to. Although they hadn't spoken to him, the old people he'd lived with had handed him a small water bladder and watched as he placed it on his mare's back. Just thinking about the water made him thirsty, but he didn't drink because he had to share what he had with his horse. Without a mount, he wouldn't last more than a couple of days.

If anyone had asked where he was going, he wasn't sure he could answer. Sweet Grass Eater dreamed of a vast herd standing belly deep in a river while they waited for the Cheyenne. Those same Cheyenne wouldn't want to hear that their outcast's dreams remained far different.

Because he trusted his mare's footing, he allowed his eyes to glaze over. The reality of what he was doing and what he'd left behind made dozing impossible, but when he put his mind to it, the vision he'd had recently came back to him.

The buffalo he'd "seen" were far fewer in number than what Sweet Grass Eater spoke of. Instead of waiting under the star grouping that resembled an antelope's horn, his buffalo—if he could call them that—were in a place he couldn't describe and might never find. The water of his dreams was a creek, not a river, but it was water nonetheless. Water and buffalo.

Maybe.

Unless ghosts and not Heammawihio were responsible for his visions.

No! He would *not* think about what would surely happen if his dreams were lies. He would *not* think about the fate, not just for the Cheyenne but for all Indians.

"I WAS SO different then. All I thought about was the look on my husband's face when he spotted the new drawings on our tepee." Calf Woman walked around a prairie-dog mound before continuing. "When I think of how I boasted—I was foolish."

"Not foolish," her sister corrected. "No one knew what would happen. If we had, we would not have been so careless."

"No, we would not have." Calf Woman glanced back at the horses she was leading. "You carry one of my husband's arrows," she said, changing the subject. "He gave it to you?"

"Three. I gave two to Knows No Fear. Nightelk wanted us to have something that would make our hearts strong."

Today the band traveled as if they were all tied to a single, short rope. Calf Woman was both heartened by their presence and bothered by the anxious looks on so many faces. The dead grass underneath crunched with every step, and although that was all the horses had to eat, they seldom took a bite. She still had horses, which made her rich in comparison to someone like Long Chin, whose lone mare hadn't gotten up this morning, but possessions that once brought her a sense of pride no longer did so.

"I did not want my husband to go," she admitted. "He has had his warrior years. It is time for others to take his place. When he would not change his mind, I asked him to take Black Eyes with him, but . . ."

"Nightelk would not be happy riding alongside old men."

"In truth, I am not certain anything would bring him plea-sure these days. He has changed, become somber in ways he has not been since Plays with Shadows' death."

Plays with Shadows had been their firstborn. She'd died in the middle of her second year.

"This summer has changed all of us," Walking Rabbit said. "Do you think—I cannot believe Lone Hawk capable of murder. Not a man who risked his life looking for a lost child in a fire."

Calf Woman shrugged. "I have tried to ask myself the same question, but it makes my head hurt."

"When Plays with Shadows died, I was a girl myself, but I knew you and Nightelk grieved. When does the pain be-come less?"

Unable to speak, Calf Woman wrapped her heavy arm around her sister's shoulder. They walked like that for sev-eral moments.

"The pain is always there," she finally admitted. "Time dulls the worst of it, but the hole in my heart—nothing will ever fill it. I wish I could tell you different."

Walking Rabbit took a less-than-steady breath. "I wish you could too. To never know—to think about what she must have endured before—if only I could shut my mind against that!"

LONE HAWK'S THOUGHTS settled not on the question of what would happen if he ran out of water before finding a creek but on the reality of his aloneness. He had his horse, but the quiet mare wasn't another voice, shared thoughts and words. He found only brief distraction in the insects scurrying out of his way.

Grey Bear was dead. He had to accept that just as he still fought to accept that the wilderness had claimed Follower. It was hard to comprehend that Grey Bear had forced himself on the maiden he professed to love, and he prayed her life hadn't been ruined as a result, but if Grey Bear had placed his seed inside her . . .

Grey Bear! Sweet Grass Eater had given his grandson that name because bears were powerful and mysterious creatures that sometimes healed their own wounds, but Grey Bear hadn't been able to heal his self-inflicted wound. Instead, he'd died.

Shaking his head, Lone Hawk looked around. Although the endless nothing of his world overwhelmed him, he also found peace in its familiarity. Over the seasons, he'd seen untold animal bones and knew the plains were unforgiving, but they also fed and nurtured and would again, in time, if the Cheyenne learned enough of its secrets.

"Talk to me," he ordered his mare, startling her. "Give me another place for my thoughts."

She had nothing to say, but then she suddenly lifted her head and stared upward; he did the same.

A hawk.

WHEN THEIR FATHER briefly walked alongside them, Little Bird asked Long Chin if he knew where her mother's digging stick was. He said he didn't and soon wandered away, leaving Little Bird and Touches the Wind alone.

"Why did you ask him that?" Touches the Wind asked. "He did not help pack our belongings."

"I know." Little Bird stepped over a long, thin line of ants. Her bare feet were covered with dust.

"Then why?"

"Because—does he still think of her?" She sounded on the verge of tears. "He never talks about our mother. Maybe—maybe he did not love her."

"Of course he did," Touches the Wind reassured her younger sister. Her lower back ached, probably because she hadn't paid enough attention to where she'd placed her sleeping blanket last night. "Once," she amended. "But sometimes things change."

"Like it did after Momma got kicked?"

"I wish you had known her as she was before. Her laughter—I always laughed when she did."

She looked down to judge her sister's reaction, noting that Little Bird walked as their mother had during the last years of her life, as if her body had become too heavy for her.

"I wish I could make your memories different," she admitted. "For you to remember falling asleep in her arms and her telling you stories and making you laugh and—"

"It is you who did those things."

"Because I love you. Because I knew she was sick and in pain."

Little Bird slid one foot after another, then, finally, looked up. "I love you," she whispered.

Blinking back tears, Touches the Wind hoisted her sister onto her back, but before long, she had to put her down. By then Little Bird had become if not her usual happy self, at least no longer as sad. She asked if skunks had so much supernatural power because Heammawihio felt sorry for them because of the way they smelled and wanted them to have something to make up for it.

Touches the Wind, who'd never considered that, agreed with her sister. Little Bird thought it was good that warriors often tied stinky skunk tails to their horses' tails to repel their enemies when they went to war.

The girl's voice droned on and on like an insect hum. The small presence beside her both comforted Touches the Wind and filled her with anxiety about tomorrow and the day after that. She'd been drinking less water than her body needed so there'd be enough for Little Bird, but she didn't dare let herself become so weak that she couldn't be there for her.

Nightelk, Sweet Grass Eater, Two Coyotes, please, be successful. Find favor with the gods so they will—

Something that was both presence and pressure touched her nerve endings, and although she instantly knew what that something was, she turned her entire attention to it, inhaled the clean, hot air and pulled it down and through her.

Lone Hawk had told her how Hawk led him to Little Bird during the fire. In turn, she'd told him that she'd always felt part of the wind. They'd come together in that thing, and if she hadn't begged him to try to stop Grey Bear from killing himself, would they be walking together today, sharing Wind? Looking for Hawk?

She scanned the sky, but although she saw a small, distant dot, she knew better than to hinge her hopes on something that might not be. The wind, however—the wind was real.

Listen to me, it seemed to be saying. *Listen and learn.*

What do you want me to know?

Wisdom is within you. Only you can find its truth.

"I am a maiden, only a maiden," she insisted. Little Bird stared up at her. "I am not wise enough. I do not know what you are saying."

Feel me. Know I am here. That wisdom exists.

"What wisdom? Please, I—who are you?"

Nothing.

"Please, what is it? Strength? Or—danger?"

Still nothing.

GREY BEAR RODE beside him. Not his physical self, of course, but Lone Hawk had the unshakable sensation that the man who'd died in his arms had sent something of himself, maybe part of his soul, to travel the same journey.

When he'd first sensed the presence, Lone Hawk believed it came from the hawk he now followed, but no bird of prey had ever touched his senses this way. Perhaps Grey Bear had left earth before saying everything he needed to and was trying to reach beyond the Hanging Road on his way to Heaven to . . .

Only, because he'd committed suicide, Grey Bear was forbidden to spend eternity there with his ancestors. Instead, when his journey along the Hanging Road came to the fork in the Milky Way, he'd have to walk into nothingness.

Was that why his soul was here? Because it fought nothingness?

"I cannot change your journey," he told Grey Bear. "When you plunged your knife into your heart, you knew what you were bringing upon yourself. Your choice—but did you have one?

"I ask you," he said once he'd gathered his thoughts, "was your guilt over raping Seeks Fire so great you could not see beyond that? You hated yourself, that hate greater than the fire that destroyed our village? If so, I cry for you, but my tears do not change what happened. Or where you are today."

Lone Hawk's thoughts had been like small creatures caught in a great flood, but now that he'd spoken, he felt a little calmer. Hawk hadn't deserted him, and he thanked the bird for showing him a way to go—the right way, he hoped—but until he'd made his peace with Grey Bear's soul, he couldn't concentrate fully on where he was headed.

"Do you know what happened to me?" he asked. His mare twitched her ears. "Is that why you are with me, to say you did not mean for your act to touch me?"

He waited for his mind to settle again, but it didn't. Instead, the sense that he wasn't alone increased. After checking to make sure Hawk remained overhead, Lone Hawk studied his world.

No one knew how far the plains extended to the west or what lay at their end, but that was where Hawk was going. As long as the men he'd once believed he'd spend his life riding beside traveled in the same direction, so would he.

He again took note of Hawk, the bird's presence comforting him; at the same time, he forced the necessary question. What if Hawk had to leave him in order to drink or kill? Would Hawk return?

Lost in thought of how far Hawk might have to fly in order to find water, Lone Hawk was slow to realize he was no longer alone. The other man, mounted on a long-legged horse, armed and naked except for a loincloth, was so far away he couldn't make out the paintings on the animal that would tell him whether he was looking at friend or foe. But could he call anyone a friend?

The newcomer made no hostile gesture. Still, Lone Hawk held his mare to a slow walk, the distance between him and the other man decreasing at a shadow's pace. When he was still out of reach of the strongest arrow, he stopped and stood on his mare's back, shading his eyes.

Four horizontal stripes decorated the other horse's flank, proof that the rider had counted coup four times. Marks resembling teardrops had been painted on the slender neck; the rider was or had been in mourning.

Lone Hawk used the index finger of his right hand to chop at his left index finger, signifying he was a Cheyenne, but instead of identifying himself, the other man urged his horse a little closer.

Then, every move measured, the man pulled an arrow out of his quiver, placed it in his bow, and pointed it at Lone Hawk's chest. Still, Lone Hawk stood his ground.

The man closed nearly half the remaining distance, but instead of sighting down his arrow's length, he met Lone Hawk's gaze.

A wide white streak of hair identified him.

CHAPTER 28

 The day seemed to go on forever, but finally evening came. Seeks Fire offered to help the mother of three young children, but her mother-in-law had already taken the baby out of its cradle board and was cleaning its bottom with grass.

Although she longed for the easy conversations that had always marked their relationship, Seeks Fire didn't feel strong enough to face her parents' concerned looks. After drinking the amount of water allotted to her, she went looking for Touches the Wind but couldn't find her. Little Bird, appearing more asleep than awake, was with several of her father's relatives while Long Chin sat nearby, complaining about his aching legs.

Not asking herself what she was doing, Seeks Fire made her way to the edge of the encampment. A couple of boys who'd been on their first hunts but weren't seasoned enough to join the men this time had already positioned themselves as guards. They sat clutching large spears, and when one's head fell forward and he jerked upright, she pretended not to see. Just the same, she wondered if she could add her eyesight to theirs.

Glad to have given herself a task, she watched as shadows spread over the women putting together simple, sparse dinners and the tired horses. Legs Like Lightning, who hadn't been killed to carry Grey Bear into the afterworld because Sweet Grass Eater had spared the stallion's life, was among them.

She'd never complain the way Long Chin did, but he wasn't the only one whose legs throbbed. Any other time, she could walk all day without discomfort, but her body needed more nourishment than she'd been able to give it lately.

Sounds as familiar as her own heartbeat eased over her. Her people had become like scrawny rabbits, hardly worthy of a predator's interest. If a rabbit couldn't find enough to eat, it died, its carcass picked clean by vultures. If that became her people's fate . . .

Feeling her head sag forward, she thought vaguely about straightening and then gave into the great weight. She'd seen men so exhausted that when they slid off their horses after a hunt, they'd been unable to stand. Before she could only imagine what that was like, but she now knew; nothing mattered except rest. And an end to her belly's growling.

Soon the hunters would return with . . .

But without Grey Bear at their lead could they . . .

Of course they could! Sweet Grass Eater was leading them toward his dream, and Nightelk was there as well as Two Coyotes, who . . .

Sleep settled over her. Grateful, she buried herself in it, her breathing deep and slow. She had a vague memory of curling up on her side and using her arm as a pillow, and then, despite the uneven ground, she left her physical world.

Her new one was pale gray like a winter morning. Neither hot or cold, it offered gentleness and peace. Perhaps she'd become a girl, a laughing child.

A puppy emerged from the foggy borders of her world and licked her hands and feet with an excited tongue, but when she tried to pick it up, it wiggled free.

She'd go in search of flowers. Yes, spring flowers filled with sweet smells and no bees. Perhaps she'd collect a handful and take them to her mother, and her mother would teach her the skills necessary for joining the Quilling Society. Yes, she'd like that, women sitting together boasting about their sewing skills while they painstakingly fastened decorative porcupine quills on cold-weather robes.

A pleasant humming filled her mind and ears, not the songs sung during the noisy Sun Ceremony but more like what a mother crooned to ease a child into sleep. Maybe her own mother had found her and was singing to her. If she'd had the strength, she'd turn toward the sound and give thanks, but her body felt so heavy.

She hummed along with the sound-maker, became part of that other person, shared something without words, was touched.

Touched?

Layers of sleep fell away, but she still hadn't returned to the earth-world and drifted somewhere between two places. She was no longer alone; she knew that. If the presence had been a threatening one, she would have broken free of her dream—if that's what it was—but this thing without substance felt nonthreatening, strong and yet soft.

A hand was placed on her shoulder, strength flowing from it and into her. The hand filled her, silenced her empty stomach, and cleansed her of fear. She wasn't a child after all but a woman—a woman seeking something a child had no knowledge of.

More layers peeled away until she was once again aware of sentry boys and cooking smells and thirsty horses. Her arm under her head had fallen asleep, but she couldn't think how to sit up. The touch remained, stronger now, message and truth.

Grey Bear?

WALKING RABBIT LOOKED up when Seeks Fire approached. For a moment Seeks Fire was incapable of uttering a word. However, instead of hurrying away, she dropped to her knees beside the other woman and busied herself straightening her dress.

"You should not be by yourself," Seeks Fire offered. "Your sister wants you with her."

"Calf Woman's thoughts must go to her husband," Walking Rabbit said. "I have taken her from him long enough."

Nightelk can become your husband as well, Seeks Fire thought, but she didn't say those words. Silence filled the air.

"A thing happened to me that—does Porcupine ever come to you?"

"He is dead."

"I know." Afraid she'd caused her sister-in-law grief, she gave her a small smile. "But in ways that are not easily explained—sometimes when I think of my brother, I hear his voice and remember the way he looked at me when I'd done something foolish as a child. It feels good to have those memories."

"Yes, it does."

"Then you have them?"

"Of course." Walking Rabbit glanced up as an elderly woman shuffled past.

"I know you do; I should not have asked but—please do not think I have lost my senses, but does it ever feel as if he is touching you, standing beside you, next to you in bed?"

Walking Rabbit stared at the ground for several minutes, her body motionless. "Sometimes," she whispered. "He was my husband for years; just because he is dead does not mean he has gone away. Whenever I look at our children . . ."

Walking Rabbit could no longer look at Follower. "You

see him in Knows No Fear?" Seeks Fire ventured.

"Yes."

"I think—I think the same thing happened to me."

"Porcupine came to you?"

"Not my brother but—Grey Bear."

Instead of expressing disbelief, Walking Rabbit nodded. "What was it like?"

Seeks Fire described what had happened. "I cannot be sure," she amended. "Perhaps it was only a dream, but I felt so weak and then he touched me, and I became stronger than I have ever been—like him."

"Lone Hawk killed him. Perhaps Grey Bear cannot go to the afterworld until he knows Lone Hawk has been punished."

The words faded, were nearly lost. Then: "No, that is not how he died."

"What are you saying? Nightelk saw—"

"I know what happened," Seeks Fire interrupted, "because I was part of it. I—I did not think I could speak of it again, but I must."

"Speak of what?"

The explanation of what had really led up to Grey Bear's death took much longer than describing her "dream" had, but in the end, Seeks Fire felt cleansed. It was almost as if Grey Bear himself directed her words, giving them shape and substance.

"I do not know what to say," Walking Rabbit admitted when she was done. "For Lone Hawk to be banished for something he did not do—I hate that!"

"I feel so responsible for—Do you understand why he ordered Touches the Wind and me to say nothing?"

"We *must* believe in Sweet Grass Eater. His dreams are all we have."

But the priest wasn't the only one who dreamed. Seeks Fire had too—of Grey Bear, whom she no longer hated.

Later, when she spotted Touches the Wind giving a nursing mare an extra drink of water, she started toward her friend, but Touches the Wind was staring off into the distance, her head thrown back so the Wind could caress her face.

SURROUNDED BY DARKNESS, Nightelk listened as Sweet Grass Eater chanted. The priest had said little during the day and had dozed off and on. He must have found his riding naps restful because his voice was forceful.

"The dream rode with me; it rode with me," Sweet Grass Eater singsonged. "The buffalo—ah, the buffalo. They wait, wait for us, growing fat and sweet tasting. As the sun sets, it kisses the rich fur, warms soft hides for us to sleep on this winter. This I see; this I see."

"Do you believe him?"

Nightelk scooted over to make room for his son. He'd had little chance to talk to Two Coyotes today because the younger man and Black Eyes often traveled ahead looking for buffalo signs.

"Do I believe in his dreams?" Nightelk asked.

"Not that. I am certain he has them, but are they what we must have—or something else?"

Instead of prompting Two Coyotes to continue, Nightelk waited. When his son was ready to speak, he'd do so.

"Everyone looks to Sweet Grass Eater for wisdom and direction," Two Coyotes said at length. "I do not remember when his words did not guide us, but when I look at him, I see an old man bowed by his grandson's death, a man forced to watch his tepee burn. A man who has turned the Sacred Arrows over to another."

"Do not tell him that," Nightelk cautioned. "Sweet Grass Eater needs to remain within himself."

"I know. And I want to believe him, but today I went as far as my horse could travel. I saw nothing that made me believe buffalo have been here—nothing that might show me where to look for a stream, and Black Eyes' nose was never still but—"

Was Two Coyotes afraid? If he was, their fear might flow together and strip both of them of courage.

"I pray tomorrow will be different," Nightelk murmured. *If it isn't, it is because my sin was too great.*

"When this is over," Two Coyotes asked unexpectedly, "will you marry Walking Rabbit?"

"She does not want me."

"Not right after Porcupine's death, but she is so alone now, and you have much to give her, wisdom and understanding. She could cry in your arms and find peace."

"She deserves a younger man who can give her more children and live to see them become adults."

Two Coyotes pondered that. "She may not want more children. Perhaps she cannot bear the thought of losing another."

"To be alive means to want to see new life begin, to know something of you will live after you are dead. She has already lost one husband. I do not want her to bury another. If she married someone younger, you—"

"See these!" Sweet Grass Eater boomed. He held up a handful of arrows. "These were to be Grey Bear's. I blessed them and rubbed them with sweet grass to make them pure. When we reach the buffalo, they will be the first to kill."

Two Coyotes sighed. "I want to believe him," he whispered. "With everything in me, I want to embrace his words, but if we do not soon find game and water, we will all die."

ONCE NIGHT ENVELOPED him, Lone Hawk stretched out on his blanket and waited for the Milky Way to reveal itself. When it did, instead of asking himself if Grey Bear had somehow found his way to it, his thoughts returned to Whitehair.

The Pawnee warrior had stared at him for a long time, his eyes revealing nothing. Lone Hawk had returned the stare. Whitehair was lean almost to the point of gauntness, his muscles barely covered by skin. Still, he held himself erect and proud, part of his surroundings. Lone Hawk had guessed he'd looked little different himself, perhaps not quite so thin but with the same resigned awareness of how little the plains offered. As the moments ticked by, he ceased to see a Pawnee, an enemy, but simply another determined and desperate man.

At long last, Whitehair had lifted his hand in a simple wave and ridden away.

Distant hoofbeats jerked him from the memory. He jumped to his feet, fighting the accompanying dizziness. After bending over to retrieve his weapons, he faced the sound. Moonlight tinged the plains, but it was difficult to determine how far away the approaching rider was. The horse—Legs Like Lightning—traveled at a fast and confident walk.

"Who is it?" he called out.

"Lone Hawk?"

Shock slashed down his spine. "Touches the wind," he managed, "what—what has happened?"

"Nothing," she said, and dismounted.

On horseback, Touches the Wind had looked more like a warrior than a maiden, but now she had to tilt her head to meet his gaze.

"Nothing? What are you doing here?"

"Legs Like Lightning found you," she said instead of answering him. "I begged the stallion to guide me to you and he did. I thought—he was Grey Bear's, and I did not know if he would listen to me, but I could think of nothing else."

Her words tumbled together. Although he wanted to shake her and demand an explanation, wisdom told him to wait. That the horse had found him in the middle of this vast nothing had to be the work of the gods.

"I told my sister to stay with Knows No Fear, to not be quick to tell others what I was doing, but if I did not return by night, for Little Bird to go to Seeks Fire and Walking Rabbit. I took Legs Like Lightning because I needed a strong horse and because—because . . ." She looked down but made no move to sit.

"One time you and I spoke of things that come to us," she whispered. "Like Wind and Hawk."

"Yes." Did anyone know she was here?

"It happened today, only different."

"What happened?"

Touches the Wind hunched forward, then straightened. As so many times before, she turned her face into the wind. The moon touched her features, and he saw that she was smiling, peaceful.

"I will always be Wind's daughter," she said. He had to strain to hear. "I want Wind to know that and to thank Wind for showing me there are things beyond this earth. When I speak of Heammawihio and Maheo, the children cling to my words, but because I keep it to my heart, they do not know of what exists between me and Wind."

Lone Hawk felt himself being pulled into her words, perhaps feeling her emotions. That she was here still seemed impossible, but he'd deal with that later, after—

"Today what touched me was not just Wind but—but also Grey Bear."

He nearly recoiled from the name and everything associated with it, but he forced his mind to open up again. "Tell me."

"Something touched me. At first, I did not know what it was, could not believe that Grey Bear's spirit had any need for me. But then he spoke to me and everything changed. I— I wonder if he did the same to Seeks Fire."

Spoke. "What did he say?"

"Not words. His thoughts became mine. Lone Hawk, he spoke of wisdom and strength, and although I did not fully understand, I felt both wise and strong. And then—do you believe me?"

The intensity of her question caught him off balance. "You believe what happened, do you not?" he asked.

"Yes."

"No questions?"

"None."

"Then I do too."

Her sigh was a gentle breeze over spring-wet new grass. "Thank you," she said.

Taking her hands, he pressed them to his chest. Despite their small size, he felt their strength and believed their separate strengths were flowing together. "Why me? Why not wait and tell Sweet Grass Eater?"

"Maybe Grey Bear's spirit told me to come to you because he knows that together we will know what to do."

"His spirit?" he asked barely comprehending. "He hated me."

"He said nothing about that." She shook her head. "When I hear my words, I do not believe I am saying them, and yet—Lone Hawk, Grey Bear's spirit spoke of more than strength and wisdom and that he wanted me to find you. He also warned of danger."

"To you?"

She dug her fingers into his chest as if trying to draw strength from the fighting-hardened muscles. "My sister— babies and old women. Everyone. Was that Grey Bear's truth? He wanted me to bring you back to the band to protect them?"

"I have been banned."

"That does not matter! I cannot bear to see any more mothers mourn missing children or cry over broken bodies. If your presence prevents that—if only I understood!"

He'd been afraid during battle; although he'd never told anyone, he couldn't deny the muscle-stripping fear. What he felt now went beyond that. "I am only one man. The hunters—"

"Legs Like Lightning did not take me to them. Grey Bear sent me here to you; I believe that. We must trust—must trust his wisdom."

Trust Grey Bear, who'd only filled her and now his head with questions? Still, how could he turn his back on her desperate plea?

"Not tonight," he told her. "The horses must rest. And us."

"But at dawn?"

"At dawn we will decide."

A FIERCE WIND came with the morning. Nightelk stood with his back to it and tried not to think what it would become once it inhaled the day's heat. From the look in the other hunters' eyes, he knew they were thinking the same thing.

Two Coyotes hadn't rebraided his hair since leaving the women and children. As a result, strands had come loose to swirl about him, making him look wild. Determination continued to square the young man's shoulders, but how much longer would that last?

"He called out several times," Two Coyotes said, indicating where Sweet Grass Eater had spent the night. "I thought about waking him and taking him from what was bothering him, but maybe he needed to stay within his dream no matter what it revealed."

"Maybe." Talking had opened a cut at the corner of Nightelk's mouth. He was careful not to lick it. "After this morning, there will be no more water for the horses or Black Eyes."

Two Coyotes' gaze flicked to the rising sun. "And soon, none for us."

Nightelk loved all of his children and believed he had no favorite, but there was something about Two Coyotes—perhaps Two Coyotes represented what he'd once been, young and confident, yet realistic and calm.

"I am glad I have not seen my daughter for several seasons," Two Coyotes said. "When my wife left, my arms felt empty because I had no baby to hold, but perhaps it is better this way."

"Your time will come again. Just because she did a crazy thing does not mean there will not be another. Walking Rabbit—"

"That is not what I am talking about. I never want to leave a wife and children the way Porcupine did. To have my life end knowing I will never see my babies become men and women—" Two Coyotes gave his head an angry shake. "A warrior *must* not think of such a thing! As long as I can see and there is strength in my arms, I will hunt."

He would, Nightelk thought, but not just because of his determination. If the Sacred White Calf's spirit demanded more deaths as payment for its death, Two Coyotes would *not* be the one to pay the price. He would. He *would!*

"Take my water," he told Two Coyotes.

"No, you need—"

"Your life is worth so much more than mine that I cannot speak of it. You are worthy of many more years, not me."

"The Cheyenne need your wisdom."

"They need your skills more." He came within a whisper of telling Two Coyotes what he believed was the cause of their desperate condition, but the words wouldn't come. "I gave you the gift of life. I give it to you again."

Two Coyotes opened his mouth, but the argument Nightelk expected didn't come. Instead, resignation, understanding, even agreement slid over his son's features. "I do not want this," he said.

"I have seen enough of life. I am ready for what comes next."

Do not tell yourself that!

Shaking, Nightelk jerked upright. Two Coyotes was studying him with a startled expression; they were alone.

"What is it?" Two Coyotes asked.

Nothing, he wanted to say but couldn't. Compelled by some force he barely comprehended, Nightelk closed his eyes and went deep inside himself. At first he felt nothing except his own body, but then . . .

Do not turn your back on life. It is precious—and once lost cannot be reclaimed.

This new sensation didn't breathe, no heart beat. Still, someone else's thoughts had slipped into him. Whether they were a gift or a warning he couldn't tell.

Death hurts. Arms are empty. Eyes see nothing. The loneliness—is the greatest pain.

Grey Bear, Nightelk said inside his head. *Is it you?*

Yes.

"Father. What is it?"

Perhaps Grey Bear had been frightened off by Two Coyotes' voice, and maybe he'd said all he'd intended to. Whichever it was, Nightelk felt himself hollowing out and then taking back control of himself, sensing the wind again.

Before he could decide what, if anything, to say to his son, someone announced that Sweet Grass Eater wanted to speak to everyone. Joining the others, Nightelk noted that the old priest's dry hair hung in limp tangles around his wrinkled neck, but his eyes were bright. Once the others were seated, he began.

"I knew the wind would be angry today," he said. "My dreams told me so."

"What else did they say?" Wolf Robe asked. "Did you see where the buffalo are?"

Sweet Grass Eater pursed his lips. "You think it is such a simple thing," he chided. "Perhaps you believe there is a wide, marked trail, but you forget, these are no ordinary buffalo but gift-beasts from Maheo."

The priest hadn't said that before. Instead of pointing that out, Nightelk tried to empty his mind so Grey Bear could again enter it if he wanted.

"Now that trust and belief have brought us this far, Maheo speaks to me of other things," Sweet Grass Eater said. "This drought came because there was no Arrow Renewal Ceremony this year."

Jerked back to the here and now, Nightelk frowned.

"Of all the ceremonies, none is more important." Sweet Grass Eater nodded. "From the beginning of time, it has been thus. All the Cheyenne bands draw slowly together. No one rides from one another telling each one what they must do, where they should go, what the others are doing because everyone knows—knows in the way that animals know to grow their hair long in winter. On their way to the ceremonial meeting place, each band stops four times, to pray, to smoke to the four directions and to the Great Medicine Spirits above."

With each passing moment, the day became hotter and the wind punished.

"Maheo is angry because those things did not happen this year."

Getting to his feet, Nightelk stood in front of his priest. "There was no Arrow Renewal because by the time the summer sun was at its highest, the streams were drying up. There wasn't enough water for everyone to come together, or enough grass to sustain so many horses. It was decided that we would wait until next summer."

"The decision was wrong," Sweet Grass Eater insisted. His eyes were narrowed but still determined. "Without the ceremony, we are doomed. The buffalo will not show themselves."

Had Sweet Grass Eater's mind deserted him? Nightelk came within a breath of saying that when another thought—this one perhaps coming from Grey Bear—struck him.

What if the old priest was right?

CHAPTER 29

"I am the pledger," Sweet Grass Eater intoned. "I come humbly and with a pure heart, begging forgiveness because the great gift to the Cheyenne was not given the ceremony it deserves."

Naked, Sweet Grass Eater stood with his eyes shut and his head toward the heavens. All around him, other men did the same. His heart threatening to break through his chest, Nightelk struggled for composure.

"Maiyun," the priest continued, "you gave us the Sacred Arrows so we would have power over buffalo and human beings. The Arrows are our soul. When they prosper, so do we. Within them is the spiritual power we need to survive. When he returned from the Sacred Mountain, Mutsoyef taught us that the Arrow Renewal Ceremony must last four days and bring together all Cheyenne; we know that."

Sweet Grass Eater fell silent, giving Nightelk time to question, again, what they were doing. Standing surrounded by the tribe's men lent him strength and pride, and yet this wasn't a true renewal ceremony because there was no Offering Lodge where people could leave their gifts to Maiyun, no special lodge poles supplied by men with good reputations. Warriors hadn't gone to two men selected because they were brave, generous, good, and even-tempered to request a loan of their tepee coverings to be placed over the new lodge poles. Sweet Grass Eater didn't have the necessary paints to paint himself red, but most telling of all, the Sacred Arrows weren't here but back with the rest of the tribe.

"Maiyun, look into our hearts and see that they are pure."

Nightelk shuddered, but although he feared his presence would prevent Maiyun from hearing or believing the priest, he couldn't make himself leave. These were his people, his life.

"You know where the Sacred Arrows are," Sweet Grass Eater continued. "You understand why we left them behind, not because they are unimportant but because we believed they were safer there. But this—"

Despite himself, Nightelk opened his eyes. Sweet Grass Eater had bent down and was holding up the arrows he'd been making when Grey Bear died.

"These were created with a priest's hands, a man who has spent his life following your ways. Please, see them and understand that our souls are with them—and you. Please, understand our great need. Guide our feet to the food gifts you have always provided."

Sweet Grass Eater's voice became tear-clogged. "These were to aid in my grandson's success. I will not speak of his death because I pray that does not matter today. I also pray the power of the Sacred Arrows will find these and power will come to them. I wish—" He swallowed.

Heat pounded onto the top of Nightelk's head and he was already tired of battling the wind. *Hurry, hurry, hurry,* he kept thinking, but ceremonies could never be rushed. Besides, without a sign from Maiyun, how would they know where to go today?

"I wish there was time for smoking the ceremonial pipe and for these men to pray to their spirit-helpers. My ears need to hear drums and songs, and I believe you wish that as well. Maiyun, look down on us and see our desperation."

The words sent a chill through Nightelk. He sensed Two Coyotes beside him but didn't look at him.

"When I went to sleep last night," the priest went on, "I prayed I would again dream of the path we must take and that as we rode along it, we would see countless buffalo tracks, but—I did not."

Two Coyotes grabbed Nightelk's forearm.

"Instead, my night was filled with visions of arrows. And you. This morning I come to you naked and humble asking for a sign that we are worthy. That it is right for us to continue to live. That you will show us how that must be done."

Nightelk felt exhausted. At the same time, the awful weight around his heart seemed a little less oppressive. Not asking himself what he was doing, he left his son's side and walked over to his belongings. He selected two arrows and held them up to the sky as Sweet Grass Eater had done.

"Maiyun, I stand before you and those who are like brothers to me and offer up my weapons as well," he said. He glanced at Two Coyotes, who regarded him somberly, then continued. "You alone know what is in my heart. You alone must tell me whether that thing should remain inside me or spread out so my brothers can see it."

A gust of wind threatened to spin Nightelk around. "But I wish you to understand this; I have been made a peace chief and those with wisdom say I am worthy of responsibility for the Sacred Arrows. I did not want to do so because of what is in my heart, but when I touched them, I became like a father holding his newborn—protective and filled with love."

Feeling more exposed than he ever had, Nightelk met each pair of eyes in turn, finishing with his priest. "I bear the weight of Porcupine's death, and perhaps every bad thing that has befallen us since then. While others faced Pawnee, I rode after buffalo. I believed my arrow was flying to a cow's heart. Instead—"

The wind beat at his flesh, burning him. He fought the

need to hide from it and whatever force might be behind it. Desperately wanted to be silent.

"Instead I struck a white calf."

Sweet Grass Eater's gaze darkened. At the same time, the old man seemed to shrink into himself. No one spoke or moved. Black Eyes stared at him. Nightelk closed his eyes and let the day's heat seep into him.

"Today, surrounded by my brothers and son with starvation stalking us, I beg forgiveness. If the gods demand my life in payment, I offer it."

TOUCHES THE WIND no longer expected the wind's message to bring her comfort. Yesterday as Legs Like Lightning took her to Lone Hawk, she'd filled her thoughts and prayers with her spirit. Wind had answered by pushing gently at her back.

She'd tried to tell Lone Hawk that she'd accepted her unseen guide and had felt no surprise when she found him. He hadn't told her she was wrong, and if he'd felt doubt, his eyes had kept their secret. He'd joined her prayer of thanksgiving, and then she'd stood beside him and echoed his words to Hawk.

But that had been yesterday. This morning Wind was full of angry energy—either that or Grey Bear with his need for battle had returned.

Legs Like Lightning occasionally nibbled at nearby grass, but much of the time the stallion stood with his back to the wind and his head lowered, perhaps listening to his master's spirit. If they returned to the band, they'd be walking into Wind.

"Have you decided what we should do?" Touches the Wind struggled to keep panic out of her voice.

"No." Lone Hawk ran his hand down his braids. "You heard whispers of danger, but who were they for?"

"I do not know." She moaned. "I trusted in Wind and Grey Bear's wish that I look for you; I did not ask what would happen after that. I should have."

But would that have made any difference? he wondered.

Last night they'd prayed together. As a result, he'd felt peaceful and been given a long stretch of dreamless sleep. Oblivion hadn't lasted long enough, but perhaps that time of peace had been a sign.

"I came to your band to learn from Sweet Grass Eater but spent much of my time becoming a hunter and a warrior," he admitted. "If I had remained at his side, perhaps I would know more about things I cannot see or touch. Hawk is my helper, but I do not understand him."

"I feel the same when Wind comes to me, grateful and blessed but without enough wisdom."

He wondered which of them had the thought first, not that it mattered because when their hands met, he knew it was right. Grit stung his face, forcing him to duck his head. She did the same.

"I do not know the words the spirits need to hear," Touches the Wind admitted. "Perhaps none because the spirits can reach inside and feel my thoughts."

"Perhaps."

"Wind." Her tone softened and became wistful. "Touch us with your strength. Believe our hearts are good and open and fill us with wisdom. Let us see into tomorrow and know— know the truth."

Her fear of tomorrow became a palatable thing. Hoping to comfort her, Lone Hawk drew her close, but she wasn't the only one trembling.

"Are you here, Grey Bear?" His question startled him, and yet it had to be asked. "The gods know the truth about how you died and you cannot go to the afterlife?"

Touches the Wind tensed.

"Grey Bear, if you have placed your anger and sorrow behind you, touch me. Let me be part of what is happening."

It was impossible to dismiss the punishing blasts and hot smell, but Lone Hawk worked his way past those things to a sense of nothingness. The plains were everything, future and past, life and death. He stood in the middle of it all, waited. Prayed.

In his mind he saw the vast curtain of stars the dead traveled on their way to the afterlife. The stars felt both cool and warm, soft breezes to walk on. Songs from those who'd taken that journey surrounded him.

The need to open his eyes first touched and then pressed at him. When his vision cleared, he wasn't surprised to see a hawk. Unlike before, it now had to move its wings constantly in order to remain overhead. Its wind-tossed feathers gave it a wild look.

"Hawk is here," he said.

"He heard our prayers." There was no hint of surprise in Touches the Wind's voice. "Hawk, the air is full and alive, touched in ways I have never before felt. What is happening? Please, what must we do?"

A violent current must have caught the bird because it suddenly shot upward and nearly disappeared. A moment later it descended again. Its small, sharp beak opened and it emitted a thin cry.

"Hawk." Lone Hawk released Touches the Wind so he could reach for it. "I am blessed by your presence, but I do not understand—"

The hawk's second cry cut him off in midsentence. Before he could gather his thoughts to continue, Touches the Wind grabbed his arm and pointed.

They were no longer alone. While they'd prayed and waited for messages from Hawk, three Pawnee had approached. Because he'd armed himself as soon as he'd gotten up, Lone Hawk had readied an arrow almost before his brain registered their presence.

"They come to kill us?" she asked.

"I do not know," he said, and told her about yesterday's meeting with Whitehair.

"Perhaps they believe we have food and water," she ventured. "When they see how little there is, will they leave?"

Instead of telling her he didn't know, he watched the Pawnees' slow, steady approach. Even before he spotted the telltale white streak, he knew who the man in the middle was. Although they were all armed, their bows remained slung around their chests, and he dropped his to the ground.

"Lone Hawk." She gasped. "You should not—"

"This is not about foe fighting foe."

"How do you know?"

By way of answer, he pointed toward Hawk, who'd positioned himself above the newcomers. "If they were our enemies, would he do that?"

"You cannot be sure! It is one thing to pray to one's spirit and feel blessed by its presence, but these are Pawnee. Whitehair killed Porcupine and Jumps Like Ants."

Rage nearly swamped him, but he fought past it. "I believe he did not know about Jumps Like Ants. A true warrior does not kill a small child."

Touches the Wind remained beside him but not so close that she'd hamper him if he reached for his weapons. The Pawnees' horses walked with their heads down, their gait uncertain. The men looked only a little stronger, and the two on either side of Whitehair rode hunched forward.

Whitehair stopped. A step later, the other two did the same, looking to Whitehair for guidance. Whitehair lifted his hand in greeting.

"Can you trust him?" she whispered.

"I must. Stay here. I will meet with him."

Lone Hawk waited for her protest, but she only ran her fingers down his arm. Leaving his weapons behind should have made him nervous, but all he thought about was Hawk watching overhead. With each step, his feet crushed dry, sparse grass.

Whitehair said something, the unfamiliar words running together.

"I do not understand," Lone Hawk said. "Why are you here?"

The man was almost Nightelk's age, with deep lines at the corners of his eyes. His nose was large and his sunken cheeks made the bones there stand out. An old scar ran along the top of his right breast.

When Whitehair reached behind him, for a heartbeat Lone Hawk thought he'd hidden a weapon there. Then the Pawnee wrapped his arm around Follower and gently lowered her to the ground.

She took a step, stumbled, fell.

"Follower!"

As Touches the Wind sprinted toward the girl, Whitehair leaned down, his hand extended. Lone Hawk grasped it, felt dry strength.

"ON THE ARROW Renewal's fourth day, the Sacred Arrows are unwrapped and laid out for everyone to see. The pledger carries a forked pole to the Arrow Lodge and the high priest fastens the Arrows to the pole. The pledger leaves then, wailing as he slowly walks to a point some distance from the front door. He carries the Arrows. When he has reached where he has been told to go, he places the sacred wrapping on the ground and arranges the Arrows on it. Then all is ready.

"Priests bring offerings that have been in the lodge and boys bring even more gifts. The women are inside their tepees and do not see because this part of the ceremony is for males only. Each in turn looks at the Arrows, but it is not easy because the Arrows give off a blinding light. When even the smallest boy baby has passed by the Arrows, the warriors dismantle the Sacred Arrow Lodge and set it up again, this time over the Arrows. This new lodge is Sweet Medicine's Lodge, home of Sweet Medicine himself."

Sweet Grass Eater's words became vibration and sensation. In Nightelk's mind, the ceremony became real, guided by memories of countless ceremonies. Occasionally thoughts of the time they were wasting intruded, but who was he to say that riding and looking accomplished more than this abbreviated version of the sacred ceremony? If Sweet Medicine and the gods blessed them for this, perhaps the buffalo were waiting.

And if they weren't?

"I want to become one with the priest's words," Two Coyotes, who was sitting beside him, whispered. "But my thoughts are with you."

"Me?"

"On what you held inside for so long. It was not your intention to kill White Calf, was it?"

"Never!" Nightelk looked around to see if the others had noticed. Several glanced at him and then returned their attention to Sweet Grass Eater.

"I knew that but needed to hear you say it."

"Why? I do not understand."

"If you do not, it is because your thoughts have become tangled, and you cannot free yourself."

Father and son had hunted together before but not for a while. What Nightelk now felt for his son went beyond pride.

"I hate feeling like that," he admitted under his breath. "But whenever I tried to reach for sunlight, guilt overtook me."

"Because guilt had become everything. But you were wrong to think that way."

Wrong? How simple Two Coyotes made it sound.

Although Sweet Grass Eater hadn't finished, Two Coyotes indicated he wanted them to leave the group. Nightelk nearly pointed out that they risked angering the gods, but a man proud of his son doesn't turn his back on that pride.

"If that thing had happened to me," Two Coyotes said once they could speak in private, "I would have been like you, ashamed and afraid."

Ashamed? Afraid? Those things and more. "My dreams are full of blood staining a white hide. Even when I am awake, they remain with me."

"Because you held the shooting to yourself." Two Coyotes touched his shoulder, indicating he wanted them to sit down. "There are no words to speak of killing what is sacred."

Nightelk shuddered. Dirt caught in the wind's grip sullied the air, but even with that, the image of red flowing over white threatened to overwhelm him.

"Listen to me," Two Coyotes insisted. "It is my way to let people have their thoughts and not try to change them to my way, but today I cannot do that. When Sweet Grass Eater speaks of the Arrow Renewal Ceremony, you know what his words will be even before he says them, do you not?"

"Yes."

"And when the decision was made for this hunt, you knew how to prepare yourself, what weapons to bring?"

"Yes."

"You know who Maheo is, what Heammawihio gave us, what we owe Sweet Medicine."

"What are—"

"Do you know those things?"

"Yes."

The stern look left Two Coyotes. "Why?"

He could barely think. "They have been part of me since infancy."

"Yes." Two Coyotes smiled. "Because you are Cheyenne."

Light-headed, he waited for his son to continue.

"You walk Cheyenne, think Cheyenne, want to be nothing else."

Without knowing he was going to do it, Nightelk began tracing a circle in the dirt.

"Bad things have happened to us this summer." Two Coyotes started a circle of his own so close to Nightelk's that the curves touched. "But with all my heart I believe that the death of a white calf is not why."

"You do not know that."

"Even before you went on that hunt, there had been no rain for a long time. That is why the different bands did not come together for ceremony. There may be a reason for this rainlessness, or it may simply be part of the great cycle that is life. This is what I know, I believe." His hand stilled.

Nightelk too stopped what he was doing and stared deep into large, dark eyes.

"Nightelk is Cheyenne heart and soul. The gods know that."

With everything in him, he wanted to believe his son. Maybe he did, but the knowing didn't bring rain.

CHAPTER 30

◆ Crying and laughing, unsure where her sobs ended and the child's began, Touches the Wind clutched Follower to her breast. His eyes glistening, Lone Hawk dropped to his knees and wrapped his arms around them. The wind tossed debris over them, and the long, pale grasses danced with each gust. In Touches the Wind's heart, the plains had never looked more beautiful.

When, finally, Follower straightened, she relaxed her hold but kept a hand on the small arm. A thousand questions and prayers crowded her mind.

"They were good to me," the child said. Her voice rasped. "I did not want to be with them. I wanted—I cried for my mother, but the one with white hair held me, and I stopped crying so much."

She was vaguely aware that Lone Hawk was no longer with them but had gotten to his feet and walked away.

"Whitehair?" she repeated. "The Pawnee who returned you?"

Follower nodded. The sun had burned her cheeks and forehead and her nose was peeling. Her dress was covered with dust and she had no shoes; unkempt hair clung to her neck. She was the most beautiful child Touches the Wind had ever seen.

"I—their words were nonsense. They did not know what I was saying but—but they were good to me. Where is my mother?"

Sobbing, Touches the Wind hugged the girl again. Holding her safe and warm against her, she prayed that Walking Rabbit felt her emotions and knew her daughter was alive.

"We will take you to her as soon as we can," she promised. "But much has happened since you—since the fire."

Follower trembled and burrowed against Touches the Wind. She remained like that until Lone Hawk returned.

"Here," he said, his voice as rough as Follower's had been. "This is for you."

As Follower drank from the too-empty bladder, Touches the Wind feared she'd continue until she made herself sick, but she didn't. When she returned the bladder to Lone Hawk, he looked at it for a long time.

"My heart sings," he told the girl, his eyes still swimming. "I have known happiness in my life, but seeing you—my prayers have been answered."

"I prayed too," Follower admitted. Then, with Touches the Wind and Lone Hawk sitting on either side of her, she explained that when she and Little Bird realized the fire was coming toward them, they'd panicked and in their panic became separated.

She'd run until her lungs felt as if they were on fire. Then she'd fallen and was struggling to get back to her feet, crying as she did, when a man on horseback appeared. His body paint identified him as Pawnee, but when he picked her up and placed her on his horse, she hadn't fought.

"We have been so many places," she said. "Even though they shared what they had with me, I did not want to stay with them, but I did not know where to go." Her tears had dried but now they began again.

"You did what was right." Lone Hawk pushed dirty hair back from her forehead. "What was wise."

"My—my mother will not be angry?"

"No! Never!" Touches the Wind choked back more of the tears she might never be done shedding. "Follower, your mother loves you with all her heart. She—" She'd been about to tell Follower that Walking Rabbit had been devastated, but didn't want to add to the girl's concerns. "When she sees you, she will not ever want to let you out of her sight."

"Where is she? The Pawnee rode and rode and rode. They went so many places and I was afraid . . ."

"What were you afraid of?"

"That—that I would never see Cheyenne faces again."

How had the girl held onto her sanity? Only one explanation made sense; the Pawnee, especially Whitehair, had understood and been there for her.

"He is not what I thought he was," Lone Hawk said, his words heavy.

"He is Pawnee," Touches the Wind offered. "But that does not mean he does not have a heart."

Lone Hawk started to frown, then nodded. "Yes, he does."

"Where are they?" Follower asked. Her attention flicked from one of them to the other and then back again. "Our people. Are they close?"

"No. Not close." The thought of trying to explain everything overwhelmed Touches the Wind and took her from the question of what had compelled her to come after Lone Hawk and onto what they should do now.

"The village is no more." Lone Hawk's voice was gentle. "Most of the men are out hunting." He indicated west of them. "Everyone else is following, but slowly."

Follower sighed. "Sometimes the Pawnee rode slow. Other times their horses ran and ran. I was not always on the same horse, not always with Whitehair." Another sigh. "It made me dizzy."

Touches the Wind couldn't help laughing. "It would make me dizzy too. Lone Hawk and I must decide where we should go today. You will let us do that?"

Instead of answering, the child looked at Lone Hawk and then back at her. "Are you married?"

"No."

"But you are together."

"Yes," Lone Hawk said.

Follower clamped a hand over her mouth. "Does your mother know?" she asked Touches the Wind.

My mother is dead. "It is all right," she said instead. "This summer is not about us but about living."

The girl considered that, frowned. She started to say something, stopped. "Little Bird," she whispered. "And my brother—did the fire . . ."

"They are fine," she reassured her. "Your mother and Seeks Fire are taking care of my sister."

"Oh." She rubbed her nose, dislodging a little of the dry skin.

"Touches the Wind?" Lone Hawk said.

Dismissing Follower, she met Lone Hawk's gaze, waited for him to continue.

"Forces beyond ourselves brought us together," he told her. "Perhaps those same forces returned Follower to us." His eyes glazed. "I see two trails, one that continues the way my dreams directed me. The other leads back to our people and Walking Rabbit."

"There is another trail. The one the hunters are on."

"I am no longer one of them."

In his heart he still was. "I wish Hawk would return, show us the way to go," Touches the Wind said.

"Maybe if we pray, he will."

When Touches the Wind stood up, she realized she'd been sitting so long that her legs had gone to sleep. Gritting her teeth against the sharp prickles, she continued. "Is it right to wait for spirits to guide us, or should the decision come from us? Your buffalo dreams—"

"May or may not have meaning."

"What else do we have?"

His mouth thinned. Then he turned his back on her and walked away. The nearly empty bladder dangled from his fingers. When he was a considerable distance from her, he held the bladder up to the sky. As he did, the wind captured his hair and slammed it against his cheek, but he seemed unaware.

Wind, she prayed. *You are my spirit. My guide and comfort, wisdom. I beg you; do not let this child die. Let her mother's heart find joy. Let me—I want to become a mother myself, not nothing.*

She searched for more to tell Wind but what else was there? With Follower at her side, she pulled her surroundings into her. The air didn't feel quite as heated as it had yesterday, and its smell seemed to carry hints of spring. Although she couldn't see them, she heard birds singing and the insect chorus was pleasant.

The buffalo who'd once passed this way had left behind faint reminders of their existence, and if it had been winter, she'd collect the dry dung for a warming fire. A spiderweb hung from several grass blades and was angled so that the tiny strands reflected the sun's light. She showed it to Follower.

Did the afterlife look like this?

I am a child of these plains, she told Wind. *This land is my mother, the air my father. If they say I have lived long enough, so be it. And—and if they say it is time for the Cheyenne to end, so be it.*

"Touches the Wind!"

Lone Hawk's cry jerked her back into reality. Just the same, her prayer lingered in her mind.

"What is it?" Follower gasped. "Oh, oh, oh no!"

A silver-tipped grizzly stood nearby. Its massive shoulders spoke of power beyond comprehension, and its mouth hung open, revealing teeth capable of crushing life out of the strongest man.

Lone Hawk didn't back away from it. Neither did he reach for his weapons. She wanted to cry out to him to be careful, but what difference would that make?

Her legs and arms and the pit of her stomach screamed at her to grab Follower and run. Instead, listening to her heart, she silently compelled the child to remain where she was and then walked to where Lone Hawk stood.

"He was not there and then he was," Lone Hawk said. He didn't look at her.

"He was lying down?"

"I do not think so."

That made no sense, and yet maybe it did. The grizzly had barely moved; there was a strange calmness to it, almost as if it had expected to find humans in its territory and understood they presented no danger. It was beautiful.

"He should not be here," Lone Hawk said.

"What?"

"There is no water, no game large enough to feed him."

Her breath caught. She tried to concentrate on the wind, but it must have fallen silent. Besides, nothing mattered except the great creature. She'd never call its expression peaceful, and yet bit by bit fear seeped out of her.

"What does it want?" she asked.

"I do not—perhaps for me to come closer, but everything I have ever been tells me not to. Its eyes . . ."

She'd never gazed into a bear's eyes before so she had no way of making a comparison, but these didn't belong to a fierce killer. Instead, they seemed . . . human.

"Lone Hawk? Please, make it go away!"

Follower's cry prompted Touches the Wind to judge the distance between girl and bear. If the beast charged Follower, she'd throw herself between them.

"What do you want?"

At Lone Hawk's question, the bear lifted its head and then, the movement filled with power and grace, rose onto its hind legs. It was male.

Be careful.

Perhaps Lone Hawk heard Touches the Wind's silent plea because, for a heartbeat, their eyes locked. Then he again faced the bear.

"I am here," he said. "I open my heart and mind to you."

Although she strained to catch something, anything from the bear, it now looked carved from bone.

Was that the wind? Unwilling to tear her eyes off the grizzly, she didn't realize Legs Like Lightning had approached until the stallion walked past her, heading unerringly toward the bear.

THE THOUGHT OF having to summon enough energy to continue walking made Seeks Fire shudder, and she saw the same dread in the eyes of other women. Even the usually energetic boys complained that they were tired, and besides, did anyone know where they were going?

"My mother wants to talk to you," Knows No Fear explained once he was close enough for her to hear. "Just you."

"Did she say why?"

"No." He pursed his lips. "Maybe she is falling ill."

"What! Why do you say that?"

He rubbed a hand along the side of his neck. "She is different."

Different.

"No, I am fine," Walking Rabbit said when, a few minutes later, she joined her sister-in-law. "I did not say more to him because—Little Bird, we will not be leaving for a little while. Do you think you could look for some roots?"

Walking Rabbit waited until the girl was out of earshot. "I did not want her to hear this because she would not understand," she explained. "In truth, I do not either."

"Understand what?"

"Me." She pressed a hand to her breast and her eyes strayed to the horizon. "Today I feel lighter, my heart not so heavy."

"Not heavy?"

"Ever since Follower disappeared, my heart became a great rock. Sometimes the rock bleeds. But today . . ."

Seeks Fire wanted nothing more than to tell her sister-in-law that her own heart too felt lighter, but days of perhaps purposeless traveling and not enough water might be responsible. She said so.

"I know," Walking Rabbit admitted. "My mouth is dry and I feel myself becoming less because there is not enough moisture inside me. I am afraid—we are all afraid. But my heart—" Again she covered her breast. "Would my heart lie to me?"

"I do not know. If your day is made bearable because of what you feel, that is good."

On the verge of adding a caution, Seeks Fire changed her mind. Walking Rabbit looked as tired as she herself felt, and yet something had changed about her. Perhaps it was nothing more than the too-seldom-seen brightness in her eyes, but Seeks Fire wanted to believe it was more than that—a returning to life.

"I try not to think of my daughter because that brings me too much grief," Walking Rabbit went on. "But today when I speak her name or see her in my mind, I am at peace."

Maybe because Follower had reached the afterlife. "You are ready?" Seeks Fire indicated the several loaded travois.

"My feet are bruised and my legs tremble, but I do not care. I wish you could feel the same way. Put Grey Bear behind you and start to walk forward."

"Today is not about Grey Bear. I will not let him in my thoughts."

"Can you do that?"

Seeks Fire started to shake her head. Instead, her attention was drawn to the sky. "A cloud," she said, disbelieving.

A few minutes later, Calf Woman and several of her friends joined them. They said little about the cloud, and yet everyone continued to glance at it. As time passed, the soft, high mass grew in size but remained a clean white, not dark the way clouds became when they were about to release rain. As clouds always did, its shape shifted, and yet something about it remained the same—at least Seeks Fire believed it did.

A mounted warrior lived in it.

"WHAT IS HE looking at?" Nightelk turned to acknowledge the man who'd just spoken. Hair in Ears, one of the less successful hunters, pointed at Black Eyes. Although the dog kept pace, his attention wasn't on where they were going.

"The cloud," Nightelk said unnecessarily. "I would like to believe he smells rain in it, but a single small cloud cannot put an end to the drought."

Hair in Ears shook his head. "I just hope he knows to stay away from my horse. Dogs are no good on a hunt. They are such excitable creatures and bark when they should be silent."

Not bothering to point out that Black Eyes barked only rarely, Nightelk waited until Hair in Ears had returned to his companions before turning his attention to the dog. Hair in

Ears might be right; Black Eyes spent much of the time looking upward and could get tangled in a horse's legs if he
wasn't careful.

Instead of admonishing the dog, however, he studied the
cloud. It struck him as clean and newborn, untouched by the
dust and dirt that surrounded him. It would be peaceful to
be a cloud, he thought, to drift wherever the wind took it, to
have no concerns.

"I wish I could believe more of its kind will join us," Two
Coyotes said. He'd just returned from a short ride to the
south, where he'd been looking for tracks. "At least it is
something different to stare at."

"You saw nothing?"

"There is an old deer trail, abandoned."

From the sun's position, Nightelk knew they were reaching the day's hottest point. Despite the toil all this walking
took on the horses, he'd never tell Sweet Grass Eater he was
wrong to insist on pressing on. This morning, as Two Coyotes guided him from guilt to acceptance, he'd truly believed
they'd find game—any game—before it was too late, but the
day had dulled his optimism.

"The other scouts have not yet returned. Perhaps they have
found something," Two Coyotes pointed out.

Nightelk nodded and then studied his son's horse. The
mare had given birth in the spring, but her foal had lived
only a few weeks. He hoped she was pregnant again, and yet
would she live long enough to give birth?

Weary of questions about survival, he let his thoughts
drift. Calf Woman was too slow and heavy to care for their
horses by herself, but there was no shortage of boys willing
to help. Maybe Knows No Fear had assumed that responsibility in addition to watching over his mother's small herd.
He'd just begun to create an image of Walking Rabbit in his
mind when Black Eyes whined.

He glanced at the dog and then up at the cloud. Two Coyotes did the same.

It was no trick of the eye; the cloud had indeed formed

itself into something—a warrior on horseback. When Black Eyes headed toward the cloud, father and son did the same.

TIME SPED AHEAD and then looped back on Touches the Wind. Because she'd spent her life keeping pace with the sun, she knew how long she, Follower, and Lone Hawk had been on the move, and yet the measured pace that had always defined her life no longer existed.

When she looked at Follower now, she accepted the girl's reality, so that wasn't the reason. Part of her sense of unreality came from being with Lone Hawk, but it was the cloud itself that took her from the world she'd always known.

Although it remained in the same place, it continued to expand and take over more and more of the sky. It was still white, and yet she didn't fault it for its barrenness.

Its shape never changed.

"The warrior is still there," Follower said. She'd been riding with Lone Hawk, and by the way her little body sagged, Touches the Wind had assumed she'd fallen asleep. "Do you see him?"

"Yes, I do," she admitted when Lone Hawk said nothing.

"His arrows are so big, and his arms never grow tired of holding them and his bow. Do you think my mother sees him?"

"Honey, I know you want to be with your mother. You understand why we are not going to her?"

The girl, tears in her dark eyes, nodded. Touches the Wind ached to take Follower in her arms again, but Lone Hawk had pointed out that Legs Like Lightning should carry as little weight as possible to keep him strong.

Strong? Without water, death was a certainty.

"Lone Hawk?"

He turned, reluctantly it seemed, from his obsession with the cloud.

"By the time we stand under it, our water will be gone."

"What do you want? For us to turn around? To do something different?"

Seeing Little Bird again and being surrounded by her people, even drawing a few words out of her father meant more than she could possibly explain, but conditions were just as bleak there as here.

"It is too late for that."

His clenched teeth were his only response.

"The end is near," she said. Why should she try to keep the reality of their situation from Follower? Surely the girl knew how desperate things were. "Our end."

"Do not say that!"

"I must. Neither of us can change what tomorrow will bring. There is only one thing."

"What?"

Her attention once again strayed to the warrior-cloud. Her world had always been filled with spirit-signs and messages. In order to keep harmony with their surroundings, the Cheyenne held ceremonies, prayed and danced, believed. Everyone chose a spirit-helper, and she'd felt compelled to share ancient stories with the children. How could she possibly ignore what was happening now?

"The cloud calls to us, but together we are slow. On Legs Like Lightning, you may reach what is under it in time," Touches the Wind told Lone Hawk.

"Leave you and Follower? No."

Although she ached to press her hand against his cheek, she kept her grip on the reins. "This is not just a cloud."

"What is it?" he asked, although she sensed he already knew what she was going to say.

"Grey Bear remains with us. He has become a cloud and—"

"Grey Bear is dead?" Follower interrupted. "How is that possible?"

"It is," Lone Hawk said gently.

Follower's gaze went to Lone Hawk and then to Touches the Wind before settling again on the cloud. "It is him," she said simply.

"Listen to her." Touches the Wind's voice shook. "Lone Hawk, this cloud does not exist just for us. Perhaps Sweet

Grass Eater and the other hunters are heading toward it. You must join them."

"Sweet Grass Eater follows his dream."

"But if he believes that that is his grandson, the cloud has become his dream. If you go to them, on Grey Bear's horse, they will accept you."

"You do not know that."

"I look at what Grey Bear has become and see not today but what happened long ago, when the Cheyenne turned from the ways of their beginning and the Sun Dance had lost its meaning."

"I do not want to hear old stories. I must decide—"

"I am trying to help with that decision. The Sun Dance exists so the earth will be renewed. Again and again we nurture the world so it will not fade into nothing, but we would not know to do that if it had not been for Tomsivsi. You are like him."

"Do not say that!"

"I must," she insisted. "Look at this land. It is wasting away and in danger of becoming nothing. The animals know that, which is why they have left. If we are to go on living, Tomsivsi's journey must be repeated."

"There is no Sacred Mountain here."

Why couldn't Lone Hawk simply accept her words, but even as the question formed inside her, she knew the answer. She was, after all, saying things no one ever had.

"Listen to me, please. At the time of Tomsivsi, there was famine. Vegetation had died, the animals starved, and the land became barren and dry. The Cheyenne who are our ancestors were on the verge of starvation. Tomsivsi, after much prayer, went to the Sacred Mountain with his wife where the Great Spirit taught him the Sun Dance and gave him the sacred horned buffalo-skin hat."

"I already know the Sun Dance. My scars—"

"Do you want to throw my words away?" Desperation drove Touches the Wind on. "You are so much hunter and warrior that all you think about is what that hunter and warrior is capable of? What about Hawk? When he came to you, you believed."

He had, Lone Hawk was forced to admit. He hadn't wanted to hear her words, not because he thought she was talking nonsense, but because leaving her and Follower behind terrified him.

"You look at a cloud and say it is the same as when the Great Spirit covered Tomsivsi with wisdom?" he asked.

"It is! It has to be. What—what else do we have? Tomsivsi received instruction from Maiyun and the Thunder Spirit. Thunder comes when there are clouds, but it is more than that. When the Great Spirit was finished with Tomsivsi, he told him that when he left the Sacred Mountain, the heavenly bodies would move. Roaring Thunder would awaken the sun, moon, stars, and—and rain will bring forth fruits of all kinds."

"And the animals came forth and followed him home," he heard himself finish.

But can what happened in Tomsivsi's *time be repeated?*

CHAPTER 31

Sweet Grass Eater lost his balance and would have fallen if someone hadn't grabbed him. Just the same, the priest continued to stare upward. His face, in shadows, had a transparent quality. It was, Nightelk decided, as if the years had fallen away, leaving the old man's skin as clear and smooth as a child's—but too pale.

"My heart beats so I think it may escape from my chest," Sweet Grass Eater announced. "I try to think on the meaning of this"—he pointed at the warrior-cloud—"but something like this has never happened before. I need to pray and smoke on it."

When no one said anything, Nightelk left his horse and stood in front of the priest. "There is no time." Keeping his voice firm, he fought desperation. "We stopped to rest our horses, but we must go on. My priest, you believe the cloud shows where your dreams said we must go. Embrace that wisdom and let it guide us now."

Sweet Grass Eater took a long, deep breath, the effort highlighting his rib cage.

"Nightelk," the priest said. "You speak with the urgency of youth, not age's wisdom. Think. I covered us with words and memories of the Arrow Renewal Ceremony, and the cloud appeared. But now I must seek more wisdom so no harm will befall us during our journey to the shadow of my grandson who has become a cloud."

With that, the old man lowered himself to the ground. Nightelk ached to grab him and pull him to his feet, but what he saw in Sweet Grass Eater's eyes stopped him. The priest was exhausted. Spent.

"I embrace your wisdom," he made himself say. "The ceremony led to this miracle." He indicated the cloud. "But your grandson was a man of action, not prayer."

Instead of telling him he was wrong, Sweet Grass Eater remained silent. His neck veins pulsed. Perhaps he'd injured his eyes from staring at the sky so long, and maybe the cloudiness in them was caused by something else.

"I was made keeper of the Sacred Arrows," Nightelk said. "I am not perfect. I have not always walked the way our ancestors and the gods created, but I am Cheyenne." He glanced at Two Coyotes and received a nod in return.

"A Cheyenne willing to die, but my death will come during action, not prayer." He held out his arm and turned it this way and that. "There is still strength in me, but that strength will not last. I rode with my priest because I believed in his dreams. I still believe in them—even more now that we have been given this sign."

The gathered men looked at the cloud and then back at their priest. Even the youngest looked spent, and the horses were in no better shape. His forehead wrinkled in concentration, Sweet Grass Eater scanned the men's faces before locking his gaze on the cloud. His hands trembled and he kept swallowing.

"My priest." If Nightelk hadn't been sensitive to the old man's dignity, he would have lifted him in his arms. "You reached deep inside you for the strength to guide us. I am deeply grateful to you for that, but you have said we must do something I cannot. Today prayers and ceremony must wait."

"Without prayer and ceremony, we will fail."

Sweet Grass Eater's voice had suddenly become strong again. Nightelk waited.

"You think I am an old man close to death," the priest said. "But you are wrong. My name comes from our prophet Sweet Medicine who learned from Maiyun and the other gods. His wisdom guides me—should guide all of us." He reached for his tobacco pouch. "I prepare myself to receive my grandson's wisdom. All should do the same."

In the past whenever an elder proclaimed it was time for ceremony, Nightelk had joined in without question. Several men, perhaps prompted as much by their own need to rest as the call to prayer, formed a circle around Sweet Grass Eater, and he felt himself start to sit. Then the priest's last words echoed inside him.

Whatever else Grey Bear had been, he'd never been blessed with spirit-wisdom. That might have changed now that he no longer lived on earth, as witness the cloud—but if Grey Bear was still a warrior . . .

A warrior!

"Today each man must follow his own heart," Nightelk said with conviction. "My heart will find no rest, no peace, if I stay here. If I have not prepared myself for what waits under the cloud, so be it, but I will *not* die without trying to fill my people's bellies."

ALTHOUGH EVERYONE WATCHED the cloud and talked about it in hushed, barely hopeful tones, Seeks Fire didn't join them. Instead, driven by a need she couldn't understand, she made her way to a slope and sat there. The camp dogs, who usually wandered about looking for something to eat or fighting among themselves, lay panting. Some people had freed their carrying dogs from the travois while others hadn't bothered.

Most of the horses slept standing up although many of this year's foals were stretched out near their mothers. Seeks Fire tried not to study the little ones too closely or allow them to touch her heart since foals were the first to die during times of not enough food. She'd already tied a filly to her mother because otherwise the little one wouldn't keep going.

A gust of wind forced her to shut her eyes briefly. When she opened them, she went back to studying the people who made up her world. Her parents, always proud of their position of wealth, had aged recently. She wished she'd taken note of that earlier, but she'd been consumed, first with thoughts of Grey Bear and the possibility of becoming his wife and then the rape and his death.

What did it matter? Without food and water . . .

Licking her lips, she noticed how dry they felt. Perhaps she should ask Easy Singer for a little of the mix of herbs he applied to wounds. After drawing up her knees and resting her hands and head on them, she turned her attention to the cloud. The air had cooled a little; she was grateful but refused to allow herself to pray for that to continue.

She wasn't with child. This morning she'd woken to discover that her bleeding had begun. At first, relief had overwhelmed her, and she'd had to fight tears, but this afternoon her need to cry came from a different source.

Grey Bear had died without creating life. His years had been so short, and although his accomplishments would be talked about for many years—if the Cheyenne had years— in time he'd fade from memory. It would have been different if he'd had a child, her child.

The thought brought her to her feet, an act that briefly made her dizzy. This morning she'd done what she could to clean her dress but hadn't taken time with her hair and didn't care what her face looked like. She was different, no longer concerned with herself, no longer a maiden thinking maiden thoughts.

Her parents needed her strength and willingness to work and would need those things more and more. She needed to grieve over Grey Bear's death, needed to untie the filly and leave her behind so the mare would live.

A low, distant rumbling pulled her away from the hard decision. Looking at the cloud, she accepted that something of Grey Bear continued to live in it—and that it was no longer white and clean but had darkened. The rumbling came again, stronger this time.

Wild hope raced through her, but she forced it away. To dream of rain was not just foolish but dangerous.

"Do I hear you, Grey Bear?" she asked. "Have you joined your voice with Thunder's?"

The hum of voices had stopped with the first thunder call. It began again but now was different, more animated. Several dogs lifted their heads and looked around.

"I am here, Grey Bear. I pray you can hear me because there are things I want you to know."

A memory of the last time she'd seen him made her shudder, but she pulled herself past the rape.

"I do not hate you. I did then and am not ashamed of what I felt, but I have walked past that, perhaps become wiser; I hope so. How I wish you had had time to do the same thing, not become so full of self-hate, not believed you should die because of what you did to me."

The warrior-cloud seemed to take a breath, grew. "I do not understand what is happening," she admitted. "But perhaps I should simply accept. Grey Bear, if you are still here, I pray you can look into Cheyenne hearts and know we are desperate. I pray you are still a warrior, a hunter."

The great crash began as a low murmur but quickly grew until the sound filled her. Dogs either barked or growled. One horse reared and others trembled. A baby started to cry.

"Thunder Spirit! I hear you! Welcome you."

She waited with her nerve endings on fire and her heart

beating so fast it scared her. The great blast went on and on, power building on power until she wondered if it would consume everything. Finally, though, it ended.

"You cannot be finished. Please, do not leave us!"

A few days ago Touches the Wind had told the children about Tomsivsi who'd gone to the Sacred Mountain in search of wisdom. Thunder, who'd been there, had shared much of his knowledge of the ways of the universe. Today she needed to cling to Tomsivsi's story and make some of his knowledge hers, and yet Thunder was more than wisdom.

He was also the giant bird that carries deadly lightning in its talons.

And lightning had started the fire that had destroyed so much and taken Follower.

LONE HAWK FOUND Legs Like Lightning's backbone sharper than he'd expected. The stallion was also the strongest horse he'd ever ridden. Someone had made sure he'd had enough to eat and drink, and although the thought of other horses suffering so Legs Like Lightning could have enough bothered him, he was grateful.

When he heard the first thunderclap, he hadn't asked himself whether it foreshadowed rain, but the sound continued along with occasional flashes of lightning—perhaps deadly lightning.

Clouds were changelings. This one was exceptional because it remained still as death for so long, but it was right for it to shift and change—and grow.

His world had darkened along with the cloud, shadows growing so slowly that his eyes easily adjusted. It felt good not to have the sun burning the top of his head, and with the air cooler, he could go longer without needing to drink.

Just the same, perhaps because there'd been so many days of heat and more heat, he couldn't quite make himself believe that this afternoon was different. Clouds came and went. Thunder roared and then whimpered before becoming nothing. Lightning seared the sky and sometimes touched the earth, causing grass to catch on fire instead of bringing rain.

Rain?

He filled his lungs but caught no hint of the blessed smell. Instead, he tasted energy—lightning's energy.

"Hawk, you are my spirit and I call to you now. Are you part of this? Have you become something different perhaps, no longer a bird?"

He shook his head in an attempt to shake off the unwanted thought, but it returned. Grey Bear's spirit-helper had been a grizzly, the most powerful creature on earth. If Grey Bear hated him enough, could what he'd become after death have caught and killed Hawk?

"If you wish me dead, tell me!" he insisted. Thunder grew and grew. He spoke not over but through it. "Is this your challenge? If it is, I accept, but do not let others die because you hate me. Whitehair returned Follower to us. She should not, *must* not die without feeling her mother's arms again. Grey Bear, I face you, I, no one else!"

To the west, perhaps under where the warrior-cloud had come to life, a great lightning tree exploded into life. Legs Like Lightning had been concentrating on where he was going, seemingly oblivious to the thunder, but now the stallion's head came up and he stared. Lone Hawk couldn't count the lightning-branches, could barely comprehend. The sky itself and the vast, glowering cloud that dominated it looked as if they'd caught on fire.

"Thunder Spirit! I am humble before your power."

Under him, Legs Like Lightning trembled, and he readied himself in case the stallion panicked. One lightning-branch ended, but another was born in its place and then another. A hawk would become cinders if so much heat and energy touched it, and yet he felt himself growing stronger.

"Grey Bear, hear me! I am not afraid of you, not afraid of death. If you believe nothing else of me, believe that!"

Legs Like Lightning continued to stare upward, but he'd stopped shaking. He sucked in noisy breaths.

"Has your master touched you?"

The wind had become a misbehaving child who tosses its

possessions about. He tried to smooth Legs Like Lightning's mane, but a spark caused him to jerk back. Perhaps Grey Bear had had a hand in that.

Lone Hawk had reached a long, narrow valley flanked by gentle gray hills. Near the end of the valley was a hill higher than the others he rode toward. As Legs Like Lightning began the easy climb, his thoughts returned to what Touches the Wind had said as he left her and Follower.

"You must become more than you have ever been," she'd told him. "I believe this; if we are to survive, we must reach into our past and embrace that wisdom."

He did that now. Became Tomsivsi who'd gone in search of wisdom. Tomsivsi had climbed the Sacred Mountain to receive instruction from Maiyun and Thunder Spirit. He, Lone Hawk, had no mountain to climb; this hill would have to do.

Reaching the highest point, he let go of the rein and stood on Legs Like Lightning's back. Ignoring the stallion who'd twisted his head to look at him, he lifted his bow and arrows over his head. The wind caught his braids and sent them streaming out behind him. Air raced across his chest.

"See me, Maiyun! See this Cheyenne warrior and know his heart is pure."

Thunder bellowed. Before it finished, lightning bled across the cloud and turned it from black to gold.

"Maiyun, see my Sun Dance scars. Know that I am Cheyenne. Like Tomsivsi before me, I come before you seeking truth so my people will live." My people, he thought. Although he'd lived with the Bow String Society for a number of years and fought and hunted alongside them, some part of him had always remained separate. It no longer did.

"I have been with a maiden, Touches the Wind. We do not understand the forces that guided her to me; that is for you, Heammawihio, and the other gods to know. She is so named because she feels one with the wind. I wish to be like her, to be connected with what is around me. Hawk may have made me his brother, but it is not enough that I speak to only one creature. Maiyun, I am here! Newborn."

His arms ached, but he didn't lower them. He could have called out to Hawk, but Hawk, like all creatures, had been created by Maiyun.

"I have tried to walk the Cheyenne way, but it is not always easy. If I have done something to offend you, I apologize. The hand I had in Grey Bear's death . . . I believe his soul has not found peace and is restless, may have—" He swallowed and forced himself to continue. "May have become a *mistai*."

He felt a prickling down his back. Maybe Grey Bear's ghost was here.

"Maiyun, I and every creature who has ever lived on these plains would not exist if not for you. My gratitude knows no end, and if it is your wish, I offer myself in sacrifice so others will live."

The thought of dying before he could become a husband and father weakened him, but he fought his way past the emotion. Eyes closed so he could concentrate on Maiyun, he tilted his head back. His throat was exposed; if Maiyun or Grey Bear's ghost wanted him dead, so be it.

The first raindrop struck him on the forehead.

CHAPTER 32

To Nightelk's relief and gratitude, as soon as he and the five accompanying him took off, Black Eyes trotted after him. At first he remained convinced he was doing the right thing, but the cloud had grown so he was no longer sure of its birthplace. Two Coyotes remained nearby, saying little. The other men were young and unmarried with the recklessness of youth.

Although he was grateful for the relative coolness, the unrelenting thunder and lightning concerned him; on a day not different from this one, the prairie had caught fire. As memories piled inside him, his hold on his son's words faded. Two Coyotes believed the spirits wouldn't punish him or those he held dear, and yet starvation faced them.

In an effort to escape the sense of dread, Nightelk concentrated on his surroundings. The air smelled of many things, but in with that of lightning and dead prairie lived rain. He'd felt a few drops and it was raining far to the north, but he'd lived through enough summer storms to know isolated drops meant nothing.

Black Eyes kept lifting his head and sniffing, and he occasionally looked up at him, but Nightelk couldn't tell what he was thinking. Since the lightning began, the hair along the dog's back had stood on end.

"Thunder makes too much noise," Two Coyotes said unexpectedly. "I cannot hear anything else."

"You think our enemies are around?"

Two Coyotes shrugged. "If they are, they are of no consequence to me."

"Unless they have found buffalo."

"Unless they have found buffalo." Two Coyotes shielded his eyes and scanned their surroundings. "I see everything and yet not enough."

Perhaps there wasn't anything except this endless nothing. That wasn't true because the land could hide a great deal, and yet he felt alone. Scared.

"You do not want me to talk?" Two Coyotes asked. "I take you from your thoughts?"

"Yes, but I need that." Nightelk stared at the vast cloud until lightning escaped from it. "I do not know if my decision is the right one. If I am leading us—"

"We do not know whether any direction is the right one. Perhaps all buffalo are gone."

Gone. No more. It seemed unbelievable that the massive herds that blackened the land could cease to be and yet . . . "Perhaps."

Lost deep inside himself, Nightelk was slow to return to his world. He was grateful to the clouds—the warrior-cloud had multiplied until the sky was covered—for hiding the sun and making him less aware of the march of time. Perhaps this half day would last forever, late afternoon sliding into night without being noticed. Still, the time would come when all strength left not just him but everyone. When that happened . . .

At first Black Eyes' whine was nearly lost under the greater sound of thunder, but the thunder finally rolled away, leaving the dog's warning. The large head rose and fell, turned this way and that. His mouth remained parted but he didn't seem to be panting. Was he laughing?

Without warning, Black Eyes started running. Afraid he might lose sight of the dog, Nightelk prodded his horse into as much of a gallop as she was capable of, every step jarring his tired body. As he prepared to call out, the dog slowed and looked over his shoulders at him. The few raindrops that had been teasing the thirsty earth increased in number, bringing with it the blessed smell of wetness. But that wasn't all he sensed.

The first sound was a wolf howl, distant but unmistakable. Then lightning chased away the gloom long enough for him to catch sight of several birds. His eyes burned from trying to see that far and the muscles at the back of his neck cramped. Black Eyes waited until he'd caught up and then kept pace.

Finally he heard—buffalo.

NIGHTELK WAS LEANING forward on his now-motionless horse when Two Coyotes joined him. He glanced at his son, then gave in to the need to take in the barely visible herd feeding on either side of a slow-moving creek. For a long time, neither man spoke.

"They are a gift," Two Coyotes whispered. "A gift from Heammawihio, and Maheo, creator of life."

Far from the thousands upon thousands that gathered together in spring, there were nevertheless at least thirty animals. And they'd found water.

"The warrior-cloud led us to them," Two Coyotes said after several more minutes of silence. "They are life."

"Life."

Two Coyotes fixed his gaze on him. "Are you all right?"

"I do not know." Nightelk spotted three prime bulls, calves old enough that they often wandered away from their mothers, the hulking figure of the dominant cow. Although none appeared crippled, neither were any spring-fat. "Finding buffalo when there have been no tracks . . . coming across water when we all thought there was none . . ."

"The buffalo arrived from a different direction; that is why we saw no sign of them. And we have never been here so how could we know of the creek?"

Two Coyotes explanation made sense, and yet Nightelk couldn't shake off everything that had happened today, particularly his conviction that their only hope of survival lay not in joining Sweet Grass Eater in more prayer but standing under the warrior-cloud's shadow.

"We must give thanks," he whispered. "Let the gods feel our gratitude."

"Later. Now we must return to the others—tell them."

Two Coyotes was right, of course, but although Nightelk had participated in more hunts than he could remember, this afternoon he felt part of not the job ahead of them but the dark and maybe angry cloud. The rain.

"Thunder and lightning did not stampede the herd." He made no attempt to keep wonder out of his voice. "Those things should have."

Two Coyotes lifted his head so the raindrops could land on his face. "Yes. They should have."

Nightelk did the same. Several fat drops landed in his eyes and he had to rub them to clear his vision. He was still blinking when a too-familiar prickle at the back of his neck caused him to sit up and look around.

"What is it?" Two Coyotes asked.

"I am not sure. Something . . ."

A man rode toward them from the north, but before the newcomer had come close enough for him to see whether he was a Cheyenne, the clouds opened up. Rain cascaded over them; instead of trying to find shelter, Nightelk remained beside his son, laughing.

DESPITE THE THUNDERSTORM, Lone Hawk heard the laughter. He didn't ask himself what Nightelk and his son were doing here or whether they knew that not just Cheyenne had found the buffalo. Neither did he question the force that had guided him. As for the rain . . .

Thunder, bringer of summer rains, thank you. Heammawihio, you are more powerful than the sun. No one knows more about how nature works. I thank you too.

Nightelk, oblivious to the water running off his nose and chin, smiled at him. His hair hung sodden around his neck. "Welcome," he said.

"I did not know if you would speak to me." Legs Like Lightning's flesh shivered as the stallion tried to rid himself of the water.

"Your leaving happened in another time. This"—Nightelk pointed at the seemingly unconcerned herd—"is all that matters."

"They are life," Lone Hawk agreed.

"What are you doing here?" The question came from Two Coyotes.

Lone Hawk took a breath, but nothing about today was simply explained. "I see only four hunters besides us," he said instead. "Where are the others?"

Nightelk's explanation of why Sweet Grass Eater and the rest of the men had remained behind awakened more questions than answers, but that, like an explanation of what had drawn him to this spot, could wait. The cloudburst showed no signs of letting up; after endless days of being hot, he was rapidly becoming cold. Some of the buffalo, particularly this year's calves, had stopped grazing and were moving about restlessly.

"They may yet stampede," he said although Nightelk and Two Coyotes had to be aware of the possibility. "They will not go far because, even terrified, they will not leave water, but our horses may not have the strength to keep up. Besides"—he looked in the direction he'd come from—"the Pawnee are here."

"How many?" Two Coyotes asked.

"Six. Whitehair among them."

"Ah! Do they know you are here?"

"Not yet."

"Not yet?" Despite the quick question, Nightelk's features remained impassive.

Lone Hawk pulled wet air into his lungs. "There are enough buffalo for both tribes."

"You want Cheyenne and Pawnee to hunt together? That has never happened before."

Encouraged by the lack of judgment in Nightelk's tone, Lone Hawk went on. "This summer is like none other. Perhaps our grandparents knew such drought, but it has not happened in my lifetime."

"It was nearly as bad when my firstborn died."

He acknowledged Nightelk's comment with a somber nod. "When that happened, did you think of the differences between Cheyenne and other tribes?"

"All I cared about was feeding my family, finding water."

"That is how it is for the Pawnee."

Two Coyotes frowned. Behind him, Lone Hawk noticed the four approaching Cheyenne hunters. They looked up at the rain, at him, back into the rain again.

"How do you know so much about the Pawnee?" Two Coyotes asked. "They are our enemies."

"They are not today." Lone Hawk grew tense in anticipation of what the others might say or do, but he wasn't an outcast today; he couldn't be! "I have looked into the eyes of starving Pawnee men. When I did, I saw not those who killed Porcupine but desperate sons, fathers, and husbands."

Father and son glanced at each other but remained silent.

"Follower is alive," he told her. "Whitehair brought her to Touches the Wind and me. They will soon be here."

"Alive?" Nightelk mouthed the word.

"Yes."

"A blessing. If—if only Walking Rabbit knew."

"Yes." He agreed. "Touches the Wind sent her the truth with her thoughts, but they may not reach her."

"No, they may not." Instead of turning his attention to what they'd come here to accomplish, Nightelk stared in the direction Lone Hawk had come from. A father's smile touched his lips. "Her heart will beat again. Follower is well?"

Lone Hawk nodded. The other men were now close enough that they recognized him. None of them spoke. "You are our leader," he told Nightelk. "What is it to be? Do we share this gift from Maheo with the Pawnee? Do I hunt by your side?"

In the slow and measured way of mature men, Nightelk looked at each of his fellow hunters in turn before speaking. "Today we ride in a new way," he told them. "A way planned by the spirits—and by Grey Bear."

"My father, someone must let the others know."

"Yes," Nightelk said. "The decision is yours, but I hope you will ride to those with Sweet Grass Eater and then to the women and children."

"Me?"

"Your words will carry weight and—"

"And you do not wish me to risk my life hunting buffalo today," Two Coyotes finished.

"I need today's sun to set on your living body."

Lone Hawk hadn't thought about his own father for a long time, but the sudden need to stand beside him became so fierce it nearly brought him to his knees. He prayed his spirit could see him.

"Take Legs Like Lightning," Lone Hawk told Two Coyotes. "He is still strong." *Maybe because Grey Bear's strength now lives in his horse.*

As Two Coyotes and Lone Hawk dismounted, Nightelk addressed the hunters through the still-driving rain. "We hunt. Pawnee and Cheyenne together."

*   *   *

Two Coyotes's stallion had known ten more winters than Legs Like Lightning, but although the one-eared dun couldn't keep up with a running buffalo for long, Lone Hawk vowed to make that enough.

Under Nightelk's lead, six Cheyenne circled south around the buffalo, leaving the northern half of the creek and land to the Pawnee. They were still on their way when the Pawnee swept down on the herd. Shutting his mind off from everything except this moment, Lone Hawk scanned the beasts until he found one he wanted and urged the aging stallion into a canter. His hands closed around his bow and arrow, became one with the weapons. Satisfied the cow was running too fast to change direction easily, he drove his heels into his horse's side.

Something that was a cross between a sigh and a grunt accompanied a gathering of muscles; the canter became a gallop. Sitting tall and straight to increase his understanding of his surroundings, Lone Hawk breathed in rain-scented air. Lived. Hunted.

"Maheo, thank you!"

His first arrow struck the shoulder bone; the wound wouldn't kill her. He quickly aimed again and fired, but his horse had already begun to slow. He could only pray his weapon had penetrated deep enough to reach the liver. Instead of turning and going in search of another kill, he followed as the buffalo's increasingly aimless run took her toward the setting sun. He could no longer see the other Cheyenne when the cow's legs went out from under her, and she collapsed onto the sodden earth. She tried to regain her feet, then fell forward onto her nose. After jumping from his wheezing horse, Lone Hawk crouched near the buffalo. Water cascaded off him.

"Your life for my people's," he told the buffalo. "Your flesh so Cheyenne children may eat. Go in peace. Know you have served us well."

Coyote Man had told Yellow Haired Woman not to feel

pity for an animal's suffering. Still, he prayed she would find
a quick death. When her great chest stopped heaving, he
covered a sightless eye with his hand.

"Maheo, today I feel you beside me. Your strength became
mine." He paused and then continued. "Grey Bear, I feel you
too. I choose to believe that some of what I felt was your
strength. Thank you."

BY THE TIME Lone Hawk returned to where they'd discovered the herd, no fewer than ten buffalo lay dead or dying.
Two of the Cheyenne hunters weren't there, and he surmised
that, like him, they'd gone after fleeing buffalo.

For the most part, the Pawnee remained north of the Cheyenne, but one had followed a wounded calf until it died near
where Nightelk had been standing when he'd given the order
to attack. Lone Hawk saluted the young Pawnee now in the
process of slitting the calf's throat. The boy hunter returned
his wave.

As was sometimes the way of buffalo, the uninjured ones
hadn't run to safety but were now trying to return to their
companions. Mindful of his horse's endurance, he waited
until a half-grown bull calf, its hair no longer newborn red,
approached. Its eyes were wide with fear and it pranced
rather than walked.

"Come to me, come to me," he crooned softly.

His stallion lifted his head and shook it as if disgusted
with the calf's stupidity.

"Hear my voice," Lone Hawk continued. "Hear it and be
confused. Walk into my weapon."

Perhaps the calf heard him because it turned and stared at
him, its mouth drooping and water dripping off its nose.
Then, quick as an antelope, it spun away. Lone Hawk, anticipating that reaction, once again commanded his horse to
run. Catching up to the calf didn't take long, but the ligh-
terweight animal ran first one direction and then another
while his horse was slowed by the slippery grass. He'd begun
to wonder if he'd ever get a clear shot at the space behind

the last rib when the calf unexpectedly wheeled and headed toward him. Even as he and horse dodged to one side, he released his arrow. A moment later only a few feathers protruded from the calf's soft, vulnerable throat.

At least, Lone Hawk thought a few minutes later, he hadn't had to run this buffalo down. Because it lacked a full-grown bull's stamina, its feet had immediately gone out from under it. Its flesh, although not as plentiful as he would have liked, would be tender.

There'd be no more chasing after buffalo until the old stallion had rested. Besides, although his quiver was still nearly full, his mind was no longer filled with hunting. Even with the rain, Touches the Wind should have no trouble following Legs Like Lightning's tracks; she knew what direction he'd gone in and should now be close enough to hear the sounds of hunting.

After remounting, he left the dead calf. The sounds, smells, and sights barely penetrated, and he gave no thought to whether he was getting closer to the Pawnee. He idly studied several heads but no one's hair had turned white.

"Lone Hawk."

Alerted by the awe and disbelief in Nightelk's voice, he turned. The peace chief sat still as death on his rain-slicked mare, his entire being focused on something half hidden behind a clump of bushes. Lone Hawk came closer but didn't speak. Positioning himself beside Nightelk, he stared in the same direction. Was that the sound of Nightelk's heart pounding?

White Calf. Strong. Alive.

"A sign?" he managed.

Nightelk drew in a long, unsteady breath. "I pray."

Breathing quick and deep, Nightelk handed Lone Hawk his bow and arrows, swung off his horse, and started toward the calf. Lone Hawk took up the loose rein, but although he'd never seen a Sacred Calf, this was between Nightelk and the creature.

With every step Nightelk took, Lone Hawk expected the calf to bolt, but it had become as still as Nightelk had been when he'd first seen him. The distance between the two shrank and shrank again. Then Nightelk slipped between the bushes and the wet growth kept the secret of what happened next.

Long moments later Nightelk reappeared. As he did, the calf backed out of the bushes and trotted away.

"The scar," Nightelk whispered. "I—I touched him everywhere—he let me. I found it."

"It was where your arrow struck?"

Nightelk nodded. "Not old. Clean with healthy flesh all around the wound—as if—as if it had been treated by a skilled medicine man or . . ."

"I do not have words for what we saw," Lone Hawk told Nightelk as the older man climbed back on his horse. "Perhaps there are none."

Nightelk didn't respond.

Wise without knowing where the wisdom had come from, Lone Hawk waited as Nightelk's eyes lost their faraway look and his breathing returned to its usual cadence. They remained silent.

Finally Nightelk took back his weapons. "It is time for me to hunt," he said. "Will you join me?"

He shook his head. "I need to find Touches the Wind and Follower."

"I thought you would say—"

"What is it?"

"Someone comes."

Not just someone, Lone Hawk acknowledged as the newcomers approached, Sweet Grass Eater at their head. When he saw Lone Hawk, the old priest reached for his knife.

"Two Coyotes told us," Sweet Grass Eater said, his lips thinning, "about the buffalo. And him." He thrust his knife in Lone Hawk's direction. "He has been banned. He should not be here!"

"He killed two buffalo. The spirits brought him to us."

"Spirits! No. *Mistai*. Ghosts."

"You do not know that," Nightelk countered.

"You question a priest!" Sweet Grass Eater's eyes bulged

so they reminded Lone Hawk of the cow as she lay dying. "I will *not* have him here! This—this animal who murdered my grandson is no longer a Cheyenne!"

"He is a man," Nightelk said.

"Be careful what you say, Nightelk," Wolf Robe warned, coming to stand beside Sweet Grass Eater. He pointed his knife at Lone Hawk's heart. "This one was once my friend, but no longer. He has been found guilty of a crime without forgiveness. We cannot have both him and the grandfather of the man he killed in one place—this place that has brought us life when we thought we were dying. Choose!"

"There is no need," Lone Hawk said. "Because I leave."

CHAPTER 33

When the rain began, Seeks Fire, Walking Rabbit, and Calf Woman stood together, crying in relief. Soon, however, they hurried toward their belongings so they could spread hides for collecting water on the ground. Because the other women, children, and old men did the same, soon the entire area was covered. The moment a hide filled, it was gathered at the corners and the water poured into waiting bladders.

The downpour didn't last long, but by the time it ended, no less than nine bladders were so full it took several people to wrestle them onto the waiting travois. Seeks Fire made sure her parents had enough before going to check on Little Bird and Long Chin. The still-dour Long Chin was doing little of a helpful nature, but Little Bird, water dripping off her braids, was trying to keep a bladder neck open so Sleepy Foot's youngest wife could pour the last of her rainwater into it. Seeks Fire took over, expertly tying the bladder closed.

"You have done well," she told Little Bird as the girl sucked on the end of her braid. "Your sister will be proud of you."

"I wish she was here. Last night I dreamed she had gone so far she could not find her way back."

Seeks Fire embraced the girl, laughing because their wet dresses stuck together. "It was only a dream," she said with all the conviction she could muster. "She will never leave you."

"But she did."

Although she managed to distract Little Bird, Seeks Fire couldn't shake off the impact of those simple words. With all her heart, she believed the spirits were directing her friend's actions, but she wished the other woman had told her what came before her younger sister.

As soon as animals and humans had had enough to drink, everyone started moving again. The clouds had disintegrated, which meant the sky would be clear tonight, stars and moon keeping total darkness at bay. Seeks Fire didn't know whether to dread night and the inability to keep moving or to be grateful for the opportunity to rest. She was trying to decide what, if anything, she could allow herself to eat when she spotted Knows No Fear and Feet Like Rocks racing toward them.

The boys' excited announcement came down to one thing. Two Coyotes had returned.

Nightelk's son waited until everyone could hear him. "There can be no sleep tonight," he announced. "Not if we are to feast."

Feast. The wonderfully impossible word echoed inside Seeks Fire, making it difficult to concentrate on what he was saying. Although several women prodded him for details, Two Coyotes' explanation remained simple. As he spoke, Seeks Fire formed a mental image of miracle buffalo around a dying but not yet dead creek.

"Pawnee are there as well," he said, "but there is no fighting because Cheyenne and Pawnee share the meat."

"Share!" Long Chin pushed himself through the crowd. "The Cheyenne will *not* do without."

"The Pawnee are more than warriors. They are also old men and girls, like your daughter. Maheo does not care whether babies are one tribe or another."

Was this the first time she'd truly listened to Two Coyotes' words and the deep, calm tone behind them? He'd been older than she while they were growing up and then he'd married and gone off to live with his wife, and she'd forgotten about him. Since his return, he'd filled his days with men's pursuits, and she'd paid little attention to the gossip about how his ex-wife must have been touched by a ghost, because why else would she divorce a competent and wise man?

"Touches the Wind found you?" Seeks Fire asked him when she finally caught him alone. "She left on Legs Like Lightning and now you ride him. She—she is not dead, is she?"

"No." He'd looked somber, almost stern before. Now his features softened. Why hadn't she noticed how handsome he was? "She is all right, at least she was when Lone Hawk took the stallion and followed the warrior-cloud."

She didn't understand any of this. Hoping to prompt him to continue, she touched his wrist. He didn't pull away but looked down at her. "Where is Walking Rabbit?" he asked.

"Walking Rabbit? You—what do you want with her?"

He leaned closer. When he took her hand in his, it felt right. "Follower is alive."

"Follower? Alive?" Light-headed, she rested her head on his shoulder. "How—it is a miracle."

"Yes, it is. You will come with me, help me tell her?"

"LONE HAWK, PLEASE! You cannot leave."

"Our priest has spoken. I remain an outcast."

Oblivious to Follower who anxiously watched her and Lone Hawk by turn, Touches the Wind struggled to say something, anything that would change his mind. When she'd first seen him riding toward her, she'd had to bite the inside of her mouth to keep from crying out in relief and joy; how quickly that had changed.

Although she was still some distance from the killing site, the circling birds and howling wolves left no doubt of what was happening. To have Lone Hawk tell her he wouldn't be joining the celebration was almost more than she could bear.

"After everything we have been through—Nightelk did not speak in your defense?"

"His thoughts were on the miracle of the Sacred White Calf; I did not want to take him from that place. Touches the Wind, I came to live among the Bow String Society because I wanted to learn from Sweet Grass Eater's wisdom, but he hates me. I cannot tell him the truth about Grey Bear."

"You must!"

Follower drew away in alarm, prompting her to tell the girl that their discussion didn't concern her and plans to reunite her with her mother hadn't changed.

"Lone Hawk," she pressed, "we did not tell Sweet Grass Eater the truth about Grey Bear's death because we feared people would lose confidence in his dream-powers, but the buffalo have been found. Everything has changed."

"No, it has not."

"How can you say that?"

Although she could have reached out and touched him if she'd had the courage, he looked so alone that her heart ached.

"It would destroy him to know his grandson will never be welcomed into the afterlife. To know his soul must spend eternity seeking peace and acceptance—I cannot do that to him."

"What about you? And me?"

"You?"

"Both of us. Something happened between us, a coming together of our separate strengths, wisdom, and hope from that joining."

"Yes, it did. Someday, I pray, I will understand, but . . ."

"But what?"

"You and I are only two people. We cannot put ourselves before what it is to be Cheyenne."

Did he have to whisper like that? Closing her eyes, she surrendered herself to the still-damp, gently moving air. She didn't expect it to calm or renew her, and yet as the moments faded one after another, she stopped thinking about how tired and hungry she was, now much pain filled her.

Follower was alive. It had rained. There were buffalo. If her heart remained empty and she never saw Lone Hawk again, at least she—and her people—had those things.

"I do not want this for you," she told him. "The thought of you alone—"

"Maybe I will become a Pawnee."

"What? No!"

"Whitehair and I have touched each other in ways I do not understand. If I am no longer Cheyenne, maybe I can learn to be Pawnee."

"They are our enemies."

"Not today," he said, and told her about the Pawnee hunters. "Such a thing may never happen again, but those who saw it will never forget, will be changed by it."

"Yes, they will," she was forced to admit.

Did he have any idea how proud and calm and accepting—how alone he looked? How much she loved him.

"You have no water or food," Touches the Wind managed. "You cannot ride away empty-handed."

"You will give me what I need."

When she stared uncomprehendingly, he went on. "Soon you and Follower will have more to eat and drink than your bellies can hold. You no longer need the little you and I combined."

Combined. That's what she wanted, for her and Lone Hawk to become one. Create new life.

Heartache pressed around her, but somehow she found the strength to lift Follower onto the horse Lone Hawk had given her. Somehow she remained dry-eyed as he helped her up as well. What she didn't have were words.

He must not either because although he stood on tiptoe so

he could kiss Follower, he didn't look at her. Lone Hawk was still standing there, surrounded by nothing, when Touches the Wind rode away.

WHEN HE HEARD someone call out, Nightelk's first thought was that Two Coyotes had returned, but then he spotted Touches the Wind and Follower. Leaving the carcass he'd been working on, he hurried over to them. As soon as he extended his arms, Follower slid off the horse, and he caught her to him, breathing in her sweet miracle smell and covering the top of her head with kisses, sending his prayer of thankfulness to the Sacred White Calf. Still holding her, he looked up at Touches the Wind. Her eyes were filled with pain.

Someone had brought along wrapped hot coals. As it got dark, the men gathered enough dry grass and buffalo dung that they were able to start a fire and place rocks in it to heat. One by one, black-eyed warriors and hunters touched and spoke to Follower. Sweet Grass Eater ran the back of his hand over the girl's cheek, tears flowing down his own cheeks.

Someone cut the stomach out of a carcass, and Touches the Wind filled it with water, which she warmed with the hot rocks. When she placed strips of meat in the water, the smell caused Nightelk's mouth to water.

Sweet Grass Eater gave the first strip to Follower and then ate himself, followed by the other men. By then the horses had drunk from the muddy creek and were wandering around in search of what little grass the buffalo hadn't eaten. In the distance, light from the Pawnee's fire served as proof that they were doing the same thing. Nightelk needed to return to the carcasses and begin the tedious cutting his wife and other women had always done. However, his arms and legs and head wanted to remain where they were, doing nothing, thinking of nothing except his full belly; he let them.

He was aware of dozing off and dreaming of a small, pale calf with gentle eyes. He awoke to the sounds of snoring all around and somehow managed to spread out his sleeping blanket before collapsing on it. Black Eyes curled up next to him. His last thought was of Walking Rabbit and what she'd say and do when she saw her daughter alive.

The sun had been up for a long time before Nightelk finally roused himself. Although he was initially concerned the others might make fun of him for sleeping so late, he soon realized he wasn't the only one. A couple of the younger men had taken it upon themselves to round up the horses, but for the most part the Cheyenne sat and watched as Touches the Wind repeated last night's meal preparation.

"Yes, I saw him," she said when Nightelk asked her about Lone Hawk. Her eyes looked hollow and her voice was lifeless. "He told me what had happened and then—and then he left."

"I should not have let him. Nothing is as it was when he was banished."

"That is what I tried to tell him, but he is afraid the truth will destroy Sweet Grass Eater."

"It may."

"I do not want that for him. Lone Hawk . . ."

"You love him."

She blinked and stared at the ground. Follower, who'd remained with her through the night, hugged her.

"Yes," she whispered. "But it is a love that lives alone."

Nightelk struggled for the words to comfort her, but before he could find them, Black Eyes started barking. A moment later someone called out a greeting.

"Follower." He grabbed the girl and swung her up and onto his shoulders. "We go to your mother."

He expected to have to search for Walking Rabbit, but she, Two Coyotes, and Seeks Fire rode at the front of the line. There was something about Two Coyotes and Seeks Fire—as if their bodies were speaking to each other.

The moment Walking Rabbit spotted her daughter, she vaulted off her horse and ran. Tears clogged Nightelk's throat; he managed to place the girl on the ground just as Walking Rabbit dropped to her knees and enveloped her daughter. He heard something like the whimper of a wounded animal. Walking Rabbit's eyes streamed tears, and she looked alive. Fully, joyously alive!

Sinking to his knees, he wrapped an arm around first the mother and then the child.

"Maheo, thank you!" Walking Rabbit sobbed.

When she looked over at him, Nightelk covered her trembling mouth with his own. Seeing them, Calf Woman hugged herself and smiled through her own tears.

"YOU TOOK MY grandson's horse!"

"Yes."

"And gave Legs Like Lightning to *him* to ride. I saw it!"

Touches the Wind had never been the subject of Sweet Grass Eater's anger, had never seen the priest like this.

"The warrior-cloud called to Lone Hawk," she told him. Speaking Lone Hawk's name made her falter, but after a moment, she continued. "He saw and heard, believed."

The priest glared at her. "Legs Like Lightning lives because I could not bring myself to kill him. The stallion and my grandson share the same heart and courage; I needed those things near me."

"I know you do."

"You lie! If you did, you would know he must never touch Grey Bear's stallion!"

In a strange way, arguing with Sweet Grass Eater was easier than asking herself how she'd face the rest of her life without Lone Hawk. Besides, she'd done what she had, and nothing would change that. Instead of trying to explain that Lone Hawk's horse had been tired, she concentrated on remaining calm.

The rest of the tribe had traveled through the night, and although they were occupied with drinking and eating and looking over the dead buffalo, it wouldn't be long before they fell asleep. She hoped most of them weren't paying attention to what she and Sweet Grass Eater were saying to each other.

"It is not enough that Lone Hawk is never again allowed

to walk among us," the priest continued. "He *must* be punished for——"

"Lone Hawk has already been punished enough."

Sweet Grass Eater reared back and glared at her. Although deep down it didn't matter, she refused to lower her gaze and learned something she didn't want to. At the core of Sweet Grass Eater's emotion wasn't anger after all but grief.

How could it be otherwise? If Grey Bear had been alive, he'd have participated in the hunt. Afterward, he would have gone to Seeks Fire, made her his wife, spilled himself inside her, created new life.

"I do not want Grey Bear to be dead," she told his grandfather. "His life ended too soon, before he could become a father." She'd only had a moment to speak privately with Seeks Fire, but it had been long enough to learn that her friend wasn't carrying Grey Bear's child. "I mourn with you," she finished.

Sweet Grass Eater shook his head as if confused. "You cannot know what I feel. My loss—my heart is broken."

"My mother is dead," she whispered. "My heart broken." He didn't have to know that her heart ached, not just for her mother but also for Lone Hawk.

Sweet Grass Eater continued to regard her, his face clouded by emotion. She was slow to notice that Seeks Fire had made her way to them. Two Coyotes stood just behind her.

"I have listened to your words, my priest," Seeks Fire said. "There was a time when I believed I would become your grandson's wife and you and I would be family. That did not happen."

"Because he murdered Grey Bear!"

"The how of Grey Bear's death is not what today is about." Although Seeks Fire's arms were stiff at her side, she sounded calm. "Instead, we must speak of Legs Like Lightning and Lone Hawk."

Sweet Grass Eater spat. When he looked around at the hunters who'd remained with him, they did the same.

"Lone Hawk is dead to me," he said. "Dead to all of us."

*   *   *

SEEKS FIRE CLEARED her throat. "You say Lone Hawk is like dirt beneath your feet, but you are wrong."

Sweet Grass Eater pushed himself to his feet, staring first at Seeks Fire and then at Lone Hawk. His fists clenched and his face turned red. He opened his mouth but nothing came out. Around him, other men began to mutter.

Lone Hawk paid no attention to them but waited for his priest to speak.

Not long ago Seeks Fire, riding a tired but still-willing Legs Like Lightning, had overtaken him. Her explanation had been simple. She wanted him to return with her. He'd told her he could no longer call himself Cheyenne, but she'd silenced him with her eyes.

If Two Coyotes, Nightelk, Walking Rabbit, and Follower hadn't been with her, maybe he would have turned his back on her, but he couldn't. No one had spoken during the short ride to where the clan had gathered, and although he spotted several Pawnee watching them from a distance, he'd easily dismissed them. Now he waited. Touches the Wind hadn't taken her eyes off him since he'd ridden up.

"I was to be Grey Bear's wife," Seeks Fire told everyone who'd gathered around but mostly Sweet Grass Eater. "Although I pretended not to care when he looked at me, every time he did, my heart beat faster. My parents wanted the marriage, as did you."

Sweet Grass Eater nodded.

"But it did not happen because he is dead," Seeks Fire continued.

"Dead at *his* hands!"

"Only Grey Bear and Lone Hawk were there when your grandson died, and Lone Hawk has remained silent about what happened." Sweet Grass Eater started to say something, but she cut him off. "I do not care; it does not matter."

"How can you say that?"

"Because I look into tomorrow. My priest, I want your

eyes and heart to see what I have done. Legs Like Lightning is part of Grey Bear; you yourself said that."

A wary expression crept over Sweet Grass Eater's features.

"You were right not to kill him; Grey Bear's strength and courage should not die."

Confusion now replaced wariness.

"This one"—she ran her hands over Legs Like Lightning's neck—"walks where his master no longer can, sees with his master's eyes, carries Grey Bear's heart."

"He does." Sweet Grass Eater blinked rapidly.

"I do not say those things to bring you sorrow," she continued, "but to beg you to listen to Grey Bear's wisdom."

Lone Hawk allowed himself to look over at Touches the Wind. She gazed openly at him, her expression hiding nothing of her emotions.

"If Grey Bear blamed Lone Hawk for his death, his horse would not allow Lone Hawk on his back," Seeks Fire said. "But he has, twice."

Sweet Grass Eater said nothing, gave no indication he'd heard. Although he'd earlier believed he had no choice but to ride away, Lone Hawk now ached to speak. Was Seeks Fire right? Did Grey Bear live inside his stallion?

"I must say something." Touches the Wind stepped forward. "When it came to me on the wind that I should take Legs Like Lightning and go in search of Lone Hawk, I did not question the command. My heart listened and believed. Learned. After I found him and we were trying to decide what the spirits wanted us to do, the Pawnee returned Follower to us."

Looking around for Follower and Walking Rabbit, Lone Hawk spotted them, as they'd been earlier, near Nightelk. The only difference was that now Walking Rabbit and Knows No Fear were with them. Walking Rabbit had her arms around both of her children.

"Yesterday was a day of miracles," the maiden he loved went on. "It rained. Buffalo sacrificed themselves so we would live. Pawnee and Cheyenne hunted together. None—

none of that would have happened if not for the warrior-cloud."

Sweet Grass Eater frowned, and Lone Hawk remembered Nightelk telling him that the priest hadn't believed there was a message in the cloud. Risking it all, he spoke.

"You do not want to hear my voice; I understand that, but there is something I must say."

"No."

"Yes. You and the hunters were not the only ones who saw the cloud. So did I. That is why I took Legs Like Lightning from Touches the Wind. So I could ride to it."

Sweet Grass Eater sucked in a breath. "Ghosts. Ghosts are among us."

"Ghosts did not control the warrior-cloud." Lone Hawk pulled in a deep drink of rain-blessed air. "Your grandson did."

"Grey Bear?"

A sudden need to embrace the old man nearly overwhelmed him. Touches the Wind's eyes glistened, and he knew she understood and felt the same way. "My priest, your grandson's spirit, which now lives in the sky, called to me. His stallion carried me to buffalo and the life-giving creek. This is what I believe. Will always believe."

THE WIND HAD gone somewhere to rest after yesterday's storm, but it was back today and full of energy. Although he wasn't sure how much longer he could ignore his body's need for rest, Lone Hawk had given in to the need to walk.

When Touches the Wind joined him, he took her hand. There were uncounted things they needed to talk about—the fact that, by holding her hand, he'd committed both of them to marriage, what Sweet Grass Eater might have seen when he took his face in his hands and stared into his eyes, whether Two Coyotes and Seeks Fire were falling in love, how soon Walking Rabbit and her children would become part of Nightelk and Calf Woman's family.

For now, however, he let whatever force controlled him take him—them—where it wanted.

Touches the Wind slowed, and when he looked at her, he saw that she'd turned her head so the breeze caressed her eyes, nose, lips. She was smiling in a way he'd never seen before.

"What are you thinking?" he asked.

"Maybe I do not have any thoughts." Her smile softened, held. "I feel the wind and I am complete. For a moment I tried to look into tomorrow, but I do not want to."

"My tomorrow will be different from what I thought it would be," he admitted.

"Yes, it will. He is not a hateful man, just one wounded by grief."

"I wish I could take some of that from him."

"Only time will heal him—that and believing that a part of Grey Bear is still here."

They started walking again. If they turned around, they'd be able to see their people, but Lone Hawk preferred it this way—feeling nothing except the plains. Thinking of her and the day when he'd hold their children, telling those children about the summer of drought, Wind, Hawk, Grey Bear, a girl stolen by fire and returned by Pawnee.

"Lone Hawk, look."

A man and horse came toward them. Without thinking, Lone Hawk positioned himself so Touches the Wind was behind him. Because he was looking into the sun, he was slow to realize that the man was Pawnee. He held up his hand, signaling peace.

The Pawnee did the same, then dismounted.

Whitehair was taller than he'd thought, and the painful thinness had faded. The Pawnee nodded at Touches the Wind before standing in front of Lone Hawk.

"I thank you for Follower's life," Lone Hawk said. "And for caring for her as if she was your own."

Whitehair nodded and held out his hand. Lone Hawk grasped it.

Then he looked into the man's eyes.

Grey Bear's eyes.